ASCENSION

ASCENSION

OLIVER HARRIS

Little, Brown

LITTLE, BROWN

First published in Great Britain in 2021 by Little, Brown

1 3 5 7 9 10 8 6 4 2

Copyright © 2021 by Oliver Harris

The moral right of the author has been asserted.

A CIP catalogue record for this book
is available from the British Library.

Hardback ISBN: 978-1-4087-0995-5
Trade paperback ISBN: 978-1-4087-0994-8

Typeset in Palatino by M Rules
Printed and bound in Great Britain by
Clays Ltd, Elcograf S.p.A

Papers used by Little, Brown are from well-managed forests
and other responsible sources.

Little, Brown
An imprint of
Little, Brown Book Group
Carmelite House
50 Victoria Embankment
London EC4Y 0DZ

An Hachette UK Company
www.hachette.co.uk

www.littlebrown.co.uk

For Taehee

ONE

They unloaded the coffin last: grey plastic, of the kind hospitals have for mass-fatality incidents. It had been at the far end of the C-17 aircraft when it landed at Brize Norton an hour ago, bare, untagged. Six men carried it into the cargo bay. It wasn't clear to anyone present what procedure to follow, because no one had any idea who it contained.

Flight Lieutenant Trevor Hughes was responsible for the loading and unloading of all aircraft. He had walked through the plane's stale air, checking equipment and coordinating its discharge. It was only when the tents and packs had been cleared that he'd seen the coffin, secured by webbing at the back. A sealed box of possessions sat beside it.

'Picked it up at Cape Verde when we refuelled,' the aircraft's warrant officer said. 'Nothing's written on the docket. I was told there'd be someone here to meet it.'

Hughes shook his head. He took pride in his job, but it depended on clear lines of communication.

'Got a contact? A regiment?'

'Nothing.'

'What am I meant to do with it?'

'Unload it, I guess.'

Brize Norton was the sole airbridge to all British forces serving internationally. It was a portal through which the UK military could inject itself into the world, and whatever remained of

1

those missions at the end flowed back. It was a border, and, as at any busy border crossing, a settlement had grown, with its own hotel, fire station, medical centre, and post service. It ran like clockwork, never more so than surrounding a repatriation.

No one had told Hughes about a repatriation.

Usually there would be a hearse waiting, a chaplain, flags at half mast, wreaths for the bereaved. The flight lieutenant didn't feel qualified to receive the dead alone. Something had gone wrong, but not as wrong as to whoever lay inside the box. Hughes had a ritual he performed when bodies returned, and he performed it now: He touched the coffin and said, 'Welcome home.' Then he added, 'Whoever you are.' He turned to the warrant officer. 'Find something to cover it.'

The warrant officer removed a sheet of hessian from a broken refuelling hose and draped it over the plastic. With the help of four other men, they moved the coffin swiftly out of the plane, onto a luggage truck. Hughes was painfully conscious that the everyday noise of the airfield continued, oblivious. Once inside the cargo bay they placed it on a gurney with the box of possessions on the rack beneath it.

Hughes checked his messages and emails but there was nothing about a corpse returning. He made calls, steadily moving up the chain of command. A squadron leader radioed back, equally puzzled.

'No ID?'

'No, sir. I'd appreciate it if you could ascertain who's responsible and notify them of the situation.'

'I'll see what I can do.'

No one came. It couldn't stay among the cargo. Hughes remembered the gymnasium once being used as a temporary morgue – a row of nine arrivals from Helmand, stately enough on the parquet floor – and he made the decision to transfer the anonymous coffin there while they sought its owner. He enlisted the help of twenty-year-old Jack Trafford, a leading aircraftman from the specialist reserves, and they wheeled it through the back corridors together.

People stopped playing as they entered the sports courts. Games concluded and the place emptied. The two men waited.

Both were tired at the end of a long shift. Trafford had been hoping to get to the staff bar. Hughes had a six-month-old daughter at home. But the coffin lent their evening a solemnity that eclipsed those concerns. It spoke of events far away, a reminder that this was no normal airport.

Hughes radioed again. Again, a message came in: Guard it for now, someone would be tracked down.

No more flights were due in that night. The clank of gym equipment could be heard next door, occasional grunts and laughter. The negligence became an increasing source of anger for Hughes: that a corpse might become misdirected mail. The vast machine of the military was nothing if it forgot the meaning of these deliveries.

He checked the blank docket again as a morbid curiosity grew. Hughes took the knife from his belt and levered the top of the coffin open. He stood back as the gases dispersed, covered his mouth and nose with a hand.

The corpse belonged to a man in his mid-forties, six foot something, with long ginger hair and stubble. His eyes remained partially open but clouded. He wore shorts and a T-shirt. Nothing about him seemed military. No more than two or three days dead, Hughes guessed, but his face was blue-grey and swollen, with haemorrhaging around the eyes and also around the throat, where purple marks had begun to blacken in the shape of a ligature.

A spook? Caught up somewhere? Had the RAF done someone a favour by bringing him home? The mystery seemed bound to the absence of anyone to receive him. But it didn't solve the problem they faced. Hughes replaced the lid, then opened the cardboard box and looked through the dead man's belongings.

They were divided into clear evidence bags marked POLICE PROPERTY. No indication which police. Included among them were several metres of thin yellow cable. It took Hughes a second to realise what it was. The cable had been severed twice: once above the knot, once across the noose, exposing copper wiring inside. He tutted.

Other bags contained more clothes, a small guitar that Trafford said was a ukulele, and finally a wallet. Governmental ID in the wallet gave them an identification at last: Rory Bannatyne, Engineering Consultant, UK Government Infrastructure and Projects Authority.

'Works for the government,' Hughes said.

'On time travel?' Trafford asked. 'Look at this.'

Money had spilled from the clothing: small change and one crumpled note. Trafford flattened the note in his palm.

A young Queen Elizabeth II gazed up. The paper was cherry red. It looked like money from the 1940s or 1950s: Elizabeth II with her life and half the twentieth century ahead of her. On the reverse, the ten-pound note bore a technicolour sunset and two old sailing ships cruising toward the watermark.

'He's come from the past.'

The coins, likewise, were definitely sterling, but unlike any Hughes had seen before. The ten-pence piece was larger than current ones, and had dolphins on the tail side. A two-pence piece bore the image of a donkey carrying wood on its back.

Finally, among some books and toiletries, they found a postcard, stamped and addressed to a 'Nicola Bannatyne' but with no message written. The front showed a landscape of black rock and the name *Ascension Island*.

'Where's Ascension?' Trafford said.

But his colleague had been distracted by the rapid clip of a

4

woman's heels. They turned to see her enter: tall with an air of civilian seniority, her long brown hair tied back, flanked by two Force Protection officers.

As she drew closer you could see she was flustered, looking ahead of her to the coffin as if late for an appointment and ready to burst into apology.

None came their way. The older of the accompanying officers told Hughes and Trafford they were dismissed. Trafford raised an eyebrow at Hughes and marched off. Hughes looked at the coffin for a final time. He didn't feel confident the body was about to get the respect it deserved. But this was not his problem anymore.

It was only once outside the building that Hughes realised he still held the ten-pence piece with the dolphin. It looked even more magical in the airfield's floodlights. He returned to the gymnasium, wondering how best to return it, and saw the woman standing very still beside the coffin. The lid had been removed again. Her guards remained a few metres away, eyes averted, so there was something oddly intimate to the scene. She held the blank postcard, and Hughes wondered if she was able to discern some message that had escaped him, a message that the man had carried all the way from Ascension Island and that had survived his own will to live.

TWO

Kane paused with the marker in front of the whiteboard, then wrote *Ecstasy*. Beneath it, to form a triangle, he wrote *Finding* and *Being*. He turned to check the faces of the nine individuals who had chosen to spend the last hour of a sunny Monday afternoon listening to him rather than absorbing the beauty of Oxford outside. The turnout was low again, but then he'd made the lecture as niche as possible: 'Sufi Influences on the European Tradition.' The room was in a remote corner of St John's College, because he wanted to see who would find it. More people found it each week, and he no longer knew each attendee by name. But still he had noticed the man at the back as soon as he arrived.

He was young, dressed smartly, with the fine features of eastern Africa and a deep, attentive gaze. Kane hadn't seen him before. Newcomers turned up, of course, in spite of Kane's bid for obscurity – sometimes lost, sometimes merely misguided. But instinct told Kane this was an employee of the Secret Intelligence Service.

For the last year Kane had been the subject of an inquiry under way deep within the entrails of Vauxhall Cross, MI6's headquarters. After ten years working undercover on behalf of the British government, it wasn't about to let him leave without a fight. His exit hadn't been made any easier by a final escapade in Central Asia that broke a lot of rules. And while Kane knew that he had saved more faces and more bloodshed than his bosses would admit, he carried an aura of danger now. Hence he was currently at risk of being found guilty of appropriation of operational funds, disobeying orders, and the magisterially nondescript 'unauthorised absence,' which was one way of describing a battle for his life in Kazakhstan. He was forbidden to leave the country and no doubt monitored while he was here, all pending a decision as to whether to press charges. This hypothetical prosecution was insurance against him speaking out. It meant there was always the prospect of a decade in a high-security prison if residual loyalty wasn't enough to keep him onside. The god they worshipped was not the law, but silence.

This humiliation remained invisible to his students. Kane was reduced to travelling the world through its languages, just as he had done twenty years ago – a hunger for losing himself in other cultures that had led him into intelligence work in the first place. His doctorate had begun well. The college had been surprised by his existing range of knowledge and had pressured him into teaching a couple of courses. His former bosses at MI6 even had the audacity to suggest Kane keep an eye out for potential recruits. And if he had taken down the maps of the Middle East from the walls it was simply to help him remain focused on the present. An acknowledgement that beneath the bandage of his new life, old wounds refused to heal.

The students weren't sure what to make of him. In self-conscious moments he wondered if they detected a fracture. When Kane had been working undercover, he knew what to wear. Now he didn't. He knew that they believed something had gone wrong in his life, but also that there must be something they could glean from his lectures for their own self-advancement. These were bright kids. They wanted a ticket into their future, the perpetuation of achievement that had borne them this far, oblivious that others would use this for their own ends. So as a secret favour, Kane gave them something beautiful and useless: a history of poetry. And they wrote it down as if it would help them.

'While Europe saved its love for God, the Middle East was articulating the spiritual complexities of human romance. That's why we're looking at Persia today, and in particular at the knot of ideas within this word *wajd*. Sufi writers believed that it had its roots in *wa-ja-da*, which means devotion but also discovery and even being itself.' Kane picked up the board marker again, then added *Grief* at the bottom. 'Alternatively, *wajd* can mean "grief" or "pain"' because the experience can only arise through separation.'

Students typed sedately, filling their MacBooks with thirteenth-century mysticism. Kane kept his focus on the regulars. He had allowed himself to believe that if he conformed enough to this new cover, the intelligence service would forget he was here. But they never forgot.

The man at the back was a few years older than most of the audience, but it was his clothing and physicality that made him conspicuous. He leaned back in his seat, leg crossed, tie neatly knotted. He nodded appreciatively when his eyes met Kane's, writing occasionally in a black notebook. As Kane began to wrap up, he returned the notebook to his jacket, withdrew a phone, and punched in a message.

'Let's leave it there,' Kane said. 'Next week we'll touch on the Cathars. For those who've not come across them before, they were a Christian sect who believed that any God responsible for creating this world must be an evil one. They refused to have sex because reproduction perpetuated existence. You'll like them. Take a look if you're keen.'

His audience stared uncertainly. A few students ventured a smile.

'We're done,' Kane said. 'I appreciate your attention.' Laptops slammed shut. Bags unzipped. The suited man eased himself forward. A few students thanked Kane as they left. Next time, he thought, he would ask them why they returned. If there was a next time.

'You didn't have to subject yourself to that,' Kane said when it was just the two of them. He collected up his notes. 'You have my number.'

'I'm Daniel. Pleased to meet you, Elliot.'

Kane shook his outstretched hand. Up close, he seemed younger – not so far off the students after all. The suit had been misleading.

'Pleased to meet you, Daniel. What do you want?'

'Kathryn Taylor is outside. We have a car.'

'Kat Taylor?'

'That's right. Okay to say hello to her?'

They walked through the corridors in silence. Kathryn Taylor had been a colleague of Kane's in Oman, a one-off job, seven or eight years ago. They'd got on well, not seen each other since. It didn't make much sense.

Taylor stood beside a silver Audi across the road from the college entrance. Seeing Kane, she flicked her cigarette into the gutter and approached, caught between a smile of reunion and the anxiety of whatever necessitated it.

'Elliot.'

'Kat, been a while.'

'You're okay?'

'I was.'

'I know. I realise this is a bolt from the blue. I could really do with a moment of your time. I apologise for gate-crashing this scholarly refuge. Are you up for a drive?'

'How long will this take?'

'Couple of hours. We'll talk when there, if that's okay.'

No suggestion of where 'there' might be. No suggestion he might decline the invitation. Surely not back to Vauxhall Cross. Taylor was already climbing into the driver's seat.

Kane stood for a second amid the flow of students and tourists, imagining the protest he might make, the appointments he might have had. But he had no appointments; perhaps they knew that. The facade of his new life was already crumbling. He got in the back of the Audi and Taylor started the car.

'He was fascinating,' Daniel said, once they'd set off. 'Did you know, Arabic has at least eleven different words for *love*, and each of them conveys a different stage in the process of falling for someone?'

'I had no idea. That's beautiful. How are the students, Elliot?'

'Very young.'

'Isn't everyone these days?'

Taylor drove cautiously, one eye on the mirrors, continuing out of town. Kane wanted to get some purchase on the situation.

'How have you been?' he asked.

'Up and down,' she said, tightly.

'Where are you working now?'

'South Atlantic desk. I run it.'

'Congratulations.'

'Thanks.'

Kane thought through world affairs: the newspapers he'd tried not to read, and, when he did succumb to a browse, not to decrypt. Nothing pertaining to the South Atlantic came to mind. It had certainly never been his domain. He wasn't as up to speed with world news as he used to be, but then his job no longer fed a hunger for omniscience.

The three of them lapsed into silence. Kane watched Oxford slip away. They didn't drive east to London, as he'd expected, but west, onto the A40. He checked Taylor in the mirror and saw anxiety.

The job on which they'd worked together involved tapping a cable running from Seeb in Oman under the Strait of Hormuz to Iran. Taylor had led a team of three – herself, Kane, and an eccentric technical specialist by the name of Rory Bannatyne.

Bannatyne was an expert on the discrete diversion of fibre optics. But he needed to get into the facilities that housed them, which demanded insider knowledge. Kane had gone over for two months to run an asset inside the Omani security services who had access to the information they needed: computer systems, building security, and personnel. Kane was essentially a conduit for this intelligence while something complicated happened at high-security junction points.

He received a commendation for the work without knowing much about what had been achieved, and the success earned him a posting to Libya as the country began to implode. He remembered Taylor as ambitious. A year or so after their job together he heard she'd stabbed someone in Algiers. Depending on who you spoke to it was an agent or a fixer who'd turned on her or got overfriendly; one person had described it as an abduction attempt, another as a sexual assault. Either way, she put a knife in his throat. Kane assumed that was connected to her being in HQ now. It may also have been connected to her marriage falling apart, although from what she'd said in Oman it hadn't been in a great place to start with. And now apparently she was running the South Atlantic desk. Not one of the prestigious departments, but it wasn't teaching poetry to undergraduates, either.

They continued improbably into the Cotswolds. Then he realised where they were going.

Kane sometimes walked in this area, but he tried not to venture west of the A34. Too many classified places: the ley lines of military intelligence webbed and thickened in this corner of England. He knew of at least ten sites of various levels of secrecy, but none like the one they now approached.

Government Communications Headquarters appeared out of the landscape like a vast space-age tumulus – a stadium landed among the Cheltenham suburbs, with half a mile of tarmac between its secrets and the rest of society. The processing and monitoring hub of a surveillance empire, GCHQ and its network of satellites and ground stations eavesdropped on every square inch of the globe. It was classified to an extent beyond anything in MI6, but then, it was more effective.

They passed the first discreet security camera, then reached an entrance ringed by barbed wire. A guard checked Taylor's pass, peered at Kane, raised a barrier. A few seconds later they paused as another camera stared through the windscreen, and then two metal posts sank into the ground and they drove down a ramp into the visitors' car park.

Kane had only been in once before, and that was more than ten years ago. A familiar curiosity returned, with a familiar caveat: being let into secrets is one thing, being let out, another. The car park had its own security centre, where they handed in their phones. Kane signed a visitors book and took his temporary pass. They received a guide, a young woman in a cardigan and heels who said 'Follow me' and led them up a flight of stairs into the largest secret intelligence headquarters outside of the US.

A veneer of normality was now allowed to present itself. Beyond an atrium with sofas and potted palm trees, the HQ opened out into two levels of communal seating lit through a glass ceiling. A floating walkway circled the space, ivy creeping up its supporting columns. The architectural theme, without trace of irony, was openness.

Kane had been given a tour after the terrorist attacks of July 2007, in the spirit of encouraging cooperation between the services. Barriers were being forced down between the traditionally rivalrous MI5, MI6, and GCHQ, with the idea that joint teams could work together and share leads. GCHQ was the last of the three to emerge from the shadows, and some were surprised to discover it was twice the size of MI5 and MI6 combined. It emerged reluctantly, highly protective of its techniques, not wanting to compromise its ingenuity.

Kane hadn't expected ever to return. Now the four of them strode through the headquarters, with their guide angling her face toward various cameras in order to open doors. No one paid them any attention. Plenty of staff still wore casual clothes: not quite the vibe of ten years ago – no shorts and flip-flops – but the Starbucks was still surreally there, and some staff carried gym bags and squash rackets. And in the empty centre of the circular building was the garden with its memorial to dead colleagues, a reminder that in the new era of warfare, there were software engineers on the front line too, that hackers sacrificed their lives with increasing frequency.

On that first visit, Kane had been led down a few flights of stairs, past an underground road to the cavernous computer halls that made the offices on top seem like a thin disguise. They didn't go down this time. He tried to remember the layout of the ground floor. There was a section devoted to math and crypt-analysis, a separate wing for activities that fell under the opaque banner of 'Enterprise' – new technologies, biometrics, AI – and a busy department dedicated to linguistics and translation. But they went to none of these. Two more punch codes led them away from the natural light to an anonymous department with its own reception desk.

The guard stationed there lifted a receiver, called through, told them to wait one moment. Their guide departed with a smile. Daniel spoke to Taylor and took a seat at the side. It was the last time Kane would see him that day. Taylor turned to Kane.

'Elliot, before we go in, I need to tell you: Rory Bannatyne's dead. That's partly what this concerns. He killed himself.'

'Rory?'

'I didn't want to speak in the car. I'm sorry.'

Rory Bannatyne was the officer who'd worked with them on that job. Kane recalled him more vividly now, a tall, ginger-haired man with intense green eyes – soft-spoken, watchful, gentle, charismatic. He was what they called a tailored access officer, which meant his background in the special forces had been put to use alongside advanced electronics and computing skills: that is, he could break in to places and then understand the wiring inside them. He was housed in the National Technical Assistance Centre, a rarely sighted subunit of the intelligence service that worked on intercepting signals data. There was something else, Kane now remembered: a minor upset Taylor had covered up, involving a girl in his hotel room. This had never entirely fit with Kane's direct experience of the man, but then they hadn't known each other well.

'Is this to do with Oman?'

'No, not exactly. They don't know anything about that. For now.'

'What happened?'

'I want to see what you think. I don't know what to make of it.'

'And I'm connected?'

'Not yet.'

The guard lifted his phone again, then pressed a button.

'Dominic's waiting for you.'

The door opened. A small, bright-eyed man stood on the other side, clean-shaven in a tight white shirt with the sleeves rolled up. He had a laptop and papers under his left arm. He shook Kane's hand vigorously.

'Dominic Bower. Thanks for coming in. Please, this way – grab a seat.'

He directed them into a conference room with glazed glass walls and a long table set with sparkling water and pens. At one end of the room was a projection screen. Bower shut the door, dropped his belongings at the head of the table, plugged a cable into his laptop. In Kane's experience, men who had built a career in the shadows were either predictably pallid or, like Bower, they acquired a proud flush as if swollen with secrets and the status this bestowed. Kane glanced at the paperwork he'd dropped, saw his own signature.

'Formality first,' Bower said. 'Wanted to be double sure – you're read into Echelon, is that right? Strap 3 clearance?'

Echelon was the data interception program that spied on the world's communications. Strap 3 clearance meant that you knew the access points at which GCHQ tapped in to the global fibre-optic system, one of the most classified projects they ran.

'That's correct,' he said.

'Inducted 2014.'

'Yes.'

Bower studied Kane's authorisation again.

'You worked with Kathryn in Oman.'

'Briefly.'

'A great success.'

Taylor shifted uncomfortably in her seat. Even without the eventual complications, these things were never straightforward. But the tap got put on the cable, and, for all Kane knew, it was still whispering secrets into ears within this very building. And from the point of view of those individuals at their workstations, no doubt it was a success.

'I'm glad you think so.'

'It's that background that made us think you might be able to help.'

Bower opened the laptop and clicked. A map appeared on the projection screen. Kane thought it was the Isle of Wight at first, then saw military bases marked.

'Ascension Island,' Bower began. 'Familiar with it?'

'South Atlantic.'

'That's right.'

Familiar would have been an overstatement. Kane knew it as an obscure bit of UK territory, a surviving outpost of empire: one of Her Majesty's rocks in the middle of nowhere. It had been a military stepping-stone during the Falklands War, and housed a joint GCHQ-NSA listening station. That was the extent of his familiarity.

'One of the most remote inhabited islands in the world,' Bower continued. 'Roughly halfway between Africa and Brazil. Been ours since 1815. The airbase is rented out to the Americans, but there's a few RAF around as well. We share its signals intelligence facility with the NSA, and there's a BBC Relay Station. That bit's ours.'

'Busy little island.'

'About to get busier.' He clicked and the display changed. The title now was OPERATION VENTRILOQUIST. The screen showed a line across the South Atlantic, captioned *TA3 Meridian subsea cable*. 'As of 2022, Ascension will be a landing point for a new transatlantic fibre-optic cable. It has some history in this role – the island's provided landfall for communication cables since 1899, when the Eastern Telegraph Company exploited its position for their first transatlantic line. But Meridian will be a game changer. There's never been so much data set to travel through one cable.

'Rory Bannatyne was over there to draw up plans for interception, to establish how we might achieve equivalent access as we've enjoyed elsewhere. Superficially, he was a UK government telecommunications consultant, liaising between the island administration and the cable company. In reality, he was drawing up proposals for a restricted processing facility. The cable company isn't one of the cooperative ones, so the process of establishing access is a little more complex. But it hasn't stopped us before. By all accounts, the assessment went smoothly. Bannatyne got us comprehensive intelligence on the company, the island, the individuals there, and he drew up plans for access that will work, we believe.' Bower sat back, as if this was where his concerns ended and the responsibilities of MI6 began. 'I'm not sure how much Kathryn has told you.'

'The day before he was due to return, he hanged himself,' Taylor said. 'Close to where he was staying.'

Bower watched Kane for his response. Kane merely nodded, trying to picture the melancholy end of a man he'd barely known.

'I'm sorry to hear that. What's it got to do with me?' he asked.

'We need to move to the next phase,' Taylor said. 'That means we need to know Rory wasn't compromised, and that he didn't encounter any complications that may connect to his death.'

'So you can proceed with tapping the cable.'

'Yes.'

'Are you saying you want me to go out there?'

'I'm not comfortable committing more personnel to the project without an investigation,' Taylor said. 'I'd like someone to take a look.'

'We're ready to go,' Bower said. 'The engineers are selected. The operation is poised to start.'

Kane studied the map of the island again, which was taking on new import. He had come here braced for questioning of some kind. It seemed there was only one question: *Will you go?*

'Are you aware,' he said, 'that I'm not currently allowed to leave the country?'

'We know,' Taylor said. 'Leave that side of things to us.'

This created the first itch of temptation. But Kane was conscious of being steered fast into a scenario no one knew very much about.

'Any suggestions that Rory did have trouble over there?'

'No, nothing.'

'Maybe he didn't want to leave,' Kane suggested.

Taylor and Bower both stared at him.

'Maybe,' Taylor said. Bower glanced at his watch. Kane got the impression that in GCHQ things operated with a technological efficiency that didn't allow for glitches such as suicide. And there was something unspoken in the room. Taylor hadn't confided about Rory's previous mishap, he thought. Now he saw why. This was one reason she'd come to Kane: for discretion.

'If we are going to send someone else out there, I wanted an officer already read into Echelon,' Bower said. 'Which I think is reasonable enough. And you had some acquaintance with the man. Perhaps that will help the two of you come to a conclusion regarding what happened. We have a fortnight, then the window for installation becomes trickier since the cover we've established won't work. I'm getting considerable pressure over this, as you can imagine. People want the data flowing yesterday.'

A fibre-optic cable between Africa and Latin America. Kane considered what this would give them: all traffic between two continents set to shape the next century. Thousands of calls in any single second. That meant serious intelligence product. At the heart of the intelligence world was a competition between the agencies: Each morning the prime minister got separate reports from MI5, MI6, and GCHQ, and the quality of these insights determined budgets and careers. GCHQ had a lead it needed to maintain. The human factor was a rare inconvenience.

'Have you ever been to Ascension Island?' Kane asked.

'Me?' Bower looked amused by the question. 'No.'

'You?' Kane turned to Taylor.

'No.'

He nodded again, looked at the map.

'How long was Rory over there?'

'Coming up for six months,' Taylor said.

'Regular communication?'

'Regular enough. We had an encrypted satellite link. Neither of us wanted to be on it daily, but he was in touch. There was nothing to suggest this was going to happen.'

'I assume someone on the island investigated it.'

'To a basic level. The conclusion was as you'd imagine: straightforward suicide. And of course they may be right. Either way, it's not clear why this happened. And there are additional questions around his belongings, whether everything got returned, if there might be something he left behind that could tell us the tiniest bit about what happened.'

'Who's in charge over there?'

'Technically it's the governor of Saint Helena, which is an entirely separate island around eight hundred miles away. But it's part of the same territory, as the FCO defines it. The governor's represented on Ascension by an Administrator. The island has two full-time police officers, assisted by a couple of volunteers. It's not set up for a thorough investigation of any kind. Obviously, the RAF and the American military base have their own security, but they deal with military matters.'

'Anyone else there know the real reason Rory was on the island?'

'No,' Taylor said. 'This was way beyond any potential clearance. There's only six people in this building that know, and three in Vauxhall: me, my assistant, and the chief.'

Kane had been in high-level, compartmentalised secrecy before, but nothing like this. He could see how it left you with little room to operate, reduced your own outlook.

'How many people live on Ascension?'

'"Live" may not be the word. There's eight hundred people stationed on the island at the moment: three hundred Americans on the base, fifty UK military, some BBC and cable engineers. Most of the others are contractors – maintenance, catering, the usual – and those tend to be workers who've come over from Saint Helena. They often bring their families. But no one's given permanent residency. And there are very few tourists. Until a few years ago, civilians weren't allowed on at all. So, we're fairly sure we know who's on there.'

Kane's mind drifted briefly to the library in which he would have been sitting if it weren't for this, to the concluding lectures in his account of secular poetry.

'How long would I be over there for?' Kane asked.

'No more than a month,' Bower said.

'I have commitments at the university,' he said. Bower looked puzzled, then realised what Kane meant.

'The PhD,' he said. 'Yes, we appreciate that. I'll leave it between you and Kathryn to make any necessary arrangements. A sabbatical, perhaps.' He smiled flatly. 'There would be a full briefing later this week. You would be paid at the rate of external contractors, which I believe is considerably more generous than for staff. Kathryn will sort your cover and handle any logistics. Obviously this would retain the same level of security. I'm assured your assistance here will help offset any ongoing disciplinary concerns.'

Kane failed to hide a mixture of disdain and incredulity. Bower seemed taken aback.

'I understand disciplinary proceedings are ongoing,' he said, more hesitantly. 'You are still technically under investigation. Is that not right?'

Kane had stopped expecting the worst of everyone, he realised; stopped seeing the world as interlocking power games.

'That's right,' he managed to say.

'You'd be doing us a favour, is what I'm saying. And, of course, with a project of this significance ... we wouldn't forget.'

Bower closed his laptop, then excused himself and left Kane and Taylor to catch their breath and shake their heads.

'I had no idea he'd do that,' she said, quietly, as they headed back toward the outside world.

'It's fine.'

'It's not fine. Let me drive you back.'

THREE

She exhaled once they were in the car, glanced at Kane when they'd cleared the last barrier.

'It's not your fault,' he said.

'The whole thing's my fault.'

She drove, jaw clenched, knuckles white.

'Bower is very determined,' Kane said.

'We all are. Fibre optic's the gift that keeps on giving. We've got more data coming in than the NSA itself. He can't see why Ascension shouldn't be exactly the same.'

'Nor can I.'

'You think Rory just lost it? We should proceed as if nothing happened?'

'He'd spent six months operating alone on a lump of rock. I suspect he was unstable to start with.'

'He was brilliant.'

'He wasn't without issues, was he?'

She didn't answer.

'No one else in Six working on this?' Kane said.

'No.'

'You're really overseeing the whole thing alone?'

'That was the agreement. Until the interception facility is in place, at least.'

She seemed sensitive about talking in the car, so Kane didn't push it any further. He thought about their previous collaboration, about a very beautiful, domed, and expensive Oman, pre–Arab Spring. Kathryn had been managing the operation, which she could have done remotely if less effectively, but she insisted on being there. Rory Bannatyne was technically brilliant. His skill with fibre optics seemed connected in some obscure way to the intensity of his green eyes, his love of music, his quiet charm. The image of him hanged felt cruelly bizarre. As ever, it was hard not to implicate the world of secrets that they served. There was a touch of Prometheus to it all: playing with godlike powers that had been loaned to you; feeling the heat of a guilt that wasn't entirely your own but to which you were exposed. Rory Bannatyne had enabled schemes beyond the natural order of things, a mutation that could give a person troubled dreams.

Kane had responded to his dark talent in the only way he knew how: He probed. He wanted to know what exactly was going on under the Strait of Hormuz. Eventually, over a bottle of Laphroaig, Rory opened up. Kane could see him leaning in, with his shock of wavy ginger hair and his strong, freckled arms.

Fibre optics had arrived just as GCHQ was hitting a problem, Rory said. The British had excelled over the years at intercepting microwave satellite communications, but the dawn of universally available encryption had started making that a lot more complicated. Underground fibre-optic cables changed the game. On one hand, they were buried deep, but at the same time they were physical, which meant you could infiltrate the system at vulnerable points. When GCHQ wanted to tap a new international cable, engineers like Rory were installed in the relevant communication companies to plan where the splitter would be connected. The splitter diverted the light carried on the cables into a secret 'black room' under control of GCHQ.

The whole thing depended on having physical access to the major junction points, and, by a feat of historical felicity, this put the UK at an advantage. When fibre-optic cables began to be laid they followed the paths of the old imperial telegraph system. These, logically enough, connected the great stations of empire, with the United Kingdom at the centre of the web.

Not only did fibre-optic cables now carry more than 90 per cent of the world's data, but eighteen of the most important came ashore in Cornwall. The Americans had recognised that. They had cash, the UK had places. Over the last few years, millions had poured in from the NSA's Foreign Partner Access budget, and windowless structures appeared on farms near Bude and Porthcurno, crammed with deep-dive processors that could turn a tsunami of data into searchable information.

The major cable companies received tens of millions of pounds to turn a blind eye to men like Rory installing hidden connections. But when the companies weren't cooperative, you needed other means. That was where Kane came in.

Seeb was part of a GCHQ network in Oman, focused on cables under the Strait of Hormuz. The strait was a narrow point in the Persian Gulf, busy with undersea cables: one carrying Iranian communications, one with Iraqi traffic, another handling all Yemen's voice and text data. The UK had a tight relationship with Oman involving three joint military training bases and a logistic support centre in Duqm, but much of it was cover for GCHQ interest in the strait. This time around, because the relevant cable company was Chinese, they had to hack in to their network, which brought a whole new level of complication, along with the need for Kane to run high-sensitivity human sources. *So here we all are*, Rory had concluded, sipping his whisky, eyes twinkling.

The actual technical details wouldn't have meant anything to Kane, but he now appreciated the background. On the next round they talked poetry. Rory knew a lot of poems and songs by heart, a quality Kane rated above most others. A large man, he sang with a high, delicate vibrato, his whole physicality changing as if this, not speech, was his natural medium.

Kane returned to the UK when his own contribution had been completed. Taylor and Rory stayed on. Her marriage was already rocky, and he could see they were developing a friendship born of two people glad to be away from home. Kane had learned little about the subsequent scandal: he knew that Rory Bannatyne was caught doing something he shouldn't, Taylor had paid some money, kept police at a distance, sent him back to the UK. Which was all standard procedure: protect the Service at all costs.

The operation wouldn't have succeeded without Rory. *A great success,* as Bower had said. Which meant big kudos for the three of them. Rory Bannatyne helped their respective careers and disappeared back into the shadowy National Technical Assistance Centre – shamed or relieved or furious, Kane had no idea. Kane lost himself in the dog days of the Arab Spring. Taylor continued toward her incident in Algeria. None exactly lucky, now that he thought about it. Perhaps Oman had put some curse on them.

They reached Oxford and Kane directed Taylor to his home. When they arrived, she got out of the car and looked around the small terraced street. He rented the upstairs flat of a neat, attractive house. The road was narrow, with the tightly packed houses lending a sense of both crowdedness and seclusion. Seven p.m. A mild night. Kane wondered for a moment if she wanted more from him than operational assistance. On the quiet street Taylor looked smart and successful and bigger than this provincial world. She also looked like she didn't want to be alone just yet.

'I can't imagine living here,' she said.

'It takes no imagination. This is my life. Come in for a bit.'

'Are you sure?'

'Of course.'

They went up to his rooms. His first visitor, and suddenly he felt aware of the mustiness. She studied the place much as she'd studied the street, hands in her coat pockets, head turning. Most of the pictures and decorations belonged to the landlord, a former professor now based in France, and Kane had adopted them as he would the furniture of any cover ID. He felt Taylor search for traces of a partner, a life, a past.

'No mementos of your service to the country?'

'No. Want a drink?'

'More than anything. But unfortunately I don't do that anymore.'

'Something soft?'

'A tea would be nice. Black, no sugar.'

She continued to browse the shelves while he put the kettle on.

'How long have you been here?'

'Almost a year. A year without spying. There should be awards: abstinence from the service. Is that tasteless?'

'Because I'm a recovering alcoholic? No, we still have a sense of humour. Although I'm not sure anyone knows that about me anymore. I heard you had a bit of a crazy time too.'

Kane thought back to the events of eighteen months ago: the search for a missing colleague in Kazakhstan, a woman he'd loved and who he'd failed to save. It wasn't a search of which his bosses approved. Having burnt his bridges with MI6, he'd holed up in Jakarta for a while. One day, he decided to try returning to the UK, to face up to things: to who he was, and to the grief. He did not trust how long it could be held at bay simply by avoiding his own life. Kane was glad to have returned on his own terms, not to have waited for them to find him. The immigration officers at Heathrow had looked troubled by whatever message appeared on their screens when they scanned his passport.

Would you mind stepping this way, sir?

So they led him from his exile into three months of discussion and negotiations.

What do you want?

I'd like to study. I'd like to transfer careers. I have no intention of damaging the reputation of the service or compromising its operations.

It was testament to the healing power of state secrecy that

so much snow had been allowed to settle over those tracks. He had followed a trajectory that wasn't entirely unfamiliar: from rising star to pariah. And perhaps the quiet bathos of his current existence was typical too, and sustaining notoriety was as rare as sustaining heroism. But it wasn't without loneliness. He had lost someone special to him in that final escapade, and grief had a way of haunting you with the future you had imagined. There was a sense of strangeness about his new life that he had failed to shake, a lingering lack of faith in it, having mastered and disposed of so many personas in his professional career.

'I heard you ran away to Kyrgyzstan.'

'Kazakhstan.'

'No issues returning?'

'I'm a lot easier to keep tabs on here, as you've discovered.'

'I wrestled with whether to call on you.'

Kane nodded. He made the teas and handed her one.

'Can I smoke?' Taylor waved a packet of cigarettes.

Kane opened the window and she propped herself on the ledge. He took the sofa.

'Seeing anyone?' she asked, from behind the first veil of cigarette smoke.

'No.'

'No starry-eyed postgrad?'

'Not allowed. You? I heard about a divorce. I'm sorry.'

'No need to be sorry. Yes. Astonishingly, I'm single.'

'Your young sidekick seems nice.'

She laughed.

'Daniel's great. He's the first assistant I fully trust. He's also half my age. Too good for the Service really, with an extraordinary life story. He lost his parents in Eritrea, came over here when he was fifteen. Six wanted him to work undercover, of course: surveillance, penetrating gangs, that kind of thing. But he pressed to be interviewed for HQ, and I liked him. He's super sharp, no time for office nonsense. Part of me wonders if he's secretly tasked with keeping an eye on me.'

'He keeps an eye on you to see how you do the job.'

'Sure.' She sighed. 'He could choose better role models. I have a horrible feeling that if people start trying to figure out what's behind Rory's suicide, they'll get to Oman. They'll find out I covered for him.'

'You think they will look?'

'Maybe. Covered for him and then threw him into an isolated environment that would have been tough on anyone.'

'What exactly happened in Oman? Was it a prostitute?'

She closed her eyes and pressed the heel of her smoking hand to her forehead, then looked directly at Kane.

'It wasn't a prostitute, it was a girl and boy. Teenagers. Street kids. They were in his room and he was watching them. The hotel owner caught them and called the police. He said it wasn't the first time.'

She continued to watch Kane, alert to flickers of judgement. He was thinking. Of people, and sexuality, and the reservoirs of anguished desire beneath the surface of things.

'Rory was in the police station by the time I found out,' Taylor said.

'What did you do?'

'Signed a piece of paper and gave them quite a lot of money on the understanding it went no further. My own money. He repaid me as soon as he was back in the UK, wanted to pay me more.'

Kane saw the potential gravity of the situation. Intelligence work magnified transgressions, because small things could become very big things if a hostile power decided to exploit them. Your secrets were your weakness, and your weakness was the service's weakness. That was why they tried to empty you of them before recruitment. That was why small lies in connection with the job could spell dismissal.

'How was he, about it all?'

'Tearful, apologetic. You can imagine. You knew Rory.'

'Not so well, it seems. Did he try to explain it?'

'What was there to explain? He said he wouldn't have touched them, that wasn't his thing. Said he never did more – that he couldn't. Which I took to mean some kind of impotence but was maybe about a moral threshold. Or both. I know this sounds awful, but right then it didn't strike me as the most appalling thing. He preferred the company of teenagers. He wanted to watch them fucking. That was all.'

'How old were they?'

'Sixteen, seventeen.' Taylor reached out to grind the cigarette against the brickwork before flicking it toward the street. She picked up her mug, moved to the sofa. 'I thought he was a wonderful man. I don't know why I protected him. It would have been the end of him, I suppose, and I didn't believe he deserved that. In the context of everything I'd seen on this job, it seemed forgivable.'

Kane wondered how he would have responded. Possibly the same. Possibly he would have felt more exposed, as a man, collaborating on this cover-up.

'Know if he had previous?'

'Obviously, if there was a history of this kind of thing he would have been dropped by the intelligence service.'

'Not always the case.'

'Maybe not. I went to his home once, you know?' Taylor said. She sounded surprised as she said it.

'Really?'

'We developed a kind of friendship. Around the time everything was falling apart for me. I went to his house, in Shepherd's Bush. It was incredibly empty, I thought. Incredibly lonely.'

'How had he been recently?'

'Not entirely well.'

'No more incidents?'

'I really hope not.'

Kane felt his memory of Rory Bannatyne coming into deeper focus. Like a lot of highly talented people, he didn't entirely fit in the world of adults. He had a touch of Peter Pan to him, and perhaps the Pied Piper, too – not the first spy to draw on those personae. They were often the mercurial and charismatic ones. The service moved you from one job to another, each new mission allowing a fresh start, the fantasy of a fresh you. Rory reminded Kane of military acquaintances who gave the impression that an exterior persona had hardened so fast that it left something vulnerable inside, trapped beneath the shell. And then danger itself became a form of protection.

'You must have had risk assessments for the island, before he went over there,' Kane said.

'I was told to use existing ones produced for GCHQ. I couldn't drop in a security team. Rory was experienced enough to keep an eye out as he went along. And it's British territory. I've checked all travel in and out, searched for patterns that might suggest some kind of cell or hit team. There's nothing. At the same time, obviously we're having to check all data Rory had access to, all live projects.'

The intelligence service didn't like people killing themselves. It responded as if it constituted a form of defection. This wasn't entirely irrational: suicide pointed toward trouble – that could mean guilt over some double-dealing, or fear of blackmail in an ongoing recruit attempt by a foreign power. Records of what an officer knew were kept up to date in case of emergency, to avoid the panicked trawls of years gone by: what operations might be compromised, which individuals were at risk of exposure.

'He wasn't well,' Taylor said. 'That's what I think. He shouldn't have gone.'

'Was he drinking while there?'

She shrugged. 'Wouldn't you?'

'Where did he hang himself?'

'Off an antenna tower.'

'You're joking.'

'I wish I was. A transmitter tower belonging to the BBC, near where he was staying. There are no trees, you see. Or none tall enough. I don't know.'

'Any note?'

'None that's been found. We know nothing about his last few days. That in itself feels odd. Nothing about the hours preceding his death. I have no idea where he was, who he saw, what he was doing. You can see that that's unsettling. I would have loved to say to the police over there: treat this as suspicious, but of course the last thing we want to do is to attract a whole load of attention.'

'You mentioned things missing, belongings.'

'Yes, in particular a file I know he had. I don't believe there were sensitive documents lying around – Rory was too professional for that – but we were quite careful with maintaining an inventory, and a box file of information about the installation is missing. Nothing sensitive, but maybe someone thought it was. Or he left it somewhere. Maybe that would give us some idea of who he hung out with. I have no idea if he had friends over there, enemies, lovers.'

'When did you last see him?'

'At the briefing for the job. He volunteered, by the way. I didn't force him into it. But I passed the opportunity his way. He wasn't getting much work. Obviously no one knew what happened in Seeb, but it had affected him.'

'He said he liked islands. Do you remember? He wanted to go to Masirah Island when we were in Oman.'

'Well, he certainly got an island. Maybe too much of one.'

Kane tried to imagine the experience: working alone there,

intermittent communication with HQ. You have isolated yourself from the rest of humanity, for humanity's sake. Left with only your thoughts for company. But that's the problem.

'What else do you know about Ascension?' he asked.

'It really didn't occupy much of my time until Dominic called. The radars do their thing. It's important enough that one of the main reasons we keep the Falklands is to defend Ascension in case anyone gets too interested. This cable project is partly so we can show the US that we're maximising its potential.'

Kane removed a cigarette from Taylor's pack, lit it, and took her place by the window. A TV flickered in the living room across the road. In twenty minutes, the couple watching it would go to bed. A man would return to the house next door wearing paint-covered overalls and eat standing up alone in his kitchen. Clouds the silver of pencil lead crossed an orange night sky.

What was Ascension like right now? He imagined it silhouetted against the sea. Precious enough for the UK to cling on to. Precious as an offering to the States. The whole GCHQ-NSA relationship was fragile, Kane knew. The Americans wanted to monopolise the flow of Western signals intelligence. What did they get from the Brits, they asked? Some good mathematicians, a loose regulatory environment, then a few strategically placed lumps of rock. The UK didn't have Hong Kong to wave at them anymore. There was Cyprus, of course, its British base hoovering up data from the Middle East. Then Ascension.

'The island captures half the communications circulating the planet,' Taylor said. 'But it's not an easy place to keep tabs on, ironically.'

'The eye sees not itself.'

'Not this one. The installations are mostly managed remotely. I'm told they target long-range high-frequency radio for the most part: military, shipping, that kind of thing. The men on the ground are private contractors, on hand in case a screw needs tightening. Otherwise, we've got a permanent crew of about fifteen RAF personnel, four or five radar engineers, more subcontractors maintaining the runway. I need someone to get into the community, find out about Rory's last days. There are very few officers read in to Echelon with the training for overseas missions of this level. You're the only one I know.'

The only one who knew about Seeb, Kane thought. How much of this was about Taylor's conscience?

'He might have left something,' she said. 'Intentionally or unintentionally. A message.'

'Anything to suggest it?'

'That's my speculation. You always talked about the need for humans on the ground when it came to espionage.'

'I'm very happy being away from the field.'

'No, you're not.'

'Aren't I?'

'I don't think so.'

'I think you mean you're not.'

She considered this. 'I'm not happy. I'm certainly not craving a return to the field.'

'What are you craving?'

'Dreamless sleep. A large vodka tonic. Why haven't you sent any students our way?'

'Why do you think?'

She sipped her tea.

'You think we're all better off out of it.'

'I'm thinking you're doing well, all things considered. You're going to make it to the top. And it would be a better service if you did.'

He watched the succession of emotions cross her face. She had been ambitious – he had recognised that in Oman. And he recognised now the caution with which she handled that ambition, on the other side of personal catastrophe. A readjustment.

But not entire, otherwise she wouldn't have been here, trying to get him on this job. When he finished the cigarette, Kane closed the window.

'How would I get there?' he said. 'If I went.'

She studied his face before replying, as if to ensure he really wanted to cross this threshold.

'A flight goes once a month from Johannesburg via Saint Helena, the other island of ours a few hundred miles to the south of Ascension. There used to be a direct military flight from the UK, but that's been cancelled, so I think via South Africa is our best bet. But we'd have to move fast. The next flight is in a few days' time.'

'A few days? Jesus.'

'There's a cruise ship swinging by on Sunday, but passengers only land for twenty-four hours, so it's not much use to us. What do you think? You'd have to be there for a month, until the next flight back. We'd arrange all cover, something that gets a visitor's permit from the Administrator without drawing undue attention.'

'Like what?'

'Sportfishing.'

'I'm not going to do much from a boat.'

'But at night you'd be socialising: meeting people. Your sort of thing. Isn't that how one does it? It's been a while.' She hesitated. 'Obviously if there's more to this . . . If there's a hostile presence on the island, I'd want you to feel you were in the right place, mentally.'

'You mean do I think I've still got it.'

'Yes. Do you feel mission-sharp?'

It wasn't just a question of sharpness, Kane thought. Missions like this took a particular kind of willpower. A suspension of disbelief. He knew men braver than any, the ones you sent in when no one else would go, who one day kitted up and couldn't walk

33

out the door. And they had to step away from the front line forever because – this was Kane's analysis – they had become sane:
suddenly, painfully sane. They didn't crave the cocktail of testos-
terone and adrenaline that overrode this sanity, couldn't justify
the willingness to inflict pain on others. They were healed.

'If I say no? If this is beyond me?'

'I would understand, of course. Dominic will insist on continuing with the project regardless. I'll have to pray that that's not
foolish in any way.' She placed her mug down on the coffee table.
'Sleep on it. Have a think.'

Taylor stood up. Kane walked her downstairs, where they
swapped numbers, then hugged tightly.

'I want the final decision to be yours,' she said.

'It will be.'

'One way or another, Rory died. *Something* happened to him
over there.'

When the sound of her car had faded, Kane put his coat back
on and walked to the college library.

It was open 24/7 during term time. One reason he didn't
recruit any students for MI6 was that the current crop lacked
experience of misbehaviour. To be good spy material you needed
time falling carelessly into other people's lives. Even at this hour
the library was busy. But it remained hushed and still served as
a refuge, a place where it felt like the world couldn't reach him.
It had its own reality, separate from the clock and the calendar
and identity itself.

The security guard nodded.

'Elliot.'

'Harry.'

'Late one.'

'Can't sleep.'

The guard nodded. Grey-moustached, surely former military
by his posture. Kane had befriended him out of habit: You always

34

made sure security were on your side. He was still getting used to befriending people for no purpose. The only sounds inside were the hum of the heating system and the soft turning of pages. Did he want to leave all this for a rushed and ill-defined mission? Taylor's request was framed with the assumption that you can go on a job and return, then continue where you left off. That was rarely the case.

Kane typed *Ascension Island* into a catalogue terminal. Three results: one book on marine conservation, a travel guide that covered Saint Helena, Tristan de Cunha, and Ascension, and a history of the island.

He found the history book on its shelf at the back of the library, blew the dust off. It began with the discovery of Ascension as related by a member of the Portuguese crew that had first stumbled across it. In the spring of 1503 a fleet of ships sailed from Lisbon, under the command of the great admiral Alfonso de Albuquerque. The Portuguese had established their empire in India and set about emptying the place of spices, gold, and precious stones. When the native rulers began to fight back, Albuquerque was tasked with putting them in their place. This was the purpose of his voyage: not to find treasure but to spill blood. *We left Lisbon on 6 April 1503, in a fleet of four ships: The St James, the Holy Spirit, St Christopher and the Catarina.*

Usually they would have hugged the coast of Africa all the way down, but Albuquerque decided to swing out, to try the deep-sea route avoiding the reefs and shallows closer to shore. They sailed into the deep ocean and promptly got lost. After twenty-eight days they sighted land, but all hopes were dashed as it came into view.

We saw a multitude of ragged, craggy, sharp-pointed rocks for miles along the shore, appearing white with the dung of seafowl of several kinds. It was the most desolate land that my eyes had ever seen, like a land that God has cursed. I believe the whole world affords not such another piece of ground; most parts of it are the colour of burnt brick, reddish, the substance stones, somewhat like pumice stones; the rest like cinders and burnt earth.

The day they saw the island it was the Feast of the Ascension of Jesus Christ, according to the Church calendar, and the Portuguese crew named it Ilha da Ascensão. But they didn't stop.

The island remained unclaimed for three hundred years. Black rats got ashore from passing ships and infested it. Some goats were set down in case any wrecked sailors needed to survive. Neither softened its desolation. In 1656 a Cornish adventurer and travel writer returning from his third voyage to India confirmed the views of his Portuguese predecessors: *A more bleak and barren landscape cannot be imagined. Truly, it struck my eyes as Hell with all the fires put out.*

How bad could it be, Kane wondered? He opened a browser, searched 'Ascension' on images. The first result was a girl's face.

He didn't pay too much attention to it initially. She was smiling, pretty, with a light-brown complexion. Every other image showed variations of volcanic slopes and empty beaches. Then he saw the text beneath the thumbnail.

Search continues for missing Ascension Island teenager.

It was from *The Times*, two hours ago. Kane clicked.

Residents of Ascension Island, a British Overseas territory in the South Atlantic, continue their search for 15-year-old Petra Wade, last seen six days ago. The island, owned by the British since 1815, is considered a temporary home by 800 people. Its 35 square miles of terrain are rugged with cliffs and sea, and concerns are mounting that the teenager may have fallen while out walking, or been washed out to sea by exceptionally high tides. In a statement, her parents said: 'There is no indication Petra had any reason to disappear, and we beg every individual on the island to help look for her. We believe she may be injured somewhere.' Ascension itself has its own small police detachment, plus military who are assisting in the search.

Last seen six days ago. Kane checked a calendar online. It was the day Rory Bannatyne killed himself. His phone screen lit up: Kat Taylor calling. Kane answered, stepping out of the reading room.

'The situation's got a bit more complex,' Taylor said.

'I've just seen. Anything to suggest it connects?'

'Apart from everything?' She sounded breathless, agitated. 'The girl went missing a few hours before he died.'

'Did you have any idea about this?'

'No.'

'Still want me to go?'

'Do you think you can?'

'Yes, I think so.'

'Okay. I've just got into Vauxhall. It's going to be a long night, and there's police involvement on the horizon. I'll let you know what I can find out. If I don't speak to you later, let's speak in the morning. Thank you, Elliot. This is ... '

'We'll see what it is.'

'Yes.'

Kane returned to the books, his heart beating with a forcefulness he hadn't felt for a while. *Do you feel mission-sharp ...* The guard approached. Kane moved instinctively to cover the history of Ascension, then stopped himself.

'Looks like no one's had that for a while,' the guard said, nodding at the book.

'I'm doing some interesting research.'

'What's that then?'

'It's about an island in the South Atlantic: Ascension. Belongs to us.'

'Never heard of it.'

'Might be some travelling involved.'

'Tropical island, eh? Want to swap jobs?'

'I'll send you a postcard.'

'Jammy sod.'

The guard walked on. Kane clicked into secure browsing, searched for any more news on the missing girl, but there was nothing. Then he searched for academic research networks: colonialism, sixteenth century, South Atlantic, watching his fingers type but thinking through an operations checklist: transport, equipment, cash, ID.

He brought up a photograph of the girl again, then a map of the island's thirty-five square miles.

FOUR

Twenty-four hours after his visit to GCHQ, Kane was in a briefing room in an anonymous MI6-owned office above an insurance company in Holborn. By Thursday morning, he was walking through Johannesburg's OR Tambo International Airport, watching the crowds thin out as he approached the gate for his flight to Saint Helena, the second leg of his three-flight journey to Ascension.

In his bag were the books and research materials he had managed to acquire in the limited time available: two histories of Ascension Island, one on the Royal Marines, Charles Driver's *Chronicle of the British Empire*, and the translation of a diary left by a Dutch sailor abandoned on Ascension in the 1700s. He had a passport, driving licence, and bank cards in the name of Dr Edward Pearce, a postgraduate researcher in early modern history at Pembroke College. Two cardboard wallet files contained the notes for Pearce's work in progress: 'Islands in the Imperial Imagination.'

There'd been no sign of the missing girl. It was ten days since Bannatyne had hanged himself and Petra Wade disappeared from the world. In the absence of useful leads, Kane had read everything he could find regarding the island, as if this itself might prepare him. But it only enhanced his sense of unease. Ascension was the tip of an undersea volcano. One per cent of it was above water. Head down another few miles and you got to the rift that stretched from Iceland to the Antarctic, where continental plates pulled away from each other and the earth's boiling core welled up. One myth said that Ascension was still warm when the first humans stepped on it. That was a few millennia out, but it said something about the lack of invitation that the rock extended.

Nearly forty dead volcanic cones rose up from its surface of lava and ash. For centuries these belonged to the seabirds who came there to breed, and the giant turtles who, once a year, swam from Brazil guided by some imperishable logic to lay their eggs before swimming back again. Humans had been dissuaded from any settlement by the scarcity of fresh water. It hadn't been entirely uninhabited in its earlier days, however. Sailors visiting Ascension in 1726 discovered a tent and the diary belonging to a Dutch mariner abandoned there the year before as punishment for sleeping with another crew member. The diary recorded his descent into terror and insanity.

It took British aggression to see the island's potential. In 1815 Napoleon was imprisoned on Saint Helena to the southeast. The British garrisoned Ascension as a precaution against it being used as a base by any French troops trying to rescue him. By the time of Napoleon's death, the island had become a midocean supply station and hospital for fever-stricken crews from the anti-slavery patrols. Eventually, freed West African slaves from the Krumen tribe were brought ashore to provide cheap labour. In 1823 the island passed into the hands of the Royal Marines, and in 1899, when the first telegraph cable arrived, it brought civilians into the population. By 1921, the navy had handed over all administration to the telegraph company, who now operated under the name Cable and Wireless.

That was the most peaceful period: just two hundred people on the rock, handling the wires. Then World War II arrived and fifteen hundred US troops descended in a matter of days. They worked around the clock to build the airfield, shielding the floodlights from enemy ships. The stony ground chewed up their drill bits, and the men – four thousand of them at the height of the war – slept on the beaches and among the rocks.

When the war ended, they all left. And none of the available accounts was very clear about what happened next. A year later, some Americans returned to survey the place, and a few months after that, new constructions appeared: radars and antennae and installations more mysterious than both. The Cold War had begun.

That was how the island had been for the last sixty years: useful, secretive, silent. As NASA began to develop its Apollo programme, they built a tracking station on the island. When the Falklands kicked off, Ascension provided a staging point for bombing raids. Otherwise it was uneventful, if events meant a physical occurrence in the public domain. Saint Helenians provided a local workforce. They were known as Saints, manning the bars, teaching at the school, helping with maintenance and fishing. They came over from the sister island on temporary permits and brought their families with them. In 2005, George and Jackie Wade came over with their three-year-old daughter, Petra. George worked as a private contractor doing operational support at the airfield; his wife secured a job in the US base canteen. Petra joined the small community of Ascension Island children who attended a nursery and school in Two Boats, the village in the centre of the island.

Petra did well at the Two Boats school, which followed the English curriculum. Extracurricular activities included camping, diving, and singing. Last year, at age fourteen, she won Miss Ascension. In pictures she looked older than her years: confident, healthy with a life of sun and sea. Locals described her as lively, spirited, charming.

At five p.m. on Tuesday, 7 November, she told her mother

she was going out to meet a friend, Lauren Carter, who lived in Two Boats. Petra's father was working. School was finished. Her mother said the girl was keen to get out, but in no way upset or distressed. She was wearing denim shorts and a striped vest top, pink Adidas trainers, and an unbranded pale blue baseball cap. The day had topped thirty degrees Celsius. She took her bike.

The last sighting of her was by a shopkeeper in Two Boats roughly an hour later, who said Petra was looking for someone, or on her way to meet someone, but they didn't know who. She still had the bike with her. Lauren Carter said she never saw her; said that they had had no arrangement to meet in the first place.

Petra didn't come home. It would have got dark around seven p.m., according to Kane's research. There was no mobile reception on the island. At ten o'clock her mother got a lift up to Two Boats and began asking around. It wasn't so unusual for Petra to stay out. No one knew anything. Jackie Wade returned to Georgetown and informed the police, who had closed the station for the night but were easily found in the Exiles Bar nearby. Whether for this reason or others, the police didn't launch into a full search right away.

The island had a rudimentary courthouse and a police station staffed by a former Metropolitan Police sergeant on a two-year posting. He was in charge of one full-time constable and two volunteer special constables. The senior officer, Sergeant John Morrogh, made calls to several individuals in places where Petra might be – including the two bases – and asked them to keep an eye out. It seemed Morrogh was initially reluctant to take it seriously. Petra was known to stay at various friends' houses, hence her father himself hadn't been concerned. The thinking, it seemed, was *How far can she go?*

That question remained unanswered.

The following day, Fire and Sea Rescue Services searched, as did staff from the bases. Drones were sent up, RAF-trained sniffer dogs set loose, finally a helicopter with heat-seeking equipment. The search went on for five days before being slowly wound down without any sign of her. No sign of her bike, either. The investigation remained open.

Rory Bannatyne had been found dead at six a.m. the day after Petra was first reported missing. For reasons that were unclear, it took some time to name him as a suspect. In the end it was a suggestion by officers on the US base that prompted a closer look. The police had searched his accommodation and dug speculatively around it in case any bodies turned up, but, finding nothing to directly connect the two events, their investigation hit a dead end. From what Kane could tell, it looked like they gave up. It seemed odd.

Taylor had acquired transcripts of all interviews the police had conducted, which amounted to over fifty individuals, none of whom had very much to say. Few people seemed to know Petra well, not even her parents. Did she have a boyfriend? They didn't know. Had they had an argument with her? No, just the usual disagreements. She was approaching the end of her time at the island's school, which meant the end of the time she was permitted on the island. The parents said she was worried about the idea of leaving, but no one asked directly if she was happy. And no one asked if she knew Rory Bannatyne.

Taylor had run the names of all men on the island against the sexual offender's register and international databases of paedophiles, but none came up. Kane had checked through general records of crime on Ascension, just in case anything stood out. There were drunk-driving offences, a fight on the UK base, the theft of some potatoes, but nothing more. The island's policing and justice system was a colonial hand-me-down: British, faded by time and the sun and limited, enclosed means. For most of its occupied life, Ascension had been technically classed as a ship. This had been the only way the Royal Navy could think of to ensure discipline, and meant the captain's orders were law. While the situation was more civilian now, it retained eccentricities, with ad hoc plans to improvise court trials in emergencies. Kane had a sense that these remained untested.

One anecdote from a history of the island lodged inside his mind like a tune he couldn't shake. A cook in the Royal Marines, stationed on Ascension for two years, had eventually had a fit and was placed in the island's hospital but ran out onto the sharp rocks barefoot, cutting his legs and feet to ribbons. Found covered in blood in what the records described as a state of acute mania, he had to be forced into the police station for his own safety. Kane felt a thread among the accounts of island life: of breaking points, men and women who stopped resisting the surroundings, and the environment had torn them to shreds.

When you get there, take a breath, he told himself. Don't rush. Fight the instinct to dive in and start investigating. Settle, blend, penetrate. Six months was a long time on an island of eight hundred people – there would be those who'd liked Rory and those who didn't. People who wanted something from him, people he wanted something out of. People who might have known his state of mind. Something made Kane feel he could find out what happened that night, if only because he was starting in that unique position of a spy: an outsider with privileged insight.

The loudspeaker woke him from that fantasy.

Would passengers for Flight 301 to Saint Helena make their way to the boarding gate, where boarding has commenced ...

He got to his feet and lifted his luggage, which seemed inadequate. There was something about the journey, with its syncopated hopping to ever more remote and uninhabitable pieces of land that felt at once disorientating and like you were being fired with great precision toward a target.

The passengers on the Saint Helena flight were mostly Saints, their deep skin tones betraying ancestry suffused with

44

intersecting bloodlines: European administrators, Chinese workers, slaves from Madagascar. Kane got his first hearing of the accent, which was a historical repository in itself, sliding between Cockney, Australian, and Irish by way of West Africa.

One of the Saint Helenians took the seat beside Kane when they boarded. He was an elegant-looking man with touches of grey in his hair, a gold tooth, and a gold watch. As they took off, he kept wistful eyes on the view.

'Heading to or from home?' Kane said. The man turned.

'That's a good question, my friend.'

He had been visiting his girlfriend in Cape Town, he said. She worked at a hotel, and they were debating where things were going. He had three kids on Saint Helena, one in the States.

'I've heard a lot about the island, the warmth of the people,' Kane said.

'Oh, we're warm.' He laughed. 'You're from the UK?'

'That's right.'

'Good old UK. I wouldn't be here without you. My grandfather was a descendant of one of the Boer prisoners of war. You guys took them to the island,' he said. 'That was 1901. And British people never seem to know anything about it. Know about the Boer War?'

'Not as much as I should.'

'The British took over twenty thousand prisoners, and then didn't know what to do with them. The prisoner of war camps in South Africa were bursting. So they decided to ship prisoners to Bermuda, India, Sri Lanka, Saint Helena. You name it. The locals treated us well. Better than the British. So one way or another we ended up sticking around. Where are you staying on Saint Helena?' he asked.

'I'm not. I have to get the flight to Ascension.'

The man stared at him.

'What do you want to go there for?'

'Research. I work on British colonial history.'

'Stay on Saint Helena. We're colonial. We've got people and restaurants, too. Might be a speck in the Atlantic, but at least we're more than just a volcano.'

Something evidently troubled him about the prospect of Kane flying onward.

'Have you been to Ascension?' Kane asked.

'Not me. A lot of us go over to work. Saints go over there, think it's a privilege, an honour to be selected, and you never see them again.'

'Literally?'

'Almost. There used to be a boat service, RMS *Saint Helena*. Now it's monthly flights, and they only run those because they have to. It's in the contracts. That's a strange island.'

Kane took the comment as an invitation.

'I heard a girl went missing recently.'

The man assessed him again before nodding slowly.

'I know the family. They're back on Saint Helena now, hearts broken.'

'They went back?'

'What could they do? Searched for ten days, eleven days. They've got no other friends or family there – all their family's on Saint Helena. The island's been searched top to bottom.'

'What do they think happened?'

'They have no idea. The girl loved to swim. There's sharks. No one knows.'

He turned away, toward the window, and Kane wondered if he'd stepped past an invisible boundary, or if there was something he wasn't saying. A few minutes later the man pulled his hat down in front of his eyes and fell asleep.

When Saint Helena appeared beneath them it looked attractive, its capital nestled between two steep hills, like a river of homes running to the sea. Population 4,500, which was five times larger than Ascension. Kane felt sorry to be moving on. He tried to see the house where Napoleon was held, but they dropped too fast.

The airport was miniature, the size of a bus station, but clean and modern and even fitted with air-conditioning, and while the view from its windows didn't extend past the expanse of beige rock in which it sat, those departing for the greener interior seemed light-hearted about it. Kane watched passengers disperse to cars and buses, and then the handful connecting to Ascension were revealed. Seven British military with canvas kit bags, two US Air Force personnel: a man and a woman. There was a group of Saints, one of whom had a huge sack of provisions: fruit and vegetables mostly, wholesale boxes of chocolate bars and crisps. Finally a British couple bringing a boxed air-con unit.

No tourists. No other first-timers, you could tell. The atmosphere was altogether different now. Those remaining were people making the journey for reasons other than sheer desire, mentally readying themselves.

They boarded at nine p.m. Kane saw mailbags and boxes of frozen food being wheeled aboard, and finally a mint-condition Hyundai motorbike. The crew of their small seventy-six-seat plane seemed unfazed by the varied cargo. The flight was rocky. Kane had hoped to sleep, but that wasn't happening. His thoughts raced, working through his preparation: spreadsheets of locations and individuals, all about to become real. Four hours into the flight they began to drop toward the ocean. Kane looked to see their target but there was nothing beneath them apart from thin white strands of foam. They sank through the air until, at the final minute, a scrap of cloud appeared ahead and then a reddish-brown rock beneath it: Ascension.

Kane couldn't see how there would be room to land. As they drew closer the surface resolved itself into individual volcanic cones, then the prickles of antennae came into view. Still no sign of life, just aerial arrays and satellite dishes, and finally a runway cutting through the rock.

They touched down in a cloud of red dust, then taxied back to a small hangar at the edge of an empty airfield. The runway petered out. His fellow passengers roused themselves. Again, there was a sense of a deep breath being taken, of stiffening the sinews, steadying the mind.

Kane filed out through a few metres of blinding sun, past a sign that welcomed them to Ascension Island Base. The terminal was a boxlike structure with a handful of seats inside. An official sat sweating at a desk with a line of yellow tape on the floor to signify the border. A few metres beyond him was a small cluster of islanders waiting to greet friends and relatives, fanning themselves, all deeply tanned: men in cargo shorts, one woman in a dress and sun hat, one teenage boy cradling a Doberman. Kane looked out for a hotel rep but couldn't see one.

The immigration official wore a hi-vis vest over khaki fatigues. He checked Kane's passport and permit.

'Mr Pearce. Professor Pearce?'

'Dr Pearce.' Kane saw he had the details of Pearce's visa application already beside him. The man flicked through the passport, looking at the other stamps that the ops team had included, checked the photo again, and looked up at Kane's face.

'Here for research?'

'Yes.'

'How long are you planning to stay?'

'Four weeks. Until the next flight back.'

'What are you going to research in four weeks?'

'As much as possible. I've been very interested in the history of this island for a long time. I wanted to see it for myself, how people live here.'

The man raised an eyebrow.

'No doubt you'll find out.'

He brought the stamp down hard, leaving the image of a sea-bird, its outlines smudged by sweat.

Kane removed his suitcase from the pile. He dragged it outside, shielding his eyes against the low sun. No sign of his hotel transfer. A donkey wandered onto the runway, standing on the barren tarmac like a protest. Peaks rose up on the north side of the airfield in varying shades of red and brown and grey. A man in an old windproof red jacket with the Royal Mail logo on the back untied the mailbag and the islanders diverted their attention from the human arrivals to the post as various letters and parcels were distributed. A Mercedes minibus loaded up with the Americans and drove off in the direction of the US base. Kane helped lift the motorbike onto the back of a transit van. He watched the plane refuel, ready to leave again.

Six became six thirty p.m. The sun melted on the horizon. A hard silence descended. No buzz of nature or rustle of trees. Kane waited for the night hum of insects, but nothing came. His phone had no signal. There was one pay phone at the back of the terminal. As he was hunting for a number to call, the sun disappeared with a last, malevolent throb of red, like a jailer walking away with the key. Kane thought of the vast expanse of ocean around him and felt a rush of claustrophobia.

The immigration officer began to lock up. The postal worker moved cardboard boxes into the back of a Chevy pickup. He moved rapidly, although his limbs were thin, and there was something malnourished about him.

'Is there any kind of taxi service here?' Kane asked.

'Not here, no,' the man said.

Kane used the public phone, tried a number for the hotel, but no one answered. They were closing the airport now. The postman watched Kane hang up.

'You okay?' he asked.

'I need to get to Georgetown. Any chance of a lift?'

'I can drive you. Give me a minute.'

The man spoke to the official, exchanged some pleasantry, and led Kane to the pickup.

'Just got here?'

'About an hour ago.'

'You can forget that,' he said, nodding to the phone in Kane's hand. 'You'll get used to it. First time on the island?'

'Yes.'

The man nodded.

'Climb in.'

It was pitch black once they were out of the airport. Beyond the bubble of their headlights, the world ended. A car passed in the opposite direction. The postman raised his hand and the other driver did the same, then they were gone.

'Brought any books over?' the man said.

'Quite a few.'

'I've read every book on this island, I reckon.'

'I'll see if I can sort you out. I guess things become precious on an island.'

'On this island, most things do.'

Kane thought of the air-con unit and the motorbike. A land to which every possession had to be hauled. Historical accounts of the island were full of ships bringing cattle and birds and trees, and the anguish at finding that most of them had died on the way.

'Do you live in Georgetown?' Kane said.

'No, but I can drop you there.'

'Been on the island a while?'

'A few years now. Lost count. But that makes me an old-timer. Not many stick it out.'

'Must be peaceful though.'

'Peaceful, all right.'

They passed wind turbines turning in the moonlight, then

50

circular arrays of antennae looking like no installations Kane had ever seen before. The road was bumpy now. They bounced north past the US base. The GCHQ radome came into view, like a giant golf ball perched on top of a flattened volcanic cone. Kane wondered what work it was doing now, whether someone in the Cheltenham offices in which he'd sat just five days ago was monitoring its actions.

'Can you hear that?' the driver said. He slowed the car. Kane listened for some hum or tick from the technology but heard only a soft rustling sound. It became louder as they continued: not technology, but nature cawing.

'Full moon, you see. They've come.' The man stopped the car, rolled his window down. Kane did the same. 'Sooty terns. You can't see them very well, but there's thousands there.'

What Kane saw was a vast plain of rippling black. He could only tell it was birds by their cries.

'Wide-awakes, that's what people call them. Because they never shut up.' The postman stared out, breathing slowly. 'Yeah, they're there.'

The signals interception facility was apparently unremarkable.

'What's the thing that looks like a golf ball?' Kane asked.

'Radar.'

'Must be strange living here with all that going on on your doorstep.'

'You don't notice it after a while.'

A few minutes later they arrived at a scattering of pale bungalows. A sign said WELCOME TO GEORGETOWN – PLEASE DRIVE SLOWLY. Only two structures achieved any visible height, the spire of a church and the clocktower of the old barracks. Waves crashed beyond them.

'This is Georgetown.' He stopped the car. 'You'll be all right?'

'Better be. Can I give you some money for the petrol?'

'That's okay. Was hardly out of my way.'

Kane thanked him and got out. The man wheeled around and drove back in the direction of the airport. Kane watched the taillights fade, then contemplated his new home. All the buildings looked anonymous and identical. The sea glistened darkly beyond them, waves booming as they hit the shore. But his attention was stolen by the night sky. Stars covered it like a rash, larger and brighter than any stars he'd seen before. They stretched from horizon to horizon, unfamiliar constellations: the Southern Cross, the Great Bear turned upside down. And the spotlight moon. The rest of humanity was a thousand miles away. The moon was only twice as far.

No bright hotel sign called to him. No street signs. Georgetown was deserted. Only the occasional sound of a television disturbed the stillness. The air was briny and the heat had settled in for the night. The ground was black grit, like poorly laid tarmac. Everything had a disjointed air, with big gaps between properties and no clear suggestion of where the road ended and plots of land began. According to Kane's notes, Georgetown housed three hundred people, but that seemed unlikely right now. He had the sensation of being watched, but couldn't see another soul.

It seemed logical that the hotel would be close to the centre. Kane associated the centre with the two big buildings. St Mary's Church had a spectral luminescence, its whitewash trapping moonlight. Facing it across an expanse of black ground was the old barracks. This was the site of the original military garrison, now known as the Exiles Building. In the silver light it appeared like something from a dream, with a pillared colonnade along the ground floor creating black arches. A few hundred metres beyond it, jutting into the water, was the island's port.

Maybe the hotel was by the sea.

Kane walked to the port, which was no more than a small stone promontory protected by railings. A set of steep concrete steps sank down into the black froth. All the fishing boats were

moored away from shore, safely into the bay, and even the din-
ghies for tendering were weighted at a distance from the stone.
The sea churned, with sparks of phosphorescence moving in
cryptic forms beneath the surface.

A crane towered above him, warehouse buildings at the
back – a shipping office, fire station. The ruins of an old stone
fort remained to the side, one of the original lookout points, silhouetted against the water. No hotel.

He headed back, past the church, toward the edge of the settlement where it ran up against a wall of starless black hillside. That
was where he found the hotel. There was an expanse of empty
parking lot with a giant anchor at its centre, and a dark, bulky
building a few metres beyond it with not a single light on inside.

The door was locked. A laminated notice had been fixed to
the glass beside it:

*It is with the deepest regret that the Shareholders in the Ascension
Georgetown Hotel have decided to close their hotel and car hire business on Ascension. We have chosen to keep the business going for
the six months since the curtailing of flight links with the UK in the
hope that a worthwhile service would resume. Sadly, the air links currently proposed are inadequate for the purposes of maintaining a fully
functioning hotel and it is impossible for the Ascension Georgetown
to continue its operations any further into such an uncertain future.*

No date. The sign looked new. Kane studied the structure. His
feeling, beyond anger at the total bungling by whoever had made
the arrangement, was that if this could go wrong, anything could
go wrong. It was a reminder that, due to exceptional operational
sensitivity, he wasn't working with a full team, that the people
planning this operation had never set foot on the territory. The
abandoned hotel was a disaster, but it wasn't the worst thing that
could happen to him here.

Kane walked around to the back. The windows would be easy enough to open. He could get inside for tonight. Was there another hotel on the island? Could he get there if there was? It was past nine p.m. now.

On his way back toward the residential area, he started looking at cars – old, rusted vehicles, a couple with keys in the ignition. This felt useful to know. There were lights on in some of the bungalows. When he saw his first silhouette behind a blind, Kane knocked. He was still surprised when someone answered it, and felt obscurely guilty, catching them existing in such a strange environment, as if everything on the island must be furtive.

It was a woman in her forties, securing a pink dressing gown around herself. She had pink tubes of sponge tied into her hair.

'I'm sorry to disturb you,' Kane said. 'I've just arrived here and found myself in a bit of a situation. I had expected to stay at the hotel, you see ...'

The woman winced. 'You booked online?'

'That's right.'

'This happened with a group on a yacht a few days ago. Seems they haven't sorted out their website.'

'What are my options?' Kane said.

'There's not many.'

'Any other hotels?'

She laughed. 'No.' Then she bit her lip, thinking. 'There is one possibility.' She hesitated. 'Follow me.'

She put her lock on the latch, slipped some flip-flops on, and led Kane around the corner.

'Where is everyone?' Kane asked.

'It's movie night on the base.'

'What are they showing?'

'Something good, I guess. It doesn't really matter.'

The woman knocked on the door of a bungalow and a man

answered in Bermuda shorts and a T-shirt that said ASCENSION DIVING SCHOOL. He was stocky, with thick grey curls. He studied Kane with a touch of disbelief as the woman explained his predicament, then went back inside, reappearing a few seconds later with a set of keys and some bedsheets draped over his arm. They crossed the road to an identical bungalow, only unlit.

'The previous tenant has just left,' the man explained as they walked in. He turned the lights on. It was a family home, furnished, even some pictures on the walls: flowers, lakes.

Kane started to get a grim feeling.

The three of them peered inside each room. The man checked the taps, opened the pedal bin. They seemed curious. He opened cupboards and swept up some dead leaves from where a plant had sat beside the sink. A line of ants continued their traffic. Kane peered apprehensively at a low single bed in a small bedroom. The only bed that had retained a mattress, it seemed. It was the room of a teenage girl.

'There's not an overabundance of accommodation on the island,' the man said. 'Perhaps tomorrow you can ask at Two Boats. I don't see the harm in you being here tonight.'

'Sure. That's great.'

The wallpaper was yellow, posters of celebrities still attached, stickers on a mirror. An ornament hung from the ceiling above the bed: feathers dangling from a metal hoop with a web of threads criss-crossing it.

'It's quiet here,' he said. 'You're not too near the bar.'

'It's all I need. I'm sure I'll be very comfortable. I'm Edward, by the way.'

'Craig.'

'How much do I owe you, Craig?'

When Kane reached for his wallet, the man waved it away as if a transaction would seal the distaste.

'Not mine to let, really. Just looking after it. See how you get on. If it's just tonight, I wouldn't worry about it.' He handed the key to Kane and departed as if he didn't want to spend too long in the place. The woman took a final look around.

'Well, it's a roof over your head.'

'I appreciate it. I was planning to hire a car from the hotel,' Kane said. 'Know of anywhere else I could get one?'

'Ask at the museum tomorrow. They should be able to sort you out.'

'The museum. Okay.'

'I have no doubt I'll see you around. Welcome. I'm Linda. I'm sorry about all this.'

'Edward.' He shook her hand. 'You've been a great help.'

When she was gone, Kane returned to the teenager's bedroom and stared. He watched the dreamcatcher turning on its string, reached up and touched a feather.

In the kitchen, he lifted his case to the table, found the phone with its hidden satellite function, and tried to send confirmation of his arrival. He was supposed to get immediate notification of the message's delivery, but none came. Kane checked Taylor's bespoke file-sharing system, fitted with the intelligence service's own end-to-end encryption. He looked for an updated report, but there was nothing.

He unpacked his torch, compass, maps, first-aid kit. There were lockpicks, a pair of binoculars, a wireless mini-camera that could fit several external cases, two listening devices, the phone with digital and analogue radio scanner, the laptop loaded with software for accessing local networks and intercepting data packets, all buried deep beneath Edward Pearce's research notes. But Kane anticipated an analogue environment. He arranged some files of historical research on the table, then notes on the island, then opened the map beside them.

The island was roughly an equilateral triangle with each side about seven miles long. He was currently on the west coast.

Most of the island's facilities were around here: the runway and airbase and GCHQ-NSA. Rory Bannatyne had been staying a couple of miles north of here, at the tip of the island. Kane's visit to his home would have to wait until tomorrow.

In the centre of the island was Two Boats village, where Petra had last been seen. Beside it was Green Mountain, the highest peak. A lot of place names appeared to have been dreamed up by men in the grip of a bad fever: Dead Man's Beach, Comfortless Cove, Devil's Cauldron. Satellite images of the island only made the place more enigmatic: thin strings of road among plains of what looked like elephant hide, with some of the most powerful surveillance tech in the world reduced to white spores among the lava. But you could see the British base had a cricket pitch and the Americans had a baseball diamond, could see the cold geometry of the installations – squares and circles of antennae and God knows what else – strangely at home among the forbidding rock.

Kane put the map away and listened to the waves pounding a few metres from his new home: the slow, alternating detonation and hiss as they crashed in, sending up spray that hung in the air before collapsing like a moment of rain. Then there was ten seconds before the next explosion, as if the sea was setting about destroying the island that had appeared in its midst one day. There was something measured and vindictive about it that reminded Kane of artillery shelling. He tried to slow his breathing to the rhythm of the waves. Then he heard a child scream.

It was short, terrified, abruptly cut off. The silence that followed seemed deeper than before. Kane opened the front door and stood in the doorway, wondering if he could have mistaken it. Then he heard another cry – *No* – and the grunt of an older, larger person.

Kane walked toward the sound. The settlement still appeared empty. Had no one else heard it? He stopped, listened, heard the voice again – less like a child now but still someone very young and terrified, a boy – he was sure it was a boy or teenager pleading. Then the older man said: *What do you want?*

They were on the other side of the old barracks. Kane went to the corner to get a view. He saw the white of the church and then two figures in front of it. The struggle was between a boy of no older than sixteen and a large man around Kane's age. The boy wore a white T-shirt and shorts. He was on his knees, trying to pick himself up. The man used a foot to push him onto his side. A torch beam came from the far side of the square, where two more men were approaching.

'Get off me.' The boy had an American accent. A bike lay on the ground between the church and the barracks. The man above him lifted his head by the hair.

'What are you doing here?'

'Nothing.'

'You fucking dare to come here?'

Kane considered his options. Dive in? Without knowing anything about this scenario? That would jeopardise his cover before his first night was over. What would Dr Edward Pearce do? He'd be in bed, asleep, earplugs in.

'He was snooping around,' the man said to the new arrivals.

'No, I wasn't.' The boy tried to get up and the man stepped on his hand. The boy screamed. In the torchlight Kane saw the assailant was in his thirties, with a fade cut and tattoos, and the neat, polished muscles of military staff with time to kill. Kane's guess was a corporal or junior technician. The other two wore identical red polo shirts branded INTERSERVE, one of the subcontractors running facilities. One was a Saint, darker skinned, the tallest of the three. The other was short and squat. He held a bottle and cigarette in one hand.

'What are you doing here?' The smoker stepped closer to the boy, speaking quieter. Now the corporal lifted the boy up. The stocky man got his hand around the boy's throat. 'Eh? What the fuck are you doing?'

The boy struggled, getting a foot up and trying to kick him. The bottle fell and smashed. The subcontractor grabbed his foot and twisted the leg, and then the soldier released the boy and let him fall face down in the dirt. The Saint drove a powerful kick into the boy's stomach.

'Take his shoes,' the first man said. The two subcontractors tore the boy's shoes off. The corporal lifted the boy's head by the hair and looked like he was about to slam it into the ground.

Kane stepped forward.

'Hey.'

They all turned. One of the subcontractors aimed the torch in Kane's face.

'Who's that?' the corporal said.

'What's going on here?'

The boy watched Kane, chest rising and falling, blood and ash across his face. He looked wary, as if Kane might be the next to kick him.

'Back off,' the short man said.

'Okay. But I think that's enough for now. Let him go.'

Few people are ever up for a physical contest that holds the possibility of their losing. The mammalian brain is good at reading who has the psychological edge. Two of the men weren't fighters – the Saint was going through the motions, but you could see he was deferential to the other two. The stocky man was angry but weak. He'd run if it came to it. The corporal was the one who needed to be taken out, and he was the one who walked toward Kane. He appraised the clothes and style of Kane's cover: preppy, pallid, academic.

'I said back off,' he said. 'Who the fuck are you?'

'What's the boy done? It doesn't seem like a fair fight to me.'

The man came right up to Kane, fury in his eyes. The Saint at the back said: 'Fuck's sake. Let's go.'

The boy tried to move, then grunted in pain as the short subcontractor punched him once, hard, in the side of the head. The corporal was close enough for Kane to smell the tobacco on his breath.

'Get out of here.'

'Okay,' Kane said. He gave a placatory smile, backed off an inch, then slammed his forehead into the bridge of the man's nose. The man stumbled backwards, hands going up to his face. Kane caught his wrist and turned it so that the man let out an involuntary scream, sinking to his knees.

'Get the fuck off me.'

The other two stared as blood began to gush from his nose.

'Get off the kid,' Kane said to them. They took a step back, leaving the boy on the ground. The corporal got to his feet, looked at Kane. Kane spread his arms. Next round meant putting the man out of contention. He suspected the cartilage was weak and a second strike at the face could be excruciating. But he didn't want to kill the guy. Maybe take the legs out, get him on the ground again and fuck with him psychologically. Sensing something troublingly composed in Kane's stance, the man seemed to think twice about prolonging the encounter.

'You're a dead bastard now,' he said, walking backwards as if only the turning indicated surrender. He smiled through the blood. When he reached the other two, they continued as a group back into the darkness.

Kane helped the boy up. He got a good look at him for the first time: a mop of curly, fair hair, a smattering of acne, a child's narrow shoulders. His lip was torn, the right side of his face grazed, nostrils caked in blood. Kane found the boy's trainers but he struggled to put them on.

'I'm okay.'

Kane watched him pick up the bike and try to walk.

'Fuck.'

He let the bike fall and sat down, removing his right shoe. It was filled with blood.

'Let me see your foot,' Kane said.

Kane gripped the boy's ankle and plucked a sliver of glass out. It was bleeding heavily.

'You're going to need a bandage on that before you can do anything. Can I give you a bandage?'

The boy nodded.

'All right to come with me?'

'Yes.'

'What's your name?'

'Connor.'

'Connor, I'm Edward. I'll try to get you cleaned up and you can go home. Try not to put weight on it.'

Kane put the boy's arm across his own shoulders. He wheeled the bike with his free hand and they progressed back through the town. In the distance he could hear vehicles returning, wheels on gravel, some laughter.

'They stood on my knee. It's broken.'

'If it was broken you'd still be on the floor. Can you bend it?'

'No.'

'Keep going.'

Kane unlocked the bungalow. The boy looked around curiously when they were inside.

'You're staying here?'

'For now. The hotel's shut down.'

Connor leaned against the wall of the hallway.

'Can you see okay?' Kane asked.

'Yeah.'

'They got your head pretty hard. You're not dizzy?'

'No.'

The floor was already spattered with blood. Kane told the boy to go stand in the bath and rinse his feet. The boy knew where the bathroom was. Kane caught his own reflection in the hallway mirror and there was a speck of blood on his forehead where he'd headbutted the man. He wiped it off and stood there for a moment, listening to the taps run, thinking: I've fucked up already. All he had needed was to remain relatively incognito. This would be everywhere by morning. Had he needed to do that? Had he enjoyed it? Rory had come to this island unwell, and Kane had followed him without due consideration to his own state of mind.

He got his first-aid kit and cleaned the dirt out of the boy's foot before and bandaging up the worst of it. Any deeper and the glass would have severed a tendon. The boy had been lucky. Kane used tweezers to get some of the worst grit out of the side of the face and applied some antiseptic, then had him extend his injured leg and checked mobility.

'Know who they were?' Kane asked.

'No. Who are you?' Connor asked.

'I just got here. You need to get the cuts properly treated or they'll get infected.'

'I'll be okay.'

'Where do you live?'

'On the base.'

'The American one?'

'That's right.'

'Think you should go to the police?'

The boy laughed. 'No.'

'Why's that funny?'

He shook his head, then exhaled softly through his teeth, making a whistling sound, wincing.

'What was the fight about?' Kane asked.

'It wasn't a fight. They just went for me.'

'That's true. Why'd they do that?'

62

'Because they're arseholes.'

Kane nodded. No more information was forthcoming, and he didn't want to appear too curious.

'Are your parents on the base?' Kane asked.

'Yes.'

'Got any way of contacting them?'

'No.'

'They'll be worried about you.'

'Yeah.' The boy winced again, looked at Kane. 'Do you have a car?'

'No.'

The boy looked disappointed. Kane stood up, an ominous sensation in his gut, realising what he was about to do.

'Wait there.'

He walked out to one of the cars he'd seen with keys in the ignition – a Honda Accord from the nineties, parked outside a house with no lights on. Kane knocked at the house. No answer. He eased the driver's door open, climbed into the trapped heat, started the engine. No one came to stop him.

'You found a car,' the boy said when he pulled up.

'Hop in.'

The boy got his bike into the back, then climbed in the front.

'Whose is this?'

'I don't know. Are you able to direct me?'

'Sure.'

They drove back past the airfield.

'Those guys,' Kane said. 'People don't just beat people up for no reason.'

'Tell them.'

'They do it to other kids?'

'Probably.'

'I might be in trouble now. I could do with knowing what I've got myself involved in.'

'I don't think you're involved.'

'The one I spoke to sounded British, right?'

'I guess so. *Spoke to.*' The boy laughed. 'How do you do that?' He turned, smiling, and Kane saw his front teeth chipped and bloodstained.

'Look, when you tell people what happened, you don't need to tell them about my involvement. Okay? Just say you got away from them.'

'Sure.'

Back past the rippling sea of birds. The moon was high. Kane could see the terns spread across the lava flows between the airfield and the coast, black heads and white breasts, all facing into the wind, insomniac chatter echoing off the rocks. The boy stared ahead, testing his teeth with his tongue, sometimes emitting a soft groan. Near the airport, the signs changed to US specifications: 'Dangerous Bends', 'Wear Seatbelts'. Some ancient construction equipment had been abandoned at the side of the road, a roller with patterns of rust like leopard skin. They arrived at the gate for the base. American and British flags hung from adjacent poles. A sign planted in the lava announced US AIR FORCE. ASCENSION AUXILIARY AIR FIELD. In the distance, long barrack buildings spread out. Solar panels glinted among the cacti.

'Okay,' Kane said, as the boy climbed out. 'Take care of yourself. Get your injuries checked out properly as soon as you can. I'll see you around.'

A guard got up from a seat inside the security hut. He shined a torch in the boy's face, then at the car. Kane began to reverse away.

'Hey. Sir?'

Kane turned and kept driving. Fuck that. He'd had enough introductions for one night.

When he'd returned the car and got back to the bungalow, the door was open a crack. Maybe it didn't lock; maybe he'd left it open. Kane checked the individual rooms until he was sure there was no one inside, then tested the lock to see if the door could swing open by itself. It seemed unlikely. But the lock wasn't secure, the wood of the frame having grown brittle.

Nothing had been taken. His bag looked like it might have been opened. Kane checked the contents, then the window locks, and then he tried to clean up as much of the boy's blood from the floor as possible. Finally he plugged his laptop into the phone, typed up a report of the night's events, and sent it through to their secure dropbox. Most disastrous beginning to an operation ever. He should never have accepted it. He checked the list of military staff currently serving on the island, but there hadn't been time to source photographs, so it was anyone's guess who he'd just clashed with: his notes listed twenty-three British men, at least eighteen within appropriate rank and age range. Interserve contractors numbered thirteen, so it was a smaller group, but no more revealing.

Kane closed the laptop and stood in the front doorway for a moment, watching the stars. Then he scooped up ash from the ground and sprinkled it onto the hallway floor in a pattern that would be destroyed by any overnight entry. He put the lock back on, more for show than in the hope it would protect him. If someone wanted to kill him on this island, they'd probably succeed. They had a lot stacked in their favour.

FIVE

There were several things Taylor didn't need crashing into her schedule as Kane departed. An invitation to New Scotland Yard was high on that list.

An hour after he set off, Taylor got a message from MI6's police liaison team saying the Yard had been in touch. A senior detective had been looking into Petra Wade's case. Although forty thousand miles away, the Ascension Island investigation was technically under the command of the Yard's Specialist Crime Directorate, and while the officers stationed on the island had hit a wall, someone in London had taken an interest. From the cooler climes of SW1 they had seen reports from the US base suggesting police might take a closer look at Rory Bannatyne, and followed Rory's cover until it hit unlisted phone numbers in governmental buildings. They had approached the various branches of the intelligence service, asking to speak to whoever had been in charge of him until finally Taylor's name came up.

'Do you have any idea who he is?' the MI6 liaison officer asked her.

'Yes.'

'Are you in a position to speak to the police? No one else seems to know anything about this.'

There followed a tense conversation between Taylor and the chief of the intelligence service, Sir Roland Mackenzie. Mackenzie had taken on the role of 'C' four years ago, and while he was an imposing figure, Taylor got a sense that he supported her; beneath the old-school exterior he was a moderniser who had personally intervened to ensure Taylor's professional rehabilitation after her incident. When Ventriloquist came up, he trusted her with the project – and their shared knowledge of the scheme had created a bond.

'The Yard aren't stupid,' Mackenzie said. 'They know this is intelligence related. The important thing is we manage the reach of their inquiry.'

'I agree.'

'Have a cover story ready, something else he might have been over there for. Something that, in a worst-case scenario, isn't going to blow ongoing operations if it leaks. Don't give them that unless you absolutely have to – use whatever tactics you can. But you tell them nothing that touches on Echelon. That is a red line.'

A couple of hours later she was sitting in a cramped office belonging to Homicide and Major Crime Command. Opposite Taylor was Detective Chief Inspector Aisha Rehman, who had taken an interest in the case. Rehman was young for a DCI, suggesting aptitude, with short dark hair and the unblinking stare that Taylor had noticed in every good detective she'd met. Beside her was another inspector with greying sideburns who rolled a pencil between his finger and thumb. From the look in their eyes it was clear that when they'd smelled MI6, they'd prepared for battle.

Rehman opened a file of photos: Petra smiling, Petra as Miss Ascension, a map of the island. She spread the images as if to say: This is real. Not spook stuff. This is why police have priority over spies. Although it was never quite that simple, which was why Taylor had received C's warning, and why she had arrived at the Yard accompanied by a lawyer for the intelligence service and a GCHQ security officer on the lookout for potential indiscretions. Both were rigidly suited, bristling with their assigned duties.

The working relationship between the police and intelligence service was fraught at the best of times. The intelligence service didn't investigate or prosecute crime; only the police did. But MI6 got itself involved in it – exploiting it, investigating it, using it for concealment – and the police entered with the law's demand for knowledge before invariably hitting a wall of silence. To the intelligence service, secrecy meant security; to the police, it indicated guilt. This created conflict. And when police were occasionally tasked with investigating MI6 itself – as it had done over torture allegations – it didn't build any bridges.

Taylor needed to ensure that all lines of inquiry were vetted. She also needed to ensure a lid was kept on it. From bitter experience, it was impossible to suppress a spy angle once it was out. The press went wild. In short, she needed to ensure the investigation due to Petra Wade could take place while keeping the police as uninvolved with the details of Rory Bannatyne's work as possible. Taylor having arrived with a team hadn't impressed Rehman. Her welcome was laced with an appraisal of what she was up against.

'Petra Wade went missing in the twenty-four-hour-period in which your employee took his life. That would place him as a suspect at the best of times. But there is some further corroborating material.'

Taylor felt the adrenaline start.

'We'd like to know everything you know,' she said.

'I'm sure.' Rehman set the map beside a timeline. 'Your employee was seen with the victim several times over the last few months. Sometimes just with her, sometimes with other teenagers.'

Taylor peered across the paperwork, trying to discern where these facts lay among the fragments. This was what she'd been dreading. She hoped her concern looked like the right kind.

'Doing what, exactly?' Taylor asked.

'It's a good question. Mr Bannatyne clearly knew the girl, and he took his life in the hours following her disappearance. So you can understand that right now he's very much of interest to us. We'd appreciate some more insight into him – who he was, what he was doing there.'

'Of course,' Taylor said. 'Can I ask about the police on the island itself? To what extent are these concerns coming from them?'

'We are working closely with the Ascension Island Police Detachment. You don't need to worry about that.'

'Okay.' Taylor felt frustration at the distance again, this island on the other side of the world that she needed to know so much about. She was glad to have sent Kane. Both she and DCI Rehman were working half blind, but she had a spy on his way. 'I appreciate how this looks, and I can assure you that we want to cooperate fully.'

'We're aware that we won't be given access to everything Mr Bannatyne was working on. But we need to know some details of his life on Ascension. In particular, the time leading up to the victim's disappearance. Is that something you can throw any light on?'

'It's difficult. We were only in intermittent contact.'

'You personally?'

'Yes.'

'When did you last speak to him?'

'Two days before he died.'

'And what did he say?'

'It was confirmation that his work had gone well. He intended to come back. We discussed arrangements for travel.'

'Are you able to tell me at least roughly what his work involved?'

'Yes. He was advising on the laying of broadband cable. With any major infrastructure project, especially overseas, there are security issues, hence some degree of sensitivity around his role.'

'Is this sensitivity something that could impede our investigation?'

'There's no reason it would.'

'Has Mr Bannatyne ever been in any other kind of trouble that might be relevant?'

This was the question Taylor had been dreading.

'No,' she said, then felt her response had been too quick.

'Not that you're aware of.'

'No.'

'How long have you worked with him?'

'On and off for several years.'

'My team needs to speak to his former colleagues. We also require any computers and devices he had access to.'

Rehman was pushing her luck, and she knew it. She was feeling out the limits, shaking Taylor to see what came out.

'For obvious reasons, that's going to have to be dealt with by SO15,' Taylor said, and caught an immediate flicker of irritation. Special Operations 15 were the police's specialist counterterrorism unit and so constituted a department considered more appropriate for MI6-related investigations. They were indoctrinated, security cleared, which meant they knew what not to ask and what not to pass on. The unit was regarded by the intelligence service as a little bit more sympathetic to the complexities of their work, which was why Rehman sighed. When previous MI6 employees had died in suspicious circumstances, it was SO15 who investigated. But there was a difference between dead staff and a missing kid.

'I would regard that as obstructive.'

'The precedent's well established. I'm happy for SO15 officers to interview any government employees in the presence of their line managers and legal representatives. They would then produce anonymised notes, drawn up after the interview.'

'Petra Wade is not a terrorist. She doesn't need counterterrorism.'

'It's worked before.'

'For who?'

Rehman burned with an authority bestowed on her by civilian tragedy. By the supreme demand of justice. Around the same age as me, Taylor thought, with a similar level of seniority. She tried to imagine that career: enforcing the law. It would have its own moral compromises, of course, but also closing scenes in bright courtrooms, with fellow citizens affirming your judgement.

'I've had homicide detectives vetted and cleared to question members of the intelligence service in previous investigations,' Rehman pressed.

'It would take time and is not the normal procedure adopted. This touches on national security.' Taylor heard the round, simplistic sound of the phrase, its superior finality, and hated herself. The MI6 lawyer leaned in.

'We're not so much concerned about your end as the potential for press involvement. There will be a need for watertight security surrounding the whole thing.'

'In my experience, the press tends to be concerned that killers get justice.'

'We don't know that anyone's been *killed,* do we?' he said.

'Not at this stage.'

'Right, so let's proceed carefully.'

'I'm not intending to be careless. It's worth being clear from the start: the law does not change. As I'm sure you're aware, if you withhold information that might be of material assistance in securing the prosecution or conviction of an offender, you will be legally liable. I hasten to add that this includes the concealment or destruction of any records.'

'Of course,' Taylor said, before the lawyer could respond. 'If I didn't intend to assist you, I wouldn't be here. We want answers as much as you do.'

'We've tried to ascertain Mr Bannatyne's employment and accommodation history over the last ten years. It's proved impossible. I was told you might be able to assist with that information at least.'

Sure, Taylor thought: a guided tour of cable-tapping around the world. That wasn't going to happen. It could well lead them to the incident in Oman that Taylor had covered up. That wasn't going to happen either. It was time to give the impression of compromise.

'I'm going to do everything I can to establish what happened in the days and hours leading up to Rory Bannatyne's death,' Taylor said. 'Anything that remotely touches on Petra Wade, I will share with you. I have no intention of letting a child's disappearance go uninvestigated. We will also go through Mr Bannatyne's professional history in case there is anything that raises alarm bells or might be valuable for your investigation. As you can imagine, we have considerable means at our disposal – for assessing his behaviour both online and offline. Anything remotely pertinent will be passed to you, and we will arrange clearance so that your officers can speak to those concerned. I can make sure things go a lot faster and more effectively than they would otherwise.'

'So we just trust you. And that's that.'

'You will have to. There is no reason we would obstruct your investigation.'

The detective turned her phone on the table to check the time, then stared back at Taylor.

'What do *you* think happened?' she said.

'I don't know,' Taylor said.

'Do you think he killed her?'

'That's not my belief.'

Rehman nodded. A final look at her notepad, which remained accusingly blank.

'Anyone else on Ascension that we should know about? Before the police there stumble into more national security issues?'

Taylor paused, wondering if there was any sense in warning them about Kane.

'No,' she said. But Rehman was a homicide detective and knew how to read pauses. She let Taylor's hesitation reverberate so that everyone present could hear it.

'We're going to demand a new forensic analysis and autopsy of Rory Bannatyne's corpse,' the detective concluded. 'Obviously, that will mean delaying the funeral. Are you in touch with his family? I'm assuming you'd rather provide their liaison.'

Not much family, Taylor thought. But there was the blank postcard. *Nicola Bannatyne.*

'I'll liaise,' she said. 'And if I discover anything that could conceivably relate to the disappearance of Petra Wade, you will be the first to know.'

SIX

The street was orderly suburbia, on the less glamorous fringe of West London. Taylor removed the postcard that had been among Rory's possessions, checked the address again, then the corresponding house. A neat semi-detached property, net curtains, a No Junk Mail sign on the door.

Nicola Bannatyne was Rory's sister. They'd run a check on her: unmarried, worked at Ealing Central Library. Their parents had died when they were both young, and this seemed to have created a closeness. There were no other siblings and no partners in their respective lives. Nicola's Facebook page was sparse, but it included a photograph of herself with Rory, the only photo of him with friends or family Taylor had seen. In his personnel file, she was named as next of kin.

Taylor had spoken to Nicola Bannatyne on the phone shortly after the woman had been informed of her brother's death. It hadn't been a pleasant call to make. Taylor had introduced herself as Rory's line manager, given her condolences, and offered herself as a point of contact. His sister sounded numb, and Taylor was guiltily relieved at the absence of questions. She felt responsible for subjecting Nicola Bannatyne to a confusing grief. It was important that any queries from the sister came directly to Taylor. The postcard remained a quiet puzzle of its own. When Taylor had called the sister that morning after leaving the police, Nicola had sounded keen to see her.

Taylor pocketed the card. She'd been anxious since Kane had set off. A brief visit to her office after the encounter with Detective Inspector Rehman hadn't helped Taylor regain a feeling of control. She had messages from C's office, asking for a report on her meeting with the police, and requests from Bower at GCHQ: *Any news yet?* As if spying were as quick as hacking.

The cable project, if successful, would single-handedly put Taylor in line for one of the top jobs. It had allowed old fantasies to return: of power, of success as judged in the eyes of the world. All for a cable. It was rare to return from a setback like hers. Failure now meant it had all been for nothing. Her career would peter out in sideways moves through HQ, or find itself drained of will via postings to inconsequential MI6 stations in Africa and the Far East.

She turned her phone off, looked at the unwritten postcard, then across at the flat. *What message was he intending to send you?*

The woman who answered the door startled Taylor with her resemblance to Rory – the same sheet-white skin and green eyes. She was as tall as he had been, nervous, in a cardigan and pleated skirt.

'Nicola Bannatyne?'

'Yes.'

'I'm Kathryn. I spoke to you this morning. I worked with Rory.'

'Oh, yes. Thank you for visiting. Please, come in.'

The flat was unnervingly neat and smelled institutional. Photos of their parents stood in frames on the dresser. A wall calendar showed a church amid snow.

When they were settled with teas, Taylor said: 'I'm so sorry about what happened, the loss you must be feeling, but also, I imagine, some uncertainty. You must have questions. I knew Rory quite well, so I wanted to meet you in person. I thought I could fill you in a little more on the details. I'd also like to learn a bit more about Rory myself. It must have been a horrible shock, and so strange when he's been so far away. I know it was to me.'

'Yes.'

'Did he ever tell you much about his work?'

'No. I understand that it was difficult for various reasons. I know he worked for the government, often helping with engineering projects abroad.'

'He was a hugely valued member of our team. A special person. Gifted.'

'I'm sure. And he was doing something like that on the island?' his sister asked.

'Yes. Helping with the internet there.'

'I was told I might be able to collect his belongings.'

'You will. This isn't comfortable to say, but there's some complexity to the situation surrounding his death. Around the time he passed away, a young woman on the island went missing. It's still not entirely clear what happened to her.'

It took the sister a moment to process this. Taylor registered uncertainty and some caution, but not shock, exactly. She seemed to understand what this meant.

'You think—'

'I don't. But then, I wasn't there. You can appreciate, the police want to be thorough. And so that's created a few complications. For example, the funeral's going to have to be delayed for a few weeks. I can only apologise for the inconvenience. And let me know if it causes you any problems – if you need any help arranging or rearranging. We can provide assistance.'

The sister nodded. She had become very still, holding her tea in her pale, freckled hands. Taylor tried to imagine Rory's funeral, and it made her sad. Organising funerals was never easy when it came to dead spies. Taylor had been at officers' funerals, listening to eulogies for lives that weren't theirs, and it was painful. And at the back of your mind there was always the question: is this what mine will be like? At least, as things stood, she wouldn't have much audience to worry about. Old friends had grown away, into family-rich lives, while she didn't seem to be making any new friends in the service. And there was no growing family of her own to refresh the stock of mourners.

Nicola Bannatyne lifted her eyes from her tea to meet Taylor's gaze, but remained silent.

'Did you have contact with him recently?' Taylor asked.

'He sent me postcards. We wrote to each other every few weeks. Whenever possible.'

'Really?'

'Yes.'

'What did he say in them?'

'He'd ask for things he couldn't get on the island, and I'd send him clippings or printouts from the internet: sports scores, music reviews. He said he needed diversions.'

'Diversions?'

'Magazines. Other things . . . ' Taylor caught a look of concern flash across the woman's face.

'Like what?'

'He said . . . For the children on the island. I imagine life's tough for them. Things for the kids, gifts.'

'What kind of gifts?'

'Clothes, make-up. Sometimes computer games. Anything teenagers would like.'

'And you sent him those?' Taylor asked.

'Yes.' The sister's voice was low and cold now. She no longer met Taylor's gaze.

'Do you still have his postcards?'

'I didn't keep them.'

Taylor imagined how DCI Rehman would have reacted to this. What had the detective said? *He was seen with the victim several times over the last few months. Sometimes just with her, sometimes with other teenagers . . .*

'I have to ask – as a friend of his, as well as a colleague – has Rory had any kind of trouble in the past that you're aware of?'

'No. He was very private, as you know. I never knew anything about his life, really. But he was an incredibly kind, gentle person. You must see that. When will I get to see his body?' she asked, and before Taylor could think how to answer, the woman began to cry.

Taylor went into the kitchen to find some tissues. Then she stopped. Held to the fridge door by a magnet was a postcard identical to the one in her pocket. She took it down. This one had a message but no address. In Rory's tight handwriting it said:

Hi Nicola. Hope you're well. Weather here is cooling now. Work's mostly done and I can avoid most of the daytime glare. Sea remains too rough to swim though. This week's challenge – a psychologist called Jack Moretti – American, I think – can you find out what happened to him? Prob now in his 50s. Would be very interested to know where he is working. Anything really. Sending love as ever. Off here soon. R

Nicola appeared in the doorway.

'Oh. That came last week. Just after I heard.'

'With no address?'

'It was in an envelope.'

'Sent from the island?'

'Yes.'

Taylor made a quick calculation. The Ascension post came and went on an RAF flight approximately every three weeks. If the postcard arrived last week, it had been sent a couple of weeks ago.

'This is definitely Rory's handwriting, isn't it?'

'Yes.'

'Who's Jack Moretti? Did you look into this?'

'No. It was too late by the time I got it.'

'Has he made other requests like this?'

'Not quite like this. Usually it's just things he was curious about.'

'What was he curious about?'

'Everything. The history of the island, information on the plants, the birds. Sometimes he'd choose something obscure as a challenge. The library has access to all sorts of journals that no one uses. You know Rory – or, perhaps you did. He was always investigating something, finding a new topic of interest.'

Both glanced at the card in Taylor's hand.

'Do you think it's connected to something on the island?' Taylor said. 'Maybe he mentioned it in previous correspondence.'

'I don't think so. He hadn't mentioned anything like this before.'

'I'm going to need to keep this.'

'Do you think it's helpful? What does it mean?'

'I don't know. I'm going to try to find out.' Taylor gathered up her coat. 'We'll let you know when ... everything can go ahead. I'll be in touch.'

'And will you tell me if you find something out?'

'Of course.'

SEVEN

'Lousy weather, ma'am.' The armed guard smiled. Taylor smiled back, touched her card to the sensor, then entered her pin code and waited for the Perspex airlock to admit her into Vauxhall Cross.

Her team occupied a remote corner of the sixth floor. She'd only been leading the department for a year, since her return from sick leave. The scale worked for her. The floor was arranged by region: Russia and Eastern Europe dominating the front, a handful of Middle Eastern offices in the centre. Her South Atlantic team was small, with desks at the back plus her own office. As controller, she was responsible for twelve permanent staff including operational managers, data analysts, two technical specialists, and the requirements officer reporting to Whitehall.

Like all controllerates, it was a supply chain, collating and assessing the product brought in by officers overseas and then disseminating it in daily updates and weekly reports to the relevant customers. Their areas of responsibility centred on the Falklands, but also involved less explicitly political issues: some drug running off the coast of Brazil and oil exploration in the North Falkland Basin. She had two case officers in Latin America, one handling an agent in the Argentine defence forces, one with a source in an energy company. There was a team working on the African side, concentrated on Sierra Leone, where the

British embassy housed a small but busy MI6 station. And, as of last year, there was Ventriloquist: a GCHQ liaison job and hence the only one that didn't make the paper trail.

She glanced down a list of messages and appointments: upcoming budget meetings, IT issues, and yet another compulsory training session on new data-sharing protocol with the EU. The only message she read in full came from St Thomas's Hospital. Rory Bannatyne's body was in the care of a security-cleared pathologist: Dr Alexandra Glenning. Taylor would be notified of the outcome in due course.

She went to her own office, which had an adjoining secure communications room and a view over South London. Daniel Kudus knocked as soon as she sat down. She was always glad to see him. He had transferred from the Falklands desk specifically for the cable project when Taylor had insisted she needed one other staff member read in to the operation. Kudus had been hungering for a more front-line role. He navigated the environment of MI6 with a taciturn facade she hoped contained a measure of disdain. His eyes showed experience beyond his years. He was an outsider in the service, so she trusted him, trusted his loyalty to her, and he worked hard. He had been processing Rory's reports over the last year and had also felt the impact of Rory's death. His bearing had become more solemn, his enthusiasm more measured.

'The deputy chief was just here,' Kudus said. 'He asked to see you.'

'Gabriel came here? Did he say about what?'

'No.' Kudus had been around long enough to know the politics of the place, and that this spelled trouble. 'How was Rory's sister?'

Taylor handed him the postcard. Kudus read it, puzzled, turned it over in his hands.

'Rory sent it shortly before he died. It was in an envelope, as if he wanted to keep the contents secret. He sent her cards whenever he could, but never one like this.'

'Jack Moretti.'

'Rory seems confident he's an American psychologist. His sister never got a chance to look into this. I'm curious why Rory wanted to track him down. So let's give it a go.'

'Okay.'

'It's an unusual enough name,' she said, getting up, wondering if she needed a jacket to visit the deputy chief. 'See what you can find.'

Gabriel Skinner called her in when she knocked. He stood in front of his window, reading paperwork, boyish in stature, hair thinning. They had been equals once, at the start of their careers, possibly even friends. But never equal at climbing the greasy pole. His office contained paintings of yachts and horses, although Taylor knew he grew up in a modest middle-class home in Reading. But he had moulded himself to the role he wanted. She had always believed you needed in some way to be mediocre to devote the necessary energies to ascending the ranks of Vauxhall Cross, with all the office politics and cultivation of connections that involved. Now she wondered if she'd just been naïve. The boldness that had helped her in the field, and that she had spent years learning to perform, didn't translate to HQ, where it seemed merely irresponsible.

'Sit down.'

Power games already. She took a seat. If they were in any kind of contest, he was winning, but victory did not grant any magnanimity, in her experience. Knowledge of others' resentment hardened the ego. He had spoken out against her receiving the South Atlantic desk – 'not a departmental leader' – which hurt more than she cared to admit. It had provided a focus for her more general distaste of the man. He had made a pass at her once, a long time ago, in the artless way of cold-blooded men. She suspected that this history combined with something else aside from the standard misogyny to generate his bitterness toward her: a dislike of her time in the field; the fact that she'd recruited and run agents in Europe and North Africa whereas he'd risen through HQ. Part of the attraction of the cable op was that it had allowed her to bypass him entirely. The Vauxhall hierarchy was steep but narrow, with visibility poor both ways, and if you were clever enough you could carve out a world of your own. She thought she had achieved this.

'What horrifies me is that I had no idea he was over there at all,' Skinner began.

He held a police report, she saw.

'If you're referring to Rory Bannatyne, it was Strap 3.'

He turned slowly, silhouetted against the green-tinted daylight.

'You didn't feel I had adequate clearance?'

'It's a GCHQ operation, Gabriel. C gave the approval. No one else was due to be read in. That's standard.'

'And what happened?'

'He took his life.'

'I'm not talking about his suicide. I'm talking about the disappearance of a child. Do you see that this slightly broadens the exposure and therefore the individuals worth alerting?'

'I'm currently establishing what happened. There seemed no point broadcasting this across the building until I knew what the situation was.'

He sighed, sat down opposite her. 'The press are on this, Kathryn.'

'Really?'

'It took some hack from the *Mail* contacting our press centre for me to find out that someone had died on a job – that they connect to the disappearance of a teenage girl. That is not "standard".'

Her heart sank. The service had strong connections with the

press; they'd try to keep it under wraps for now, but she could see the headlines itching to surface: *Teen Sex Killing on Spy Island.*

'What does Ventriloquist involve, exactly?' Skinner asked.

'Much what you'd expect. Comms interception.'

'What I really want to avoid is finding myself in front of the Joint Intelligence Committee being asked to explain how the programme connects to Petra Wade.'

The deputy chief never raised his voice, which made him all the more unpleasant. Maybe the service needed people like him, Taylor had once reasoned: fastidiousness as sadism. Or perhaps he was simply an outdated curiosity, and not worth being intimidated by. Which was easier to think from a distance.

'It was cleared through the appropriate channels,' she said. 'I have followed procedure at every step.'

'Don't be obtuse, Kathryn.'

She felt the cool fury of a man who had hit the ceiling of his authority. This was why people like him hungered for the very top: you could piss on everyone. Was that what it felt like up there? She had the authority of magic words – Echelon, Ventriloquist – but he could still ruin her career. True seniority within the agencies came down to ears: who had the ear of C, of the F-Sec, of the PM. Skinner was close to Downing Street.

'What do you intend to tell the Americans?'

'Nothing.'

'Do they know about the cable plan?'

'No. We don't go to the White House for clearance on our own soil just yet.'

He briefly closed his eyes, and when he opened them he was gazing wearily down at the desk.

'Do you know what they give us for use of Ascension? Do you know their longstanding concerns about the security of the place?'

'I'm sure Washington will approve when they see the data coming in. GCHQ have a team waiting to start. I've sent an officer to establish what happened. They will find out if there's any reason to pull the operation.'

Skinner nodded, studying her.

'Did you have any previous connections with Rory Bannatyne?'

'No,' she said. 'Well, we'd worked together before, but only very briefly.'

His eyes narrowed. He sensed something, like a dog sniffing. As if this was enough, Skinner got up, moved around the desk toward her.

'What your officer will do is extract himself from that place at the earliest convenience. Suspend all operations. We're going to need to devise a media strategy. The press are very close to sending someone out there. This is what we call an almighty cock-up.'

Because he couldn't leave an encounter feeling like he was the one who'd been humiliated, he patted Taylor's cheek and watched her flinch. 'Sort this out.'

She returned to her office, his aftershave still in her nostrils, so that she had to chew some Nicorette just to clear her sinuses. Her cheek tingled nauseatingly. Enough for an official complaint. She could win – there were enough other women to call upon – but that would be promotion over. One thing rarely prized in an intelligence agency is a whistle-blower.

Suspend all operations? On his say-so? No, she thought. Gabriel Skinner didn't trump the might of GCHQ. Press interest was an issue of its own. She suspected Rehman or those around her. Fucking police.

Taylor called the MI6 media liaison.

'How bad is it?'

'Under wraps for now. Speculative on their part.'

'Anyone suggested legal instruction? Give the papers a clear warning?'

'We've been advised to tread carefully, in case it does more harm than good.'

She called SO15. Her contact there confirmed he had four officers ready to interview any intelligence service employees deemed necessary for the Petra Wade investigation.

'Hold for now. No one speaks to anyone until I say so, okay?'

She spoke to the technical assistance department that arranged the surveillance side of Six operations and confirmed what clearance she'd need to intercept communications from Ascension Island police or New Scotland Yard. It would be governmental level sign-off, extraordinary circumstances.

Slow down, she thought. The press wouldn't draw in the intelligence service in any specific way; they could use hints, allusions if they wanted. That wasn't a story. Meanwhile, she could only pray Kane somehow proved a negative: that whatever happened, Rory wasn't involved. Which meant finding another explanation for Petra Wade's disappearance. And what consequences would that bring him?

She logged in to the file-sharing system, felt excitement at seeing a report from Kane, then increasing concern as she read it. He had outlined the previous night's incident. What on earth was one to make of that? Just a very unfortunate beginning, or – in spite of the unpleasantness – a promising glimpse of whatever was going on on the island? An explanation of events that drew attention from Rory Bannatyne?

The victim of the attack was a boy called Connor, who lives with parents on the US base.

Taylor felt a pang of guilt at subjecting Kane to this mission. Behind his terse account she sensed disorientation. The hotel closing down was a ridiculous mess, and she was about to have a word with the operations team responsible when she saw Kudus approaching, a frown on his face.

'Got something,' he said. 'Maybe.'

'On what?'

'Jack Moretti. The name on the postcard.'

He spread papers on her desk.

'There's around twenty Jack Morettis I can find currently alive, mostly American, thirteen of them between forty and sixty years old. None are psychologists. But there was a Jack Moretti born thirtieth September 1971. He graduated from Stanford in 1990 with a doctorate in clinical psychology, died twenty-ninth July 2008, Los Angeles. What caught my eye is how he died.'

'How did he die?'

'He hanged himself. Seemingly out of the blue.'

Taylor felt butterflies. She moved to see the papers more clearly: printouts of a newspaper and a magazine article.

'Go on,' she said.

'The death's odd. Moretti's a respected psychologist, happily married, with one son. He'd reported no issues, according to his family. He'd just been promoted at work. Next thing they know he's committed suicide.'

Taylor brought the notes closer. The article was an obituary from the *Journal of Neurology, Neurosurgery and Psychiatry*. Moretti had been based at Harbor-UCLA Medical Centre, home of the Los Angeles Biomedical Research Institute. It spoke about his service to medicine, pioneering work in neurology and psychology, his popularity as a lecturer, sense of humour as a colleague. It mentioned he left behind a wife and son, didn't mention the cause of death.

The report, from the *Los Angeles Daily News*, gave a bit more but not much: *Mystery Over Senior Doctor Who Took His Life.*

Dr Moretti's family insist his death was entirely out of character and have demanded an investigation into the events leading up to it.

'Did Rory's sister say anything else?' Kudus asked. 'Other requests?'

Taylor decided to keep the gift requests to herself for now.

'Nothing like this. Would you see if you can get any more? Someone will have chased the story.'

'I'll try. There's been something else on Kane as well. It may be nothing. Look at this.'

He showed her another sheet, this one a log of website visitors. Just before three a.m., someone had checked Edward Pearce's university profile. The academic webpage they'd created for his cover was set to automatically record and analyse the IP address of anyone probing, but whoever had done this had disguised their device and whereabouts.

'Could be anyone,' Kudus said. 'Someone curious, maybe someone he met on the way. Or a fellow academic.'

'On a hidden device?'

She studied the log again.

'His cover looks solid to me,' Kudus said. 'It's not so unusual to use a private server. Some people have them set up as standard.'

'Send it through to technical analysis, see if they can extract any more data. I'd really like to know who's interested in him.'

Bring him back, Taylor thought. Cancel it. Do as she'd been instructed to do. But she sensed it was already too late. She wasn't going to drop everything just because Gabriel Skinner felt left out.

It was six o'clock. Taylor told Kudus to call it a day. She lingered in the office. There was a dinner party she was meant to attend that evening, an old uni friend. She would have loved, more than anything, to have a drink with someone to whom she could unload the aggravations of the last twelve hours, but neither of those things was permitted. She locked her work in the office safe and tried to remember what other people liked to talk about.

EIGHT

Hunger woke him, followed by a stab of adrenaline. Kane sat up. The room was lit by a weak blue light from the curtainless window. His watch said five forty-five a.m.

The events of the previous night returned in fragments, as if out of an alcoholic escapade: the spotlit scene by the church; the boy's wounds beneath the bare bulbs; the final sight of him walking into the US base. Kane saw himself returning the car, like a regretful thief, and sighed.

He checked the laptop for any indication his report had been received by Kathryn Taylor, but there was nothing yet. He found an old radio in the kitchen, turned it on, and listened to a man with an English accent reading messages from soldiers on deployment. *Hi, Sarah. Happy birthday* ... British Forces Broadcasting. Unmistakable. It did pop music, *The Archers*, and service-oriented news bulletins on the half hour. Kane hadn't heard it for a while.

UK prime minister in visit to new Brunei base. EU Defence Co-Operation in tatters. Mental health charity recruits veterans for new campaign.

Kane tried other frequencies and got an earful of static. He dialled back to BFB as a weatherman recited his way through the network: Gibraltar, Afghanistan, the Falklands, and finally Ascension. *Clear skies, hitting a maximum of thirty-three degrees in the shade. Going to be the same tomorrow and the day after that.*

Kane turned the radio off, checked the ash on the hallway floor. No one had been in. The door was still locked.

He searched for food. The departing family had left plenty of possessions but nothing edible. Kane unpacked the rations he'd picked up in Johannesburg airport: an apple, a protein bar, a cheese sandwich. He found his folding knife and divided the bar in two, ate half, then the apple and half the sandwich, wrapped the rest. He refilled his water bottle, pocketed the knife.

Thirty days until the next flight out. He had no idea how to play it. Worst-case scenario: some men turn up with scores to settle. He ends up in the island's hospital or its police station. Either way, his ability to operate is all but ruined.

But it hadn't happened yet.

He was determined to get a car and establish means of survival. To proceed with the existing plan as far as humanly possible. Do what he could before repercussions hit, which they would, in some shape or form. With a car he'd be able to see where Rory had been living, look for any of the messages that Taylor thought might be left behind, or any suggestion of what led up to his death. But acquiring one meant he was going to have to show his face among the local population and discover how badly he'd sacrificed any anonymity.

Kane stepped out.

Georgetown looked more ramshackle in the flat light of dawn. The buildings were weather-worn and flimsier than he'd first noticed. Donkeys shuffled through the streets, rummaging in bins. Kane counted six of them: large, smooth-coated, with sad eyes. He walked back to the car he'd borrowed the previous night and checked it was parked straight, then looked inside for incriminating traces. He opened the passenger door and wiped blood from the inside of the window where the boy's head had rested, then eased it shut.

The area where the attack took place looked very different in daylight. The barracks building had shops beneath the arches: the Turtle Nest Gift Shop, Glamour Fashion and Beauty, one charity shop selling clothes and ornaments. Some broken glass remained on the ground, with traces in the dirt where someone had raked it to the side with their boot. The black ground had soaked up the blood. Against the ash, the white church spire looked as defiant as a Klan hood. Two palm trees fanned out on either side of the door like brushes used to keep it spotless.

He kept walking. Kept an eye out for indications of the men he'd encountered, but most contractors and soldiers would live on base. This area was more civilian. Some of the homes had fashioned verandas with wicker chairs and vases of fresh flowers. A canary sang. Kane imagined remnants of a colonial routine: morning tea, evening cocktails, quinine nightmares; empty, sweaty ex-pat days, drinking against the creeping knowledge that you were in the wrong place, that your life had taken a very odd turn. The gardens contained old scrap and driftwood arranged in place of growth, with plastic paddling pools and a child's swing lending some splashes of colour.

Sleepy town. He found the post office with its red post box standing surreally outside. Close by it was a delicate pink coloured building that turned out to be the seat of government for the island, with a Union Jack on a pole sunk into the lava. Further along was a picket-fenced vicarage, then the small building signed POLICE STATION. Kane heard the boy's laugh when he'd suggested reporting the incident to the police and wondered what that was about. The station door was locked. On a side wall, someone had affixed a torn poster for the missing girl. *CAN YOU HELP?* It was dominated by the school photo image Kane had seen: bright smile, hair plaited. *Last seen at Two Boats, 6 p.m. on 7 November. If you have any information, please speak to Sergeant John Morrogh.* It looked like a second one hung beside it at some point but had been torn down.

He returned to the harbour and checked the boats. They were several hundred metres out, turning on their anchors, masts swaying. Last resort for an escape. He didn't think it was quite that desperate yet, but worth researching the option. Fishing boats for the most part, small and solid: a couple of older-looking trawlers, but mostly cabin cruisers with outboard motors. These would be pull start, no key needed – you just needed to procure a dinghy to reach them. A full tank of fuel would get you a hundred miles or so. Enough to be out of sight. It wouldn't exactly get you to Angola.

He watched the lines of rolling swell heading to shore, then turned and admired the hill looming over Georgetown taking on a murky shade of red in the dawn. Cross Hill. It looked man-made, like a slag heap. Halfway up, the remains of one of Georgetown's historic Victorian-era forts clung to its grit.

Kane walked toward the hill, and then, without fully intending to, began to climb. The red earth was like ground-up brick beneath his feet, rolling down with each step. But Kane progressed, and as he climbed he felt previous visitors alongside him making the same instinctive journey: to achieve height, to survey the parcel of land on which they'd found themselves and establish how alone they were. To set up a cross, give the place a name, and shake off the image of a hostile planet.

The fort was little more than a few stone walls now. At some point someone had hauled a couple of First World War ship's guns up the hill, and their long white barrels still pointed cautiously at the Atlantic. A few metres below them were their ancestors: a pair of bulbous Victorian cannons also keeping watch. Kane propped himself against the fort's remains and studied the sleeping town, then the sea itself, wondering how many had stood here gazing out. Men wrecked or abandoned; men discovering new worlds, new parts of existence, then setting up guns to protect them.

Kane slid his way back down. He needed a car. The museum where he'd been told he could hire one was on the road out of town: a long, flat building painted the same flesh colour as the rock behind it. It was still only seven a.m. and he didn't expect it to be open, but the door swung when Kane pushed.

Artefacts and display cases crowded the main room. An old US Jeep sat in the corner beneath a ship's bell: *Roebuck – wrecked off Ascension, 1701.* Huge turtle shells the size of shields lined one wall. Shelves sagged under the weight of telegraph equipment and rusted cannonballs.

Kane stepped inside, heard someone vacuuming at the back.

'Hello,' he called. The vacuuming continued. He turned the light on, studied the sepia photographs: Eastern Telegraph Company staff in high socks and stern moustaches. A game of cricket in front of St Mary's, circa 1920. Several photographs showed turtles tipped onto their backs, ready for slaughter. Then you reached the Second World War: American GIs staring out with guarded smiles and cigarettes behind their ears and what may have been the faintest flicker of bemusement. The BBC engineers arrived in the first colour images, with shaggy hair and tinted glasses, ready to bring the voice of Britain to Africa and South America. There was nothing about GCHQ or the NSA.

An office in the corner contained a lot of cardboard files and an old PC. Beside it was a bookcase advertising the Ascension Island Book Swap. *If you take a book, please replace it.* Warped copies of Dickens, Stephen King, Tom Clancy. The bottom shelf had a stack of issues from a local newspaper called the *Islander,* each comprising a single, folded sheet. The top copy was dated yesterday. *Marine Protection Area Approved; New Pier at Georgetown Delayed.*

Kane dug in to the pile, checked the one dated 9 November, two days after Rory died, but no hanging had been reported. Maybe it wasn't that kind of publication. No mention of Petra

Wade, either. The back page listed church services, film showings, live entertainment. There were results of a darts tournament and appeals for football players. Finally, a message from Canon Damian Duncan: *I am very pleased to say that a few females have expressed an interest in becoming members of the choir, but nothing so far from the men. We are desperately in need of more members; please think about it, even if you are only here for a short period of time.*

Kane turned back through the old issues to gauge the general tone and saw that pictures had been torn out. When he tried to discern a pattern, it seemed they accompanied stories about Ascension Island children. He found three instances over the last year: *Ascension Island scouts help out in bird survey. Young Islanders take their first diving certificate. Fifteen-year-old Petra Wade, smiling after her contest victory.* All had been robbed of their accompanying image.

'Hello?' A woman appeared. 'Can I help?' She wore a floral blouse, her greying hair tied back. Kane returned the paper to the pile.

'I was told I might be able to hire a car off you. Is this the right place?'

'Not here. We had one but it's being used.'

'That's a shame. Any idea where I could pick one up?'

'Maybe Terry's at One Boat. Know it?'

'Is it, by any chance, near Two Boats?'

'It's on the way.'

'That makes sense. Terry.'

'If he's not at the pump, try the golf course.'

No golf course had shown up on the satellite imagery. But the woman seemed sincere.

'The golf course is near a pump?'

'Petrol pump. You'll see it.'

'What's the best way to get to One Boat?'

'I take it you're not driving.'

'Not yet.'

'I'd find someone who is.'

'Okay.'

Kane stepped back into the sunshine. The day was already hot. He wanted to survey the place before it became a furnace. He walked back toward his bungalow, saw a figure at the door waiting for an answer, then the police car from which he'd emerged.

Kane stopped. The man hadn't seen him. He stepped sideways, out of sight, then circled wide of the accommodation back to the road.

He had a sense that it was worth keeping moving as long as he could. Maybe there was something important that wasn't too difficult to find. Maybe he didn't have long.

NINE

A dirt track led along the coast, north from Georgetown toward Comfortless Cove. That had been the main landing site for the original telegraph cables, and was set to fulfil the same role when fibre optic arrived. Kane followed the path and soon the buildings were behind him and he was in a world without shade. Huge pyramids of rust-red ash appeared from slopes of black cinders. Sometimes these cones appeared solid, other times you could see the surface formed of loose fragments of clinker. Black lava welled from fissures in the paler rock, looking as if it had set just yesterday. Occasional plant life broke through: low, plump prickle pear cacti and a tough grass, flattened by the wind. Then even the cactus plants dwindled and the ground resembled crushed charcoal again. But one growth survived. In the morning glare, the antennae shone so bright they appeared liquid, ascending out of the fire-blasted scene.

After twenty minutes Kane saw a sign: COMFORTLESS COVE.

Black teeth of rock encircled a pristine beach. This was the sheltered side of the island, and the sea was comparatively calm. Only the rocks preserved a moment of violence, and you could see where the lava had plunged into the water. The sea spray looked like steam. The spiky black spines contrasted vividly with the white sand, like a dream and a nightmare refusing to blend. Kane walked across the sand. When it became soft underfoot, he took his shoes off and felt the warm seawater ooze between his toes. He continued until it lapped at his ankles; then he turned around and looked for the cables.

The original nineteenth-century landing point remained only in occasional stumps of cable markers rusted to blankness. But they gave him a start. This was where they'd been dragged ashore. From here, you could see they'd followed the winding path of the ash beds between the impermeable basalt slabs, eventually connecting with the telegraph company office in Georgetown. The fibre-optic project to come had even fewer traces: a sign announcing planned commencement, some preparatory clearance of rocks. But soon this would once again be the gateway for two continents' worth of voices. It was a patch of ground that occupied the dreams of men and women many miles away, but they would never set foot here. Rory had set foot here. Kane saw him in a long line of imperial servants sweating amid the hallucinatory landscape, feeling their connection to civilisation stretched to breaking point.

The fibre-optic cables would come ashore and run along the rocks to a new landing station in Georgetown. But a top-secret offshoot would intercept them a mile offshore and run beneath the seabed, surfacing in a GCHQ processing centre due to be built near the US base.

Kane followed the predicted route with his eyes. His attention was caught by a man-made arrangement at the back of the beach: a clearing within the jagged rocks that contained a handful of chalky white headstones. As Kane got closer, he saw it was a cemetery, the stones small and narrow like steles. The names on them had mostly worn away, with only a few still sharp enough to read. *Henry Garland Harrison, Assistant Surgeon, HMS Viper* ... Kane wondered what Henry Garland Harrison must have thought as he lay dying here. Then he heard a car approaching.

It appeared slowly, a white Buick Enclave, tinted windows.

He was in clear view; there was no point in hiding. He stood among the graves waiting as the gleaming SUV stopped above the beach.

All four doors opened at once. A man stepped out, then a woman, then two kids. One of them was Connor.

The boy pointed at Kane.

'That's him.'

The man waved.

'Hey.'

A girl of five or six moved from Connor to her father and took his hand. The man had reflector shades on a cord around his neck, silvering hair tied back in a ponytail. The mother was taller and slightly younger.

Kane walked up to the road. Connor had shades on but you could see butterfly stitches where his face had been cut. His foot had been rebandaged by someone who knew what they were doing. He wore sandals but still balanced on one foot with a hand on the car door.

'You're the guy who helped Connor last night,' the man said.

'That's right. Is he okay?'

'Thanks to you. I'm Thomas,' the father said. The man shook Kane's hand vigorously. The woman smiled before also shaking his hand.

'Anne.'

'I'm Edward. Pleased to meet you.'

Both wore vests and shorts that showed lean, suntanned bodies. The man could have been anything up to sixty, the woman in her late forties.

'We owe you some thanks,' she said.

'Not at all.'

'I think we do.'

Kane sensed a mixture of emotions behind the family's stares – not just gratitude but residual anger, a measure of fear, a degree of understandable curiosity. Kane imagined the story of the previous night as it might have been recounted.

'This little monster's Carina.' Thomas ruffled the girl's hair. 'And Connor you've met.'

Carina squinted up at Kane; she looked like her mother, even with the same toughness in her stare. The boy looked like none of them. Dressed in a black T-shirt and cut-off jeans, with the shades on – a shadow in the sunlight of the smiling family.

'Connor wanted to say something too.'

'I really appreciate it,' Connor said.

'How are you doing?'

'Okay.'

'How's the knee?'

'Fine.'

'Told you it wasn't broken.'

Connor smiled. But he was wary. Kane connected to a humiliating episode, and the boy could have done without being here to relive it. The girl didn't take her eyes off Kane. She had a wistful expression, something slightly haunted that came from neither parent. From the island, perhaps. From a childhood staring at volcanic fallout.

'I'm Carina,' she said.

'Pleased to meet you, Carina.'

The parents smiled. The mother took her daughter's hand and led her down to the sea's edge. The boy eased himself back into the car.

'How did you know I was here?' Kane asked the father.

'Someone told us you'd come this way.'

'Really?'

'Linda. She helped you with your accommodation. You came in on yesterday's flight?' Thomas said.

'Yes. Not quite the introduction to the island I was expecting. Who were they?'

'Thugs.'

'Any idea what it was about?'

'All sorts of ideas. None of which you need to worry yourself about. They'll get their comeuppance. One way or another.'

'Think I should worry about myself?'

'That's what I've been wondering. I hope not.'

The man's underlying fury showed in his jaw and hands. His American accent was underlaid with something German or Scandi, which fit the pale blue eyes and maybe the sense of a gentleness at odds with his current rage.

'You'll have us on your side, whatever happens. I mean it. What brings you to Ascension?'

'I study British colonial history. Thought I should see it up close.'

'It's quite a trip to make.'

'That's part of the point. I'm writing about the people who ended up here back in the day, what took them on such a journey, what it did to them. All that kind of thing.'

'Interesting.'

'I hope so.'

'You saw these?' The father gestured to the graves. 'Yellow fever. This was quarantine. Ships came in loaded with sick men, and the men had to stay here, dig their graves, and sleep in them. If they didn't wake up, they were ready for burial. The British Marines on the island would come and drop food off for them, but about a mile away.' He waved in the direction of Georgetown. 'They'd fire a gun, beat a hasty retreat.'

'What a place to die.'

'Isn't it just? Like dying on an alien planet. And these aren't half of them. There's several hundred unmarked graves around the place. A lot of the ships were anti-slavery patrols, coming from West Africa. It was a good cause, and it always pains me thinking this was the last place they saw.'

He looked again at the graves, then shielded his eyes against the rising sun to better study Kane.

'You're living up on the base?' Kane said.

'That's right. Anne's in the military. I'm the plus-one. I do conservation work on the island.'

'I thought you might be connected to the Historical Society.'

He laughed.

'Not that kind of conservation. Trying to keep what's here, not worry about what's already gone. But you spend enough time on this rock, you start to get curious.'

Connor was sitting in the car, his bandaged foot sticking out. With the shades on, you couldn't tell where he was looking or if he was looking at all.

'Is he really okay?' Kane asked.

'He'll live.' Thomas shook his head. 'He's a lot better than he would have been if you hadn't come along. He said there were three of them.'

'Yes. Pretty sure one was British military. A couple looked like contractors. It was dark.'

'Right. We're pursuing it, of course. Don't worry about that.' Alongside his anger, there was a sense of impotence, a helplessness in proportion to the rage, which seemed odd.

'I spoke to Connor about going to the police,' Kane said.

'Yeah, I know. Things aren't straightforward here right now. There's complications.'

'Really?'

Thomas nodded slowly.

'All sorts. But, seriously, don't spoil your trip on our account.'

'Okay. But I'm concerned those guys are going to pick on some other kid. Or that they've done it before.'

'Maybe they have. I don't know. My advice is really not to get yourself too involved.'

'Can I ask something else? A slightly weird question?'

101

'Anything you want. Fire away.'

'You seem to know the place.'

'Much as anyone does. Why?'

'I turned up last night and the hotel was closed. So someone let me stay in a house in Georgetown where the family's just left. I get the feeling they left in a hurry. Any idea what happened?'

The man's eyes flicked to Kane with renewed interest. There was a wariness there, a sadness and caution.

'Connor told me where you were staying.'

'Where's the family gone?'

'Heard anything about the last couple of weeks here?'

'No.'

'A girl went missing. A fifteen-year-old. I'm sorry to tell you that.'

'Missing?'

'Disappeared. Vanished into thin air. Her family moved off the island a few days ago. They were ... broken. It looks like you're in their old home.'

Carina squealed. She was out of the sea, having her feet towelled by her mother. The reality of Petra Wade's disappearance hit Kane hard. He imagined having a daughter on the island, how it must feel if you thought the man responsible was still out there.

'What do you think happened?' Kane asked.

'No one knows. Could have been swept away, could have fallen somewhere. There's a few potential explanations, but no sign of her and it's possible no one ever finds out for sure. How long are you on here?'

'Just the month. Until the next flight.'

'A month is long enough. Listen, if I were you I'd enjoy my time on Ascension, get some good research, explore a few extraordinary geological formations, and not worry too much about the other humans or anything else.'

'Okay. I hope the other humans allow me to do that.'

'I'm sure they will. I mean the thanks. You might have saved his life. If there's anything we can do for you, just let us know.'

'Actually, there is one favour. I need to pick up a car. I was told I needed to get to One Boat.'

'Old Terry.'

'That's right.'

'Sure, we can drive you. Carina's already late for a dance class, and she's the boss around here, but I can drop you off. It's the least we can do.'

TEN

Kane got the front seat, with the mum and kids squeezed in the back. The car was crowded with boxes of leaflets and equipment labelled ASCENSION ISLAND CONSERVATION CENTRE: clipboards, torches, welcome packs. The clipboards held surveys: *Seabird Survey: Pillar Bay and Coconut Bay*. The packs were titled *Beach Cleaning for Green Turtles* and *Landcrab Monitoring*. Alongside the papers was equipment for a boat: life jackets, safety lines, a navigation light. They set off into the island's interior, past mounds of purple scoria.

'Where are we going?' the girl asked.

'Just need to drop Edward at One Boat then we'll get you to the class,' Thomas said. 'Don't worry, pumpkin.'

'We're late.'

'We're not late.'

'Do you sail?' Kane asked.

'Part of the work. Got a little motorboat. We can take you out sometime.'

'What does that involve?'

'The island's just got itself a marine conservation area. Means a two-hundred-mile exclusion zone around the island, prohibiting any commercial fishing vessels from entering. Which means the only fishing that takes place is by local rod and line. So, I'm going to be keeping an eye on that and how it affects things in the water. See the rocks there?'

Thomas pointed at the nearby scenery where lava-flows like calcified rivers swelled toward the sea.

'That's one of the newer formations. The colours tell you the age. You can see successive eruptions. The older rocks have all weathered and oxidised; they're the orangey, rust-coloured ones. The latest flows are still black. You can see they've spread more slowly, right?'

'Right. Kind of beautiful.'

'That's not beautiful,' Carina said.

'Who says what's beautiful, honey?' her mother asked.

'It's ugly.'

'To you maybe.'

'Is the island always this hot?' Kane asked.

'This is particularly hot, even for Ascension. But it's always dry. A couple of times a year, if you're lucky, you might see some rain evaporating before it hits the ground. The rocks make it feel hotter. Rocks and the lack of shade.'

Twice on the drive they passed what looked like traps for an animal. It happened half a mile apart: leg hold traps chained to an upturned white bucket on which someone had written *Poison*. Registering Kane's curiosity, Thomas smiled.

'Cat hunting.'

'Cats?'

'This place has got a wild cat problem,' Thomas said. 'They eat the birds and the birds are too precious. This is one of the main breeding places in the Atlantic. So, the cats have to go.'

'Why the bucket?'

'Stop the crabs stealing the bait,' Thomas said. 'It's poisoned, you see, but the crabs have got a taste for it.'

'That's why we don't eat the local crabs,' Anne said. They both laughed.

'What happens if you eat the crabs?' Carina asked.

'Nothing, honey. We're joking.'

'I've seen dogs around though,' Kane said. 'No problem with the dogs?'

'Problem with the dogs is the owners. No one's here for more than a few years, so the dogs get left behind. Mostly they get passed on. People inherit them. Not always, though. The dogs get used to being passed around.'

'Like a lot of things on this island,' Anne said. 'A lot easier to share and pool your resources than to haul things to and fro.'

'You said I could have a dog,' Carina said.

'We said maybe. Can you remember what the problem was?'

'The base doesn't want it.'

'That's right.'

'Why can't we live somewhere else? Jenny has a dog.'

It was another few minutes before they arrived at One Boat. Thomas stopped beside the structure from which the junction took its name: half an old rowing boat stood on its end. As Kane looked closer, he saw that it had become a strange kind of cupboard, filled with old trophies.

'It's just near here. I'll stop and you can take a look at some of the island's curiosities.'

Kane got out of the car and went over to the boat. The pile of sports trophies glittered like unwanted treasure – cheap cups and statuettes, a tangle of medals, even a silver plate. Thomas followed him. The rest of the family stayed in the car.

'People leave them there when they go.'

'Why?'

'Maybe their suitcases are full. I don't know. What are you going to say back home – "I was the best darts player on a volcanic rock thousands of miles away from all other human life"? At least they mean something here. Have you seen the Lizard?'

'No.'

'It's over here.'

A little farther along the road was a garish paint-splashed

stone, waist height. The entire rock and the ground around it were covered in coloured paint. The smell of paint hung in the hot air.

'Meet the Lizard,' Thomas said. 'Superstition has it you should paint it before leaving. Some people think the shape looks like a lizard. Never quite seen it myself.'

'What happens if you don't paint it?'

'You return.' Thomas grinned. 'You end up back here. Look, we really mean it: Thank you.'

'Anytime.'

'Pumping station's straight that way.' He pointed confidently across a wasteland that looked like the surface of Mars. 'Think you'll make it from here?'

'Hope so. I appreciate the lift.'

When the SUV had disappeared, Kane walked over to the Lizard and touched it. His fingers came away sticky. *Do people paint it when they kill themselves?* That's what he should have asked. He had collected various death rituals on his travels, curious about the superstitions they reflected. The idea that you might not die successfully was common enough, that you might fail to cross over. He'd never come across anything equivalent for successfully escaping a place. But they were the same thing, he reasoned. Not being able to leave.

No sign of the pumping station or golf course. The ground was pocked with what looked like craters from bomb tests. The temperature was thirty-two degrees in the direct sun now, the black rock giving back a suffocating heat. Something among the craters shifted and Kane realised he was looking at animals. It took him some time to recognise them as sheep: their wool was grey with ash, hanging in tatters where it had torn on rocks and cacti. Presumably these were descendants of one of the failed attempts he'd read about to farm the island. What an existence. Did they know where the last cats were hiding? He imagined being stranded here alone, castaway, and having to face slaughtering them for your dinner. Necessity would ease qualms – then it would just be a question of technique. The real challenge was hydration. It was Victorian times before the Royal Marines dug their way to a reliable water source. The abandoned Dutch sailor had found himself on a thirty-five-square-mile desert, searching the place for anything to drink with increasing desperation. *I kept constantly walking about the island, that being all my hopes.* It was a line from his diary that had got under Kane's skin. The sailor began drinking his urine, then the blood of seabirds. In one of the last entries he described slicing the head off a turtle and drinking the blood from its throat. Kane wished he hadn't read it. The landscape hadn't changed in the intervening centuries and it felt like this search for a petrol pump was the first touches of his own insanity.

When Kane finally saw a flat roof on struts with two pumps beneath it, he felt disproportionate relief. The words *Birdie's Refuelling Station* had been painted onto the canopy. Aside from the pumps there were two rusted portacabins and a fire hydrant. No one around. He walked over. The pumps themselves were locked. Kane wondered if being sent here was a joke. Where was the golf course? He turned back to the bomb craters and realised he was looking at it.

Flags had been stuck into the volcanic rock. He walked up to a flag and saw where a hole had been drilled. Someone had smoothed areas of crushed, compacted lava, binding it with what smelled like diesel oil. Sand had been arranged around the edges to demarcate the greens: fragile white outlines, like the ones around the graves at Comfortless Cove. Suddenly a cloud of black dust rose from behind a ridge. Kane heard swearing, and a moment later two men appeared carrying golf clubs, both upwards of fifty. The larger of the two wore a Panama hat. He had a pink face behind a neat white beard, and thick, hairless

108

legs sticking out from his tailored white shorts. The smaller was almost child-size, in a fisherman's hat too large for him and sunglasses with thick black lenses. They saw Kane and regarded him cautiously at first.

'Have you seen a ball?' the smaller man asked.

'I'm afraid not. I'm looking for Terry.'

'That's me.'

'My name's Edward. I was told you might be able to rent me a car.'

The bearded man grinned and clapped his companion on the back.

'A customer, Terry,' he boomed. 'Don't give him any old crap.'

'I'll give him what I've got,' Terry said.

They walked over to the pumping station. The bearded man introduced himself as Derek. There was only one Derek on the island according to Kane's lists, and that was Dr Derek Nulty, the doctor who'd pronounced Rory dead. His voice was rich, mannered.

'Come from a base?' he asked.

'No. I'm an academic. Just doing some research.'

'You're one of the environmentalists,' Terry said.

'More the history side. Human history.'

Terry nodded, still searching for his ball, tapping his club against the pumice like a blind man with a cane.

'Looks like a challenging course,' Kane said.

'Worst golf course in the world,' the doctor said. 'It's famous. Do you play? There's a tournament coming up.'

'Haven't played for a while. Willing to give it a go.'

When they got to the station, Terry unlocked a gate and led Kane to a lot at the back. There was only one car in it, under blue tarpaulin. Terry dragged the tarp off to reveal an ancient-looking white Ford Laser with rust along the joints.

'Does it run?' Kane asked.

'Let's see.'

Terry fetched keys and a towel from the office, then opened the doors and stood back as hot air escaped. The towel was wet, and when he wiped the steering wheel it sent up steam. He did the same to the seats, then got in and tried the engine.

It ran. He asked for five pounds a day. Kane gave him cash up front for the vehicle and to fill the tank.

'Don't forget to register it with the police,' Terry said. 'Where are you wanting to go with it?'

'Not sure. Just exploring the island.'

'You won't be able to take this one off-road. And mind the crabs. The claws puncture.'

'And mind the drunkards,' the doctor added. 'There's enough of them.'

Kane drove slowly at first. The steering wheel felt loose. The Check Engine sign came on, then turned off again. On the plus side, driving was on the left, British-style, and he could now cover the island in a few hours.

Occasionally another car would pass him, sometimes military, sometimes civilian. The drivers waved in a ritualistic way, eyes lingering on his unfamiliar face. He understood now: Not to wave would be odd, like being stuck in a confined space with someone and not acknowledging them. So he started to wave too. But as he headed to the north of the island, the other cars disappeared.

He continued to the place Rory Bannatyne had been living and where his body had been found.

ELEVEN

English Bay was located at the extreme northwest point of the island. It was home to the BBC's relay transmitter complex and the island's power station and desalination plant, and not much else. The road leading there was in good condition and didn't have another vehicle on it.

That suited Kane. He kept one eye out for police, the other for the British military and their subcontractors. But as he progressed, the idea of stumbling across other humans felt less and less likely.

The island's north was flatter, even more desolate, and when volcanic cones did arise they carried an eerie majesty. Vast cinder fields stretched between them and the road, plains with nothing but small jagged mounds of rock that looked as if someone had modelled a war-torn landscape in miniature. You could see where the crust of lava had cooled, then broken up as the flow beneath it continued. The process left strange shapes, like casts of once-familiar objects that had been shattered in rage. Black sticks of lava had curled like the handles of enormous teapots or twisted like the branches of trees. Kane stopped the car to feel them with his hands and they rang with the hollow chime of porcelain. He looked back down the road to see if he was being followed. Nothing moved but the heat.

He drove alongside a ridge of striped cones his map named the Sisters, their bases lapped by undulating, silky silver ash dunes. Half a mile farther north he passed a sign for Broken Tooth Crater Firing Range, pointing down a narrow dirt track toward a volcanic cone with one side collapsed. Then more urgent notices appeared: DANGER – EXPOSED HIGH VOLTAGE, RADIO FREQUENCY LINES. So he was on the right track.

Kane kept to the road and arrived at the BBC Atlantic Relay Station. It felt bizarre and strangely comforting seeing the old-fashioned BBC logo by the side of the road. The air filled with metal now, slender white poles that reached half a kilometre high with wires strung between them like an intricate net. The road divided, with one fork leading toward the power station and the other into the radio facilities. Kane continued through the BBC's cluster of flat white buildings until he saw the sea and, just before it, Rory Bannatyne's shack.

Rory had chosen a curious place to call home. In 1920 some men had tried to establish a mining operation on Ascension. What they were mining wasn't the rock but seabird guano, rich with phosphate. When the enterprise failed the works were abandoned, only to be repurposed in 1942 by US soldiers in need of accommodation. This was where Rory had moved: a rundown hut born of Edwardian industry and GI ingenuity. He had moved a week after arriving, claiming his original Georgetown billet was insecure. Here was security, discretion, and, as it turned out, a lot of beauty. Clear blue water, an empty beach protected from sight. Solitude. Privacy. Somewhere to hide.

The shack itself was barely bigger than a caravan, with a few steps up to a wooden door. The bay over which it looked carried a deep sense of seclusion. There were no BBC staff physically based here anymore. Engineers visited occasionally to check the transmitters, but they were based at Two Boats. Most of the work was done remotely. An emergency phone stood beside the beach, alongside a lifebuoy. Kane checked the phone and it appeared to be in working order. Near the phone, the sand contained a cluster of white balls that he thought at first belonged to a beach game but, closer up, revealed themselves as broken turtle eggs, with the shrivelled remains of the unborn turtles still inside. Three white oil storage tanks interrupted the view along the coast.

He walked back up the beach to Rory's home. At various points, holes had been dug, precise and deep, and after a moment Kane realised what they were.

They'd dug around the hut as well. Down to the depth necessary to bury someone. Kane made his own brief search for burial spots, but the choice was hard rock or thin sand. It wasn't terrain for burial.

The door was unlocked. Inside, Kane was surprised to find the hut still crowded with possessions. The police had opened all the drawers and storage, rolled up a rug, and pulled the furniture around. There wasn't much else to search. The bathroom still contained Rory's toothbrush and toothpaste; there was tinned food in the cupboard. Bedding had been removed, but not a half-drunk bottle of red wine on the bedside table. Kane checked the obvious hiding places: behind the air vent, then the cistern. The bottoms of the drawers were real. He upturned chairs and checked the underpanels of the seats. He had a quick look for any bugs or surveillance devices, but it felt absurd. There wasn't even a plug socket.

Kane sat on the front steps, gazing out to sea, and imagined Rory doing the same. You would feel like a true castaway. One of the self-sufficient ones, perhaps. You had met all your human needs. Except one. And in the silence and the heat it becomes all-consuming.

Rape the girl, kill her, kill yourself. It was plausible. According to Kane's notes, Rory's body had been discovered by a runway engineer, Gordon McNamara, on the morning of Sunday, 8 November, at approximately 0600 hours. McNamara was a keen scuba diver and had been hoping to fit in a dive before work, hence arriving at the remote English Bay at six a.m. He said he saw the body hanging from the antenna as soon as he got there – it was visible from the road down to the beach. The runway engineer had left his car to check what he was seeing, then rapidly returned and drove back to Georgetown to summon help. He made no attempt to cut down the body by himself: McNamara said he knew Rory had been dead for a while, as birds had begun pecking at him. Sergeant Morrogh and five other residents cut Rory down an hour later using a handsaw. The line Rory had used in place of rope was old electrical cable from the BBC store. They made no attempt at resuscitation. His body was taken to the hospital, where Dr Derek Nulty pronounced him dead. By this stage the Administrator had been informed and had alerted authorities on Saint Helena and in the UK.

Nulty estimated that the death occurred sometime between seven p.m. and midnight the previous night. That evening most of the island had been at a talent contest at Two Boats. The last people who'd seen Rory alive were two guards at the British base on Traveller's Hill. He'd been seen driving west at around four p.m., toward the interior. They knew Rory, and the car he used – a boxy blue Fiat 500 – because he was a regular frequenter of their bar. They couldn't gauge if he was agitated or otherwise, but he was driving at a relatively sedate speed, no more than thirty miles per hour, they estimated. The car was parked neatly by his accommodation when Rory was found.

The Ascension Island police found contact details for Rory Bannatyne's UK employers, which put them through to the government department providing his cover. They, in turn, immediately contacted Kathryn Taylor, as protocol demanded.

In a hurried call with Bower, Taylor had debated sending out a specialist police team under their own direction, but it would have been conspicuous and risked blowing Ventriloquist entirely. Their priority became getting his body back. It was a circuitous route. An RAF flight took the corpse to the Falklands, a second onward to Cape Verde, where it was transferred to a C-17 refuelling on its way from Belize to Brize Norton.

An initial autopsy in the UK recorded the cause of death as brain ischaemia due to asphyxiation, with reflex cardiac arrest, which fit death by hanging. A toxicology report registered 0.02 milligrams alcohol in his blood, which was equivalent to two or three drinks.

Kane felt an urge to visit the antenna he'd used. He'd seen a photograph of it in the file, but there were none in the immediate vicinity. He had to go back up to the relay station. The antenna farm began on the other side of the road. Pylons rose up to one hundred twenty-five metres into the air: high-frequency towers, antennae in circular formations, then some solitary ones – ones that looked like giant fish-scale TV antennae, one like a crucifix, with the top angled downward so it seemed to be bowing its head. Most would be involved in receiving or transmitting BBC signals. The idea had been to extend the reach of the BBC World Service, beaming to Africa until nightfall there before switching to broadcast into South America as it woke up. Not all the tech here was strictly BBC, though. This was a GCHQ outpost too, and it was unnerving being alone with the structures, knowing the power they signified, the secrets they were drawing down from the equatorial sky. There was a constant electric hum that sometimes resembled strange music, as if the wind was playing through the metallic rigging.

The fragments of clinker here were sharp, with razorlike edges that scored lines in Kane's shoes and the palms of his hands when he stumbled. What a final journey to make. How did you choose which antenna to hang yourself from? Seeing it every day, perhaps, sensing a significance that slowly revealed itself. When do you think 'That's the one'?

There it was: one of the towers supporting the high-frequency arrays. Kane approached over the rough ground, touched the metal to gauge its temperature. Then he found the first of the footholds and began to climb.

The strut from which Rory's noose had been attached was high – six or seven metres off the ground. It would have been a long drop, a sharp break. Kane hauled himself up, then sat on the crosspiece and tried to think through the logistics. Balancing while tying it, your hands occupied. Is the noose already around your neck? Secure the cable, slip off. No one around. There'd been no other cars since Kane had arrived here. You could spend an hour getting ready. But equally you could spend an hour setting up what looked like a hanging, arranging Rory's body, and then climbing back down and disappearing into the dreamscape.

If that was what happened, it meant the killer was probably still on the island with Kane now. Which meant they'd be very alert when new people turned up, and willing to go to extreme lengths if they believed they were going to be discovered. Nowhere to flee – it was you or them.

Birds tracked him overhead as he returned to the beach, white ones, fairy terns, curious companions. They hovered, dispersing only when he focused his attention on them. Early accounts of the island described how tame and fearless the birds had been, oblivious to humanity, sitting calmly among the sailors so that the men could just reach out and wring their necks.

Violence infused the place. It seemed to press up from beneath the beauty, to make the whole place a lure, a trap, and the beauty something to poison yourself with. Rory's hut sat alone, but not alone enough to escape. There was something it hadn't disclosed yet, Kane felt sure. It looked like it wanted to speak, simultaneously slumlike and idyllic with a couple of plant pots, and a chimney, and three steps up to its painted door.

Kane walked back to the steps and tried lifting the top one first. It was secure. But the middle step was loose and came away when Kane pulled, revealing a cavity below. Inside was the missing box file.

He took it out and opened it. Whatever documents the file had originally contained had been disposed of. It held only loose Polaroids of children and a school exercise book. On the front cover of the book it said: *Secret.*

Kane took it into the hut and opened it. The pages were crowded with children's handwriting and drawings, in lead pencil and biro and occasional coloured pencil. The handwriting was barely legible. The drawings were more eloquent: faces, eyes stabbed or missing entirely, mouths of broken teeth. Sometimes the figures were bleeding, sometimes wearing grotesque smiles. One had been captioned *The Dead Astronaut.* The dead astronaut appeared repeatedly, with a tortured expression behind their helmet's visor.

At the back were a couple of separate sheets in Rory Bannatyne's handwriting: lists of children, with their ages and whereabouts they lived. With these were the pictures torn from the *Islander:* the scouts, the junior divers, Petra Wade.

Kane returned to his car, threw the file onto the passenger seat, and sat for a moment, staring at the antenna field. Then he began to drive.

A few metres south of the BBC complex, he passed the police car heading in the opposite direction. Kane watched in his mirror as it stopped and turned around behind him. An arm emerged, flagging Kane down.

There was no time to hide the file, so he slid it beneath the seat and prayed.

TWELVE

'Edward Pearce.'

'Hi.'

The officer leaned into Kane's window, grey hair cropped close, face tanned, shades dark so Kane couldn't see his eyes.

'I'm John. We haven't met.'

They shook hands through the window.

'I guess it was only a matter of time.'

'Haven't had a chance to welcome you to Ascension.'

'I still can't believe I'm actually here.'

'You had some issues with the accommodation, I heard.'

'Yes. It would be nice if the hotel stopped taking bookings, seeing as it doesn't exist anymore. But people have been very helpful.'

'I see you've acquired yourself a car.'

'Just now. From Terry, at One Boat. Drives better than it looks.'

The officer straightened, looked around as if the oddness of the landscape had only just struck him.

'What brought you up here?'

'I heard it was a good beach.'

'Not good enough to stick around?'

'Just getting a feel.'

'Where were you planning to go now?'

'I'm not sure. Keep exploring. Get my bearings.'

'Registered the car?'

'Not yet.'

'I know. Because you register it at the police station, and there's only one person in there this morning and that's me.' He smiled. With the shades on, it was hard to gauge what the smile was meant to communicate. 'Want to come in and do your paperwork?'

'Of course.'

'Follow me then.'

Georgetown had woken up by the time they got back. It meant there were plenty of Kane's new neighbours to watch him tailing the police car to the station. People nodded at Sergeant John Morrogh as he drove past, nodded at Kane, sometimes with a polite but curious smile, squinting to see who he was. They looked up from gardens and magazines.

'Morning.'

'Morning.'

Morrogh unlocked the building and set about switching on a variety of fans. Kane followed him in, resisting the temptation to turn around and see the eyes on him. The station was a single room, crowded with piles of paperwork, kitchen equipment, and island memorabilia. It was sweltering. The sergeant opened a back door to try to get a breeze through, and Kane saw a tarmacked area with a second police car and a blue Fiat 500, the one that had belonged to Rory Bannatyne. The rock of the hill rose up behind it.

'Take a seat.'

Morrogh angled a rotating desk fan so that it covered both of them, took a plastic bottle from the fridge, and poured glasses of water. The fan was vigorous, but all paperwork had been weighed down with lumps of obsidian, volcanic glass, glinting with dark interiority. Papers on the wall riffled: rotas, tidal maps, road safety posters; there were children's paintings showing Morrogh and his car, and a Charlton Athletic fixtures list. Kane tried to remember the sergeant's background. According to his research, before coming to the South Atlantic, John Morrogh had served as a police officer in the Royal Borough of Greenwich for twenty-five years. He had been on Ascension for three years now, extending his contract when the initial two-year fixed term expired. No accompanying family.

Kane looked across the files and the name Petra Wade jumped out. It had been handwritten on the top grey cardboard wallet file of three, all bound by a rubber band. They were on top of loose paperwork, as if used that morning.

Morrogh fussed with various old forms and pens, eventually finding what he needed.

'How long are you staying here?'

'A month.'

'Staying in Georgetown.'

'If you have any alternative suggestions, I'd appreciate them.'

He nodded. Then he put the pen down, sat back, studied Kane like a problem. He knew about the fight, Kane saw.

'Has anyone told you what's been going on here the last few weeks?'

'You mean the missing girl?'

'Yes. Petra.'

'I saw it in the papers in the UK.'

'You're here at a strange time.'

'Are you still investigating?'

He sighed. 'Of course. As much as we can.'

'I'm in her home, aren't I.'

'Yes. But that shouldn't cause you any problems. So long as you don't go seeking out any trouble. Emotions are running high.'

'I'm certainly not intending to seek out trouble.'

Morrogh turned his attention back to the form. The pen didn't work. He smacked it against the desk a few times then gave up.

'Wait there.'

Morrogh headed off toward the shop. Kane stared at the Petra Wade file. Alone in the police station. He had two minutes by his estimation. One of the big lessons in fieldwork was to seize your chances. Always act cautious, but sometimes something can land in your lap, and the difference between the good spies and the mediocre was being prepared to take a risk. That meant not wasting too much time thinking. Kane moved the lump of volcanic rock from the Petra Wade file and opened it.

A photograph of Connor stared up.

It looked like it had been enlarged from a school photo, low res, with other pupils' shoulders cropped either side. On a sheet of paper beneath it was a list of timings – *Connor seen leaving base, 1715 7/11: suspect wearing blue jeans, grey T-shirt, white tennis shoes; 1745 Connor and Petra seen cycling together by Jenny Wightman, direction south-east on New Mountain Road* ... Then, clipped to this, a letter from US officials, beneath the crest of the US Air Force Detachment:

We fully appreciate your concern and it goes without saying that a matter like this needs to receive a stringent investigation. However, you do not have jurisdiction over members of the US base or their offspring. I understand Anne and Thomas Lindgren have made it clear that they do not consent to the interviewing of their son ...

Kane heard Morrogh's footsteps return and placed it back. The officer stepped in, set a box of twenty black biros down in the centre of the desk.

'People steal them,' he said. 'That's half the problem.'

He filled out the form.

'Terry tell you the regulations?'

'Most of them,' Kane said. But his mind was tracking back fast – to the smiling family among the fever graves. The Lindgrens. To the boy snotty and helpless on the ground. Kane tried to see him as a killer; imagine him with his hands around a girl's neck.

'Speed limit's thirty,' Morrogh said. 'Twenty in residential areas. And we mean it. We enforce that. Alcohol limit's the same as back home, no matter how hot and thirsty you get. I'm sorry I can't help you with the history of this place,' Morrogh said, handing Kane his driving permit and capping his new biro. 'I'm told there's plenty of it, though. Enough to keep you occupied.'

Kane stepped out, squinting against the light. Connor, he thought. Was it conceivable? Kane had been looking for an alternative explanation, something to exculpate Rory. This wasn't what he had in mind. Even allowing for the possibility that the boy he'd saved last night was somehow responsible for Petra Wade's disappearance, it still left the mystery of Rory's suicide unresolved. One thing was clear: people on this island knew a lot more than he did.

He walked through Georgetown and watched a group of ten young children with satchels climb into a minibus. A small crowd occupied the jetty where a fisherman was hosing a bin of tuna and marlin, passing them out to his colleague to fillet at a stone-topped table. The fish flapped and the silver knife came down. Blood trickled to the ground, which was stained with layers of it. Some of the crowd clutched money in their hands as if they'd placed bets on the outcome. They turned to stare briefly at Kane, then returned their attention to the slaughter. He walked past to the edge of the quay and looked across the boats until he saw the one belonging to Thomas Lindgren, the newest of the lot, painted with the words *Ascension Maritime Conservation*. A trip out would have been nice, but it had just become more complicated.

The gift shop in the arched shadows of the old barracks was now open, as was the beauty parlour beside it, two women standing between the doorways, smoking and talking. One of them was the woman who'd answered his knock the previous night: Linda, as he'd learned. She appeared to run the beauty parlour. He nodded and she nodded back, but her smile seemed uncertain. He decided against conversation.

Alongside the old barracks, a young man was opening parasols over two plastic tables.

'Is this a café?'

'Café, bar,' he said, smiling. 'What would you like?'

'Breakfast.'

'Only food we do is toasted sandwiches. But I can do you one with bacon.'

'That sounds fine.'

Kane took a seat and watched the boy disappear into the doorway of what looked like a bar inside the building. He tried to relax, to let himself be Edward Pearce on his first morning on an exciting research trip. Donkeys sheltered from the sun beneath the arches of the Exiles Building. A middle-aged man in Birkenstocks passed, walking a dog, and the dog sniffed at the animals. How strange that the owner would leave the island and the dog would remain. Like island lore, passed down. Like its secrets, perhaps.

A young-looking priest in a short-sleeved black shirt and collar crossed to the church and fixed a notice to its door. It was his lack of hair that originally attracted Kane's attention: a smooth, pale scalp that was the brightest thing around. The priest stepped back, admired his handiwork. Then a second man approached. He wore the same blue uniform shirt as Morrogh, but was younger than his boss. The island's other full-time police officer: Constable Sean Reid. Reid had conducted most of the interviews surrounding Petra's disappearance. The officer wore wrap sunglasses, his fair hair cropped close to the skull. He leaned in and spoke to the priest, who smiled. Then Reid continued toward the police station and the priest disappeared into his church.

Kane's food arrived. He ate it, thinking about Rory's collection of Polaroids and Morrogh's file on Petra Wade and wondering how they connected. Thinking of the fight last night and reframing it with Connor as a murderer with diplomatic immunity. What did Anne and Thomas Lindgren make of accusations being directed at their son? At the very least, it gave last night's altercation some context, which gave Kane some idea of how to negotiate any repercussions. The food was more needed than he'd realised, and made him feel, for the first time since landing, as if he might survive this experience somehow. He had transport and some sense of the island's main geography; he'd endured his first encounter with the police, had come away with dramatic new information. The kind of disorientation he felt now was the productive sort. The jigsaw was out of the box.

When he'd finished and paid, Kane went over to read the notice on the church door. *In addition to the normal 10.30 a.m. Mass this coming Sunday, 24 November, we will be having a memorial service at 5 p.m. in memory of Petra Wade. All are welcome.* He pushed the door and walked inside. The interior was surprisingly homey, with low, sloping wooden beams and walls crowded with inlaid plaques. A war memorial stood beside the door. At the front was a simple altar under a white cloth and beside this was a separate table with a vase of flowers and a framed photograph of Petra Wade.

Kane didn't want to make a beeline for the shrine. He moved toward it slowly, reading the wall plaques, aware of the priest semi-hidden in the corner, watching him. Kane found one plaque recording the generosity of a Mr Gordon Croft, whose son was buried in Comfortless Cove. Kane imagined him in 1850 writing the cheque with thoughts of an island that held his son's remains and about which he could imagine little other than that it had no church.

The largest plaque recorded the church's own dedication.

Dedicated as St Mary's on Ascension Day, 1861. Kane tried to remember his Bible. Jesus ascending back to heaven after having returned from the dead, that was the story. Returned from the dead for forty days, walking and preaching alongside his disciples, a ghost at their elbow. Then he bade his farewell again, rising up, abandoning them on earth. Kane wondered in what way the Portuguese sailors who named the island had been marking Ascension Day when the volcano came into view. He imagined a chaplain of some sort trying to stay upright as the boat rolled and the wine spilled from his communion cup. Or was it no more than an entry on the ship's calendar, one way of dividing up the blank time through which they sailed?

'Can I help with anything? Just curious?'

The priest approached, hands joined in front of him, smiling. Hard to gauge his age without any hair, but no more than thirty-five. Long eyelashes, conspicuous in the absence of any other hair. Kane wondered how he kept so pale.

'Just curious. Just arrived.'

'Welcome. Feel free to look around, to pray. Ask me if you need anything. We do services twice a week, if you're interested,' the priest said. 'Open every day. We only keep the door closed to stop the donkeys wandering in.'

'Do you get many people attending?'

'A healthy number. Though some would say it's down to a lack of alternative entertainment.' He smiled. 'But perhaps that's unfair. I hear you're a historian.'

Kane shouldn't have felt surprised. His reputation was evidently preceding him. So long as it was Edward Pearce's reputation, he didn't mind.

'How do you know?'

'It's a small island. I'm an amateur historian myself. I wondered if you'd be interested in the church. It took two hundred years to finish. You wouldn't think it, would you. The spire was initially clad with beaten biscuit tins. I'm actually writing a bit about it. Perhaps you could take a look at some of what I've written. It's very much centred on the Anglican Church abroad. I don't know if that's within your field.'

'Of course. It sounds interesting.' Now Kane walked over to the shrine. The photo was the same one he'd seen in the *Times*. In front of it, people had placed friendship bracelets, lip-gloss, sweets, a condolence book with her name drawn on the front in italic script.

'What happened?'

'No one knows for sure.' The priest's lips tightened, as if this was all a stranger needed to be told. 'It's a tragedy that has caused a great amount of anguish in this community.'

Kane opened the condolences book.

Petra, you lit this place up.

You had everything before you.

Where did you go?

More than forty pages of entries: hundreds of them. He looked for Connor, couldn't see him. Most people on the island, though: airmen, technicians, contractors. Far more than could have possibly known her. Lining up with a formal correctness, an overeagerness, as if they were providing alibis.

Solomon's Supermarket was identified by a rusted A-frame sign outside – YES, WE'RE OPEN. Inside it was larger than Kane expected, but the items on the shelves didn't add up to much of a meal – cereal, ketchup, concentrated squash, and toothbrushes. A tall Saint Helenian man behind the counter nodded at him.

'Morning.'

'Morning. Are you Solomon?'

'No Solomon here for a while.' He smiled.

Kane smiled back. 'I just got here.'

'I know.'

One empty shelf was dusted with bread crumbs. Kane had clearly missed the bread itself. He picked up crackers, dry pasta, tins of tomatoes and beans. A few vegetables wilted in plastic crates: stunted bell peppers and cucumbers with dusty soil clinging to them. He decided to skip the vegetables. A chest freezer contained some hand-labelled packages of meat. At the back was a section devoted to car maintenance: oil, hand tools, reconditioned taillights.

Kane took his groceries to the till. Yellowing copies of the *Daily Mail* and the *Telegraph* remained on the counter, ten days old. The man rang everything up and gave him his change, then watched him studying the unfamiliar coins in his hand.

'We get bread on Tuesdays and Thursdays, meat on Fridays. You'll have to keep an eye out if you want fresh vegetables.'

'I will,' Kane said. 'Thank you.'

Kane stepped into his bungalow, across the scattering of ash. Could he stay here? He didn't want to waste time looking for other accommodation, which was likely to be a room in someone else's house anyway, with all the insecurity that brought.

Connor. He thought of the boy here, injured, the previous night. Young, vulnerable. Tried to read beneath the injuries to the character, still couldn't see it.

Kane checked that the door was shut, drew the blind, then arranged Rory's hoard across the kitchen table. He looked at the Polaroids. Kids posing, laughing, sometimes oblivious to the camera, it seemed. There were nine different children in total, but three dominated: Connor, Petra, and another girl, blond, with braces on her teeth. Kane recognised the beach at English Bay behind them. Some, more worrying, were interior shots, a bedroom, Connor with his arm around Petra. There was information here, Kane felt. Rory had caught something. Kane sifted the pictures Rory had torn from the island's local newspaper, then turned to the exercise book and its drawings of some imagined horror. Its expressions of a troubled mind. Then he hid them in a wardrobe in what had been the parental bedroom.

He spent some time grateful to be out of the sun, trying to assess the situation away from the glare of the midday and the curiosity of the islanders' gazes. Had Rory been with Petra and Connor that night? What had he got involved in? Eventually, Kane gave up on rest and brought up the satellite map. Rory had last been seen passing the British base at around six thirty p.m. on the night he died. That was strange. Kane couldn't understand where you could go from there without being seen by someone else. The road west – the direction he'd been travelling in – would have taken him past the airfield and into Georgetown. Yet no one saw him again until his body turned up. Kane thought of the witness statement he'd glimpsed in Morrogh's file – *Connor and Petra seen cycling, direction south east on New Mountain Road.* He located that on the map and it placed them nearby. The three of them were converging. But where? Kane studied the map and decided he needed to take a look at the area in person.

THIRTEEN

Vauxhall Cross at seven a.m. on a Friday morning was peaceful. A few keen analysts digested reports in time for morning briefings, security officers patrolled. The Thames slid murkily by outside. Taylor stood at her office window and watched the traffic junction below, around which the humans waiting to cross appeared small and defenceless.

After Kudus's alert about someone probing Kane's cover she'd done what she could, instructing their resident signals expert to look into it, then spent an anxious evening in awkward conversation with an old university friend, her lawyer husband, and the man they had hoped to set her up with, maintaining her side of a dinner party conversation about London property prices and governmental incompetence while thinking about Kane and the missing girl. She'd had awful nightmares all night, then come in to find yesterday's headache in paper form on her desk.

Dominic Bower at GCHQ was keen to impress on her that work on the cable had begun. The black box processing centre parts were ready for shipment, disguised as components for the cable station. Their optical splitter was to be housed in a secure building adjacent to the island's telescope observatory. He needed an update from her end. The next message was from DCI Rehman, restating her demand for access to Rory Bannatyne's former colleagues. Then Gabriel Skinner: 'Could you confirm that you have suspended operations? Why am I under the impression that you haven't?'

Fuck that. He couldn't stop her. She replied, *Further discussion regarding the GCHQ programme should be conducted via the chief's office. Talk to C.*

Finally, reports from the overnight signals team: There'd been no more searches on Edward Pearce identified. No other evidence of attention on Kane. They were still working on determining the source of the original probe.

At eight thirty a.m. Kudus came into Taylor's office, handed her a printout from the news archive: *LA Times*, 2 March 2009. The front page was dominated by a picture of Barack Obama, but a column on the right carried the headline: *Mystery over doctor's suicide. Family of US govt psychologist demand answers.*

'Dr Jack Moretti,' Kudus said. 'As we know, he died twenty-ninth of July 2008, age thirty-eight. Buried Cedar Lawn Memorial Park, California. All that's uncontroversial. It's not easy finding out further details, but someone's had a go.' Kudus tapped the printout. It was dated nine months after Moretti's death, a follow-up story.

'A journalist did some digging. So, we've got a few additional facts: Moretti hanged himself in a wasteground behind a couple of foreclosed homes in Antelope Valley. His parents demanded answers, because nothing made sense to them. He'd been happy, then he hangs himself. Why? Where had he been that day? Why was he in Antelope Valley?

'Turns out he'd been there for work. He hadn't been physically based at the hospital for a couple of years. The work address they're given is 1349 El Monte Road, Los Altos Hills. That's the official address used for a facility called Lake Ravenna. It's a secure site sixty miles into the desert, run by the US Air Force. A very secure one.'

'Okay.' Taylor had the distinct sensation of slipping into the black side, both ominous and promising.

'They ask to collect his belongings from this place and are told, in no uncertain terms, that that's not possible. Eventually they do receive a bag of belongings, but items are missing. Moretti's family hire a lawyer to represent them – Charles Becker, from the firm Markman, Becker, and Reith. Becker steps in, requests the police file, then when that's refused, he goes sideways, presses for information relating to any other suicides connected to Lake Ravenna. This is blocked, but the pressure he's exerting has an effect. To get him off their back, the military eventually release a pathology report. And it puts Moretti's death at twenty-ninth July, six days before the family were informed. Turns out it wasn't handled by the police at all – it was the US Air Force Office of Special Investigations.'

Taylor felt the story darken further. The OSI provided independent investigative services outside of the traditional military chain of command. They covered everything too sensitive for the regular teams: national security issues, espionage, terrorism. She brought up a map of Lake Ravenna on her PC.

The lake itself was an unreal turquoise, blank and flat, shaped like a kidney. The facility that took its name extended to the west. Taylor wondered why she couldn't see fences, then realised she was looking at less than a tenth of it.

'It covers three thousand acres, stretches from Palmdale in the north down to Quartz Hill,' Kudus said. He zoomed out. There were individual clusters of buildings miles apart. Then several more miles of blank, beige scrub before you got to the double-layered outer fence, where you could just about see security booths on the gates. Mountains to the east created a defensive wall. But even here you could see the fence extended over the rock. Within the perimeter were several individual airstrips, each accompanied by aprons of tarmac and the blank oblongs of vast hangars over a square kilometre each.

'Plant Twenty-One alone, where Moretti was listed, has three hundred square kilometres to play with. It has a runway complex shared between several private contractors. There are eight production sites specially suited for what they call "advanced technology", leased from the air force on a government-owned contractor-operated basis.'

'What's a psychologist doing there?'

'Fair question. So now Moretti's family want to see where he worked,' Kudus continued. 'And, of course, they're refused. They ask for access to belongings they say are missing, including a journal of some kind. The air force spends three months denying it ever existed, then they say it's accidentally been destroyed.'

'I bet.'

'It gets stranger. Moretti's family want to know exactly what he was working on. Did it somehow place him in danger? Or create unnecessary stress, leading him to take his life? Is it even possible he was killed because of objections?

'At this point the government gets involved. They assert executive privilege and claim the federal court has no jurisdiction over the matter. When Becker requests the files documenting the air force investigation into Moretti's suicide, he gets another stone wall. A district court judge takes his side, however, and orders them to be handed over, so now the air force refuses on the grounds of national security. Protocol is that in this kind of situation a judge is allowed to review the documents so any compromising information can be excised, but the air force wouldn't even permit that.'

'Deep black.'

'Deep black something.'

'Where's Moretti's wife in all this?'

'Not sure. The people driving this are his parents. They're the ones who hire the lawyer. They're the ones who eventually got paid off. Healthily, it seems. Lake Ravenna kept its secrets. The end. Or, until Rory started thinking about it.'

Taylor lifted the printout. It carried a photo of Moretti wearing a lab coat, pens in the top pocket. He was smiling, a little care-worn, with black hair and thick dark eyebrows. A man who looked like he could have been a GP or a pharmacist but had answered the patriotic call out to the military-industrial desert. To LA's dark research sprawl.

... A psychologist called Jack Moretti – American, I think – can you find out what happened to him?

What had made Rory suddenly curious, during his final days alive? Taylor turned back through Kudus's notes. She reasoned that most of the people Moretti's family were in contact with wouldn't have known much themselves. Taylor had worked closely with the US in enough roles to have gained some insight into how things operated. Once above 'top secret,' operations branched out into special access programmes, each with its own security channel. That covered new weaponry research, special forces, black ops. You were read in to the information compartments one by one. The idea was to prevent anyone but a tiny handful from having a complete picture.

The investigative journalist who'd done the digging was called Lee Perryman. According to his web page, Perryman was now a professor of journalism at Berkeley. Taylor called the office number on his university webpage, listened to it ring for a minute, then left a message, asking him to get in touch with her.

She returned to the hanging at the heart of it all. *In a wasteground behind a couple of foreclosed homes in Antelope Valley.* Studying Google Maps, she tried to identify the wasteground in question on satellite view, but it looked like it was now a playing field.

'Was it on his way home?'

'I don't think so, not according to the family. I can't get a residential address. I think he may have been staying on site.'

'No suggestion of what he might have been doing there?'

'Nothing that I can find.'

Hanged himself out of the blue . . .

She called the direct number she'd been given for the patholo-gist taking another look at Rory's corpse, Dr Alexandra Glenning.

'I wondered if you'd had any fresh insight,' Taylor said.

'I was about to call you,' Glenning said. 'I can't promise answers, but I may be able to give you some new questions. Can you come in? This is something that should probably be done in person.'

St Thomas's was the major Westminster hospital, surreptitiously serving all manner of governmental needs, and as such it had secure areas: subterranean facilities, secret morgues, dedicated clinics. They also had pathologists vetted by the military and government to work on sensitive corpses.

Rory Bannatyne was a sensitive corpse. Taylor was met at the front, led through by Glenning herself, a brisk middle-aged woman with a Scots accent. Former army medic, Taylor guessed. She knew Glenning had overseen the Berezovsky autopsy and consulted on a couple of intelligence service suicides.

'The body's been badly looked after. There's traces of everyone who came into contact with it. Was he in military hands?'

'Yes.'

'On a plane?'

'Yes.'

'Okay.'

They arrived at a post-mortem examination. It was operation-theatre white, with a camera and mic suspended above the slab, a twenty-seven-inch screen at the side, infinite drawers and cupboards.

Taylor wouldn't have recognised the corpse on the central slab. Rory's head had been shaved, with a neat line where they'd sewn the scalp back up after opening the skull. His body had been covered by a thin blue sheet, which had then been arranged so that his paper-white arms were free, and his hands sealed inside clear plastic bags.

'I'm not going to be able to give you anything definitive, but I don't think he killed himself.'

The screen was attached to a MacBook. Glenning turned it on, entered a password. What looked like an aerial shot of a landscape appeared, dry but for the occasional cobalt blue lake. For a second Taylor wondered where this was, then realised she was looking at flesh.

'This is his neck,' Glenning said. 'The colours show bruising and rope burn.' She clicked through to another image, even more microscopic. 'These are fibres. There's been another material involved in the strangulation, not just the cable. That's my belief. At some point his hands have been on the ground, with weight on them.' Now she clicked to what looked like a tray of jewels: microscopic traces of rock and dust, reds and yellows and blacks. Volcanic particles.

'Where *was* he? If I'm allowed to ask.'

'Certainly not around here. Why?'

'This is trachyte. It's volcanic rock, rich in silica and quartz. It was dug into the skin of his palms.' She clicked through again: more of the shades Taylor was beginning to recognise as bruising.

'If you look at his lower back, significant pressure has been applied here. If he had been on the ground, face down, then this could potentially indicate someone applying pressure with a knee while strangling him.'

Finally she led Taylor deeper into the room to where a vacuum-sealed bag sat on the side counter. It contained a portion of the cable noose. Glenning indicated with the top of her pencil.

'The knot is a running slip. Most hanging deaths involve a fixed type of knot. Ninety-five per cent or so will be half hitches, overhand knots, granny knots. This is more in the style of a bow-line, quite sophisticated. I'd say it was made by someone who has used knots professionally or knows a bit about them. You don't have to tell me if the deceased falls into any of those categories, but I thought you might be interested.'

'Very.'

'The knot was placed over the back of the neck. The cable was doubled, looped twice, which isn't so unusual when using a thin material like electric wire. But, again, you could consider it a sig-nature of sorts. Other than that, there's very little I can tell you at this stage. I'm not sure the blood tests will turn up anything more. In your email you asked if he might have had any recent contact with a young woman, sexual or otherwise. I'm not seeing any evidence he had close physical contact with anyone other than a possible assailant. Certainly no evidence of recent sexual activity.'

Even though it had begun to rain, Taylor walked back to work along the river. She needed to think before she got there.

Rory Bannatyne was most probably killed. That meant she had an issue. There was no way of keeping the murder of an officer localised; it was big news, demanding a big investigation. It would have to go to Skinner first. She didn't relish that meeting. Then perhaps the chief himself. How would the conversation go?

So you think he might have been killed? And then framed?

All I have so far is this.

Are we aware of any hostile parties on the island?

No.

And what about this missing girl?

That bit's not clear.

What preparations were made in advance of the operation proceed-ing? Was Rory Bannatyne the best man for the job? Do we know much about him at all?

Taylor thought back to the morning when Mackenzie had

assigned her to the South Atlantic desk. She'd been called in to see him, first day back from sick leave. She'd thought he was going to fire her, but he said he wanted to see a more enlightened approach to trauma in the service. That was the box in which he'd put her experience, which was okay with Taylor. He said: Be open with me. That's all I ask. We can't afford to crack in private.

Taylor watched the river. She passed people taking pictures, kissing, living their lives, and wondered why she had been assigned the clandestine work of preserving this peace on their behalf.

The office was still mercifully quiet. Taylor opened her safe and found the report from the Ascension Island police concerning Rory Bannatyne's suicide. She read it again, trying to see it as a murder. If the same person killed both Rory Bannatyne and Petra Wade, how did the sequence of events play out? Say Rory had been killed, transported to the antenna, strung up to look as if he'd been hanged. At some point the girl was killed too and disposed of by other means. Without knowing the island, Taylor couldn't move toward any more certain hypotheses, no matter how many maps and photographs she studied. Only someone there could assess the logistics.

Kane's only report so far had been ominous: involved with an attack on a boy called Connor. Whether or not it pertained to the objective of his mission over there, it suggested an environment on the edge of control. She was wondering what to make of it when she saw her message light flashing. Lee Perryman's West Coast accent filled her office when she pressed play, the journalist who'd dug into Moretti's apparent suicide. He'd left a personal number, which he answered promptly this time.

'You're looking into Jack Moretti?' he said.

'Yes. I realise this must be strange. My name's Kathryn Taylor. I work in the British civil service. For complicated reasons, I've become quite interested in Jack Moretti, and it seems you're one of the few people who've investigated what happened.'

'The civil service, right.' Perryman sounded good humoured. He sounded like he saw through bullshit. 'Who exactly am I speaking to? Are you police? Government?'

'More government than police,' she said, making her own attempt at a knowing humour.

'Okay, well, this is going back a bit.'

'I know.'

'What's going on over there?'

'Moretti's death may connect to something that's happened more recently. That's what drew my attention.'

'Really? Like what?'

'Like another death.'

'Can you tell me what's happened?'

'Not at this stage. But I'm very happy to keep you in the loop if anything progresses. Obviously, this is just speculative for now.'

There was a moment as he inhaled noisily and she imagined a fresh notebook being opened.

'This other death – is it a government employee?'

'I can't go into details.'

'No one ever has when it comes to Jack Moretti. I can dig out what I've got. But it's questions for the most part. I was moved off the story before it even began to make sense. And it was made clear to me that that was for the best.'

'By who?'

'Well, my editor, for one thing. Plus everyone I spoke to who might have known anything about it.'

'But you've still got your notes?'

'Notes, sure. I don't know what use they'll be to you.'

'I'll take everything. Just in case.'

'Tell me again what made the British civil service interested?'

Taylor decided to give him some crumbs.

'A man took his life, a colleague of mine, in fact. It turns out he'd been looking into Moretti. So I'm just curious what drew his attention, and what he found. All I know so far is what's available on open source, and that's enough to tell me there's a lot being suppressed.'

'And if I send through what I've got, you'll keep in touch?'

'Of course.' She could hear pencil on paper. Taylor gave him her personal email address; she didn't want this coming through MI6 systems.

'In the files, are there pathology details for Jack Moretti?' she asked.

'I'm not sure. Like I say, it's been a while. But I've got copies of the original police report, from just after they found the body, and that involves photos.'

'I'd love to see them.'

'Okay,' Perryman exhaled. 'Jack Moretti. Never expected him to walk back into my life.'

The journalist was as good as his word. He sent through a zip file ten minutes later and an email with a public key for encrypting any further communications. Taylor clicked through the files: interviews, notes, reams of Moretti's psychological papers. Finally she got to a smudged copy of the original police report, compiled in the hours before the investigation was taken off their hands. It contained several pictures, including two of the abandoned lot where he'd been found, five of the body itself, and one of the rope. Taylor checked a magnified version until she felt sure: It was doubled. It was the same knot.

Kudus came in as she was staring at the screen.

'This is from the American journalist,' Taylor said. 'Moretti's noose. Rory's was tied in exactly the same way.'

Kudus studied the image.

'What's the implication?' he said, carefully.

'That possibly the same person was responsible – for killing them and staging a suicide.'

'Okay.' He sounded sceptical. 'What would the logic be there?'

'I don't know. Rory requested the name of a man who died by hanging a few days before he was found hanged himself. Neither death makes much sense. But the new pathology report makes it seem likely someone else was involved in whatever happened to Rory.'

Taylor described Glenning's assessment: the dirt on Rory's hands, bruising on his back, the sophisticated knot.

'What would you do about Kane?' she said. 'Given all this?'

Kudus considered the question. 'Has there been anything more to suggest he's being monitored?'

'Nothing that's shown up.'

'Let him know what we know. Keep him updated on potential surveillance. Let him know about Moretti. If it's nothing, then it's not going to occupy his time. If Moretti connects, Kane's the one in a position to find out what's going on there.'

'Better position to get hurt, too. But I agree.'

When Kudus was gone, Taylor messaged Kane. She sent through a summary of the new pathology report with a cover message explaining the conclusions. At least he would be informed, she told herself. Then she briefly outlined her interest in Jack Moretti and wondered how crazy it sounded.

She needed to go to Skinner, tell him about Glenning's conclusions before they reached him independently. She took a deep breath, preparing herself, then a call pre-empted her. It was C.

'Kathryn?'

'Yes?'

'Is it true that you worked with Rory Bannatyne in Oman, July 2015?'

Taylor froze, feeling a cold dread spread inside her.

'Yes,' she said.

'Could you come up to my office?' He hung up before she could answer.

FOURTEEN

Kane passed the RAF camp at Travellers Hill. He identified the guards' hut from which Rory had been seen alive for the last time, then continued along the road in the direction Rory had been driving, slowly now, looking for an explanation as to how the engineer could vanish and then reappear hanging off an antenna. Then Kane saw the turn-off.

It wasn't clearly marked on the map. This seemed to be because the road was not used much anymore. It had been built to US specifications, with a solid yellow centre line, and had evidently been busy enough at one point, because the line had needed repainting, a second ghost line faintly shadowing the first. But the traffic had stopped a while ago, and vegetation had begun to reclaim it.

Kane waited to see if any other cars were nearby, then turned onto the abandoned road. It snaked into the hills, climbing steeply through a series of switchbacks. He passed a huge crater ringed with coloured bands of rock so that it looked like a racetrack, then rattled over a dry streambed. The Atlantic Ocean appeared ahead of him, a flash of light between gravel mountains. Then the road twisted inland again, rising into ever-increasing desolation.

Soon he was on little more than a dirt track. The car shook complainingly. He wasn't confident the suspension could handle it, let alone the wheels. Terry's words echoed: *You won't be able to take this one off-road.* Was he still on the road? The idea of getting stuck on a long-forgotten stretch of tarmac in the blazing heat wasn't appealing. No reception; no emergency phones here.

Kane pulled over and wondered at the wisdom of continuing on. He had nothing definite to suggest Rory came this way. He climbed out to stretch, and the sun on his head was like a blow. For a bizarre second he thought he heard Rory's voice. He was somewhere in the centre of the island. Peaks surrounded him. Large black birds with narrow bodies and pointed wings circled in the air above him. They soared high and steady, and brought with them a raucous screaming that sounded like machinery grinding. Kane searched for any shade, for a moment's respite from the heat, then gave up and climbed back into the car. He licked the sweat off his lips, drank the last of his water, and decided to give it five more minutes before turning back.

Three of those minutes had passed when he reached a dead end. The road parted around some abandoned concrete – a crumbling, disused building guarded by the stumps of dead palm trees. On its far side, the ground gave way entirely and a deep crevice opened up with sheer, ridged sides. According to his map, it was known as Devil's Ashpit.

Kane got out and wandered the ruins. It had once been a compound of some kind, constructed beside a ravine that tumbled away down to a dried-up inlet. Man-made blocks lay scattered about: seven or eight concrete pedestals, and foundations where further buildings had been. Only one survived intact: a single-storey sprawl of peeling white paint; the size of a school or headquarters. The front doors were secured with a padlocked bolt. Windows on either side had been covered with black panels. He pulled at the doors and the sound of the bolt rattling startled birds from the nearby rocks.

Kane circled the building and peered down into the ravine. A few hardy bushes clung to the sides. There were traces of whatever had been constructed beside it, bricks and some metalwork tossed down and forgotten. It was too hot now. The long-winged black birds circled above Kane's head and seemed excited to find him hanging around. They were waiting for his luck to run out, and the cries sounded gleeful. His mouth was dry. It was time to head back. If Rory's last journey brought him here, Kane had no idea what he'd found.

Two Boats was a blessed relief. The village was situated in a gentle valley ringed by volcanic cones. Originally set up by the BBC, it was one of the few places on the island from which you couldn't see the ocean but you got a breeze off Green Mountain, and with its boxy white houses and cinder lawns, its school and community centre and speed bumps, the place was the closest the island got to suburbia. The name had come from two longboats that had once been sawn in half and set on end to provide shade for people making the day's hike from Georgetown to Green Mountain to fetch water. A zigzag path still led up the mountain behind the settlement like a jagged fracture.

Two Boats was where Petra was last seen alive.

Kane stopped the car at the edge of the village and walked in, past rows of polytunnels and a fenced sports court. The day was finally softening into a more manageable late afternoon. He found the island's only other grocery store, Jam's Convenience, which contained the same tins as Solomon's, and the same crumbs from absent bread. One man sat behind the counter with a handheld electric fan and a book of crosswords, a younger man stacking shelves. Kane bought a litre bottle of water and drank half of it gratefully in the shade of the shop's veranda. The community centre next door advertised Zumba and aerobics and Bridge Night. Beside it was Ladybirds Preschool. The sound of children playing floated from the windows.

There was a strong possibility that the men from last night were based around here. Kane could feel his muscles tense as he walked, keeping an eye out for the red polo shirts. But he wasn't going to achieve much trying to avoid people, and the heat had emptied the place anyway.

The island's school had been built at the southern edge of the village. It had whitewashed buildings arranged around a lawn like a bowling green overlooked by a small clocktower, all of which lent the place some degree of formality. The entrance was open. Kane checked he was still alone, then walked in, past a framed photograph of the queen circa 1970, into a large hall with gymnasium markings on its polished floor. One teacher's voice escaped a classroom in the far corner of the building – a man talking mathematics. It was quarter past three and Kane figured the class wouldn't be finishing in the next five minutes, so he explored. Most of the rooms were open, empty, with whiteboards and maps of the world, dogeared British textbooks on shelves. There was something about the place that made him uneasy. The relative coolness felt unnerving. Kane studied the class photos on the wall until he saw Petra Wade. She sat beside Connor in the front row of last year's photo. Kane took a photo of his own using his phone, then encrypted it.

Artwork had been displayed along the walls of the central hall. A lot of the more accomplished pictures were by the same individual. Kane recognised the style from the exercise book Rory had hidden. They were signed Connor. These images were less horrific – mountains, wildlife, portraits: several of Petra Wade. Kane tried to read obsession in the fine pencil lines. An obsessive eye, for sure. A talent. Somewhere, deeper within the building, a door opened and closed, and Kane made his way swiftly back outside. This wasn't where he wanted to be found loitering.

*

144

The most eye-catching thing in Two Boats was the blue of a swimming pool visible through the entrance to a small bar that styled itself the Two Boats Club. The club had a yellow sloping roof and a board outside advertising lunches, snacks, and dinners. A poster promised live bands and discos with 'mixed music.' The menu offered what it called Saint dishes: tuna fish cakes or 'Plo' curry.

The woman managing the place was fifty or so, flip-flops and a pink T-shirt that said *Saint Helena*. The only other customer sat nursing a Coke at the bar, holding a fan, wearing a billowing white dress and sun hat and large shades. Both smiled at him, and both smiles faltered as he came closer. They'd heard something, he could tell by the reaction. But it was too late to back out.

'Do you do coffee?' he asked.

'Sure.'

'What do you recommend to eat?'

'Fish cakes are the speciality.' The woman spoke politely but not warmly. Kane ordered fish cakes and an iced coffee, took a seat far enough from the bar to let the women continue talking, close enough to hear them. A message came in to his phone as he waited, via its satellite function: the code that meant Taylor had uploaded information. Kane logged in and saw Taylor's messages. He read through the details of the second pathology report and Taylor's terse conclusion: *I don't think Rory killed himself.* That lent a sharpened edge to the day. More puzzling was her subsequent message. Kane skimmed through it quickly. Rory had been interested in someone called Jack Moretti, a man who had hung himself in similarly mysterious circumstances a decade ago. Kane stared at Taylor's notes, trying to figure out what he was meant to do with this information. Part of him wondered at Taylor's state of mind, and what the implications were for himself if she was losing the plot. His instinctive response was that this wasn't the input he needed from HQ.

Let me know if you come across any reference or connection to Moretti.

That was profoundly vague tasking. He closed the message down as the manager came over. She looked at him again as she set the coffee down.

'New here?'

'Yes. Flew in yesterday. I'm Edward. Pleased to meet you.'

'Pleased to meet you, Edward,' she said, without conviction or an introduction of her own.

The coffee was good. He'd read that Saint Helena produced some of the most expensive coffee in the world, and wondered if he was sampling it. The fish cakes were spicy and fresh. Kane was thinking of spending the last of the afternoon assessing the state of play, avoiding heat exhaustion and maybe reading a bit more history on the pretext of living his cover. The woman fanning herself at the bar didn't take her eyes off him. Eventually, under the pressure of her stare, he looked up and nodded.

'It was you, last night,' she said.

'Me?'

'In the fight.'

'In Georgetown, you mean?'

'Yeah.'

'I tried to help some kid who was getting beaten up. I wouldn't call it a fight. I'd only been on the island about an hour. What was it about?'

'That boy's no good. That's all you need to know. I'm not saying it was okay what the men did, but you should know: That boy's not a victim.'

'Really? What's he done?'

The women exchanged glances.

'Heard of Petra Wade?' the manager said.

'I saw the posters at Georgetown.'

'Well, maybe that tells you.'

146

Kane frowned.

'You think that boy . . . ?'

Silence fell. Finally the woman in shades said: 'Everyone who's been on this island for more than a week knows it was him.' She turned back to her drink.

'Why hasn't he been arrested?'

'That's a good question.' She looked meaningfully at the manager, who raised an eyebrow.

'Seriously,' Kane said. 'I don't understand.'

The customer turned again on her stool.

'His mum's an American general. He lives on the US base. So he's protected.'

'Though maybe not forever,' the manager said.

'Why not?'

'There's only so much evidence they can ignore.'

More people came in before Kane could get her to expand on that. It took Kane a second to recognise the man who'd given him a lift from the airfield the previous night. He was accompanied by a woman of a similar age in loose cotton clothes and sandals. The man looked at Kane. Kane raised his hand in greeting and the man nodded back hesitantly, removed his cap and wiped the back of his arm across his brow.

The four islanders spoke together quietly. Kane heard the name *Lauren* being repeated. *Will she? . . . Could she? . . .* A Lauren Carter came up in police reports as the girl Petra had been intending to visit the night she went missing, a 'best friend'. Her father worked as an RAF vehicle technician, Mum helping as a teaching assistant at the school. Lauren was the second girl in Rory's photographs, Kane felt sure.

When eventually the postal worker and his companion left, Kane gave it a minute, then went up and paid.

'Seemed like they had news.'

'Maybe.'

'You said there was only so much evidence they could ignore.'

'That's right.'

'What do you mean?'

'Someone might have seen what happened. Another girl.'

'Really?'

'Yes. Question is if she has the courage to say.'

'Why wouldn't she?'

The woman in white fanned herself violently.

'Because the murderer is still on this island with her. Still at her school. Because last night he was out looking for her. You saw him. You see what's going on?'

Kane stopped in the doorway before stepping into the white heat, put his shades on, heard the women behind him.

'Of course they were together. They always were.'

'Inseparable.'

'The three of them. Always.'

Lauren Carter, Kane thought, walking back through the village. The police had been confident that Petra never made it to Lauren Carter's house, because it would have meant her passing the community centre, which had an exercise class outdoors between five and six p.m., and no one saw her.

Kane went back to the community centre. He tried to establish the route Petra would have been expected to take, and therefore the location of Lauren Carter's home. A narrow path ran alongside the centre toward the northern edge of the village. He followed it, past more attempts at cultivating growth, until a residential property came into view. It stood alone, with a lot of rusting machinery in the front yard – a washing machine, a Kawasaki motorbike – all in the process of being assembled or disassembled or both. Kane stepped past the repair work to an open window and stopped. A girl sat just inside the window, staring vacantly into space.

Kane recognised Lauren from Rory's Polaroids. He hadn't

148

expected her to be there, but there she was, sitting alone in the front room. Now he felt overly hasty and conspicuous. Her fair hair was plaited. She wore a pink hoodie though even in the shade it must have been hot. She sat very still.

Kane listened for sounds of anyone else in the house. He tried to think of some pretext on which to speak to her. For the first time in his operational career, he came up blank.

He stumbled on the loose ground and she turned sharply. Her lips parted and he saw the train-track braces on her teeth.

'Sorry to disturb you,' he said. The girl watched him. He stepped closer. 'My name's Edward. I just arrived on the island. Got myself a bit lost.'

The girl nodded slowly, as if the truth of this was deeper than he realised.

'Is there a garage near here?' Kane continued. 'Somewhere I can get petrol?'

'I don't think so.'

'But this is Two Boats.'

'Yes.'

Kane took his map from his bag and unfolded it.

'Could you show me exactly where we are?'

She got up. As she approached the window, he saw her expression change. Kane turned and saw a man with shopping bags approaching through the front garden.

'What are you doing?' he said.

'He's lost, Dad.'

'What do you want?' Lauren's father stared at Kane, red-faced and breathless.

'I just drove here from Georgetown but I need petrol, and I wasn't sure where you're meant to fill up. First day on the island. Someone said One Boat, but I'm not sure where that is.'

'One Boat's that way, back past the store.'

'Okay. I must have missed it. Thank you. And thank you, too.'

Kane turned to the girl, who had stepped back deeper into the shadows of her home.

He felt the man staring at him as he walked away, through the village, through blinding sunlight. Felt the heat of the father's stare and an irrational guilt, entwined.

What had Lauren Carter seen?

Inseparable. The three of them.

Quite a place to grow up. Eternal summer. Kane thought of the exercise book and imagined children trying to make a world out of the stark landscape – a world of adventure in which you were explorers navigating your way out; a team, shipwrecked here together, learning how to survive. And the island, becoming smaller by the day, would eventually banish you. Everyone is ejected from childhood, but few with such geographical finality. How did it feel, knowing this fate was on the horizon? People think they are returning you to a larger world, but they haven't felt the trade winds in their hair as they cycle down volcanic slopes. Kane thought of Connor, with all his awkward adolescence, coming of age here, the volcanic peaks sharpened with new desire.

Kane ducked into the store again, grateful for the cooler air. The two men, old and young, remained as they had been, one with his crossword, one beside the shelves. Kane picked up more water and some snack bars. As he was paying he heard a familiar voice.

'Any chance of leaving these leaflets here? Almost turtle season. Need all the volunteers we can get.'

Kane turned to see Connor's father in the doorway, holding a stack of leaflets.

'No, thank you,' the shopkeeper was saying – saying it as soon as Thomas came in so that their voices overlapped. 'No, thank you. Not today. Not here.' The man didn't look at Thomas Lindgren. For a second, Thomas seemed stunned. In that moment he looked around the place as if seeking support, noticed Kane. A rapid sequence of expressions followed: recognition, then blankness. Kane realised Thomas was doing him a favour.

'Okay.'

When he'd left, the shopkeeper shook his head. The shelf stacker dropped his empty boxes by the counter.

'Does he really think—'

'Either he does or he doesn't. Or he won't admit it. Not to himself, maybe.'

'We're expected to pretend like it's not happened?'

'No.'

Kane cleared his throat.

'Isn't he with the conservation centre? I saw him in Georgetown.'

'That's right,' the shopkeeper said.

'What's the problem?' Kane asked.

'No problem,' the man said. 'No problem at all. Have a good afternoon.'

Kane walked back to his car, pondering his next move and how to translate this situation into a report for Kathryn Taylor. She would be relieved to have an alternative suspect. He could imagine her leaving the mystery of Rory's fate intact. Just before he got to the road, he saw Thomas sitting alone in a patch of shade cast by a crossroad signpost, with his box of leaflets beside him. He stared at nothing, wearing a look of emotional exhaustion. Kane stopped. For a moment he couldn't help watching him. Was that a man whose son had killed someone? Would you feel the crime was in some way your own, that you had brought a killer into existence? At the same time, Kane knew this was his opening. On any mission you sifted the lives around you, feeling for the weak, the vulnerable, those who would give you a way in. Thomas's nightmare was his window onto the island; the man's outsider status, his fear and resentment and desperation, made him perfect for cultivation as a source. He was already in Kane's debt, trusted him implicitly.

'Hey.'

Thomas looked up.

'Hey.' Then the look of concern returned. 'I wouldn't hang around with me. Not here.'

'Why?'

'They not tell you in the store?'

'Not in the store. I heard some stuff in the café. Sounded like a lot of rumours and not much sense. Is that what last night was about?'

'That's what I'm assuming.'

'What's going on?'

'A hell of a lot more than some people realise.'

An engine growled into earshot. Ahead of them, on the road leading away from the village, a van stopped suddenly. It looked like it had been used for refuse collection at one point, with a caged tipper back, but now said *Extermination* across the front doors. Kane smelled rotting fish, then saw the traps in the back of the vehicle.

'Stay still,' Thomas said. 'They won't see us.'

Four men got out, one carrying a bolt action shotgun. They wore the red polo shirts Kane had seen on the attackers last night. He recognised the two men. The gun was mounted with telescopic sight. They all moved to inspect something at the side of the road, their shadows long on the ground, crouching to a patch of sand arranged around an upturned bucket. So these were the cat hunters. One man produced a glass bottle and found a syringe. Another, in thick red gloves, reached into the sack of raw fish. They injected poison into the fish, then placed the fish on top of the bucket. Then they drove on.

'There you go,' Thomas said. 'But who's going to kill the rats when the cats are gone?' He spat into the dust.

'Where can we talk?' Kane said.

'Not here. Let's get out of the village.'

'Where?'

'Have you seen Green Mountain?' Thomas asked.

'Only from beneath.'

'Let me show you Green Mountain. We can talk up there.'

FIFTEEN

The mountain path rose gently for about six hundred feet then took off – incredibly steep with hairpin bends and sheer drops on the outside. But the reward was living nature. Slowly the steep slopes beside them became green with ferns, cedar, gorse. It spread upward. The greenery thickened around them until they were beneath a canopy of overhanging trees.

'Shade,' Thomas said. 'When did you last feel that? Shade from a tree. You feel the climate start to change?' The air had become sweeter, cool and moist. Fleshy leaves dangled clusters of red flowers like miniature chandeliers, others like bright purple bells. 'This is one of the most ambitious experiments on earth.'

The trees around them were eucalyptus, with pine in the distance and thick tangles of blackberries and raspberries lower down the slopes. There didn't seem to be any logic to it, as if a collection had spilled and plants grew up randomly. Pairs of small blue butterflies appeared and disappeared.

'You know Darwin came here? It was part of his world tour. He said it was one of the most desolate places he'd seen. At that time there was nothing growing whatsoever. But he went back home and talked to his friend, Joseph Hooker, from the Royal Botanic Gardens. They thought if you could kickstart some foliage up here it might trap the moisture from the winds, let it drip down to ground level. Then you had the beginnings of something; a water supply at least. So they shipped plants from

Argentina, Europe, South Africa: eucalyptus, bamboo, banana trees, scotch pines. And it worked. The water dripped down. You got soil, you got more plants; life began. You're in the world's largest artificial cloud farm.'

'Incredible.'

'People come here to see about terraforming other planets. If you can do it here, you can do it anywhere. But that doesn't mean it's not a nightmare from an ecological point of view. It looks like paradise, right, but you scratch the surface and there's none of the interrelationships you'd expect in a real forest. Meanwhile all of the species that were originally here are vanishing. Turns out it wasn't desolate at all – it was just fine.'

They passed a gate set into moss-covered stone walls with an older building beyond it. Kane could just make out the crest of the Royal Marines engraved above the entrance. It stood high above a hillside with great clumps of bananas and bulbous mangoes ripening in the sun. Green Mountain, Kane remembered, was the legacy of the Marines as well. Military energy diverted into the creation of a farm and water supply.

'It would take thousands of years to get a fully functioning ecosystem here,' Thomas said. 'At the moment it's a completely unmanaged mess of invasive species. The whole island is.'

'Stunning, though.'

'Stunning mayhem. Meanwhile we're killing the cats to protect the birds.'

'So we saw.'

'I wasn't joking with what I said. It's only going to lead to more problems.'

'Seriously?'

'You know the whole place was once crawling with rats? They've been here since the first ships arrived. That's why the cats were introduced in the first place. It's just a shame that the cats prefer eating the birds. We've already lost some species here forever. Anyway, it turned out the rats chewed at the cactus seed-lings and once the rats started to die the cactus ran wild – the donkeys spread the seeds. Ideally we'd eradicate the donkeys, but no one wants to do that – they've become a part of the place. So now they're trying to introduce various insects that might want to eat cactus. God knows who brought the cactus over.'

'There was an old lady who swallowed a fly.'

'Right.'

They climbed higher. Thomas was in good shape. Kane was glad he'd kept up a habit of long walks while in Oxford.

'But it *is* stunning. You're right. I can never believe the guys on the base who never explore. They haven't seen even half the island. Collect their pay cheques, enjoy the cheap beer, counting down the days. But they're younger ... Maybe they don't realise how special it is. This is where the boss lives,' Thomas said.

They passed a colonial-looking building with its standard-issue lawn and flagpole. A signpost beside the entrance directed people to two separate paths: INVALIDS and CONVALESCENTS.

'The Administrator?'

'That's right. Originally a naval sanitarium.'

Kane looked for signs, but couldn't see any evidence the Administrator was home. Her Majesty's representative, Nigel Horsley: career diplomat, ex-ambassador to Gibraltar. Kane tried to imagine the diplomatic trajectory that led him here, and the reason someone would accept the post. In place of global heft you got a kingdom of your own – perhaps that was it. An idyll that was yours to rule.

The Royal Marines building was far below them now. They'd climbed more than five hundred feet. The path became rougher. Now the mist came down as they continued up the final steep track.

'Here's the cloud.'

Kane had never walked into a cloud before. The dampness

appeared like a living presence, wreathing around them. Leaves held beads of moisture. The ground was muddy, with a wall of bamboo on either side, and a rope handrail for the final ascent to a small pond.

'This is it: the Dew Pond. This is what we were to depend on if everything else went. Our emergency supply of water.'

The pond was clouded with water lilies supporting delicate blue flowers. Goldfish flashed in the gaps between them. Thomas sat down on a bench.

'You kept up,' he said, smiling. He caught his breath then retrieved a flask from his bag and drank. He offered Kane the water.

'This is my bit of peace, this place. That's how you make somewhere home: You find your bit of peace. All you can ask for.'

Kane drank, gave the flask back.

'How long have you been on the island?'

'Eight long years.'

'Miss the States?'

'Know where I miss? Finland. Haven't been there for forty years. But I remember the air.'

'Helsinki?'

'Much further north. Do you know the country?'

'No. I've always wanted to go.'

'I'm from a little place called Inari. I'm a country boy.' He stared into the pond. Sweat dripped off the end of his nose. 'What were they saying in the café?'

'Sounded pretty crazy.'

Thomas laughed gently, as if embarrassed by Kane's caution.

'About the girl who went missing,' Kane said.

'About Connor.'

'Yes.'

Thomas nodded, leaned forward so his elbows were on his knees, still gazing into the pond.

'So people are saying my son's a murderer.'

'No one seems to know anything.'

'People think they know.'

'They said he was with her that night.'

'He was. They were friends. They were together that evening, sure. He didn't kill her. Do you have kids?'

'No.'

'Okay. Well, it's not easy for kids here, as you can imagine. As far as Carina's concerned, it's all she knows. But Connor remembers the States. Even before all this happened I knew he needed to get off this island, start building a life for himself. The more he developed here, the harder I could see it was going to be for him to adapt anywhere else.'

'So what happened?'

'He was with Petra. They were messing about. He says he doesn't exactly remember what happened, he'd been drinking. At some point they met up with a guy called Rory Bannatyne – a Brit, working over here on installing broadband. He's not here anymore because the night Petra went missing he hanged himself.' Thomas turned to Kane, spread his hands as if to say *Draw your own conclusions*. Kane's heart raced hearing Rory's name for the first time on the island. He had to check himself, check his cover.

'Really?'

'What do you make of that?'

'It would put him pretty high on my list of suspects.'

'Right.'

'Was he ... dodgy? Why was he meeting with teenagers?'

'Dodgy? Is anything here not dodgy? This is the thing – this is what I'm trying to tell you, Edward. Do people ever call you Ed?'

'Not really.'

'Okay. Something's gone wrong on this island. I appreciate you need to write your book and I'm sure you'll get some good local colour for it, but don't try understanding more. Can I ask you a question?'

'Sure.'

'Do people in the UK know about this place?'

'Hardly at all.'

'It's not like the Falklands, right?'

'No. I don't think many people know it exists.'

'You see, we're living on a secret. It's not healthy. This whole place is a dirty secret. Officially, nobody is a citizen of Ascension. Even if you've been here for decades, you're a temporary visitor. You're a job, that's all. And if you have kids here, as soon as they leave school they have to find work on the island or leave. And they take their silence with them. You can't belong here – you can't choose to grow old and die here.'

'Why?'

'Ask your government. They don't want attachment. A few years ago there was talk of changing things up a bit; Ascension was trying to be democratic. Then that all stopped. Now they only let people bring their families if it's essential. Mostly, everyone's being replaced by contract workers. People come and go. And without attachment, you have no principles. A lot of men here get bored, look for distractions. Teenagers, too. Anyone tell you details about Petra?'

'What kind of details?'

'Petra got herself a bit of a reputation. She was a good kid but she'd gone wild, as teenagers do. She was fifteen, you know, and always was a precocious kid, always liked attention. It was normal teenage stuff, but this isn't a normal place, and people knew her, knew a bunch of those girls who were looking for opportunities to party and express themselves, shall we say. They'd get alcohol off the bases – I'm not sure exactly how. One time I know Petra was found on the UK base and various reprimands followed, although it doesn't seem like she did anything apart from use the pool there. But she was still technically a kid. You'd see her and her friends getting rides from adults all the time. First time I saw Petra in the front of the police car, I thought the obvious. But she was laughing, having a great time.'

'When was that?'

'End of last year maybe. I said to Connor: Is this normal? He told me there were invite-only parties on the island, out away from the main centres. Usually it was just the girls who'd get invited but one night he was there and they got the girls drunk. This is the tragedy: the only place they can go wild is with a bunch of middle-aged men who've been alone on an island for a year. That's fucked up. Connor said he saw a maroon Land Rover parked up by this party, at one or two in the morning. Now, the only person on this island who drives a maroon Land Rover is the Administrator. So what the fuck do you do with that?'

Kane wondered. He could see how the Land Rover made a very different situation out of the whole thing. That and the police being close to Petra. Very different, very deep.

'Was the British engineer involved in all this?'

'I think he'd been sucked in.'

'To what, exactly?'

'To that. To the culture here. I only met him a couple of times. He struck me as someone who was here to escape something, willing to throw himself into whatever escapism offered itself.'

'Really?'

'Don't get me wrong, he was pleasant enough, intelligent. Quite charming. He certainly charmed the local kids.'

'What do you mean?'

'Kids loved him. He'd mess around, giving them medals and tasks. Like he was running a scouts club. But a lot of the adults loved him too. He played the ukulele and sometimes he'd sing. Any entertainment's going to win you points around here. I was never quite so sure, but then I was never in the bars at three a.m.'

'And you think he killed Petra Wade? That's why he killed himself?'

'I'm not saying he did or didn't do either. I'm saying whatever happened, he might not have been alone.'

This was a new option. More complex than solitary innocence or guilt. Rory had got involved in something.

'What would he do with her body?'

'It could be anywhere: taken by sharks, taken by birds, taken by rats. I don't see how anyone could have successfully buried anything here – it's rock all the way down, but there are places you could hide a body, perhaps. It's not a big island, but there wasn't a big search team. We get rollers. You heard about them?'

'No.'

'They're coming in again now. Giant waves, nothing to do with the trade winds – they appear without warning, from the northwest. Huge. Ships can't dock. The whole island's locked down. In the past there's been people swept out by them. And the sides of the island plunge straight under the water, totally sheer, which means there's a vicious undertow. That's why the rocks and beaches are all picked clean. Everything's sucked away, nothing's left: There's no flotsam. A body in the water isn't necessarily going to be washed up, not necessarily seen again at all.'

He stood up, walked to the pond's edge, hands in his pockets.

'That's where I think she went, but I don't think that's how she ended up there.'

'Did Connor tell the police all this?'

'I told the police. Connor won't go near the police now, for obvious reasons. John Morrogh's done his fair share of ill-advised socialising. He knew Rory. I don't know what else he knows, but I imagine a scapegoat would always come in handy. I told him all this and he said he'd look into it, but has he?'

'I don't know.'

'Me neither.'

Thomas squatted to peer into the pond, moving the water with his fingers. Kane thought of the sheer sides of the island, the hungry sea, the hungry rats. In the diary found on Ascension Island, the abandoned mariner had recorded his nightly fear that the rats would eat him as he slept. They'd colonised the place. It was one explanation as to why his own skeleton was never found.

'I heard something else at the café,' Kane said. 'Apparently there was another girl who might know what happened: Lauren something.'

Thomas straightened.

'Who said that?'

'The woman who runs the place. She said this girl knows something. She's been too scared to talk until now. Apparently, she was very close to Petra.'

'Lauren's close to Connor as well. What did they say she knew?'

'I don't know. But she'd been scared and now she might go above the police, straight to other authorities – straight to the UK.'

This was clearly news to Thomas. He nodded, looking almost hopeful.

'Well, that would be something. Did she see it?'

'Maybe. She's just been too terrified to talk.'

'I bet.' Thomas shook his head. 'Then I really hope she's okay. Because, whatever Lauren knows, it's not that my son is a murderer. Which puts her in a very vulnerable situation. She needs a guard. Shit.'

Thomas stared anxiously back at the water. Kane imagined they were thinking the same thing: They weren't in a position to guard Lauren Carter. Kane wondered who she would try to speak to, who it was safe to speak to.

It had got late. The setting sun pierced the bamboo and ignited the spaces between the lilies. Thomas circled the pond distractedly.

'No frogs today. You watch the ecosystem here like it could fall apart at any minute.'

The sunset crept up on them as they made their way back, first as a general thickening of light, and then the bamboo thinned out and there was a view down a thousand feet across the lava plains. Both of them stopped.

The sun was dissolving into the Atlantic, becoming blood red as they stared. Kane had never seen a sun so red. But equally breathtaking was the effect it had on the landscape. Volcanic mounds caught fire and the ground revealed itself as pink, purple, and blue.

'It drops so fast here,' Thomas said.

The evening mists rose from the heated rocks, softening the outlines of the peaks so that the island looked like a crumpled sheet. And, just as silently, the sense of confinement came in off the darkening ocean like a breeze.

SIXTEEN

They parted before getting into Two Boats.

'Listen,' Thomas said. 'It's probably best if you keep a distance from me. I don't know what's about to happen. I probably can't show my face much anymore. If you hear anything I'd appreciate you letting me know – just come to the base. But don't put yourself in danger. And don't believe what people say.'

'I won't. I'll see if I hear anything.'

'This is a great island in many ways. I'd just really avoid the wrong crowds.'

'Okay.'

Kane drove back to Georgetown. In the beam of his headlights the roads crawled. The crabs had come out, with orange legs and purple pincers, scuttling across roads and pathways toward the sea. Human life had also roused itself, free of the oppressive sun. Lights had turned on in homes and other buildings. The rocks dissolved into the night and the thin, electric forms of civilisation became visible like an X-ray.

Kane imagined the patterns of desire and secrecy becoming visible too, webs of lust, guilt, shame. Morality shaped itself to the environment at hand. In his experience, no one's ethics were stronger than those of the people around them. Groups released themselves into depravity as one. That didn't mean Connor himself might not have woven some tall tales, but there was a ring of truth to what his father said. Adults turning from the radars, from the secrets of nations and armies to the mystery of girls becoming women.

Just before One Boat, Kane passed a young man in US Air Force fatigues who flagged him down. The airman had been trying to transport crates on the back of a motorbike, but the ropes had snapped.

'Could really use a lift to the base.'

'Sure. Jump in.'

The young man filled the back seat with boxes of mushrooms and got in.

'Mind if I smoke?' he said.

'Go ahead.'

'You smoke?'

'I'm fine.'

No matter how many war zones Kane visited, the childlike youth of military personnel never failed to surprise him. The man couldn't have been older than twenty.

'How long have you been here?' Kane asked.

'Four hundred and seventeen days.' He laughed. 'Oh boy.'

'Many to go?'

'Two hundred, I believe. Join the air force, see the world. Didn't tell me the world was like this.' He whistled softly. Kane thought of the generations of young men before him, in slightly different uniforms with similar looks of youthful stoicism; back through World War II and the Napoleonic Wars, staring at the same rocks.

'How's business on the US base?'

'All nice and quiet. Better than Iraq, that's for sure.'

'Did you serve in Iraq?'

'No, sir.'

'What do you do for fun here?'

'There's the Volcano Club on the base. That's got cheap beer. There's a gym, burger place.'

'Ever mix with the locals? Must be some nice young ladies around.'

He gave Kane a sidelong glance.

'Not that I'm aware of.'

'What about the Brits? Get on with them?'

'Don't see them that much. There's a bit of tension right now.'

'Really?'

'Think so.'

'What's that about?'

'Just the same old rivalries I guess.'

They passed one of the traps and the car filled briefly with the stink of rotten fish.

'Oh, man.'

'I heard that's for the cats,' Kane said.

'Right. We're down to the last few. That's what they say.'

'Bet those last few are pretty canny.'

'Sure.'

'Imagine being the last one. Alone on a rock with no one but people trying to kill you.'

The airman nodded.

'Reckon a couple of us on the base could finish them in a night or two, but that's not allowed. Which sucks. They used to hunt the goats here. That's what I've heard from some of the old-timers. See any goats around?'

'Not so far.'

'Exactly.'

Kane dropped him at the gate to the US base. The man thanked him profusely, offered his cigarettes again, then a free meal at the Volcano Club anytime. Kane circled back to Georgetown. The place felt different when he arrived. The priest walked past with a bag of shopping. At the front of the vicarage he put his bags down to check the flowers he'd cultivated. Someone waved to him from outside the post office. There was a laugh from somewhere, a couple of men stopping to chat in front of the church. One passed over a newspaper. Kane thought he could hear the radar turning up on the hillside, a clicking sound. He mentally parsed his cohabitants into instigators, fellow travellers, those turning a blind eye, those helpless and scared.

He spent an hour or so lying on the bed in the bungalow feeling his sunburn throb, letting the island grow fully dark, then showered, typed up an update, and sent it through to Taylor. His thoughts turned to the name Jack Moretti for the first time since he'd read Taylor's report. No more on this odd thread. He searched online, saw the obituary, wondered what on earth a psychologist in LA should have to do with Rory Bannatyne, aside from their chosen means of suicide. Again, he felt that frustration at having been delivered nothing but more puzzlement. Not what he needed on this island. He boiled pasta and ate some of the provisions he'd bought, sitting in the Wades' small kitchen, feeling insensitive. Four weeks of this, he thought.

When he'd eaten, Kane stood in front of the bungalow and tried to remember the southern night sky. He found the Southern Cross, then the Jewel Box cluster beside it. He'd seen it once through a telescope. It was like a hundred sparkling blue jewels around a single red star. Just a bit farther to the right was the Coalsack, a dark nebula. Kane waited as more stars came into focus. The galaxies seemed to sink back, gaining depth. He thought of the early explorers reading these, their eyes on the stars as they sailed, as if the map of the world was written above them. The abandoned Dutch mariner had grown to fear the night sky; his diary made frequent references to the stars. Once his lamp had broken and he had no means of creating light, the stars had begun to appear terrifying. He associated them with the screaming of the birds, who he believed were accusing him of his crimes. A cursed place, Kane wondered, or simply blank, so that it became a mirror to your heart, with nowhere to hide.

Sink into the milieu: That was what he needed to do. What he was trained to do. Thomas's warnings were a prescription for action. If there was something rotten at the core of Ascension, Kane needed to go there – that was his job.

At nine p.m. he walked back through Georgetown. People sat in their small homes eating meals, watching TVs. He wondered about bars, about prostitutes. He'd seen smaller communities support the trade, with a lot fewer military around. It was time to get in with the wrong crowd.

The Exiles Bar had a string of coloured lights around its doorway; otherwise he wouldn't have seen it was there. But he might have heard the laughter from inside. This was the bar where the police had been drinking when Petra Wade's mother first tried to report her missing. Kane wondered who was in there now and how they'd respond to him. It seemed likely that this was where the two subcontractors had appeared from last night. Kane pushed the door and walked in.

The bar contained three people and none of them were the assailants from last night. One was the doctor Kane had met on the golf course, Derek Nulty, his bulky form propped on a stool that didn't look adequate for it. Leaning against the bar beside him was a lean man tanned the colour of hard wood, his Hawaiian shirt unbuttoned to reveal a shark's tooth necklace. A young Saint polished glasses behind the bar. All turned to watch Kane enter, the drinkers with the unsteady glint of men interrupted in the midst of a joke.

The barman smiled at his new customer. He couldn't have been older than eighteen, in a white shirt and waistcoat. The bar was framed with flags and netting and faded photographs of happier times which lent its present emptiness an air of decline.

'Evening,' Kane said.

'The historian,' Nulty said. 'We met, I believe. How's the car?'

'Not bad.'

His companion had a leery smile that creased his face. Kane ordered a beer, nodded at the tumblers of dark rum on the bar.

'Can I top you up?'

They looked at their glasses then back at Kane.

'Why not?' the doctor said. 'Not often a new customer walks in.'

'You're the professor,' his companion said.

'That's right.'

The drinks were set before them and they raised a toast to newcomers.

'Welcome to the volcano.'

'What do you think?' the man with the shark's tooth asked.

'It's different.'

'It's different.' He grinned. 'Where are you staying?'

'Well, it was meant to be the hotel. I've been put in a bungalow along the way. Looks like a family just left.'

There was an exchange of glances.

'Craig put you there?'

'That's right.'

'Kind of him. Make sure you lock your door at night.'

'I heard it was a friendly place.'

'Oh, yes.'

'That's the problem.'

This caused sudden hilarity. The doctor's laugh was a rasping, asthmatic wheeze that didn't match his speaking voice. Then it stopped, and his expression became serious. He placed a hand on Kane's shoulder.

'There's something you need to know.' He turned to his companion. 'Do you think he's ready?'

'Don't tell him, Derek.'

'Better sooner rather than later.'

'He's just arrived.' The younger man watched warily.

'Neil Armstrong.' He extended a finger toward the rocks outside. 'This is where they filmed it – the moon landing.'

His friend grinned.

'It was here,' the man continued. 'The whole thing.'

'That must be why the flag was rippling,' Kane said.

'You're on the moon, my son.'

'Not over the moon, for sure,' his friend said.

'The dark side of the moon,' the doctor said. They all drank. The barman watched Kane as if he hadn't seen any sober Englishmen for a while and it was a marvel.

'Spent much time on an island before?' the doctor asked.

'Not like this one.'

He leaned close, and Kane could smell warm and sour breath.

'Watch out for the wives.'

His companion shook his head. 'Fuck's sake, Derek.'

'I'm serious. A good-looking man like yourself.'

'That hotel,' the tall man said. 'It's the end of this place, now that's gone.'

'Certainly seems quiet out there tonight,' Kane said.

'Quiet's one way of putting it.'

'What brings you guys to Ascension?' Kane asked.

They looked at each other.

'He's the doc.' The thin man nodded at the fat one. 'So don't get sick while you're here. I'm an electrician. Frankie.'

'Good to meet you, Frankie. Valuable profession. Live in Georgetown?'

'Travellers Hill, by the RAF base.'

'You work on the base?'

'That's right. Dull enough that I have to come hang out with this old fart.'

'He's after his Viagra prescription,' Nulty said.

'Like there's anything worth that.'

'Warn the donkeys.'

Kane grinned. Eighty per cent of spying is pretending to be drunk with men you wouldn't choose to drink with. This wasn't new territory. Frankie was missing teeth and his nose had been broken and reset at one point, skin leathered by sunny postings. Kane had crossed paths with a lot of Frankies in Afghanistan and Iraq: tradesmen who'd got on the khaki circuit. Camp followers, who enjoyed the sense of being on the road, the stories they could tell when they got back home, the subsidised lifestyle.

'Seriously, though,' Kane said. 'Where are the ladies? Where are these wives? Beautiful as you guys are.'

They hesitated, as if struck by shyness, but it wasn't shyness. They were calculating something.

'Are you married?' Nulty asked.

'No. You? You guys single?'

The doctor said he was sadly divorced. The electrician grinned and said he was single on the island.

'What do you do for fun?' Kane asked.

'Oh, there's options.'

'Really?'

'Steady yourself, my friend, the night is young.'

They asked Kane about the UK, about news there, then what he'd heard about the island before coming over. Talk turned to the loss of the airbridge with the UK, and Kane got a sense that they felt abandoned, that the island was floating away. 'Cast adrift,' the doctor said. But he didn't seem too sorry about it.

'They've done it elsewhere,' Frankie said. 'Sterilised the place. Swept it clean when it suited them.'

Kane wondered where he meant exactly. Diego Garcia? That was a colonial possession the British had emptied for the sake of military installations and American radar. How much did the people of Ascension think about their Pacific sibling? Twinned with Diego Garcia wasn't a heart-lifting proposition.

'We are the endangered species here, make no mistake,' Nulty said. 'The island now has more antennae than people.'

It chimed with what Thomas had said. Was this neglect of the island's population the vague background to a lower-level corruption? There was a sense that civilian time was almost done here, a fin de siècle guttering, a last hurrah. Kane finished his drink and insisted on buying another round, insisted on them all accompanying their pints with shots.

'You really have Viagra?' he said.

'Of course. It's a bestseller.'

'Prozac?'

'Prozac, diazepam. Why? The place got to you already?' The doctor laughed and laid a fleshy hand on Kane's arm. 'My treasure chest is always open.'

'What about contraceptives?' Kane said.

'Essential service.'

'The pill?'

The doctor studied his face, nodded.

'You're very curious.'

'I'm trying to imagine life here,' Kane said. 'The doctor must know all the secrets.'

Nulty smiled. 'A few.'

'What's the craziest thing you've dealt with while on here?'

He considered this, downed his rum.

'A case of telepathy.'

'Telepathy?'

'Man said he could read people's minds. He'd been stung by a jellyfish and the poison got to his brain. But he voiced people's thoughts with some degree of accuracy for twenty-four hours or so. Had to be airlifted off when he started speaking prophecies that upset the ladies. Filth, but also what we eventually determined was an African dialect. That was the strangest thing about it. The man had never set foot in Africa. Claimed to be possessed by the slaves who'd worked here. Possessed by their voices.'

The doctor shrugged. A silence fell. Each man seemed to feel the darkness lapping at the bar, a darkness filled with the ghosts of men far from home, severed from their lives.

'My round,' the electrician said eventually.

The clock behind the bar ticked toward ten thirty p.m. No sign that closing time was approaching. Kane wondered if this was enough progress for one night. He'd made his first foray into companionship. It hadn't been an entirely unproductive day. They drank a final round, then the doctor checked his watch. Frankie checked the clock. They looked at each other.

'Are you thinking what I'm thinking?' Frankie said.

'Shall we?'

'Fuck it. Let's do it.'

Both turned to Kane.

'How do you feel?' Nulty asked.

'Okay,' Kane said.

'Think you can drive?'

Kane thought of Sergeant Morrogh's warnings about drunk driving, then of the winding roads thick with crustacean life. But he wasn't here to keep his nose clean.

'Sure.'

'We need a lift,' the doctor said. 'We shall introduce you to the fairest sights on this isle, but we need wheels.'

The electrician grinned.

'Fairest sights man ever did see.'

'A place you'd never find.'

'If you can drive us there.'

'Fancy going to a party?'

'I'd love to go to a party,' Kane said.

SEVENTEEN

The men directed him north, away from Georgetown into darkness. The doctor sat beside him, the electrician in the back. The road was full of potholes and little pinpricks of light where the land crabs were still flowing. Kane concentrated on keeping to the road. The white-painted stones along the edge were a lifesaving device, he realised. Then they stopped and there was no way of telling where the road gave way to the rocks.

Nulty lit a small cigar and held it out of the window.

'Listen to that,' he said. 'The waves.'

'Rollers,' Kane said.

'So you've heard about the rollers?'

'A bit.'

Both men peered out toward the sea.

'Kill your headlights,' Nulty said.

'Are you sure?'

'Go on.'

Kane killed the headlights, slowed.

'Can't see her,' the electrician said.

'She's out there.'

'Who's that?' Kane asked.

'The *Crystal Symphony*,' the doctor said. 'A cruise ship. Comes a couple of times a year.'

'Meant to be docking here in the morning. But she won't make it with a sea like this. A lot of people will lose money.'

'The passengers come onto the island looking for turtles,' Nulty explained. 'On here for a few hours, but they'll buy anything with a turtle on it.'

'They give them lectures about the turtles when they're on the ship. Get them all excited.'

'But the Administrator has said no go,' Nulty explained. 'Order is not to use the wharf until the swell dies down.'

'So long as the tanker gets here next week,' Frankie said.

'We get oil deliveries,' the doctor explained. 'Like milk deliveries, only through a big hose. It's quite a sight.'

'I bet.'

'Did you know, when the Americans scarpered at the end of the Second World War they left so much oil behind, it kept the island running for fifteen years. Did you know that?'

'I didn't know that,' Kane said.

'There's some history for you.' The doctor sucked his cigar and looked out to the sea. The men grew quieter as they approached the north coast, until it was just the electrician giving directions onto ever smaller roads winding through the rocks. Kane wondered what environment he was about to enter, what he would have to turn a blind eye toward for the sake of maintaining cover. If there were children present, he wondered what his response could be. He'd had to suppress moral objections before while playing a role, but nothing like this. He was also aware that he may be being lured somewhere for other purposes. The doctor and the electrician would know the men Kane had confronted last night. He thought back over the previous couple of hours and wondered if there'd been any opportunity for the two men to coordinate this behind his back. *Directed into isolation, five men on one, a blow to the head* ... When Kane heard music and voices ahead, he felt both relief and caution.

'This is it.'

Kane pulled in beside several cars already parked up. He

thought of Thomas's account of the secret parties and looked for the Administrator's Land Rover, but it wasn't there. Nor were either of the police cars, although there was an army-green RAF truck.

A hand-painted sign had been stuck into a crack in the ground announcing KLINKA KLUB. The club was a tin-roof shelter built onto a ledge overlooking the sea. It had a large patio with a concrete barbecue pouring flames and smoke into the night, and steps down to the beach. A few men kicked a ball around on the sand. Rollers smashed the shore behind them, creating an epic backdrop. A crowd clustered around the barbecue, and a few queued up at the hatch that served as a bar. Thirty or forty people in total, with more cars arriving as Kane walked in.

'Welcome to the Klinka,' Nulty said.

The setup didn't feel clandestine. Kane didn't see anyone underage. Most looked like they'd come off the bases: a lot of sunburnt men in T-shirts and shorts. He recognised some from Georgetown, some from the flight over. There were older men who must have been GCHQ-NSA, technical specialists who'd found a comfortable niche in the intelligence world and hunkered down. The women were outnumbered but made up for it in noise and colour. He saw Linda, the woman who had helped him the previous night, and the manager from Two Boats. Everyone seemed in party spirits. The air smelled of sun cream and sweat. A generator fed a sound system, and a space in the corner contained a small drum kit and a guitar on a stand.

The doctor and technician went off in the direction of the barbecue. Kane ordered a beer. It turned out to be happy hour – two-for-one drinks – so he gave his second one to an RAF lad beside him at the bar.

'It will be warm by the time I get to it,' Kane said.

'Then you're drinking too slow,' the officer replied with

a grin. He was tall, with cropped blond hair and a broad Yorkshire accent.

'Over here long?' Kane asked.

'Been six months.'

They chatted about the facilities on the British base, which included the island's only hairdressers for men, a mess bar, and what the man claimed was the best pool on the island, which doubled up as an emergency supply of fresh water: 'So don't piss in it.'

He introduced Kane to some of his fellow military personnel, all of whom looked well refreshed. Kane could feel the last couple of hours' drinking being counteracted by a watchfulness born of the new environment. Pace yourself, he thought. Keep control, see where this goes. People around him were drunk. Rehydrating-with-tequila drunk; Friday night on a volcano drunk. He turned toward some laughter and saw a donkey with its head over the side wall being fed beer.

Kane mingled, alert to people's responses, to his own bearing, projecting relaxation, bonhomie. A group of four Saints arrived – two men and two women, in sequins and cowboy hats – and they took up the instruments and began to play covers of pop songs. There was some tentative dancing among the crowd, then less tentative. The woman who'd been feeding beer to the donkey climbed onto someone's back. The Two Boats Club manager danced with a barefoot man in a torn pink T-shirt – then another man cut in and there was laughter as she was passed around. The atmosphere reminded Kane of drinking in war zones, the sense of fate having thrown you together, created a little club you could join by helping make a party out of unpromising materials. And the bigger things going on around you were like a cloak.

At some point Kane got chatting to a nurse from the RAF base who said she'd come over to save money and get a tan. She spoke rapidly and not entirely coherently, trying to persuade him to get involved with a running club – 'more a drinking club with a run attached if I'm being entirely honest' – then about her life and her ex. She leaned in, the ice in her G&T rattling.

'I have always believed you regret the things you don't do, so here I am. And I don't regret it,' she kept saying.

They got some air up by the road, away from the music, over-looking the beach.

'Nothing like a Klinka party,' she said.

'Been to a lot of them?'

'Fair few. Not many choices around here.'

'Must be a bit strange. So many guys about. Not that many ladies.'

'I guess so. It doesn't really bother me, to be honest.'

'Things ever get out of control? I've been around a few bases. I know what it's like.'

'Depends what you mean by out of control.' She smiled. Then the headlights of an arriving car drowned them. It stopped hur-riedly, with an urgent air.

'Who's that?' the nurse said. She checked her watch. It was almost one thirty a.m. A man and woman got out; there was an anxious exchange with a couple of RAF men smoking nearby. The nurse went over, returning a moment later and rolling her eyes.

'One of the local kids has done a runner. You've not seen a girl around, no?'

'Who is it?'

'She's called Lauren Carter.' The nurse sighed. 'Obviously, with what happened ... '

Kane's stomach lurched. Lauren Carter. Lauren who knew what happened, who was ready to speak. What had Thomas said? *She needs a proper guard.* Beyond the party, the night was a textureless black now.

'Do you know her?' Kane asked.

'Everyone knows Lauren. Let's get another drink.'

They went back inside. The crowd had thinned slightly. Kane sensed that a few people now knew of the search and weren't sure how to respond yet. Maybe they shared the nurse's insouciance. But people were drinking as if last orders were about to be called. Now Kane tried to remember who had turned up when, who might have been using this as an alibi. He started to think through his options, how to respond without drawing attention to himself.

The band played on. The nurse leaned in close to him. After a moment he realised she was saying, 'Do you dance?'

They danced. She took Kane's hand and he twirled her. While he was twirling her, the police walked in.

Morrogh was accompanied by his shaven-headed deputy, Sean Reid, and a third man in a hi-vis bib that said *Ascension Police Volunteer*. As the volunteer stepped into the light Kane saw his bruised face and recognised the corporal he'd headbutted last night. The man's gaze met Kane's. He held it for a few seconds before scanning the rest of the crowd.

The room became quieter and this ripple of hush attracted attention. The police went to the bar, spoke to the staff. They got Cokes, sipping them as they looked around, as if counting off faces. Morrogh accepted a beer towel from the barman and mopped his sweat. The barman signalled to the band. After another minute the song ended and Morrogh went to the microphone.

'As some of you know we're currently trying to locate the whereabouts of a girl – Lauren Carter. Fifteen years old. Ran off this afternoon. I'm sure most of you know her: blond, dental braces. At the moment there's no need to panic, but we'd appreciate people keeping an eye out. Anyone here seen her in the last couple of hours?'

There were shakes of the head.

'Where was she last seen?' one of the RAF men asked.

'Last we've got is at her home. That's Two Boats. There's a possibility someone entered the home. We don't want to speculate at this stage. She may have gone to Georgetown, but there's no sign of her around there at present.'

No one knew anything, or had any suggestions, it seemed. Kane looked around the faces for reactions, got blankness. The police officer moved back into the crowd and people returned to their previous conversations. But there was a self-consciousness now, spreading to the men at the back. The atmosphere had changed. The military bristled, alcohol fuelling a new machismo in the face of this challenge. The young Saints stiffened with a dutiful responsibility. One of the musicians packed their guitar away.

The nurse disappeared toward the beach. Kane went to the bar, where the officer who owed him a drink passed him a rum and Coke. Kane found himself amid a group of air support officers.

'Who is she?' he asked.

'Don't ask.'

'She'll be hiding somewhere.'

They exchanged careful looks. Kane glanced around for the men who had brought him here – the doctor and electrician. The doctor was talking to one of the musicians, the electrician was elsewhere, maybe down on the beach. Kane stepped out. He needed to get back to Georgetown, get his map and torch. Get a full satellite link with London in case Taylor had any information from intercept. They needed to establish access to police communications: see what was going on, how deep and dark things were on this island. They could do that from the UK end. The Administrator's comms would be more complicated.

The coals of the abandoned barbecue glowed. No one was playing football anymore. The waves crashed in. Kane could hear a whispering anxiety among the crowd behind him: cautious, pragmatic but real.

I'll take the car.

People are coordinating the search from Georgetown.

From what I hear, her dad popped out for a minute and when he came back she was gone.

Free round to whoever finds her.

The narrow, winding roads were about to be filled with a lot of drunk people moving fast with their minds elsewhere. Kane headed back to his own vehicle.

The night air was hot and soft and the wind felt like someone draping a sheet over your face. Where the volcanoes had been there were just black gaps cut out of the night sky. As Kane began to drive away from the club, something stepped into the road in front of him. He slammed the brakes. It was the donkey. The animal looked unsteady on its hooves, gazing at Kane through the windscreen. It hissed at him before stepping slowly out of the way. When he later thought of that moment, it seemed like the donkey was trying to warn him of what was to come.

A minute further along the road an approaching car flashed its lights and stopped beside him. The woman in the front leaned out.

'Seen a girl about? Blond, fifteen years old?'

'No. I heard. I was going to take a look around.'

The snarl of an army helicopter came into earshot, its searchlight drawing closer, then away as it began to comb the island.

Georgetown had entered crisis mode. People had gathered in front of the church, which was open and spilling light; more people, including military, in front of the bar and the police station. The sea looked black and vicious. Torch beams criss-crossed one another on the beach. It was two a.m.

Uniforms appeared in Kane's headlights as he drove through,

a few aircraftmen writing on clipboards, gripping Maglites between their teeth. One officer was giving instructions to RAF Operations Support: dog handlers, communications engineers in short-sleeved blue shirts. Others were marking up maps or distributing torches and batteries out of a box. The sudden efficiency of it all created the impression that this was what the island had been waiting for.

When he was almost at the bungalow, Kane saw movement ahead: a small crowd centred on his accommodation. A dog barked. He slowed the car down and a torch was shined through his windscreen.

'It's him.'

Suddenly there was a lot of weaponry pointed Kane's way. Kane could see more men running over. The door of the bungalow was open.

'Step out slowly. Hands up.'

He stepped out of the car. The group by his bungalow included Lauren Carter's father, peering anxiously at the doorway. As Kane watched, a man in RAF uniform appeared from inside, holding the pink hoodie that Lauren had been wearing when Kane saw her earlier in the day.

'Leave it,' Morrogh shouted, running over. 'Don't touch anything. Put it down where it was.'

Lauren's father pushed past the RAF officer into the bungalow. Morrogh stopped, breathless, at the door.

'Is she in there?' he asked.

'No,' the man with the hoodie said.

Morrogh turned to Kane.

'Where is she?'

'I've no idea,' Kane said. 'I just got back here.'

Lauren's father reappeared.

'Where is she?' he screamed. He ran toward Kane. Three RAF men held him back. A throng of people had gathered across the road, staring at the bungalow and at Kane with his hands up. A military flight came in low, deafening, momentarily casting the whole scene as small and absurdly terrestrial. Then Morrogh nodded to the police station.

'Leave the car. Come with me.'

EIGHTEEN

Taylor walked up the stairs to the chief's office, his words ringing in her ears. *Is it true that you worked with Rory Bannatyne in Oman, July 2015?* When she arrived at the top floor she was surprised to see Skinner standing in the corridor. Perhaps she shouldn't have been, Taylor thought. He wore his coat and scarf, still damp from a shower of rain. Taylor wondered where he'd come from, and what he'd just told Mackenzie. He didn't say anything, just watched her walk in.

Sir Roland Mackenzie's office was minimalist. He didn't put on the stuffiness or pretensions of his predecessors. Taylor closed the door, took a seat as instructed. On the expanse of desk between Taylor and the chief of the Intelligence Service sat a single sheet of fax paper that spelled the end of her career in cramped and smudged Arabic.

'You paid this fine to the Omani police,' Mackenzie said.

'Yes.' She felt like a child, cornered. Events were moving too fast for her to regain any poise.

'There's no trace of any incident involving a Rory Bannatyne and yourself in our records.'

'That may be the case. It was dealt with on an unofficial basis.'

'Rory Bannatyne was your man over on Ascension.'

'Yes.'

'He was your man in Oman, too.'

'We were working together, yes.'

'What were you doing paying fines to the Omani police?'

'I was averting an operational crisis.'

'Is this document real?'

'I'd need to check,' she said, hearing herself sound unconvincing.

He handed it over. She recognised the emblem of the Omani police – a dagger and two crossed swords: *Royal Oman Police, Muscat Governorate HQ. Penalty Payment. 400 dinari ($1038 US).* Then her signature. Her thoughts were, simultaneously, *This is my time in MI6 over* and *If I am responsible for a girl's death, professional concerns are trivial and it's ridiculous of me to care.* But the question she wanted to ask, above all others, was *Where did this come from?* Who did this and why now? It would take digging, by someone who had access to personnel files. Senior-level access. Someone like Skinner. But still this was a lot of effort just to destroy her.

'Have you informed the police about this?' Mackenzie asked. 'With regards to the current situation?'

'About GCHQ operations? No.'

'That he was a sex offender.'

'No.'

'You need to go back and inform New Scotland Yard. Then tell GCHQ to freeze any new activity on the island until this Petra Wade situation has resolved itself.' He took a deep breath. 'It was ill conceived in the first place. That was my mistake – to give you the green light.'

'Freeze everything?'

'This is a potential disaster. The fallout if he killed her is unimaginable. The press wouldn't stop digging until they knew what he was doing there. The island would be thrust into the spotlight. What is the situation now, with regards to the police investigation?'

'They've requested interviews with Rory Bannatyne's

colleagues, details of his career history. I've suggested we might coordinate via SO15, for security reasons. But there are a lot of question marks, and it's an evolving situation.'

'And the Americans? What do they know?'

'Only the cover story, as far as I'm aware: that he was over there to consult on broadband.'

'This has potential to cause real damage in multiple directions. Suspend Ventriloquist with immediate effect and begin sharing relevant information about Rory Bannatyne with Security Branch. We're going to have to contain this somehow, and that's going to need cooperation.'

'This is Gabriel's doing,' she said, gesturing at the Omani document. When Mackenzie didn't respond, Taylor continued. 'Why is he interfering?'

Mackenzie stared at her. 'This is me,' he said, finally. 'I'd like you to take care of all loose ends by the end of tomorrow, please. Then we'll speak again.'

He looked at her with some sadness in his eyes. Not pity, she thought. Please, not pity.

'Okay.'

'I spoke up for you. To keep you in the service. Give you a second chance.'

'I know.'

'You're making me wonder if that was wise.'

Taylor returned to her office. She felt she was already fired, that her status had evaporated in an instant and she may as well pack up her personal possessions and leave. How would she phrase it to Bower? How could she break the news that his dream had collapsed? *There's been a complication. It's me, my life.* That would be her farewell to the immense power of GCHQ. Power that seemed wedded to the world's future, and thereby to her own, to an aggressive kind of progress.

She picked up the phone. *Call Bower. Tell him it's off.* She dialled. He wasn't at his desk, which felt like a temporary reprieve. She left a message.

'Dominic, it's Kathryn. We've had some major hiccups at this end, and I need to speak to you asap.'

Hiccups, for Christ's sake. Kudus appeared, holding his laptop.

'You okay?'

She tried to think what to say. He saw her expression and frowned.

'Got a minute?'

'Why?'

'Look.'

He showed her the laptop screen. It contained a photograph of Kane: Kane in a T-shirt with the unmistakable black rocks of Ascension behind him. He held a pair of sunglasses. There was a small rucksack at his feet. The picture was clearly taken without his knowledge, from a distance, going on the basis of the quality. Someone had been waiting for him to remove the shades. They wanted his face.

'Where did you get this?'

'It was sent to a facial recognition company called Percepta Biometrics a couple of hours ago. We keep tabs on them – they're used by a lot of interesting players, some less reputable than others. Because I put out an in-house alert on Edward Pearce, including Kane's face, this got picked up, passed through to me.'

'Any idea who sent it to the company?'

'No.'

'Do we have a client list for Percepta Biometrics?'

'No client list. We're in their bank accounts, but that's a heavy trawl.'

Her phone flashed: Bower calling back.

'Did Percepta get a result?' Taylor asked.

'I don't think so,' Kudus said. 'There's no other images of him in their database that I can see. I can't find another image of Elliot out there under his own name. He has no social media. Any search is going to be directed to the Edward Pearce front.'

'Get me data for this company: phone numbers, email addresses, anything.'

'It's here.' He passed over a sheet with the relevant information, including the encryption technology they were using. She lifted the phone.

'Dominic.'

'Kathryn, you said there was a problem.'

'Yes.' She took a breath. 'I need you to do me a favour. We've got what looks like possible countersurveillance on the island – someone checking on Kane. I don't know who, but I know that they've taken photographs of him and sent them through to a facial recognition company called Percepta Biometrics.'

'Your message sounded like there were internal issues.'

'I'm managing those for now, but it does mean we need a result on this fast. People are developing anxieties about Ascension. They could throw a real spanner in the works.'

She gave him the details they had for Percepta. The company used various encryption tools but none of these were invulnerable. If you had a lot of time and expertise they could be hacked, or you could simply steal the keys, as GCHQ had been doing for two decades now by various means.

'I can explain more later,' Taylor said. 'But I'm not in a position to put in a formal request. That would draw attention to Ventriloquist.'

'I would have to go through appropriate channels, Kathryn.'

'You're the UK head of Echelon, Dominic. You don't have to go through anyone. We've got a few hours, then I'm going to have to consider reporting that the island's insecure and future operations are inadvisable.'

'Let me try,' he said.

Taylor hung up. That wasn't the conversation she'd meant to have. She researched Percepta Biometrics, without uncovering much other than it was registered in Montserrat and boasted a database of three billion faces. She studied the photo and wondered where in the island Kane was when it was taken. If she sent it through, he might be able to identify the moment and therefore the camera operator.

She messaged Kane with the image attached, then waited for his reply, refreshing and reconnecting the system. There was still no word by the time Bower called back an hour later.

'I can't see any direct communication between Percepta Biometrics and Ascension Island, but I've got something.' Taylor felt a jolt of electricity.

'What have you got?'

'Percepta's European office received seven emails from a computer in London this month, and this same computer has been contacting a device on Ascension for the last two weeks.'

Yes, Taylor thought. She savoured the sweet rush of a result – of knowledge, meaning power; meaning the correction of a power imbalance. Her heart raced.

'Any details?'

'I've got a physical location, some search history. But the computer concerned isn't used much, and a lot of what it does is encrypted.'

Bower sent through the data: seven pages of contact information. But the bit Taylor cared most about was up front. The computer communicating with both Ascension and Percepta was housed at 9 Russell Square.

Whatever she'd been expecting, it wasn't that. Russell Square, Bloomsbury: traditionally home of intellectuals, now split between tourism and academia. She'd spent a happy postgraduate year at the University of London, but the address didn't mean anything to her. On Street View it was a part of a grey stone terrace. Glossy black door, no sign visible. A prestige address, but unrevealing. Yet from Bower's data, she knew that a computer there had had contact with a device on Ascension Island at eleven a.m. today, and with Percepta three times between midday and four p.m.

She searched through the rest of the data he'd sent for any other clues. As well as the IP address, he'd established a landline phone number at the Russell Square property. Last call made from the number was to Oman.

Kudus saw her staring.

'What's the significance of Oman?' he asked.

The bare reality of that call was like a punch in itself. A punch from an anonymous attacker.

'Something I can't talk about right now,' Taylor said. 'What can we get on this address?'

Kudus ran a search.

'According to Land Registry, Nine Russell Square has been owned outright since September by a company called FSF Holding Limited, registered in Guernsey. Dead end, as you'd imagine. Not on any of our records. No idea what, if anything, FSF stands for. What do we do?'

Taylor needed to know who was there, why they were targeting her.

'Nothing,' she said.

'What do you mean?'

'I want you to step away from this.'

'Step away?'

'Let's get a drink.'

The HQ's Terrace Bar offered the possibility of a discreet conversation. It was also the only place you could smoke, overlooking the river, underused in winter.

'What are you having?' Taylor asked. 'These are on me.'

He asked for a lemonade. She got one lemonade and one soda and lime. They took their drinks to a far corner of the outdoor terrace with a view of Parliament across the river.

'Not very wild, are we,' she said.

'Not in this way, I guess.'

'They used to make us drink on training,' Taylor said. 'Tell us we had a night off, hand out free booze, then suddenly announce we had to do memory tests, things like that, see how we performed drunk. Did you have anything similar?'

'No.'

'I imagine they've had to tone it all down now.'

'Is there a problem, Kat?'

'Not with you, no. With everything else, yes. That's the problem.'

'Can you explain?'

'Rory shouldn't have gone to Ascension. I made a mistake, and it's caused a lot of complications. There's trouble behind the scenes – trouble for me – and I want to keep you out of it. It's not your fault, and it shouldn't have to damage your career.'

'What's happening?'

'I took a risk and I don't want you exposed to the consequences. You might be called in to answer some questions very soon. About me. If they ask what you've been working on you don't need to mention Ventriloquist.'

'I didn't come here to duck and run at the first sign of trouble.'

'There's a difference between a challenge and a fuck-up. There are moments for heroism – this isn't one of them. Trust me.'

'And you won't read me in to what's happened?'

'No.'

He stared out toward the river.

'Do you think I don't fit in here?'

'Do you want to fit in here?'

'Yes.'

'I think you fit in fine. You've been incredible over the last year. I want you to stay in the service, that's the point.'

'If you're in trouble, Kat, let me help.'

It made her smile.

'You've been through some things in your life,' she said, after a moment, carefully.

'Have I?'

'I'm not asking you to talk about personal stuff. I'm saying, I admire you. The fortitude. It will see you well.'

'Thanks.'

'How did you get through it? The tough times?'

Now it was Kudus's turn to consider. He turned the bottle of lemonade on the table, picking at the label.

'I didn't have a choice.'

'I guess not.'

'That was how it felt. I had to keep going or it would have all been for nothing.'

'That's the worst, isn't it,' Taylor said. 'That things might be for nothing.'

'Yes.'

Both watched the river and the floodlit Houses of Parliament, floating amid the darkness like a hallucination.

'I'm out of here,' Taylor said. 'Out of Vauxhall Cross, I think. I'm going to assign you to the Argentine oil exploration job. Clive has the file. Give it a read. Let's say you've been working on it for the last couple of weeks. Okay? This is serious. This is how the service works. We're dominos: I fall, you fall.'

'I think I could help if you told me,' he said.

'I'm sure you could.'

He met her eyes a final time, as if they might contain a more promising message, and when he didn't see one, he got up.

'If there's nothing more I can do, good night, Kat.' He walked away. Taylor finished her soda, went back to the office, looked at the Russell Square address. She had a sensation of cold clarity that was familiar; it was the feeling when she was about to drink. To dive into her self-destruction. The sense of a decision being taken on her behalf.

NINETEEN

Russell Square looked elegant in the darkening evening. The street lamps had come on but the air was mild, and students and tourists hurried along the pavements. Taylor found the address.

Number 9 Russell Square looked entirely anonymous, sheltered among buildings now used by the universities. The academic side of the area had expanded since her time here. Being in the centre of London, expansion meant filling in cracks and crevices, taking over the existing real estate of mansion blocks and terraced townhouses. Number 9 stood between a Bureau de Change and the International Programmes Office for the University of London. Its single black door was newly painted. No identifying sign, but lights on inside. It had the security camera you'd expect covering the entrance, a video door phone system with electric lock, and a discreet infrared motion sensor beneath a security lamp. There was nothing whatsoever to give any indication of what went on in there. Blinds had been drawn over the windows. So that was her game plan exhausted. Was she meant to approach? Ring the bell? What did she have to lose?

That was always a stupid question in the spying business. She was still alive, for one thing. She thought back through old training exercises: Get inside this house, that office, that club. Challenging but artificial because they missed one factor: the possibility that the object of your interest might be willing to hurt you very badly.

She was pondering her options when a pair of workmen in overalls brushed past her and opened the door. It was unlocked. She glimpsed protective sheeting inside.

Taylor followed them in.

Her heart thumped. To the left of the entrance was an empty reception desk, to the right a waiting area with a blank pinboard and empty pigeonholes. She couldn't see where the workmen had gone, but the whole place was being refurbished, with ladders stacked at the side and a smell of fresh paint. She could always say she was looking for the university office next door, Taylor reasoned. Simple mistake. And if that didn't work, she was a government employee. She wasn't the one hiding behind a front. If whoever was here wanted to cause her trouble, let them try. They'd picked the fight. Taylor needed to know who she was up against.

She continued deeper inside, past open doors revealing empty offices and the occasional larger room with stacks of new furniture still wrapped in plastic. She looked for post, paperwork, anything that might give her a lead, but it was bare. Then she saw a steel security door blocking the corridor ahead of her. It looked out of place, as did the discreet surveillance camera fixed to the wall beside it.

Kathryn suspected the real business of 9 Russell Square, whatever it was, began on the other side of that door. But this was as far as she was getting today. Taylor was making a final appraisal of the security when she heard voices coming closer. People were approaching from behind the door.

She backed into an empty office just as the door opened and they came into view. She had seen them, though, which meant they might have seen her. Taylor swore silently to herself. It had been three individuals: a middle-aged woman in a black skirt, a gangly, bespectacled man in a blue jacket, and a shorter, slightly older man in a grey suit. Their voices continued, jovial.

'Well, you must join us another time,' one of the men said.

'This is your night,' the woman said. 'You enjoy it.'

'I hope you will celebrate somehow.'

'Indeed.'

'Right. Showtime.' Someone clapped their hands.

'See you later.'

Taylor watched the two men pass the office doorway. It appeared they had left the woman to whatever went on behind the security door. The older man swung an umbrella. He had neat grey hair. She tried to recall their faces again. The men had looked an odd couple. Both in high spirits, though. Taylor thought she recognised the older man. A public figure of some kind.

'She's great,' one of them said as they passed.

'One of the best around.'

'Knows her stuff.'

'And no shrinking violet. You're okay to walk?'

'It's barely a minute away.'

Taylor stepped slowly into the corridor. The men were almost at the front door now, about to leave. She wondered what showtime involved, wondered if it would throw some light on this setup. Taylor waited for the door to close, then left the building a few seconds behind them, in time to see the two men enter the square itself. *Barely a minute away.*

She followed them.

The man she had recognised was a politician, Taylor felt sure now: Geoffrey Payne, secretary of state for Business, Energy, and Industrial Strategy. Who was he with? What were they up to here? This is crazy, Taylor thought. They crossed the square diagonally, and she checked her pace so as not to get too close. First rule of tailing: Never do single-person mobile surveillance. The idea of successfully pulling it off without being noticed was a joke. But it was a winter evening in busy Central London.

Neither of them was conducting any countersurveillance. She could potentially follow them for miles without becoming conspicuous.

She didn't have to go that far. They left the square and continued along the side of the British Museum to its front before entering the gates into the museum's grounds.

Taylor stopped, momentarily thrown. It was seven p.m., past the museum's closing. But security remained on the gates conducting bag checks, and a handful of people were crossing the front grounds to the steps. Beneath the pillars she could see a small queue to enter the building.

An event? There were enough people arriving to lend her some cover. She was wearing her work suit, which was sharp enough to blend in. Taylor thought she might at least try to find out what it was – that this might give her some insight into 9 Russell Square. She showed her bag to the security and crossed toward the museum. A corporate event, Taylor decided, scanning the attendees. She climbed the front steps, glancing at her watch as if late. Security just inside the doors amounted to two young staff with clipboards. No name badges to collect, Taylor was relieved to see. She approached, unsmiling, governmental ID at the ready.

'I'm with Geoffrey Payne,' Taylor said. 'You won't have my name down.'

There was an exchange of looks between the young man and the slightly older woman beside him who saw Taylor's ID and gave a nod.

'Of course,' she said. 'Have a good evening.'

The sight inside took Taylor's breath. Coloured lights swept across the pale stone walls of the Great Court. Acrobats descended from balloons suspended above the heads of several hundred people. Beneath them, a contortionist in silver balanced on a giant mirror ball. Projections wrapped around the rotunda of the Reading Room: *Financing the New Age of Exploration.* Then the words disappeared and in their place was the burning exhaust of a rocket launch.

Taylor followed the crowd as it channelled toward the Egyptian sculpture gallery. There were more guests in here, crowded closer together, talking over the sounds of a string quartet. Ramses II stared impassively past the Rosetta Stone at the musicians. Drinks and canapés filtered through. Taylor took a glass of orange juice. She read identifiable types around her: government, City, media, finally the self-styled entrepreneurs: younger, tieless, eager. She searched for her target pair, contemplating cover stories she could give if challenged. Snap cover needed to be convincing but obscure enough that no one would expect to find you online. An investor on behalf of a wealthy individual could work; she knew enough of them, wrapped in tangled webs of advisers and investment vehicles. They turned up most places and were usually welcome.

After a moment, she clocked the two men from Russell Square in the centre of the room. They were partly eclipsed by the group that had gathered around them. Payne had an unmistakable Westminster bearing, simultaneously gauche and unctuous. The younger man had removed his jacket. He looked intelligent, awkward, excited. Why had they been running checks on Kane, thirty thousand miles away? Why digging up her past transgressions? Taylor wondered if she'd made a mistake. But the conjunction of a senior politician with an offshore-owned property suggested something was going on. The Oman element put Taylor in the crosshairs, but it also gave her a sense of purpose: If they wanted to confront her, they could do it directly. They could come out from behind the holding company, show her what they were made of. She was running on anger and adrenaline. At the same time, something told her that these weren't men who got their hands dirty with security, that neither of them knew her face well enough to recognise her.

They split up. A lot of people wanted to speak to the younger man. The MP moved away, joining a separate cluster of guests. Taylor made a mental note of the people that the two men interacted with, noting who appeared acquainted, who might have information, who might even engineer an introduction. A 'bump' as they called it, get talking apparently accidentally, establish cover, draw closer to your target. Taylor was assessing her options when someone grabbed her arm. She turned to see a man in his sixties wearing a pink tie and a wavering smile.

'I believe I saw you at the expo last week,' he said.

'Really? I don't think it was me.' She smiled.

'Oh. You're not with the *Financial Times*?'

'No.'

He laughed. 'Apologies. A senior moment. I thought your face looked familiar. Are you in the business?'

'On the edges,' Taylor said, catching her breath again, focusing on her story. 'And you?'

'Empyrean.'

'Remind me what Empyrean do.'

'Space burials. Funerals: memorial ashes sent into orbit. That kind of thing.'

Taylor felt her eyes widen. She moderated her surprise.

'How interesting,' she said.

'Very popular. Surprisingly popular.'

Taylor introduced herself using the investor cover and his eyes lit up.

'I must send you one of our packs.'

'Please do.'

Financing the New Age of Exploration, she thought. Was it possible she was at a networking event for the space industry?

'Two years ago, this was in a Holiday Inn with about twenty

people,' the man said. 'And we were the only ones offering funerals.' He looked wistful. 'Soon they'll say it's a bubble. Enjoy it while it lasts. This is your nuts man.'

He stopped a young man as he was marching past.

'Michael, you must meet Suzan. She's an investor. I was saying you're the nuts man.' He winked. 'Michael's the nuts and bolts of it all.'

Michael was tall with a receding hairline and gleaming brow. He grinned, reached into his pocket, and produced a thick silver screw, which he gave to Taylor, closing her hand around it.

'If you've ever struggled to thread a nut onto a bolt in an awkward spot, you know how frustrating it can be. Imagine doing that in a space suit; imagine doing it in zero gravity. That's an AstraNut.' Taylor opened her hand and gazed at it with what she hoped was appropriate awe. 'No threads, no issues with rust, paint, damage. Used on oil rigs, used in the Arctic.' He took his phone out and showed her an image of a contraption like a spinning top, floating in outer space.

'That's the world's first space hotel, launching next year. How many bolts do you think that will need?'

'A lot.'

Taylor cast an eye around the room while they spoke. The younger, awkward-looking man still stood among a group of eight or nine individuals. Hard to reach. He was the one speaking, but he didn't like making eye contact. Payne's eyes roamed everywhere. He chatted to a man in a corduroy jacket, glancing distractedly over the man's shoulder as he spoke. MI6 had worked to bury a sex scandal when he was trade secretary, she remembered. It had caused a flap just as he was set to negotiate a deal with the Saudis. One of those handkerchief-in-the-breast-pocket politicians whose traditionalism was entirely at ease with the bleeding edge of corporate enterprise. Money being as traditional a anything, she guessed. As power. His eyes met

Taylor's. Payne smiled before she had a chance to turn. No sense he recognised her. Taylor held his gaze a beat, allowing herself the slightest of smiles before gently looking away again.

'No nuts, no insurance,' Michael was saying. 'That's why we work closely with the guys trying to set up an insurance framework.'

Taylor nodded, planning her next move. The funeral director had found someone else to buttonhole. After another few minutes on the intricacies of galactic policy cover, Taylor pointed to the man in the centre of the crowd, the younger one from 9 Russell Square.

'Do you know that guy? I swear I recognise him.'

'Stuart Adair? Sure.'

'Who does he work with?'

'He's the founder of Quadrant. They're doing okay. We're trying to get them to use AstraNuts. Could save them a lot of time and money.'

'What do Quadrant do?'

'You must know them. One of the main sponsors of this whole thing. All sorts of space magic.'

Now that he'd said it, she could see the name on various stands and banners: *Quadrant Space Technologies.*

'Of course, Quadrant. I'm being dim. Probably need some rehydration.'

Taylor excused herself and went to get another juice. When Payne noticed her by the drinks, he caught her eye again. He kept his head bowed, as if deep in discussion, but a second later began to move away, a hand on his interlocutor's elbow, a pat on their back. Then he was beside her.

'Stick close to the wine. That's my policy.' Payne smiled, topping up his glass.

'It's a good one.'

'I remember coming here as a schoolboy. Seems a bit of a

shame to see it used for corporate nibbles. Bit of an insult to the gods.'

'I'm sure the gods have seen worse.'

'Indeed. How are you finding it all?'

'Fascinating.'

'If you don't mind a bit of snake oil with your Chardonnay.'

'Nothing snake oil about Quadrant,' Taylor said, with a smile of her own this time. This caused him to regard her more carefully, but not without amusement. Now Payne introduced himself, by which he meant: *Who are you?*

'Suzan Wicks,' Taylor said, shaking his hand. 'I'm an investment manager.'

'Is Quadrant a company you've got your eye on?'

'For sure. One of the reasons I'm here.'

'Between you and me, they would be a wise investment. A British company that's going places. That has that vision thing. You know what I mean? Stuart's a genius.'

'What's he got up his sleeve this time?'

'Making space viable. Finding solutions to problems.' Payne winked and leaned in. 'Junk.'

'Junk.'

'Space junk. Where there's muck there's brass, and there's a lot of muck in space right now. It's a little over my head, but I know intelligent people when I see them. It's a very clever gambit. But that's just the start.'

Before he could expand, Payne's attention was diverted by someone standing behind Taylor. She saw his eyes slide and a new smile grow. Then she heard a voice that sent a shiver up her spine.

'May I cut in?'

'Markus,' Payne said. 'What an unexpected pleasure.'

Taylor turned, slightly horrified to gaze up into the eyes of Markus Fischer, officer for the German intelligence service.

Fischer was tall, smartly dressed, immaculately groomed, befitting his long-term cover as an international banker. This, she assumed, was how Geoffrey Payne regarded him. She hadn't crossed paths with Fischer for six or seven years, but they knew each other well. He met Taylor's eyes and appeared to bury his own reaction.

'I hope I'm not interrupting . . . ' Fischer began.

'Not at all,' Taylor managed to say. She stuck a hand out quickly. 'Suzan Wicks.'

Fischer smiled with only the hint of a raised eyebrow.

'Pleasure to meet you, Suzan. Markus.'

His eyes bored into her. This happened, of course. Certain environments brought out the spooks, and she was never surprised to find Berlin sniffing around. But it was a different feeling being caught winging it, off-road. This was dangerous, but also possibly an opportunity. She'd met Fischer in Geneva many years ago. Alongside his activity as a globe-trotting financier, he remained a senior officer within the colossal Bundesnachrichtendienst, or BND, as Germany referred to its intelligence agency. Taylor was one of the very few people who knew of this double life. She wondered what he was doing here and hoped he felt equally exposed, so she might exploit the potential awkwardness. She suspected Fischer had more insight into this scene than she did, but he didn't have to know that.

'I wanted to catch a word with Geoffrey before he disappears,' Fischer said.

'I've monopolised him enough. I needed to freshen up anyway. Geoffrey, it's been a pleasure. And I wish you luck.'

The MP shook her hand again, releasing it regretfully, insisted she take one of his cards, and offered her lunch if she wanted to continue the conversation.

Taylor cut through the crowded room, trying to think why Markus Fischer would turn up here. She went to the bathroom, locked herself in a stall and ran searches on her phone for Quadrant. The company's website was as slick and opaque as she expected: sliding full-screen images of the stars with a variety of mission statements. *Quadrant Space Technologies provide advanced space engineering solutions that integrate an innovative proprietary portfolio of satellite technologies and disruptive business solutions.* It listed offices in London, along with testing and production facilities in Oxfordshire. There was some information on their patented ClearSky debris solution, but all it told her was that investment had been made and things were set to proceed in the coming months. Nothing about why it should cause her problems.

By the time Taylor returned to the sculpture gallery, Fischer's conversation with the MP was over and the German stood alone, admiring the Rosetta Stone. She went over. They stood side by side, gazing at the hieroglyphs.

'I owe you one,' she said quietly.

'We owe each other. Let's get out of here.'

Fischer taking the initiative shifted her momentarily onto the back foot, but this was what she'd had in mind. She needed insight, which meant taking a risk.

'Be at the end of the street in fifteen minutes,' Taylor said. 'The far corner of Russell Square. I'll pick you up.'

TWENTY

Germany's BND was as cool and effective as you'd expect from an intelligence agency born out of the ashes of postwar Berlin, second only to the CIA in scale but several fathoms further below the radar. To the British, they were mostly regarded as an ally but not always. They didn't have MI6's legacy of global coverage, but they spied the hell out of Europe and had been increasingly energetic over the last few years.

When Taylor met Fischer in Geneva, she was running an agent in a private bank with a lot of interesting Russian clients and he was establishing himself as a high-flying money man with fingers in several pies. That was ten years ago. He was a heavy drinker, shrewd gossip, bon viveur. She'd been tipped off about his real employer, and it seemed he knew she wasn't simply embassy staff, which didn't stop some good-natured, flirtatious, and mutually beneficial information sharing. And there was plenty to share. Geneva attracted every intelligence service in the world: the Russians loved the ease of agent rendezvous and low levels of police surveillance. The US hammered at the UN's European headquarters. Germans and French went heavy on the WTO, while MI6 tried to keep an eye on all of them. Markus Fischer had provided a convenient entrance to various worlds, but Taylor never kidded herself it was out of the goodness of his heart.

She stopped on the corner of the square and Fischer appeared from the darkness and jumped in, checking the road behind them, exhaling when they were on the move.

'Your car?' he said.

'Yes.'

'Head toward the river.'

Fischer loosened his tie. He slid the seat back, lowered the sun visor, ran a hand across the fabric, looking for microphones, then flipped it back up.

'How are you, Kathryn?'

'That's a good question.'

'Enjoy the party?'

'Where are we going?'

'Cross the river. I have somewhere in mind.'

Taylor turned onto Waterloo Bridge and continued into South London. They needed a location that was both secure and discreet. If Fischer had a suggestion, she'd have to take it.

'So, was that your first taste of New Space?' he said.

'First taste of something.'

'What did you learn?'

'There are approximately two thousand bolts in a space hotel.'

'Michael Greenwood. Funny guy. But their contract with India's Galactic Tourism could be worth a cool sixteen million.'

'Doesn't seem to be a shortage of money around.'

'Never is when the future's at stake. Know what Geoffrey Payne said to me?' Fischer imitated the MP's cut-glass accent. 'There's one thing of which I'm certain, and that's the generation being born now will look up and see lights on the moon, and they'll feel a lot more free and a lot more prosperous than us.'

Fischer laughed. She wondered if he was drunk. Wondered who was luring who.

'Can you think of anything worse?' he asked. He told her to turn off the Old Kent Road at the next lights, twisting in his seat as she did so to check the road behind.

'Keep going.'

They continued through the back street of Bermondsey, then out of the estates toward the shiny towers of Surrey Quays. He told her to slow, checked the mirrors a final time.

'Here is fine.'

Taylor pulled up alongside the old docks. The residential towers were dark. Geese slept on the ornamental squares of water between them. When they were out of the car Fischer lit a cigarette and looked around. The street remained deserted.

'Follow me,' he said. They cut into a small side street, to the entrance of one of the glitzier blocks, where he dropped his cigarette, tapped a fob to the entry system and the door opened. He unlocked a mailbox in the foyer, put his phone inside, nodded to Taylor, and she did the same.

They ascended in a glass-walled lift with London beneath them, neither speaking. The flat was on the seventeenth floor. Fischer switched the lights on and looked around. It was showroom plush, safe house cold: floor-length windows, slat blinds, slices of a London view. Fischer opened kitchen cupboards, then the fridge, studying the bottles inside. He took a sticker off two new wineglasses and rinsed them.

'Make yourself at home.'

He poured them both red wine. Taylor went to the window to gather her thoughts. In Geneva, Fischer had operated out of a comically vast but barely furnished apartment on the Quai du Seujet, with the Rhône out one window and the Jura Mountains out the other. She felt momentarily nostalgic thinking about it. Exciting times. Or just young times, with so much future ahead that small mistakes seemed sure to be washed away.

Fischer gave her one of the wines, then collapsed onto the sofa with an arm along the back, brogues up on the coffee table.

'So what took you to the event?' he said.

'You first.'

'I was working.' He said it with a slight smile. 'You seemed to be getting on well with Geoffrey Payne.'

'Until you came along.'

'Spying on your own MPs?'

'Maybe there's more to Payne than meets the eye.'

Fischer leaned back, watching her carefully.

'I suspect there's plenty more. In fact, I thought you might be able to fill me in.'

'It's not going to be that easy,' she said.

'But you're here. You want something from me, don't you, Kathryn.'

'I'd like to know about Quadrant.'

He stretched, studied her again.

'Quadrant, indeed. Majestic, mysterious Quadrant. Yes, I'd certainly like to know about Quadrant too. What have you heard so far?'

'They clear up junk.'

'Will do. So they say. Been working on a system called ClearSky for the last three years, but it's just gone big-time. Eco space. Green space. You've cried about the oceans, now let us remove the debris from low earth orbit. It's an eye-catching initiative, enough to get them a hell of a lot of funding upfront. A strange amount of funding. Something's very wrong there.'

'Go on.'

'Are we going to be open with each other, Kat?'

'I wouldn't be here otherwise.'

'Until recently, Quadrant were at risk of bankruptcy. They'd always struggled to attract investment. There'd been seed funding but that had gone. Then there was a very rapid turnaround. In February last year, the company received an injection of one hundred twenty million dollars from two venture capital funds about which I can get very little information other than that one's registered in Delaware and one in the Cayman Islands. That was a few days before your government announced a further twenty-five million would go to the company via the UK Space Agency as part of an attempt to boost the space industry in this country.'

'Something must have attracted them.'

'Right.'

'Maybe Quadrant have got groundbreaking technology.'

'I hope so. The following week Payne flew to Brussels, attended a meeting of top European policy makers and announced that all UK cooperation in the European space programme was off.'

Fischer watched Taylor's reaction. She tried to remember if she'd seen this in the news. There had been a lot of negotiations, a lot of cancellations, too.

'The European space programme's world class,' Fischer said. 'Navigation systems, high-precision positioning, space surveillance and tracking. The UK were central to it, of course. You had access to research grants, manufacturing contracts, prestige. But no, suddenly the word goes out: You guys would explore alternative options. No more data sharing, you'd do your own thing. My bosses came to me and said: *What's going on? How are they going to afford that? This is insane.*'

Fischer's incredulity seemed genuine, but Taylor took a mental step back. Lesson one: ask yourself what's *their* game? Why are they talking to you at all? Germany was an ally, but one with its own ambitions. So she added a pinch of salt and kept her mind open.

'I started looking into it,' Fischer said. 'And I got to Quadrant. They've been channelling a lot of resources to Geoffrey Payne and he's not been shy in returning the favours. Those resources came out of nowhere, as far as I can tell. But whoever's behind it has clearly been pushing for total autonomy. Why? There are bigger players in the UK space industry but none as strange, none operating in such secrecy. When do you start talking?'

'In a minute. Tell me what else you know about the money trail.'

209

'One of the funds that propped up Quadrant when it looked like it might go under is called Celestus Ventures. They were lead investor in the last financing round. From what I can tell, they have twenty-five active portfolio companies, all space-related, and they put seventy million into Quadrant without blinking an eye. They don't appear to seek any control. They don't answer their phones, either. Quadrant must have something pretty incredible in development. So that's one thing that took me to the British Museum, but I didn't find anyone who could shed any light. So I'm really hoping my luck changes now. Your go.'

'Nine Russell Square.'

'So you do know something.' Fischer sat back and appraised her. 'It's an interesting address. Can you throw any light?'

'Owned by FSF Holdings, based on Guernsey. Geoffrey Payne and Stuart Adair were there this afternoon.'

'Is that right?'

'Yes.'

Fischer considered this. 'Know what FSF stands for?'

'Go on.'

'The Free Space Foundation. Nine Russell Square is going to be the foundation's prestigious new home. They fund research into space policy, advise government on space law, promote investment in the industry. Advocacy work. All sounds very proper, and it's where you'd expect to find an official research centre, but it's shady. More a lobbying company than anything academic. No official university affiliation. Trace the cash back and you get to Quadrant. It seems to be a useful address for a lot of Quadrant business that they don't want in their head office.'

'Like what?'

'There were eight rival companies working on space debris, all in the running for the UK government funding. In the weeks leading up to the funding allocation at least six of them were subject to surveillance: employees bugged, computers hacked.

The trail ran straight back to the foundation and onto Quadrant. They've targeted the European Space Agency and they've targeted the UN's Office for Outer Space Affairs. We know that. They play dirty. They also play rich. Since Quadrant's recent windfall they've used the Free Space Foundation to make almost half a million in political donations.'

'What do they get for that?'

'Payne's been helping Quadrant acquire UK launch facilities. That involves a lot of licensing and planning applications, but the foundation's generosity has paved the way. Doors seem to open for them. There's a well-established institute for the development of space policy just around the corner. It's respectable, independent. Until last year they were advising the government on its space strategy. Then suddenly they weren't. In the last couple of months foundation staff have held regular meetings at both the Foreign Office and Department for Business, while a lot of experts in the field have been closed out.'

'So the foundation does have staff.'

'Sure. They've brought some pretty ruthless minds on board: former property lawyers, aerospace lawyers, a lot of individuals with a background in maritime law. The thinking seems to be that if you can draw lines in the sea you can draw them in space, carve out ownership. Last month Geoffrey Payne got them an audience with the attorney general.'

'To do what?'

'Get on the front foot. Space is going to be a trillion-dollar economy. Someone's going to have to establish law up there. Who owns the moon? According to the UN Space Treaty of 1967, everyone and no one. So, do you need a licence to operate there? Who's going to give you a licence? Anyone want to tax it? A lot of the existing treaties date back to the Cold War. It's more about stopping people from putting nukes in orbit than establishing a competitive free-market environment. Space, the province of all mankind: That's great, but not very commercially viable. According to the treaty, astronauts should be treated as envoys of humanity. What does that mean? All of them? There's a hell of a lot of people heading into space in the next few years who really aren't envoys of humanity. So who polices them?'

'And Quadrant are pushing this discussion.'

'So it seems. But why? A year ago, they were just another small start-up chasing the New Space dollar. Where's their power from? Why are they suddenly steering the UK's space strategy?' Fischer let silence fall as if it might coax her. 'You haven't touched your wine,' he said, finally.

'I don't drink.'

Now he looked at her with renewed curiosity.

'It has been a long time, hasn't it, Kat.'

'You seemed to know Payne well.'

'Turns out we're members of the same London club.' Fischer smiled. 'What are the chances?'

'Does he know someone called Gabriel Skinner?'

Fischer hesitated. 'Payne met with a man called Gabriel Skinner the day before flying to Brussels.'

'Where?'

'At a private address in Central London. It's not the first time they've met. Skinner's a colleague of yours, I believe.'

Taylor stood up and went to the floor-length window. The sparkling lights of the city twinkled beneath her. She admired the darkness of the Isle of Dogs, then the towers of Canary Wharf behind it, pointing up at the stars.

'There's an island in the South Atlantic,' she said. 'Called Ascension. Has it come up in connection with any of this?'

'Not as far as I'm aware.'

'A girl went missing there a couple of weeks ago. Heard about that?'

'On Ascension? No, I don't believe so. Why?'

'Something's not right about it. Someone on the island has been doing surveillance on one of my officers. I traced the activity back to Nine Russell Square. That's the only connection I have so far.'

Fischer frowned, scratched his jaw.

'Is the connection solid?'

'Yes.'

'Does this girl connect to space in any way?'

'Not as far as I'm aware.'

The German officer took a deep breath as he pondered this.

'I'll look into it. I think we can help each other, Kat. I'd like to know what Quadrant are up to, what makes them so special. You're in a good position to find out what's going on.'

'What do I get?'

'Just possibly, you get your career.'

Taylor felt a new sharpness in the air.

'What do you mean?'

Fischer glanced down, picked some fluff from the floorboards and flicked it away.

'Tomorrow they'll try to fire you,' he said, without meeting her eyes. 'They plan to use Oman and what happened there, all that nonsense.'

Taylor stared at him until he was forced to look at her.

'What do you know about that?' she said.

'Grapevine stuff, Kat. I'm not a stalker.'

'Were you there for me tonight? Were you following me?'

He put his glass down, walked over to her. 'I can help you win, Kathryn. I can help you defeat the people trying to destroy you. They're up to something, and when we know what it is, we can judge to what extent they deserve their secrecy.'

'Is this some kind of trap, Markus?'

'If it is, it's not necessarily the worst one to be in.' He watched her from up close. Taylor felt cornered, but in that situation you fight with what comes to hand, and what she had was an offer.

'Let's say I get you information on Quadrant,' she said, carefully. 'What then?'

'It depends what it is. We would manage an appropriate response. That might involve exposing criminal behaviour or merely threatening exposure. That could be enough to stop them. Same principle they've used with you. If things became heated in any way, we would get you out of the country. For the time being, at least.'

Things felt suddenly very big and very real.

'Time isn't going to change the fact that I've leaked national security secrets, Markus. That's a fourteen-year prison sentence.'

'No one's going to prosecute you. Not if you're in the right. They wouldn't take that risk.'

'Any idea what they might do to me then? Geneva hasn't softened you that much, has it?'

'I understand the magnitude of what I'm asking you to do.'

'I wouldn't take any money.'

'No, I assumed not.'

'This is about finding out what happened on Ascension.'

'For sure. I'll start investigating from our end immediately. Perhaps we're after the same thing.'

His eyes held an entirely different light now, as if every moment she had spent with him he had been acting and now he'd stopped.

'You really don't know anything about Ascension?' Taylor said.

'I would tell you if I did. But you've made me very curious.'

'Okay.'

They arranged secure means of contacting each other and a backup plan in case something went badly wrong. Fischer was insistent about this, as if he knew of dangers he wouldn't share. Taylor said she'd see what she could do and stepped back into the night, trying to decide what she meant by that.

TWENTY-ONE

She went straight back to HQ. No time to waste. Betraying your country wasn't something to dawdle over. Ten p.m., office to herself, windows dark. Security had nodded to Taylor as she entered but she didn't feel too conspicuous. Intelligence work was a global and unpredictable enterprise; various demands meant people came and went at all hours. Everyone had something that might pull them in at midnight.

First on her list of checks was Markus Fischer himself. She ran him through the system to see if he came up as active, hostile, or monitored. Vauxhall's counterintelligence on rival European agencies was substantial, and they had good penetration of both the French DGCE and German BND. There were no alerts on Fischer. Records had him based in Frankfurt since 2015, no suggestion he was currently in the UK, which made her wonder what paperwork he'd travelled in on, and why.

She studied the Quadrant website again. The company had been set up in 2014 by Stuart Adair, originally a professor of space robotics at the University of Southampton. In the late 2000s, he led a group of researchers experimenting with miniature, manoeuvrable satellites. In 2012 he attended the European Conference on Space Debris and, seeing the scale of the problem, redirected energy toward devising a system for orbital sustainability. Quadrant was formed two years later as a spin-off company to transfer the results of research into a commercial enterprise.

The website included a cute personal bio. Adair recalled attending Space Camp in the US as a child and meeting the UK's first astronaut, Helen Sharman, who gave him a handwritten note with the message, 'Space is waiting for you.' This note became the inspiration to pursue his dream. From what Taylor could tell, childhood dream segued rapidly into commercial vision: *Quadrant seeks to create a freer and more prosperous life for each generation by using the unlimited energy and material resources of space.* According to commentators in the press, they'd lobbied hard to ensure governmental support for the rapid commercial development of the solar system. In one off-the-cuff remark to a journalist at a space expo last year, Adair had said: 'As a planet, if we don't colonise space, we doom ourselves to stasis and rationing. As a nation, we miss our chance at dominating this fourth industrial revolution.' Debris was their in.

The danger to satellites and space stations from pieces of orbital wreckage after more than 60 years of space exploration has become a commercial opportunity. Our research suggests there are 900,000 pieces of debris in low earth orbit – and even a 1mm-sized object can have a devastating effect. If we continue the way we do, some regions in space will become too risky to visit.

Quadrant's ClearSky system delivers the provision of both active and end-of-life debris removal services – cutting-edge technologies that enable missions toward capturing and removing environmentally critical debris, such as rocket upper stages and defunct satellites.

It got them big backing. Taylor browsed the information available on Bloomberg and a couple of other business intelligence platforms. The players pumping money into Quadrant had stakes in launch systems, orbital manufacturing, asteroid mining, and space tourism. Evidently, they regarded the clearance of debris as a fundamental necessity. As Fischer had described, two venture capital funds devoted to the commercial space industry – GTX Capital and Celestus Ventures – supplied 120 million dollars to Quadrant over the course of one week in April 2018.

Last month, the US Office of Commercial Space Transportation had approved Quadrant's request to launch the first components of its debris removal system: a constellation of satellites that would track objects as small as ten centimetres in length. Soon it was hoped they could launch direct from the UK. The 25 million pounds that the British government had directed to Quadrant came via a new development fund for UK spaceports. Sites were under development in Newquay, North Uist, in the Western Isles and Snowdonia.

Taylor sat back, mind spinning. Where was she when the new space age had been announced? Fixated on the terrestrial matters of the Persian Gulf and North Africa. How twentieth century. There was a lot going on to which she had been oblivious.

She kept reading. Geoffrey Payne had attended the launch of the UK Spaceport Alliance. The *Telegraph* quoted from his speech: 'As a nation of innovators and entrepreneurs, we want Britain to be the first place in mainland Europe to launch satellites. This would put the UK in an even stronger position as a leading commercial space nation, while filling the gaps in sovereign capability. Our space industry need be dependent on no one. This island has always thrived on its appetite for exploration, a willingness to seek our fortunes beyond these shores, channelling our creativity and industry and ambitions ... '

In the week after Celestus Ventures had invested several million into Quadrant, the *Financial Times* carried an interview with Stuart Adair in which he declared that he was on a mission 'to expand humanity's economic sphere in an unprecedented way.' The *FT* reported that the recent injection of capital had allowed Quadrant to invest in new facilities in Hawaii, New Mexico, 'and on Ascension Island in the South Atlantic'.

Taylor read it twice, to be sure she hadn't imagined it. There'd been no reference to Quadrant in any of the Ascension Island documents she'd seen. And there was no mention of Ascension Island on the Quadrant website when she checked. She searched through all her files on Ascension until she saw one entry in the archive of subcontractors, coinciding with the relevant period: 10 March 2018: *Ten-year lease on research facilities attached to Ascension Island auxiliary airfield, including the former European Space Agency observatory, granted to QAR Services Ltd.* QAR had taken over management of the facilities, which included the contract for overseeing their modernisation and expansion. When she looked up QAR Services on a business database it came up in full as Quadrant Astrophysical Research Services, a subsidiary of Quadrant Space Technologies.

Taylor brought up her map of the island and found the relevant facilities. Did this explain the hostility to her project from Gabriel Skinner – if, as seemed to be the case, he was close to Payne, and therefore close to Quadrant? Either way, it didn't explain what Quadrant was up to.

Intelligence work revealed the world as layers of knowledge. MI6 divided responsibility geographically, but you never had full oversight of a territory, just projects, and projects sometimes collided. The airfield lease had been signed off by her predecessor. Possibly they had seen no cause for concern: The island was full of contract-run facilities. Taylor must have seen reference to QAR Services in the handover notes without it meaning anything to her, either. She would never have had cause to look into them if GCHQ hadn't decided to expand their involvement on the island.

She brought out the surveillance photo of Kane on Ascension. Fed through to a facial recognition company via Quadrant. Did that mean they had their own security on the island, checking out newcomers? She read through the various lists of staff and personnel who'd gone over since the lease was signed, but those employed directly by QAR Services would be exempt from a visa, so not necessarily show up on records. She didn't see anything that looked like private intelligence officers. Finally, Taylor ran Quadrant through the MI6 database and got a result that made her stop. On 1 February last year, someone in the building had input an agent report that contained a reference to both 'Quadrant' and 'Ascension Island'. These were the keywords listed in the directory, from staff officer DX/3372. It had never surfaced in her own files.

The report was classified as a top security document, which meant it was accessible only via the Cleared Access Archive. This itself signalled its importance. The archive was used for the most sensitive casework, known as 'YZ' cases: information too confidential to put on the shared data system. Access was through nominated terminals in a secure room, and required clearance from at least regional controller level. Which meant she was senior enough to take a look.

Taylor headed down to the terminals, two floors underground. One night guard on the door watched Taylor sign in. The room was small and bare, but large enough that none of the four monitors was visible to anyone but the individual seated there. As it was, she had the place to herself. She typed in her own password, then input the code for the file on Ascension and Quadrant. She got a message saying *Item not found*. Taylor tried again, with the same result. It wasn't there.

But it had been at one point. Uploaded by an officer assigned the staff identification: DX/3372.

DX was an odd designation. Usually this would tell you the department number: D7, D9, and so on. Taylor had never seen DX before. She checked this ID on the personnel directory, and it came up cancelled.

As a last resort, before packing up, she emailed a request for further info to a friend in personnel, with instructions to contact Taylor directly if they knew anything about this officer. She was watchful as she began to drive home. *Cancelled* was an odd designation too. It suggested they'd either left the service suddenly or were dead.

TWENTY-TWO

Home, since the divorce, was a flat in Angel. For the ridiculous money Taylor spent on rent, she could have been closer to
Vauxhall, but she didn't want to be. Something felt right about
having the river between her and work. And something felt
right about renting; she didn't have the will to pretend she was
settling this time.

A lot of dark thoughts clattered on the journey home. Was she
now spying for the BND? How predictable it would look when
she was caught: breakdown, divorce, impending suspension.
Into the arms of another lover and all their subterfuge. But her
cause wasn't entirely self-serving.

Taylor grabbed some food from the kebab shop at the end
of her road. If she was ever found murdered in mysterious
circumstances, these would be the neighbours saying how
normal she had seemed. Normal but distracted, they might
say: anxious, kept strange hours. At home she ate, showered,
then tried to imagine how she might achieve some sleep.
She was too agitated. Alcohol would have been one solution,
screaming itself in the empty house. But she was going to have
to get through the night without it. She turned the TV on and
then off again, sat on the sofa, thinking of the various people
who had once been part of her life and wondered what their
Friday nights looked like. Her home was very quiet. How did
its quietness compare to Ascension Island? Only one voice

remained in the room with her: that of Dr Glenning. *I don't think he killed himself.*

Taylor picked up her laptop, hesitated, then put it on encrypted mode. She typed in 'Jack Moretti' and got the same results she'd seen before. She went into her personal emails and downloaded the zip file of Perryman's investigation.

The work was organised into three folders: 'Documents', 'Interviews', 'Drafts'. She went into documents. First up were the police reports, then Moretti's research papers. The ones in the public domain, which Perryman had accessed, covered performance under stress, visual perception in high-stimuli environments, decision making and memory. These finished the year he began at Lake Ravenna. There was a file of Perryman's correspondence: a lot of polite refusals, a legal threat. Interviews were mostly old friends who hadn't seen Jack Moretti for years, who said he'd become distant or his work had forced him into distance. One interview was with the police officer who initially dealt with the hanging, who said the area was out of the way, 'bums sometimes hung around' but there was nothing to suggest anyone had interfered with the body.

There were self-styled experts among the general public: *Lake Ravenna is the site of a lot of experimental work. It's split between three or four private companies. I had a friend who worked there who says they have their own pilots, runways, factories. Bigger than anywhere else he's seen.* This interviewee provided an old photograph of the site with the windowless blue hangar roughly a square kilometre in size and the height of a tall office block. *I know for a fact one company alone has around two thousand people on their books. They control five hundred acres: three separate plants, two hangars, three runways.*

Taylor looked for Lake Ravenna employees. Only two had agreed to speak to Perryman. One was a haematologist who said little other than that Moretti was a good man who may or may not have been feeling suicidal. Then Anonymous, who had a different angle entirely:

Someone said his wife was having an affair. She worked there too. Jack found out a few days before he killed himself. I think she married the other guy a few months later. Lake Ravenna's full of black tech, but I'm not sure there's anything mysterious about Jack Moretti's suicide.

That was pretty much where Perryman's investigation ended. It appeared more conclusive than perhaps it deserved to be.

Was that it, Taylor wondered? Had she woven a grander conspiracy out of some infidelity? A conspiracy of governmental schemes rather than the more personal and mundane story of emotional betrayal? It made sense. It just didn't explain why Rory Bannatyne started wondering about it on an island in the Atlantic eleven years later.

Taylor checked her doors and windows before going to bed, studying the vehicles parked outside for any unfamiliar ones. It was a few hours before her phone rang. Her body was just releasing itself into sleep and the ringtone dragged her against the weight of dreams.

Her overnight manager, Owen Hayes, sounded anxious.

'You asked to be notified of any events on Ascension Island.'

'Yes.'

'A man's been arrested. Apparently, another girl's gone missing and it looks like he might be involved.'

'Who is he?'

'His name's Edward Pearce. It's flagged on the system to notify you immediately if anything happens. So I thought I should call.'

TWENTY-THREE

The police station felt like an oven. Kane had sat there for half an hour already when Morrogh closed the back door out to the parking area. There was no lock on this door but he secured it with a heavy wooden plank. It took Kane a second to realise he was protecting him from the crowd outside. Even as they'd walked over, Kane felt the atmosphere turning nasty, heady with fear and anger, ready to explode. And he'd been thinking: Where is Lauren? Where would you take her to kill her? And why had someone put him in the frame? Framing him for convenience was one thing. Someone doing it because they thought he was a spy and wanted to stop him was quite another. Had he been too obviously sticking his nose in? Kane ran through the various conversations he'd had. People knew about last night's skirmish, of course. Maybe that was enough. But where *was* she?

Morrogh stared at Kane with an expression equal parts fear and puzzlement.

'When were you last at your accommodation?'

'About eight p.m.'

'And you've just been at the Klinka Klub.'

'Yes.'

'People will have seen you there.'

'Yes. I was there when you spoke.'

'So you knew Lauren Carter was missing.'

'Of course. I was helping look for her.'

Morrogh's unease – at Kane's involvement, at the scale of his responsibilities – made him appear less directly threatening but also less competent, which didn't necessarily help. Kane needed him to find the actual culprit. Someone was trying to set Kane up as a murderer – maybe someone who knew he'd been talking to Thomas, and that he was interested in a ring of abusers. Whoever it was, he didn't necessarily believe they'd taken Lauren Carter for the sake of framing him, but he could believe they took the opportunity to kill two birds with one stone. A police service out of its depth was to their advantage.

'What explanation do you have for the girl's clothes being in your accommodation?' Morrogh asked.

'I have no idea. Clearly someone put them there. The question is why.'

The other officer – Sean Reid – came in, accompanied by the corporal Kane had assaulted. The corporal stared at Kane. The three of them spoke quietly together, and then Reid turned to Kane with renewed ferocity.

'What have you done with her?' he said.

'I haven't done anything. I don't know what's going on.'

'Where were you this afternoon?'

He talked them through his day again.

'I came back to Georgetown around seven p.m. On the way I gave a lift to a cook from the US base.'

'Did you get his name?'

'No. He was young. His bike was having issues. He had boxes of mushrooms. After that I came home, rested, showered.'

'Changed clothes?'

'Yes.'

'What were you wearing before?'

Kane told them what he'd been wearing, and Morrogh instructed the corporal to go and communicate this information to the individuals searching Kane's bungalow.

'You hadn't been at the house in question since seven or eight p.m.,' he asked.

'No.'

'And you believe you locked it.'

'Yes, but the lock's not very secure.'

'But Craig Riley had given you the key last night.'

'That's right.'

In front of Morrogh was a notebook in which he'd carefully written timings for Kane. He occasionally glanced at the page as it might guide him.

'Had you seen anyone acting suspiciously around the house before?'

'No. But I thought maybe someone had been in last night, while I was looking around Georgetown.'

Kane could feel the pressure of the people outside. He'd seen places turn riotous before. It happened in the blink of an eye. A car pulled up and there was a rapid knock. Morrogh opened the door and Kane saw the maroon shine of the Administrator's Land Rover. Beyond it, a crowd of forty or fifty people watched the police station.

The Administrator walked in. Kane recognised him from pictures in the briefing file. Nigel Horsley was trim and tanned. He retained thick silvering hair with a slight wave to it that made it look artificial. He was the only man on the island Kane had seen wearing a suit.

'This is the suspect?' he said to Morrogh.

'Yes. He arrived yesterday.'

'Do you have your passport and visa on you?' Horsley asked.

Kane handed them over. Horsley flicked through the passport, checked the visa.

'Lauren's father says he saw you trying to speak to her earlier,' the Administrator said. 'At their home in Two Boats.'

'I was just passing. I asked for directions.'

'It's a bit out of the way to be just passing.'

'I was lost.'

'And that's all your interaction with her involved?'

'Yes.'

'Did you know anyone on this island before coming over?'

'No.'

The Administrator beckoned Morrogh to the side, where they spoke in low voices. From what Kane could hear, the Saint Helena chief was flying over with more police, one of whom had training in forensics. Some officers were on their way from the UK, but that would take forty-eight hours. A new military figure came in, this one in US-style camo fatigues. He shook the Administrator's hand, levelled a gaze at Kane, took Kane's passport, and left, returning after a minute, giving the passport to Morrogh and consulting with the Administrator. He exited with Horsley a moment later, leaving Morrogh and Reid guarding Kane.

'We need as much information from you as possible,' Morrogh said. 'Obviously we're going to have to check to see if you have any criminal record, and that means five years' worth of addresses.'

This wasn't going to go well. It was time to cautiously turn the light in their faces. 'Lauren knew Petra Wade, didn't she?'

There was a pause as the officers studied Kane, finding themselves off-balance.

'And?'

'At Two Boats people were saying Lauren knew what happened to Petra. She was going to give a report. Maybe she tried.'

'What are you suggesting?'

'Look, I'm new here. But one obvious theory is that whatever's happened to Lauren Carter it's because she knows what happened to Petra Wade. Clearly, I wasn't involved in Petra Wade's disappearance. Which means someone's out there right now, responsible for both. Do you have any idea who? Because I think they set me up.'

Just as Kane was feeling the tables turn there was another knock. An RAF crewman appeared. Kane saw what he was carrying and got a sickening feeling.

'I found this where he was staying,' the crewman said. He set Rory's box file down on the table. 'It was hidden in a wardrobe.' He opened it and removed the Polaroids of the children. Morrogh looked through, handling each photograph with horror before turning to the exercise book.

'Are these yours?'

'No,' Kane said.

'Going to say someone left these as well?'

'I found them in a hut at English Bay this morning.'

'Where in the hut?'

'It had fallen down the back of the dresser there. It was partly hidden.'

'Why were you in there?'

'I was curious. I'd gone to take a look at the beach and I saw the hut. It looked abandoned, the door was open. But obviously someone had been living there recently.'

'Did you ever know a man called Rory Bannatyne?' Morrogh asked.

'No.'

The three men conversed. There were mutterings about procedure. Then someone shouted outside: 'Let me speak to them!'

It was Thomas. Morrogh opened the door as Thomas pushed his way past the guards.

'Where's Connor?' He was wild-eyed with anxiety.

'Please, Thomas.' Morrogh tried to stop him entering. Thomas cast his gaze around the station, pointed at Kane.

'He hasn't done anything. You know that, you bastards.'

'Calm down, Thomas.'

'Has Connor been here?'

'No.'

'Has anyone seen him?'

'Not that I'm aware of.'

Thomas turned to Kane. 'Have you seen my son?'

'Not tonight. What's happened?'

'He's gone. What happened to Lauren Carter?' Thomas said. 'She's missing, my son's missing. What the hell are you doing sitting here interrogating a fucking professor who's been on the island twenty-four hours?'

'Get out.' Reid moved toward him. Thomas stepped backwards into the Administrator, turned.

'And you,' he said, up close to the Administrator's face. 'You know. You know.'

'Everyone's anxious,' the Administrator said. 'Calm down.'

'Tom, come on. Let's go home.' An American officer tried to grab Thomas's arm, but Thomas shook him off. It wasn't clear what happened next, but it seemed Thomas had taken ahold of the Administrator. They both staggered unsteadily toward the crowd. The police dived out. Thomas took a swing at Morrogh, who backed away from the blow. Reid got his arms around Thomas's neck and wrestled him to the ground. Morrogh had the presence of mind to shut the police station door.

Kane heard the shouts continue: 'Help me hold him down.'

'Get his arms.'

'They're out there,' Thomas screamed. 'And you're fucking around here.'

Kane sat in front of Rory's box file. He looked at the Polaroids, picked the exercise book up from the desk where it had been left. *Secret.* He turned through, gazing at the troubled drawings, until he came across a building. He'd seen it last time he'd looked, but it hadn't meant anything then. Low and square, it had been drawn hurriedly in pencil but was immediately familiar now as the ruins he'd seen up at Devil's Ashpit. There were even the concrete stumps on either side. On the facing page was a list: *People who saw it.* In childish scrawl: *Petra, Lauren, Connor.* There were spaces for more, but it seemed no one joined them.

Kane studied the drawing. Above the padlocked door of the ruined building Connor had added a sign that said *NASA.* Kane didn't remember seeing anything like that when he'd driven by earlier. But he knew that NASA had built a tracking station on Ascension Island in the 1960s. It had been instrumental in the moon landing. This had to be it: the ruins of the old NASA site.

Kane felt there was a good chance that Rory had been there shortly before dying. Which meant a distinct possibility it played a role in other trouble. Petra, Lauren, now Connor. It also seemed plausible that, for one reason or other, no one else was looking in that direction right now, and that if he was going to stop whatever was happening, he had to get there himself.

There was a crash as someone fell against the front of the building, then more shouts. Kane stood up, turned to the back door, and removed the plank. He stepped into the parking area, past Rory's Fiat, to the fence, which was ten feet high or so, with sloping rock on the other side but no people.

Kane climbed onto the car, then jumped from its roof to the fence. He managed to get a grip, while his feet found some purchase in the chain link, and then he swung his leg over and let himself down, heart pumping. He moved up the hill, deeper into darkness, until he could see the town beneath him. A helicopter hung above the bungalow, fixing it in a spotlight. Dogs continued to bark. The fracas by the police station was obscured by the station building itself, but he could see people moving toward it from the old barracks. He recognised men from the Two Boats Bar, including band members still in their outfits, saw the nurse he'd been talking to. Beyond them, the waves boomed and the antennae stood silently against the night sky.

He needed a car.

The back streets of Georgetown looked deserted, including the one with the Honda he'd borrowed the previous night. Kane crept down the slope, very slow and quiet. He found the car with the keys still in the ignition, climbed in, and began to drive.

TWENTY-FOUR

Taylor headed toward Vauxhall through predawn London, cramming in a hands-free mic and trying to get more details from the overnight manager.

'The missing person's a fifteen-year-old girl, Lauren Carter,' Hayes said. 'This information's from New Scotland Yard. She went missing sometime late yesterday.'

'How is Elliot connected?'

'Her clothes were found in the place where he's staying.'

'I don't understand. Are they saying he killed her?'

'I don't know. He's being interviewed at the island police station.'

The first thing she did once in the office was check for messages from Kane. There was nothing. She sent one: *Contact me asap.* What else could she say? This was why she preferred being in the field: HQ meant when things went wrong you were in the wrong place by definition. By design.

She returned a missed call from DCI Rehman.

'Are you aware of the current situation on Ascension?' Rehman asked. 'That another girl has gone missing?'

'I've just heard. What's going on? How does this connect to Petra Wade?'

'I'd like to find out. We need to speak to you.'

'You can speak to me now. Did you leak information to the press?'

'No, of course not.'

'Someone did.'

'Not us. I believe you spoke to Nicola Bannatyne, Rory Bannatyne's sister.'

'That's correct.'

'She mentioned a postcard, one that's currently in your possession.'

'You spoke to Nicola Bannatyne?'

'Yes. What does the postcard say? She claimed you were very interested in it.'

'I'll find it. I'll call you back.' Taylor hung up. She couldn't imagine where that lead would take Rehman, but she suspected the detective wasn't going to get any further than she already had, and she didn't have time for it now. Owen Hayes, the office night manager, knocked on her door.

'Were you were running searches last night? An officer code: DX/3372?'

Taylor froze.

'Why?' she said.

'Personnel called.'

'Saying what?'

'Saying you should speak to them.'

'Was it Laura Whitemore?'

'Yes.'

The previous night's transgressions flooded back. Taylor called Whitemore on a direct line.

'DX/3372?' Whitemore said.

'Yes, that was me. Who are they?'

'Are you working with the Global Issues desk?'

'No, why?'

'I don't have information on this officer; it's missing. I'm looking into that. But someone else was asking after it yesterday, in Global Issues.'

'Who?'

'Chris Hawkes.'

'Do you know why he was asking?'

'No. He just said it was urgent. He's in now, I just spoke to him.'

'This is sensitive, Laura. Does anyone else know I was looking?'

'Just me.'

'Let's keep it that way. Thank you.'

D7, the Global Issues Controllerate, had been set up as the Cold War began to wane and the intelligence service, feeling the need to rebrand, put increasing resources into investigating organised crime. A few years later, when terrorism became the biggest game in town, the department was well placed to draw in resources: Everything, it turned out, came back to organised crime – arms, drugs, money laundering.

Taylor crossed the sprawling open-plan office to Hawkes's desk. He had his phone to his ear, standing in front of a monitor filled with photographs of badly mutilated corpses. The bodies had been shot or hacked to pieces or both. One had a rope tied around his wrists. Hawkes looked wired, tie askew, his usual good looks grown pallid.

'DX/3372,' Taylor said. Hawkes glanced at her, told the caller he'd get back to them and hung up.

'Is it you?'

'No.'

'Who is it?'

'I don't know, but I'd also like to find them.'

'Why?'

She looked across the images: a man lying on the floor of an inflatable lifeboat filled with blood; two men bound together and shot in the head in what looked like a ship's hold.

'What is this?'

'Trouble. Why are you chasing it?'

'I've got an issue on Ascension Island. I believe that the officer

234

who used that personnel code knew something about the place. Where is this?'

'A long way from Ascension. I'll tell you what I know.'

The boat appeared on 2 November, a couple of miles out from Coron, in the Philippines. It sat there overnight, and in the morning it still hadn't moved. Coron was home to the Club Paradise Palawan Hotel, so there were plenty of people who noticed the boat and the fact that it didn't appear to be going anywhere or doing anything.

Club Paradise Palawan was an exclusive island resort, monetising azure waters and a pristine beach. It wasn't unusual to get boats passing, but there was something odd about this one: approximately 130 foot – not big but not small, either – with visible machinery on deck and no crew in sight. It didn't broadcast any radio signals. On the third morning, when birds had started gathering around the ship, the resort's security took their own craft out to get a closer look.

They found the first body in the water, tied by its feet to the railings. Two more on the deck itself, which was sticky with blood.

'There were three in the cabin,' Hawkes said. 'All had been tortured and shot. The men were of various ethnicities and carried no identification. The machinery, including towing winches and stern rollers, looked like it was for some kind of salvage work. The boat had been torn apart.'

'Like what?'

'Like they were searching it for something.'

After liaising with several maritime administrations, the Philippines authorities managed to establish that the vessel had sailed from Hong Kong via Manila. But it still wasn't clear what the boat was for. The local police had passed the ship's details on to Interpol. Interpol automatically contacted all organised crime units globally, including London's Serious Organised Crime Agency, who contacted the intelligence service.

Naturally enough, it came through to Chris Hawkes. Hawkes kept D7 operating on multiple fronts. Taylor liked his energy. He'd been a good agent runner, she'd heard, withdrawn from the Balkans after a cycling accident, although that wasn't the story he always told. The desk job sometimes appeared to be constricting him, but he applied the same level of enthusiasm, and he needed it. D7 wasn't as big as once promised, but every conventional target crossed over with organised crime – from Russia to the DRC – so he was kept busy. His team had seen it all, or so they thought.

Hawkes showed Taylor a plan of the boat.

'First thing I noticed: This boat is highly customised. It looks like a research or survey vessel, with a lot of onboard computing but also diving equipment and the contraptions for salvage work: generators, steel-cutting equipment, salvage pumps. Then, at the back, you get the real oddity: a separate, unmanned submersible vehicle sitting in the hold. Like a robotic sub.'

'Military?'

'Not like any we're aware of. Not naval, not used by any oil exploration, either. The sub has advanced deep-sea sensing tech: cameras, lights, sonar. The only similar vessels I could find are used for searching out plane wrecks. But the weirdest things on board were some of the objects stored in a safe nearby: there are human bones and jewellery and watches. According to notes in the safe, it's all historical. There are watches belonging to people who died in the Second World War, bones belonging to Japanese crewmen from the sixteenth century, you name it.'

'What the hell were they up to?'

'Peer behind a couple of front companies, and the owner of the boat turns out to be Jerry Lau, son of one of Hong Kong's biggest property developers. This is where it gets troubling. Lau was security vetted by us in 2016. It looks like he was on our books in some capacity, being run by officer DX/3372.'

'Who's vanished.'

'Right.

'So, what does Lau use the boat for?'

'He's a treasure hunter.'

'A treasure hunter?'

'That's his thing: searches shipwrecks for treasure. It's how he spends his millions. He'd been cruising for lost galleons or something just a week before the hit, then got called away to some business in Hong Kong. His crew were going to reconvene with him the following week. I ran Lau through our system and almost all traces of him have been scrubbed away. But since word broke of what happened in the Philippines, he's been trying to contact us. He's hiding somewhere in London and claims we owe him protection.'

'Has he said what he did for us?'

'Not to me.'

'Any idea where he is?'

'No, but I've got a number.'

'What are you going to do?'

'Keep searching for someone who knows what's going on. What put you onto it?'

'A thing,' Taylor said. 'Do me a favour – hold off searching for a moment. I'm going to see what I can do. This touches on something, and I'd appreciate you keeping it to yourself for now.'

Hawkes looked at her with wary acceptance. This happened – a polite word, a nudge: *This touches on something live.* Usually at least one of you knew what was going on.

Taylor returned to her own department. The first light of morning lay flat against the windows. The chief had called and instructed her to present herself at his office asap. That had to mean he knew about the chaos unfolding on Ascension.

Kudus was in.

'I heard,' he said.

'You shouldn't have.'

'I came in early to read about Argentine oil exploration. I got told about another girl missing. I thought it might take priority.'

'And?'

'Kane's been arrested. The girl comes up in reports as a friend of Petra Wade. Someone said you were upstairs.'

Taylor hid her relief at having an ally. She'd tried to keep him out of it. Now he was going to have to come along for the ride.

'Are you able to tell me what's going on?' Kudus said.

'I'm looking into a guy called Jerry Lau. He knows something. That's my object of interest at this moment.'

Kudus watched her run an open-source search on Jerry Lau. There was no shortage of biogs and appraisals. Lau was the second son of a construction tycoon, Lau Chao-yung, whose China Construction and Engineering Company appeared responsible for half the buildings going up in the Republic. Jerry Lau had been sent to the UK at age nine, educated at Harrow and then Imperial, where he gained a master's in mechanical engineering. He'd gone into e-finance, specifically electronic trading platforms, investing his father's money wisely. In April 2009, Lau Junior was ranked as the twenty-third wealthiest man in Hong Kong, worth 900 million dollars. He divided his time between Hong Kong and London. According to various profiles, he discovered his first shipwreck at seventeen years of age. At twenty-three his hobby had been professionalised under the name JL Marine Exploration and he'd raised further millions from people willing to invest in his maritime archaeology.

'This is not what I was expecting,' Kudus said.

'He knows something about Ascension. So did whoever was handling him.'

MI6 picked up strange people of necessity. It liked dilettantes, who were often internationally mobile, well connected, cloaked by their own eccentricity. As Hawkes had described, there was a vetting file from 2016 suggesting he had entered into some form of work with the intelligence service, but no records beyond that. Taylor dialled the number Lau had left. When it went to voicemail, she recorded a message saying she could help and gave her direct line.

He called a minute later.

'You can help?' Lau sounded sceptical, angry.

'I really hope so. Are you still in London?'

'Yes.'

'Can you meet me in an hour?'

He inhaled. 'That should be possible.'

Taylor suggested a hotel in the centre, somewhere discreet but public just in case anyone wanted to cause them trouble. He said no and suggested the corner of Pembridge Square and Chepstow Place, Bayswater. Taylor brought up a map with the phone cradled against her shoulder.

It was an expensive part of town, residential; it would be quiet but still public – inconvenient for surveillance, inconvenient for assassination. You didn't let agents dictate arrangements, but then, he wasn't her agent, and this was the only chance she had.

'Okay,' she said. 'Be there in an hour.'

She hung up, grabbed her coat.

'Where are you going?' Kudus asked.

'Out.'

'Not going to C?'

'No.'

He got his coat, joined her in the corridor. Taylor stopped.

'Please, Daniel, your career is starting. I think mine's over.

I'm doing this because someone needs to figure out what's happening on the island – for Elliot and Rory. But it will likely get me fired, at best, whatever I find. At worst, it's a lot messier than that. So please . . . '

'There's no way this is a solo operation,' he said, moving for the stairs. 'Come on. I've never met a treasure hunter.'

TWENTY-FIVE

Kane drove fast. The twisting roads were still a nightmare to drive, but empty now. Everyone was in Georgetown for the drama or hiding at home.

He almost missed the turn-off for Devil's Ashpit. Kane swung onto the overgrown road, aware that he was heading into more mystery than he'd ever faced before. He passed the crater striped like a racing track, the glimpse of blackly glinting sea, continuing toward the interior. The moon was low and swollen, and he was grateful for its light. What the hell was he heading toward?

He stopped the car before the station came into view, got out, listened. Nothing. Kane approached on foot. As he drew nearer, Kane saw what he thought was a girl with her arms out, but it was one of the decaying stumps of palm tree. Beyond it, the ruins appeared. In the cold moonlight the concrete blocks where the deep space antennae would have sat looked like ancient plinths. The front doors remained locked. Nothing had changed. Kane was wondering how he might get in when he heard a sound behind him.

Kane turned. A figure appeared from the darkness, pointing a gun.

Connor.

The boy advanced slowly, limping on his bandaged foot, gun shaking. It was a Beretta, heavy in his hand, but his finger was determinedly on the trigger.

'Hey, Connor,' Kane said. 'You okay?'

Connor's eyes were wide, terrified. 'What are you doing here?'

'Taking a look. What's going on? Where's Lauren?'

'I don't know.'

'What are *you* doing here?'

'Looking for her.'

'Okay. Where did you get the gun?'

'I took it.'

'Anyone know you're up here?'

'No. I think I'm going to be killed.'

'Who's going to do that?'

'Whoever killed them.'

'I want to make sure that doesn't happen, Connor. Do you have any idea who we should be looking for?'

'No.'

'But you know I'm on your side, right?'

'I don't know anything.'

It had been a while since Kane had had a gun pointed at him. The Beretta M9 was reliable and easy to use, one reason it had been standard issue in the US Air Force. You were taught how to respond to this kind of scenario: distract, redirect, disarm. But persuasion could work too.

'What do you think happened to Lauren?' Kane asked.

'I don't know.'

'But you're here.'

'So are you.'

'That's right. I was wondering if this place had something to do with it.'

'What made you wonder that?'

'The dead astronaut.'

Connor tightened his grip on the gun. For a second Kane thought he'd taken the wrong step. A new look of terror froze the boy's face. It wouldn't take much for him to squeeze the trigger.

'What do you know about that?' Connor said, finally.

'Nothing. That's why I thought you could help me.'

'Where did you hear about it?'

'I found an exercise book with drawings and writing in. Your drawings. A guy called Rory Bannatyne had it. Remember him?'

'He killed himself.'

'So it seems. The night he died, I think he came up here.'

'Yes.'

'What happened?'

The boy screwed his eyes shut then opened them again. He glanced around for something – help, or other threats. The gun shook violently now.

'Listen to me,' Kane said. 'I don't think you're responsible for what's going on. I think Petra and Lauren were really close to you, and I want to find out what's happened. But I need your help.'

Now the boy slid down to the ground and without releasing the gun placed his head in his hands. Kane gave it a moment, then sat beside him, which put him close to the gun without being in front of it.

'Do you know what happened to Rory?' Kane asked.

'He was looking for the astronaut.'

'I need to understand this. Talk me through it, Connor.'

The teenager straightened, breathed, staring ahead.

'We used to hang out here.'

'Okay. Who was that?'

'Me, Petra, Lauren. You know, as kids. We'd bike up here and it was, like, our place. One time we thought we heard someone inside. That's how the dead astronaut started. We were sitting right here, and we thought we heard someone in the building.'

'Someone in the building?'

'Yes.'

'Doing what?'

'I don't know. Just bangs at first, then maybe a voice.'

'Was the building in use then?'

'No. It's never been in use. Not while I've been here.'

'So what did you do?'

'Nothing. We went home, and later we started making up stories about it. Our parents were always going on about how we shouldn't come here, using rumours: Kids had gone up here and never been seen again. That kind of thing. So we added to that.'

'They said that?'

'They didn't want us getting hurt, because of the drop. It wasn't true. But it made it exciting. And we freaked each other out with the stories. That was what Rory was interested in.'

'Tell me the stories he was interested in.'

Connor turned to look at the building behind them, then rolled his neck and groaned softly. 'Can we get out of here?'

'I think this might be the best place for us right now.'

'Really?'

'Yeah.'

Connor gazed down toward the darkness of the valley, then let his head tip back.

'What is going on?' he said to the stars, voice choking.

'We're going to figure that out. Take a breath.'

Connor took a breath. The tears held as he spoke.

'The stories were like, this dead astronaut from the old days is still locked up inside there; they did experiments on him and he went mad. Stuff like that. If you saw him it would be so terrifying, he wouldn't even have to kill you ... You'd just die.' The boy hesitated. 'Or you'd kill yourself.'

'You think that's what happened to Rory?'

'Well, he died, didn't he? I don't know. That was what we said: joke stuff. Sometimes the astronaut escapes, walks around the island at night. His face is all fucked up. I'd draw pictures, and we came up with ways of protecting ourselves. We were twelve, thirteen. Then we thought, maybe the whole island's an experiment and the adults know what's going on. They're following orders. And if you talk about it you become the next prisoner. You get put in the NASA building with him.'

Both looked up as a helicopter came into earshot, searchlight combing the volcanic peaks to the south.

'They're looking for me,' Connor said.

'Looking for both of us, I reckon. But we're all right. I'll take care of them if they come. Did you ever see or hear anything else?'

'Not then. Pretty soon we stopped all the astronaut stuff. We'd come up here to drink or smoke and it was pretty much a joke.'

'But Rory took it seriously.'

'Yes.'

'Why?'

'Fuck knows. Maybe because the astronaut's come back.' The boy turned to Kane, wet eyes catching moonlight.

'What do you mean?'

'A couple of months ago Petra and Lauren were up here. They said they heard someone inside the building. They ran. That's all.'

'What did they hear?'

'A voice.'

'Saying anything?'

'I don't know.'

'And Rory was interested in this?'

'Yeah.'

'Tell me about Rory. Did he seem okay? Or like he was a bit messed up in the head?'

'Rory was cool. We'd go to English Bay to swim and he'd let us drink. He liked hearing our stories. And he knew how to do stuff. He was good at getting into places, climbing, breaking in.'

'Where did he break in to?'

'One time we broke into the BBC building and saw the old equipment and there were still some old records and amps.'

'What else did he do?'

'He got all the kids to tell him secrets – about the island or what they did and stuff. You got a medal. It was dumb. The younger kids liked it. But he was good for driving us and sometimes buying us alcohol.'

'And that's how he started hearing about the dead astronaut.'

'Right.'

'Did Rory think it was real?'

'I think he was just . . . adventuring. That's what he called it. He had his own crazy theories.'

'Like what?'

'Not proper theories.'

'What did he say?'

'Like maybe people's souls couldn't leave the island and that was why the government didn't let people die here. Stuff like that. He said there were already too many ghosts from the past, and maybe that explained the dead astronaut.'

Kane watched the helicopter illuminating peak after peak of charcoal-grey stone. He felt caught in the webs of someone else's fever dreams. But all it takes for dreams to become real is for the person to treat them as such. The border dissolved more easily than it had any right to do.

'What else did Rory say?'

'You're really interested in him, aren't you.'

'Yeah.'

The boy thought.

'He said the radars and everything, maybe they were connected. They were researching ghosts. Like, they caught voices in the air, stuff like that. He was crazy. He'd wind us up.'

'And the tracking station's always been like this?'

'As long as I can remember.'

'Who do you think comes up here? Apart from you?'

'No one.'

'But that night, when Petra went missing and Rory killed himself, you came up here. All of you.'

'Yes.'

'What happened?'

'We said we'd show Rory where we hung out, where we'd heard things. And we came up here. And I think the astronaut came out.'

'You saw him?'

'Not exactly.'

'What did you see?'

'Just the door starting to move.' He glanced at the building again.

'You're sure?'

'Yeah. Hundred per cent.'

'Where exactly were you positioned? Can you show me?'

Connor got to his feet, holding the gun as if he'd forgotten about it. He led Kane around to the side of the compound, to one of the large concrete stumps overlooking the building. His bike was propped against it.

'This is where we were that night.'

There was a rock in place, which meant you could climb up onto the old radar base for a sight line to the door of the main building. But from the front of the building you'd have to twist to see anyone up there, and at night they'd be well hidden.

'You were all up here?'

'Yeah.'

'And what happened?'

'When the door opened Petra panicked. She ran. I don't know. It was chaotic. I ran after her. I got to my bike. A few seconds later I heard her scream.'

'And Rory?'

'I don't know what Rory did.'

'You got on your bike and started to cycle.'

'Right.'

'Where was Lauren?'

'I thought she'd gone a while back, as soon as we heard the first sounds.'

'What were the first sounds?'

'Doors, metal, banging inside. Lauren ran and I thought she'd gone back home, but maybe she was hiding somewhere.'

'And what happened to Petra?'

'I think she was too slow. The Russian astronaut got her.'

'Russian?'

'The one we told stories about.' The boy checked Kane's face, registering a new intensity of interest.

'You didn't say they were Russian.'

'Sometimes the girls called him that.'

'Why?'

'They thought they heard someone talking Russian, maybe.'

'They heard Russian?'

'They thought it was. They were, like, eleven or something.'

'Know anyone on the island who speaks Russian?'

'I don't think so.'

'So that night you were cycling away. You heard Petra scream.'

'Right.'

'And no idea what happened to Rory.'

'No.'

'Do you think maybe Rory was killed up here? Then someone could have taken his body down to English Bay, made it look like he killed himself.'

'I guess.'

Kane walked to the front of the tracking station and checked the visibility of the ledge where the teenagers had been hiding, then the door once again.

'Did you tell the police all this?'

'My father did.'

'What did the police say?'

'They said they'd investigate. But they haven't. They know something – maybe about what's in there.'

Kane studied the lock.

'Got a torch?' he said.

'No.'

Kane went back to the car and searched. No torch, but he found a disposable lighter in the glove compartment.

'Where are you going?' Connor said.

'Inside. Ever been inside?'

'No. How are you going inside?'

'Give me the gun.'

The boy hesitated, then handed over the gun. Kane checked the box magazine. It was fully loaded: fifteen bullets. He took his shirt off and wrapped it around the muzzle to suppress as much noise and flash as possible. The idea of shooting a metal lock to pieces was a Hollywood fantasy, but the door frame itself was wood: a lot more fragile, with a lot less chance of ricochet.

'Step away.'

It took two shots, and then the wood was shredded enough for him to pull the bolt through. The shots had echoed off the rocks, but the waves were also loud. Nearest likely responders were on the UK base, and it would take them at least twenty minutes to get here. Kane nudged the door open with his foot.

'Oh shit,' Connor muttered behind him. 'We really shouldn't go in.'

'I think we should take a look.'

Kane stepped inside, into a corridor. The air was musty. He tried to let his eyes adjust but the darkness was too thick. He clicked the lighter.

The corridor led through the building. Its walls were scabbed with peeling plaster. Kane walked slowly, the flame animating rooms on either side: offices with empty metal cabinets, dorms with rusted iron bed frames, blackened glassware and crockery beside a cobwebbed sink. On the wall of the canteen, a crooked picture showed a space shuttle in front of two flags, a Union Jack and Stars and Stripes: *4 July 1985, Ascension Island. 'In Peace for all Mankind.'*

Kane stepped carefully into a large bare hall that must have once been the Operations Room. He could see indentations where the huge mainframe computers had been. Now it contained stacks of plastic chairs.

Then Connor screamed. Kane spun, saw the boy jump backwards. There was a scurrying at floor level as a rat dived for cover.

'Holy shit,' Connor said.

Kane looked to see where the rat went. It slid passed a door with a yellow sign reading CAUTION: ELECTRICAL HAZARD. Kane walked through, into a room with pipes and a generator at the back. Then he saw a sealed panel in the centre of the floor.

It was an iron access hatch: square, heavy-duty, embossed with diamond-shaped grips. But opened recently. You could see where the handle had scored a line in the dust. You could see shoe prints.

Kane tried to prise up the hatch, but it was locked fast. This one was too solid to shoot. It had a key lock, set into the iron, with the iron fixed to the stone floor. Kane crouched and watched a beetle cross the metalwork. He knocked. A hollow chime filled the room. Connor stood in the doorway, staring at the panel with the look of dread that Kane felt.

'Hello?' Kane called. He listened to the waves outside and the helicopter softly churning. No reply. Another beetle skirted the edge of the metal.

'We need to get some tools,' Kane said, straightening. 'Think there are any on base we could use? That you could get access to?'

'Maybe.'

'Are the British police allowed onto the US base?'

'No.'

'Okay.' Kane emptied the rest of the bullets out of the gun, put them in his pocket, and gave it back. 'Let's head there. Your parents will be worried. Who did you borrow the gun off?'

'It's my mom's.'

'Does she need a gun?'

'Everyone on base has one.'

'Going to return it to her?'

'Yes.'

'Let's go.'

TWENTY-SIX

'The girl who went missing last night is called Lauren Carter,' Taylor said as she drove. 'Her father's an aircraft technician, been on the island five years. It's not clear who she is, how she connects to Petra Wade.'

'And what's Jerry Lau got to do with it?'

'I think Lau knows something about the island. He was being run as an agent; he passed information that led to a report being filed with the keywords Quadrant and Ascension. Quadrant is Quadrant Space Technologies, who I think are the ones checking on Kane – they have a contract to run a research facility on Ascension. They're big new players in the space game, with the ear of the government. But there's something more to them, and I think Lau might know. He might even know why the whole thing's been wiped from the system.'

'He won't talk to us.'

'He'll talk to people who can ensure his safety. So that's what we are.'

The area was even wealthier than she expected. Posh London: leafy, peaceful, sinister, with rows of identical stuccoed houses surrounding locked, private squares and not many humans in sight at all.

They drove by the rendezvous point, checked for any obvious signs of danger. But danger rarely made itself obvious. Taylor parked a street away, and they split up and approached from opposite directions, eyes out for anyone waiting. Neither of them saw anyone.

They were at the corner at the specified time. Taylor assumed they were being watched. A moment later a man crossed toward them, very tall, very tightly suited in a navy blazer. A former member of one of the diplomatic wings of the police, Taylor guessed. He had that practised stiffness. He looked them over, glanced at the nearby cars.

'Waiting for someone?'

'Yes.'

'Who?'

'Jerry Lau.'

'Just you guys?'

'Yes.'

'I work for Jerry. I'm going to take you to where he's currently staying. Can I see some ID?'

They showed their government passes. The man studied them carefully, then handed them back.

'Follow me.'

He led them around the corner, onto an exclusive cul-de-sac where the houses were behind solid fences, then stopped beside an ornate but very functional metal gate higher than their heads. It opened electronically without him apparently doing anything. Inside was a gravel garden and a shiny black Mercedes, then an attractive Georgian house with ivy and security cameras and metal shutters closed on every window.

'Need to give you a quick search,' he said once the gate had slid back into place behind them. They spread their arms. He patted them down for weapons and wires. When the guard was satisfied they were not a threat, he knocked on the front door. Another guard answered, and the four of them walked in.

The house contained no personal effects. Taylor suspected it had nothing to do with Lau and that was precisely why he was here. It felt like a stage set, very beautifully decorated, with shades of plum and midnight blue on the walls and little busts in alcoves. Lau appeared, coming downstairs at the back of the main hall, shrugging on a suit jacket. He was slight and smart, wearing a black shirt, tan chinos, expensive Italian shoes. Taylor wondered if he'd dressed for them or if he did being on the run in style. His face had an unmarked, ageless quality. But he wasn't happy.

'They're legit,' the guard said. Lau appraised the pair. Beneath the evident anxiety Taylor sensed a zealous energy – someone who had monetised a childhood passion: intelligent, spoiled, gifted.

'What happened to my crew?' he said.

'That's what we want to find out: what happened to them and how we ensure it doesn't happen to you.'

'Until now it seemed you were going to break every promise you made.'

He spoke softly, with a non-native precision.

'Things have been far from ideal, and we apologise for that. Is there somewhere we can talk in private?'

'I need my security to be present.'

'I'm afraid that's not possible.'

Lau spoke with the guards alone. He returned and nodded acceptance, leading them into a dining room with a table set with candelabras. Lau shut the double doors behind them and they sat down on cushioned chairs.

'Something has gone wrong at our end,' Taylor began. 'We don't deny that, and we want to apologise. The records that should be there are no longer there. On our side, there's an inquiry under way. But obviously a lot of people are scratching their heads – whatever you were involved in was such high secrecy that even senior members of the service have not been fully briefed. That's why we're here: We need to know exactly what happened before we can begin arranging appropriate protection and compensation. Ultimately we need to know where the threat lies and how we can keep you and your family safe.'

'We need to know everything,' Kudus said.

'How much do you know already?'

'Imagine we know nothing.'

Lau exhaled, ran a hand through his hair, then stared at Taylor.

'Are you aware of the cemetery?'

'Which cemetery?'

'In the Pacific.'

Taylor and Kudus glanced at each other.

'No,' Kudus said, finally. 'Tell us about the cemetery in the Pacific.'

Lau gathered himself, gazing toward the shutters before turning his bright eyes upon them.

'May 2016, I was searching for a Second World War ship, the SS *Minerva*, in the South China Sea, the Lingayen Gulf, to be precise. I had spent years compiling a database, tracking the gold shipped by the British government to pay for weapons and goods during the World Wars. There were around seven and half thousand merchant ships sunk, and my team have identified more than five hundred that were carrying vast quantities of precious metals. Twenty are in the South China Sea.

'The *Minerva* had been carrying platinum, gold, and industrial diamonds when it was torpedoed in July 1942. That's all still down there. But if it was easy to access it would have been salvaged by now. Our mission to find it was the conclusion of two years' preparation. We'd been sailing for almost a week. On the sixth morning, just before dawn, my crew saw what looked like three fishing boats approaching, but moving way too fast. They got closer and we could see they were more like military craft: very low, ten men per boat, all masked up. And heavily armed. We knew they were either special forces or very well-equipped pirates. We were outnumbered. They boarded, all speaking Chinese. Claimed we were in Chinese territorial waters, which we weren't. We were arrested, blindfolded, taken onto their boats. Next thing I know, I'm being interviewed in a secure facility.

'I spent three days in a cell. I had no idea where I was. I was accused of being a spy. They said I was in their waters illegally, wanted to know what I was doing there, wanted to know about my work, my connections. On the third day they came to me with a deal, and it became clear what they were after. They wanted to see what my equipment could do. They wanted me to take them out, find a wreck they thought was down there, show them my technology and how it works.'

'Your technology?'

'Mapping shipwrecks at great depths with any kind of precision involves a lot of sensors – acoustic, hyperspectral, stereo. But done well it means you don't need to carry out endless inspection dives. You fit a stereo camera on an ROV, and you can have high-res 3D models in front of you on dry land.'

'ROV?'

'Remotely operated underwater vehicle. An underwater robot. These things can collect and analyse the data on their own, which means they can decide whether to investigate further: what to document, what to map. I was the only one who'd combined the whole package on a single underwater vessel. It had taken years of development.

'The Chinese threatened my family. They were willing to arrest relatives of mine. My father's business would have been destroyed. So, I agreed. And when I was taken out of the interrogation facility, I was on what I believe to have been an artificial island. There was something very odd about the shoreline, the way it met the sea. The island itself was perfectly flat. I saw buildings that might have been labs, some more like military HQs.

And there, finally, was my boat and crew, who had been through a similar experience to me, and were waiting for instructions.'

'Do you know where this island was?'

'Not for sure, but I suspect Paracel.'

That sounded right. The Paracel Islands included some of China's largest military outposts in the South China Sea. A lot of them were newly made – dredged-up miracles, studded with long-range sensor arrays, port facilities, runways, reinforced bunkers for fuel and weapons. Lau had got a glimpse of one of the most secret places on earth.

'And where did you go then?' Taylor asked.

'The next day we sailed past Guam into the Pacific. Heading into the cemetery. You really don't know about it?'

'Tell us.'

He took a breath as if wondering where to start, joined his hands, pressed them against his lips then, gazing straight at them, began again.

'Satellites die. Spacecraft die. Then you've got two choices: direct them farther away into outer space forever or let them return to earth.' He looked from one intelligence officer to the other to ensure they were following. 'Only, you don't want them falling on anyone, right? And maybe you don't want anyone falling onto them.

'The spacecraft cemetery is where they're dropped. It's the centre of the South Pacific, about as far from land as you can get on this planet, somewhere between Easter Island and Antarctica. There's been around three hundred spacecraft sunk there over the years. The Mir space station's down there, various resupply craft belonging to the ISS, some transfer vehicles from the European Space Agency. It's a junkyard over thousands of square kilometres, as deep under the sea as you can go.

'Obviously, none of them is just sitting neatly on the ocean floor. Re-entering the atmosphere is like being hit by a bomb.

The heat generated can burn metal. But that's not to say you don't get some interesting fragments. And piloted vehicles like the Space Shuttle or Russia's Soyuz capsules have thermal shielding to protect them. The Chinese wanted to know what they could find, but also what of theirs the Americans might be able to find. I was instructed to help prepare an assessment, show them how it could work. I told them it was near impossible – looking for a satellite the size of a car in the Pacific, trying to retrieve a sea drop. You needed razor-sharp trajectory prediction followed by ultrafast response using vehicles that could go deep.

'I don't know if you know how deep the ocean goes. The spacecraft cemetery is down in the abyssal zone. That's about four to six thousand metres below the surface. There's no life down there. Maybe sponges, the odd octopus or viperfish. The water pressure means diving's impossible. But if anyone could do this work, it was me. The underwater vehicle I use has speed and, more importantly, thermographic cameras. For recent drops you're not looking for something cold but something hot. And the Chinese were improving their location estimates. A couple of days before a spacecraft drops, whichever space agency is in charge of it has to notify authorities in Chile and New Zealand. Those countries share responsibility for the cemetery, and they publicise expected re-entry times and where debris is likely to fall. The Chinese had access to all that. They also had extensive systems of submerged microphones each with a range of several hundred miles. And for a while, of course, you have heat, a lot of heat. But satellites sink fast.'

As Lau described it, they'd set off – sometimes from Easter Island, sometimes from Concepión in Chile – sail three or four days, anchor at designated coordinates until instructions came in. At that point you were already above the abyss; nothing but water beneath you for thousands of feet.

'Then, as soon as we had word of impact, we'd begin searching.'

At three thousand feet you were entering what he called the midnight zone, light fading, six thousand pounds of pressure per square inch.

'There's a Soyuz trapped on a ledge at around this depth. One time I saw parts of the Japanese H-II rocket. We know of more than eighty Russian cargo vehicles scattered over one particular area. Then, past three thousand feet down, you're in the dark zone. Pitch black, close to freezing – a few invertebrates: starfish, eels. Then the trenches and the abyss, twenty thousand feet and beyond, into the unknown.'

'What were they looking for?'

'There was stuff going down there that wasn't what it was meant to be. That's pretty much as close as I got to understanding the situation. Things that looked wrong, or suspicious.'

'Have you been down there?'

'Sure. The shallower regions.'

'You dive?

'Right.'

'Down to satellites?'

'Most of my diving was in wrecks. But once or twice I took a look at the debris down there; not satellites – part of the Mir space station. It had got encrusted, but a door was intact and you could see the airlock.'

In the depth of his cold eyes was a gleam.

'Must be quite something,' Taylor said.

Lau nodded, but her curiosity had made him uneasy. He sat forward, both hands pointed toward her as if to channel his message.

'The first thing you said when I agreed to work with you was that I'd be protected. From the very start, Andrew promised me protection, precisely for a situation like this.'

'Andrew.'

'The guy who met with me.'

At the end of September 2016, a man walked up to Jerry Lau in the hotel he was staying at in Kuala Lumpar and suggested they have a drink together. This was 'Andrew,' the MI6 officer who would be Lau's handler for the next eighteen months. He said he knew Lau needed help and could provide it, extricate him from the situation in which he'd found himself with the Chinese, if he was willing to work for the British government.

Lau was keen. He didn't hear anything more for six weeks, thought they'd changed their mind. Taylor knew what would have really been going on: intensified analysis to ensure he wasn't a double agent; heavy surveillance to determine whether anyone else knew they'd made an approach. Assessment of his value; assessment of the risk. Then a plan would be painstakingly constructed regarding the best way to run him.

In November, Andrew appeared again, same place. He drove Lau to an office behind the Pudu night market, with a secure room at the back. The conversation was very much a rehash of what they'd already been through, but it concluded with arrangements including payment and secure means of communication.

'I wanted to get out of the whole situation immediately, but I was told that wasn't the plan.' Lau sighed. 'I was given means of communicating with Andrew. He made a promise – my family would be resettled eventually. But he wanted me to continue working with the Chinese. And that was how it kept going for the next year and a half.'

Of course, Taylor thought. An agent's no use in retirement. There are people in Vauxhall Cross breathing down your neck for product, finance asking you to justify operational costs. If you weren't prepared to risk lives, you didn't become an agent handler.

'What was Andrew interested in?'

'Everything. But most of all space. Chinese space tech, their knowledge of Western space tech.'

'And you were able to access that information?'

'Not much. I'm a treasure hunter, not a rocket engineer. I couldn't tell him what they were looking for. I didn't know what they had. I said to him: *It's not going to work like this.* But he said not to worry. The next two meetings were in Bali and then once in Macau. Andrew started asking about who came on board the ship, all the details of the Chinese I dealt with.'

'What kind of details, exactly?' Taylor said.

'Everything. Their ages, their technical skills, whether I heard any names or ranks, whether they brought devices with them. He asked if they swept it for bugs, if they seemed to trust me. He wanted to bug the boat. He said when I was next in Malaysia some inspectors would come on board, and I should go along with it, just do whatever they said. At Port Klang the following week, it happened. They said they were Customs and asked to see my papers. They checked all over. I assume that some of them rigged devices into the boat. I was never told what or how.

'Next search mission was in December, just before Christmas. I was told by Andrew that a similar thing would happen when I got to New Zealand. It went on like that. Very few meetings. Whatever he was doing, he was doing it with technology.'

'Did you sense that Andrew was getting something from all this?'

'I can only assume it was successful, since you continued risking my life. You subsidised me quite healthily for the privilege. Then, one day, nothing. No communication. I waited for some kind of message, and there was silence. Next thing I know, my men have been slaughtered. For all I know the equipment is still installed on that ship. If they found that, my family is dead. I was told six months at first, then two years. I was told that there was a system in place for emergencies. What if I was in a Chinese prison right now? You used me. Something went wrong your end – fine – but I believed the British government was better than that.'

'Did Andrew ever ask about a company called Quadrant?'

'No. The space company? Why would he ask about Quadrant?'

'I believe he was interested in them.'

Lau looked blank. He shook his head.

'When did you last see him?' Kudus asked.

'In Melbourne, late June last year.'

'What did he say? Was there anything to suggest the situation might be changing?'

'He told me to be prepared – the game might move. He asked about a place called Ascension Island.'

Both Kudus and Taylor nodded, restraining their expressions of interest and resisting the temptation to look at each other.

'What did he ask about Ascension Island?' Kudus asked.

'Whether I had heard it mentioned. Whether I knew anything.'

'Had you heard it mentioned?'

'No. And I didn't know anything, either.'

'Did he say why he was interested in Ascension?'

'No.'

'Have you ever sailed around there?'

'No.'

Taylor could see that Lau wasn't going to throw much more light for now. She needed to find Andrew himself, if he was still alive.

'One challenge we've got is that Andrew may have left the service or moved roles,' she said, registering Lau's expression of disbelief.

'You don't know where he is?'

'We're struggling to locate him. Andrew probably wasn't his real name. Can you tell me what he looked like?'

'He was very tall, with fair hair going grey. Probably fifty or so. At least.'

'What else do you remember about him?'

'One time he told me he had briefly lived in Russia. That's pretty much it.'

'Ever meet him with anyone else?'

'No.'

'Where was he currently based?'

'I don't know.'

'Would you say he seemed confident handling this operation?'

'Yes.'

'What languages did he speak?'

'English, Chinese. I don't know what else.'

'And he asked about Ascension Island.'

'The last time I saw him, yes.'

'And then?'

'A message cancelling the next meeting.'

'From him?'

'Hard to say.'

'Any further contact from anyone?'

'Until now, absolutely nothing. That is what I am trying to explain to you: My life is in danger and I need the help you promised. I never asked for any of this. All I wanted to do was explore wrecks.'

'We'll do what we can. Have you noticed anything that makes you believe you may be under threat right now?'

'Aside from my crew being slaughtered? No.'

'How long have you been based in this house?'

'Three hours.'

'Okay. We'll be in touch very soon with arrangements. In the meantime, keep moving.'

TWENTY-SEVEN

'He said Ascension might be a new area of interest, then disappeared into thin air forever.'

'Just like that.'

Taylor and Kudus sat in the car, looking out over Hyde Park. No update on Kane. Taylor wondered if he was physically safe, if he was sweating in a cell, if he was wondering what she was doing for him, and what she *could* do. Meanwhile, from what Kudus could establish from a call into the office, there were a lot of people looking for Taylor, from the police to her seniors in MI6.

She needed to get legitimate security precautions in place for Lau. She needed to find Andrew, if he was still alive and able to talk. The next time she stepped into HQ, it would be her last; she wouldn't be leaving it a free woman. There had always been rumours of interrogation rooms on the second basement level. She'd have a chance to find out.

Taylor tore the cellophane off a pack of cigarettes. She checked her phone. Her sister was calling, from a life far away.

'I'm meant to be at a birthday party,' Taylor said. Kudus studied her.

'What are you going to do?'

'Disappoint my family once again.'

'I mean, about this. What's your theory?'

'My theory is that Andrew got something he shouldn't have,

something about Ascension, and then he was shut down, painted out of the picture before it could spread.'

A white transit van rolled in behind them. It parked and the driver made a call on his mobile. Kudus saw it too. A few seconds later it drove off again.

'Are we being paranoid?'

'I don't know. Maybe not.'

Taylor felt a ripple of trepidation as she started the engine.

'You're going to have to go in to the office,' Taylor said. 'Tell them you've lost contact with me. Tell Chris Hawkes about Lau – where he is, what he needs. Chris is in a better position than us when it comes to arranging protection. Then we need to find out what happened to Andrew. There's not that many officers trained to handle agents overseas. Narrow that down to Chinese-speakers, someone with the confidence and experience to manage a multi-territory operation, and I think we can identify him. Product on China's intelligence service comes around once in a blue moon. He'll either have been on the China desk or working on defence technology. If the intelligence touched on space or satellites, Helen Jackson may have been receiving reports. She's trustworthy. See what you can do.'

Taylor dropped Kudus on the north side of Vauxhall Bridge and drove on, keeping to back streets. Eat something, she thought; inject some caffeine. Had she slept? Maybe an hour or two. She got a pastry at Pret and checked the news on her phone as she drank one espresso then another. Nothing on the events on Ascension Island yet. She stared at the street outside but saw only the seaweed-coiled remnants of space stations. What had Andrew got from Lau to justify those meetings? That bit didn't make sense: Taylor had no impression of what Lau delivered in terms of intelligence.

She found a public phone behind the store and called the number she had for Markus Fischer.

'Someone in Six was on this before us,' she said. 'Do you have any idea who?'

'No. We're picking up reports of trouble on Ascension. Another girl gone missing.'

'What have you heard about that?'

'Just a suspect name: Edward Pearce. Know him?'

'Yes.'

'You think this connects to Quadrant?'

'I'm sure it does. Quadrant have a lease on a research facility on Ascension Island.'

'I've just discovered that. Do you know what they're up to?'

'No.'

'We need to find out what they're doing there.'

'What's your exit plan for me?'

'We've been discussing this, Kathryn. There's something very wrong going on, and it needs to see light of day if we're to stop it. That means someone who can speak with authority.'

'You want me to be a whistle-blower.'

'We would protect you. The truth would protect you.'

She laughed.

'It's not just your career at risk anymore,' he said. 'This is growing rapidly out of control.'

'What makes you say that?'

'Can we arrange to meet?'

'I've got one more thing to do first,' she said. 'I'll be in touch.'

Kudus called half an hour later.

'An officer named Ian Latham moved from the China desk to Defence Intelligence in 2014, looks like with a focus on China's space capability.'

The Defence Intelligence desk supported military ops, defence policy, capability assessments of other countries' weapons systems. This fit what she was looking for.

'Did you get a personnel file?'

'Yes. Latham trained in 1988; he was based at Six's Moscow station in 2002, then Beijing. Fluent in French, Russian, and Chinese, left the service in July last year.'

'That sounds like our man.'

'I thought so.'

'Any idea where he went?'

'Not one hundred per cent sure, but an Ian Latham comes up as a languages teacher in Guildford. Joined the school eleven months ago. Cambridge graduate, specialist in Mandarin.'

'Any pictures?'

'No. It says he has extensive experience overseas, though.'

'It's him.'

'Maybe. I got a home address off an alumni directory.'

'You're very good at this.'

'That makes me responsible if anything happens to you.'

'Welcome to the intelligence service.'

'We can run a security check.'

'We don't have time. Send it through.'

Kudus sent through the name and address: *Ian Latham, 11 Chesterfield Grove, Bellfields.* This time she went alone.

TWENTY-EIGHT

Bellfields was a suburb to the north of Guildford, a cluster of residential streets bordered by the River Wey and the A3. It was close to the school at which Latham taught. His home address was a freshly bricked house on a private estate, quiet on a Saturday morning. Taylor rang the bell and a woman answered the door, balancing a baby on her hip. Taylor hadn't prepared for this possibility and froze.

'Yes?'

The woman was East Asian, in her late thirties, tired. She wore a dressing gown. A man appeared behind her. He saw Taylor, saw her study his face, and something triggered an alarm bell. He met her stare and very subtly shook his head once.

Taylor thought fast.

'I'm looking for Naomi,' she said. The woman frowned.

'Not here, I'm afraid.' She turned to the man. 'Is there a Naomi on the street?'

Latham stepped forward so he could see the street outside while also shielding his partner and child. He matched the description Lau had given, only older. His fair hair was thin now. He had silver bags under his eyes and a thin blue vein at the side of his head. He checked for backup, then smiled at Taylor.

'Perhaps try the house opposite. Number thirty-nine.'

'Thank you. Sorry to disturb you.'

The door closed. A van passed at the end of the street, very slowly. By the time she'd got to the corner it had gone. She checked the other cars as she walked back, listening for the tick of hot engines, looking for the silhouettes of individuals waiting. No one. But her skin prickled.

What now? Taylor kicked herself. She could have thought of some way of speaking to Latham alone. She wasn't prepared to give up just yet. She spent ten minutes circling the block, smoking a cigarette as she contemplated options, alternative ways of drawing Latham out. When she finally got back in her car, the glove box was open.

She hadn't used it today. As Taylor leaned over to see if anything had been taken, she felt the cold metal of a blade at her throat.

'Drive.'

She looked in the mirror. Ian Latham met her stare.

'Now,' he said.

'I need to speak to you about Ascension Island.'

'Trust me, that's the last thing you need.'

'I'll drive. Take the knife away.'

He sat back. It was a chef's knife, Taylor saw, razor sharp, gripped tight. She started the car, drove to the end of the road, where he told her to take a right and keep going.

'Try anything and I'll put it in the back of your skull.'

'I need to talk to you, Ian.'

'Who are you?'

'My name's Kathryn. I'm head of the South Atlantic desk.'

'Which floor's that on?'

'Sixth.'

'Describe how you get there from the pool.'

'There's no pool.'

'What do you want?'

'Information about Ascension Island and Quadrant. What they're doing there; why it's so sensitive.' She kept her voice steady, as authoritative as possible.

'Who sent you?'

'No one.'

'You're on your own?'

'Yes.'

'Then you're really fucked.' He shook his head in amazement. 'Turn right again, then in by the leisure centre. Stop at the side.'

They waited to see if anyone caught up. She could hear his breath. After a moment Latham got out. She thought he was going to run, but he climbed into the front passenger seat.

'What makes you think I have anything to do with Ascension?'

'You entered a file on the system: Quadrant and Ascension. It was product from Jerry Lau.'

'And what do you know about Jerry Lau?'

'You were running him, then got interested in Ascension – then you disappeared.'

'You need to go back to Vauxhall and forget all this.'

'There are several lives in danger. Jerry Lau's is one of them.'

'Why? What's happened?'

'His boat was found with all the crew killed. Lau's in hiding.'

'Any suggestion who killed them?'

'No.'

'Was the boat searched?'

'Torn apart.'

Latham swore quietly under his breath.

'Tell me exactly what the situation is on Ascension Island,' he said.

'An officer of ours died there. It appeared he hanged himself, but I believe he was killed. He was over there to assist with some GCHQ work, but seems to have stumbled into something more dangerous.'

'On Ascension?'

'Yes.'

This provoked a few seconds' silence from Latham.

'Is it connected to what's happening today?'

'What do you mean?'

'For Christ's sake. Drive.'

He directed her onto a rocky path, through a jumble of allotments, past an old barn and a burnt-out trailer. A sign warned of guard dogs but there was nothing moving in sight, just dilapidated farm buildings and a muddy track.

'Let's leave the car here.'

She stopped the car and they walked fast, in silence, past empty fields to a shallow wood with an abandoned fridge deep in its wet leaves.

'What was your man over there for?' Latham asked.

'Cable tapping.'

'Purely technical, or security elements?'

'He was assessing security.'

'On the island.'

'Right.'

'My guess is that your officer stumbled into Gemstone.'

'Who's Gemstone?'

'I'll tell you what I can. You listen at your own risk.' He checked his watch. 'Then I think you'll see why this isn't a situation for you to get involved with.'

'Okay.'

'Jerry Lau was a convenient cover. He didn't have much useful information to share himself, but he unwittingly provided us with cover to run an agent who was dynamite – a general in the technology division of China's Ministry of State Security. His name was Zhao Mingqiu. He was in charge of over three hundred technical spies, all focused on space warfare, but over the last ten years he'd developed doubts. There was also some hostility toward the government. A cousin of his had been arrested and disappeared. And he found the work he was tasked with increasingly troubling. It took two years for us to get close to him, another year to gain his trust. But when he began to deliver, it was a gold mine. Let's walk.'

Latham glanced over his shoulder as they set off. They walked along a barbed-wire fence beside a thin, brackish flow of oily water.

'He was code-named Counsellor. We paid him hundreds of thousands of pounds and he was worth a lot more. The only question was how to get regular intelligence off him while keeping him alive and out of the camps. We couldn't see how to establish secure procedures while he remained in his position. Then we heard about Jerry Lau – saw he was in trouble, that he might be open to an offer: someone mobile who we could both access. Zhao thought if we could get receivers onto Lau's ships, he'd be able to transfer data and we could collect it at our leisure. Like a dead drop. It was a brilliant idea. I approached Lau and we were in operation a couple of months later.'

Latham paused as the woods thinned and the blank walls of an industrial estate appeared on the far side of the water. When he was sure they were still alone, he continued.

'For over a year General Zhao was our most important agent in China. We had twenty specialist officers dedicated to processing the product he brought in: Chinese research, weapons systems, command structures, but also the details of their intelligence penetration of the West, what they knew about us. And that was where the problems began.

'We started seeing highly sensitive US documents coming up, ones the Chinese had acquired. These were classified beyond anything I'd encountered before – memos that weren't even to be seen by their Congress or senior Defence Department officials. They pertained to a program code-named Ptolemy. It was huge, and entirely off the books, involving thousands of men and women, most of them employed by private contractors rather than the military, hidden in places like Quartz Hill, Palmdale.'

'Lake Ravenna.'

'Lake Ravenna, yes.' He glanced toward her. 'You know about it?'

'I know it connects somehow. What are they doing there?'

'Preparing for war in space. As we got passed more details about these places, it became clear we were seeing a shadow space programme under the command of the Pentagon. It was pulling in five times as much funding as NASA itself. What have you heard about Lake Ravenna?' he asked.

'I came across a Jack Moretti, a psychologist who worked there. My officer on Ascension was looking into him. Does the name mean anything to you?'

'No. Is he on Ascension now?'

'He died about eleven years ago. But there are connections between his death and the death of my colleague.'

Latham frowned.

'What would he have been doing at Lake Ravenna?' Taylor asked.

'I imagine he would have been working with military astro-nauts, the crews of a space defence force. Lake Ravenna was where a lot of this research began. NASA staff would disappear off the books, maybe reappear years later with some private aerospace company. In the intervening time they were based at Lake Ravenna. They developed strategies for space combat, the vehicles and weaponry involved, everything from putting arms depots on the moon to the use of particle accelerators, space planes, kinetic bombardment, you name it. More recently it's been about exploiting the existing infrastructure up there. Disguised weapons. What Zhao saw emerging from the offices of commer-cial space companies in the West were designs that bore a strange resemblance to those he'd originally seen in development as defence systems. These were companies receiving a lot of political and financial support. That's where I first came across Quadrant.'

Latham stopped for breath. He wasn't well, Taylor realised. He looked pale and she'd noticed a slight limp begin to affect his walk. Latham asked if she had any water and when she said she didn't he took another moment before continuing.

'The documents I saw involved the movement of several million dollars to Quadrant's debris programme coinciding with new fears over China and Russia's ability to knock out satellites. There was a big push around that time to ensure space became the new war-fighting domain. A new emphasis on establishing pre-eminence up there. The Pentagon was hijacked by space hawks, and anyone who objected was moved away. A similar thing happened over here. Vast amounts of off-the-books defence spending was redirected to the companies involved.'

'Quadrant are military?'

'If they need to be. The backbone of Ptolemy is a security net hung across several players. Quadrant come with wide-reaching orbital surveillance hooked up to an automated response system. Their technique for cleaning up space is to capture defunct satellites and drag them down to the earth's atmosphere, where they get burned up, incinerator-style. But obviously you can do that with a live satellite, too. You can do it with anything. Most importantly they brought Ascension with them. Those at the top of the Ptolemy program channelled millions to Quadrant as a way of securing control of the island. There's going to be some big changes on Ascension over the next couple of years.'

'Why Ascension?'

'Because there's nowhere like it. You see, when the Chinese saw the plans coming out of Lake Ravenna, they shifted a lot of their research toward stealth technology. Zhao got us details of some ingenious means they'd devised of making military satellites disappear using mirrored surfaces or the earth's shadow, even merging microweapons with debris clouds. It was jaw-dropping. But it meant the defensive focus on both sides moved toward increasingly sophisticated surveillance.'

They reached a muddy clearing beside the river, with a graffitied bench and the burnt-out carcass of a motorbike half hidden by brambles. Latham stopped, leaned against the back of the bench.

'In 2017 there was an incident where an American satellite was disabled in a co-orbital attack. Officially it was a data relay satellite, but it had inspection equipment for spying on other craft, which was one reason they weren't able to publicise what happened. It had been shadowing the Chinese space station Tiangong-1 when an unidentified object approached, latched on, and tilted it toward the sun. All the instruments burned out within seconds. At least, that's what they guessed happened. The incident occurred in a blind spot directly over the South Atlantic, and no one could see. The Chinese knew exactly what they were doing and had timed it perfectly.

'In the next few months a lot of attention got directed to Ascension Island, because its telescopes covered the blind spot. Whoever's got Ascension would have the only comprehensive space surveillance system on earth. The US documents that Zhao was bringing us began to show back-channel discussions about bringing the UK into Ptolemy. Then we started seeing the names of colleagues coming up. And suddenly we were spying on ourselves – or, at least, on the corner of MI6 and the British government backing this scheme.'

'Gabriel Skinner.'

'He was one of the main ones. But he wasn't alone.'

'How were the Chinese getting all this?'

'That's the point. It became a very big question for us. When we saw what the Chinese had on American space defence, on Ptolemy, there was a lot of debate within Six about how to proceed. Protocol was to hand over to Washington, step discreetly away, lips sealed. But we decided that identifying the source of the leaks could give us some serious standing. And I knew that if we handed it over, we'd lose our chance. Done wrong and they'd go to ground, then the opportunity's lost forever. If someone has managed to get that level of access, they're exceptionally skilled, exceptionally well concealed. They'd been in place for years, which meant years of cover above them.

'So, we did our own search. We knew this depth of intelligence wasn't the product of hacking. They had someone close to the programme. And we put everything into establishing who they were. Was it possible there was a mole at the heart of the Pentagon? Could they be in the new Space Force itself? The problem was that Zhao had no idea, because the source wasn't being run by the Chinese. New intel came in after high-level meetings in Moscow: China-Russia meetings. That changed things, but it made sense. We knew there'd been a Soviet unit dedicated to infiltrating the US space programme right up until the collapse of the Soviet Union. China has the technical superiority now, but Russia still has the deep network of human assets. It looked like there was some kind of trade-off. So we began thinking along these lines. We redirected attention toward the Russian agencies, pulled in expertise from the Russia desk. That was when we started hearing about Gemstone.'

Latham eased himself away from the bench and they set off again, this time away from the river, deeper into woods.

'Back in 2011, the Russian desk had managed to bug a negotiation in Minsk between senior Chinese and Russian officials in which they refer to an asset by the codename Gemstone. From what was discussed it seemed Gemstone was a Russian spy, central to an intelligence-sharing arrangement. Russians needed access to Chinese space research. They could see the Chinese space programme was going to overtake their own in a matter of years. But they had this card to play: an officer who could supply regular, detailed intelligence on Ptolemy.

276

'But who were they? And where were they? We spent three months trying to sniff out Gemstone, then got the result that gave us as many problems as it did solutions. Early last year Gemstone sent through a report with high-urgency status. It included a photograph showing British officials meeting senior US commanders on Ascension, and it included speculation that they'd been in discussions regarding the future of the island. So now we knew Gemstone was probably on Ascension – they'd been able to photograph this event but hadn't been part of the group that travelled over. But we also knew, thanks to him, that the UK was preparing to join the US in an exclusive space defence programme. We asked around and couldn't find anyone who would admit to this. So what had we discovered?

'A month later, the RAF took on command and control of all UK military space operations. We began pulling away from the European Space Agency. Big changes were afoot. According to Gemstone's report, the officials he'd seen were discussing the possibility of making Ascension a high-security command site, central to a ground-based space surveillance system.'

'When exactly was this meeting on the island?' Taylor asked.

'About eighteen months ago. As far as I'm aware it's still going ahead. Ascension will connect to observatories in Hawaii, New Mexico, Alaska, and the Marshall Islands.'

The sun came out, catching them in an incongruous mesh of golden shards. Latham shielded his eyes. Taylor tried to process what she'd heard so far. The scale of it all was breathtaking, the implication and stakes involved.

'Then what happened? You raised this with superiors?'

'We knew we had to hand over. Spying on the Americans is one thing, spying on ourselves ... We were instructed to deny ever seeing any of it, of course. To erase records.'

'Did they fire you?'

'No, I left of my own accord.' Latham stopped among the trees and looked at Taylor. 'When I first began meeting with Zhao, we discovered we were the same age. We talked about our memory of the moon landing, both young boys, both fascinated by it. What an extraordinary achievement. Do you know what people said at the time? We did it. And they meant humans, as a species. Everyone.' He shook his head. 'That was one of the main reasons Zhao felt compelled to work for us. He thought China was going too far. I promised him that the risks he took would help us keep space peaceful. I think even then I knew I was lying.'

Latham looked away. Now his infirmity seemed born of a more emotional breakage, a collapse of his moral centre.

'I objected to the whole direction of policy,' he said. 'Because I also believed we were at a dangerous crossroads. It wasn't an argument that was going to be had. By that point, I'd done my time.'

'And Gemstone?'

'Gemstone was never identified. I was called back a few months after leaving and questioned by a team from the US. They clearly hadn't made any progress. I know the Space Force turned themselves inside out, even fired a few people. I'm sure they changed all their passwords too. And it's true, the leaks stopped for a bit. But that's what you'd expect. Do they have the skills for a mole hunt? No. Due to Ptolemy's unique sensitivity they weren't prepared to draw on established resources or expertise. A supposedly select handful of security officers blundered in. All they achieved was to alert the Chinese that someone had been leaking from their side. And the Chinese were more successful in their hunt. Zhao was executed by firing squad last year. Now they've come for Jerry Lau.'

Latham stared through the trees. Taylor allowed him a moment's reflection, but she had her own potential tragedies to avert and needed to keep him focused on the present.

'I think Gemstone killed my officer there.'

'I suspect you're right.'

'Did you ever establish any identifying details for them?'

'None.'

The obscurity was maddening. But this in itself told her a lot. Spies operating successfully deep behind enemy lines for more than a decade were a rare breed. It took years to train them, years for them to get into position. In that time they might do nothing but live their cover. She remembered being talked through the principles during training: placing someone so that they grew with their environment, ready to be activated after a decade or more. These were already antiquated skills at the time, belonging to a world where you knew who you were targeting one month to the next. The art of living deep. But at some point, you had to deliver. That was the pinch point: contacting your handlers. Somewhere in their life there had to be that umbilical cord, or the whole thing was for nothing.

'How does Gemstone transfer information from the island?' Taylor asked.

'It's a good question. Ascension's too remote to be passing anything physically on a regular basis, so Gemstone must have a communications setup. We wanted to assess all radio signals, but with the amount going on there, it proved impossible. I think Gemstone has an advanced system hidden somewhere, well away from the bases.' Latham shook his head regretfully. 'I reckon we were a few weeks away from uncovering them.'

'How did HQ react when you told them you'd been seeing Ptolemy documents?'

'I was told to forget it all, of course. The following week I got a call from the Russian desk suggesting that someone I'd crossed paths with in Moscow had put a price on my head. The message was clear enough: Speak out about this and everything is in place to have you silenced.'

'Jesus.'

'You can see why I'm concerned about you turning up here. People who know a lot less than what I've just told you have been killed for the sake of protecting Ptolemy.'

He shook his head and sighed.

'If you have an officer on the island, Gemstone will know. If they pose any threat to him, they will be killed. I think Gemstone's almost out of time, and they're going to be easily panicked.'

'Why? What did you mean, earlier, when you asked if this was connected to what's happening today?'

'As soon as I saw what was going on, I thought of Ascension. I wondered if someone was going to turn up, try to drag me back in.'

'Saw *what* going on?'

'The ship.' He looked at her, bemused. 'Have you not seen? The Russian ship in the South Atlantic.'

TWENTY-NINE

Kane drove Connor back to the US base. It was almost four a.m., but the island wasn't sleeping tonight. The guards at the base were out in force, which meant more torchlight in his face. Then they saw his passenger.

'It's Connor,' one of the guards shouted. 'He's here.'

'Thank Christ for that. Straight through, buddy. Follow me.'

One of the guards jumped into a Jeep and drove in front of Kane, leading him past long barracks buildings, a smattering of beige huts, and a grassless softball field with bleachers and a chain-link fence. There was a second guard post before they reached an area with detached cabins, pebbled grounds, and artificial-looking shrubs. Married quarters. Officers' quarters.

At the sound of the vehicles, Connor's mother appeared in her doorway. She ran to clasp Connor as he got out.

'Oh, thank God. Oh, Jesus. Come in.'

She told Kane to come in too. The guard wheeled away with a salute.

A lot of effort had gone in to making the cabin feel like a family home. There were shelves of CDs, magazines, ornaments. Carina's toys and dolls cluttered the floor, and the dining table was filled with picture books. Still the artificial light seemed harsh after the darkness.

'Where were you?' Anne said.

Connor looked nervous.

'He was up by the old NASA station,' Kane said.

'Connor, what the hell . . . ' She turned to Kane. 'Did the police let you go?'

'Not exactly. I had a bad feeling about the NASA station, so I headed up there. Of my own accord, so to speak. There's a good chance police still want to speak to me and will come after me.'

'They said Lauren Carter's clothes were at your place.'

'Yes. I don't know why. I don't know what's going on but it's nothing to do with me.'

'The bastards,' Anne said.

'Has there been any word of Lauren?'

'Not that I'm aware of.'

'What about Thomas? Last I saw he was getting in a situation with the British authorities.'

'They've released him. He should be home any minute.'

Connor went to the bathroom. Kane heard him being sick. Anne made some calls, came back, shaking her head grimly.

'No sign of her yet,' she said. 'Listen, I think we're going to try to leave here, get off this island . . . '

The front door opened and Thomas appeared, silhouetted against the headlights of the vehicle that had dropped him off.

'Edward,' he said.

'Are you okay?'

'Just about. There are people going crazy looking for you.'

'I could do with lying low for a while.'

Thomas looked to his wife.

'They won't come on here,' Anne said.

'Not for now.'

Anne went and spoke to the uniformed men outside. Kane heard them address her as 'ma'am.' She returned.

'They say there's a stolen vehicle here.'

'That's me. You can tell them to take it.' Kane gave her the keys.

Anne looked at them as if she was about to say something, then went and passed them to the men outside.

'We can stall them, at least,' she said, shutting the door.

'Where did you go?' Thomas said.

'He found Connor up at Devil's Ashpit,' Anne said.

Thomas took a deep breath: 'Looking for Lauren.'

'That's right. What do you know about the place?' Kane said.

'I know the kids have always said there's something odd up there, and when Petra went missing, I told the police they should take a look. Which I don't believe they ever did.'

'I want to take a closer look myself,' Kane said. 'But I need metal-cutting tools.'

'There's no way you're getting back out there tonight. You won't get much farther than the gates of the base. Seriously, they're all over this place. What happened at Devil's Ashpit?'

'We went in,' Connor said, appearing from the bathroom.

'Into the old control building?'

'We went in and there's a basement or something. That's really secured. Edward thinks we should look there.'

'I think it's worth checking out,' Kane said.

'I told you,' Connor said.

'Okay. Tell me about this basement.'

'My guess is there's extensive underground space,' Kane said. 'Someone's locked the access hatch but used it recently. I've got a bad feeling about it.'

'Fuck. What would you need to get in?'

'Something heavy-duty. Ideally an oxy-fuel torch. Maybe a circular saw or angle grinder.'

Thomas nodded, thoughtful.

'I can give it a try,' he said.

Anne frowned. 'Using what?'

'There's a plasma torch in the boat hut. There's a hacksaw, too. It's worth a shot.'

'You'd go back to Georgetown now? That's crazy.'

'Everyone's by the police station. The port's empty.'

'On your own?'

'You can't go alone,' Kane said.

'No one's looking for me. And whoever's responsible won't be up there now. Not if it's been entered. If Lauren's there . . . Fuck.'

'Thomas, are you sure?' Anne said. 'I can come.'

'What about Carina?'

'What *about* me?'

They turned to see the girl in the doorway to her bedroom. She wore pyjamas, held a stuffed toy.

'Go back to bed, sweet pea. It's the middle of the night.'

'Daddy.' Carina walked over to her father. He picked her up.

'Everything's okay.'

But the girl sensed something and began to cry.

'Who's the person?' she said, pointing at Kane.

'You remember Edward. We met him by the beach yesterday. He's a friend.'

'Hey, Carina,' Kane said.

The girl hid her face against her father's shoulder.

'How might you be getting off the island?' Kane said.

'There's a plane going to Florida tomorrow night,' Anne said. 'I don't know if we can get you on it too, if that's something you need. It may be your best option.' Anne gazed at her daughter's back, deep in contemplation. Then a radio transceiver on the kitchen table crackled into life and she picked it up, walking away.

'Command, this is Alpha 1.' She stepped into the kitchen, came back a few seconds later.

'I'm going to have to go in,' she said grimly.

'At this time?' Thomas said.

'Yeah, at this time.'

'What's going on?'

284

'Issues. I can be back in an hour.'

'Well, I need to take a look at Devil's Ashpit before it starts getting light.'

'I can keep an eye on things,' Kane said.

'Are you sure?' Anne said. 'I won't be too long.'

It wasn't the worst option, he reasoned. He needed means of communication to alert Taylor to the tracking station and the new territory he'd found himself on. From Kane's experience of US bases there'd be decent internet – both laptops around and public PCs. Maybe a free phone. Maybe something in the Lindgrens' cabin. And then? The police and Administrator were a problem. His total absence of trust in them was a problem. Most of the potential plans of action involved revealing that he was more than an academic. He needed at least three men, armed, who would take orders that superseded those of the police and possibly any senior military personnel. That might involve establishing an autonomous chain of command from the UK.

Carina was howling now. 'Don't go, Daddy.'

'I've got to go do something, sweetheart. I'll be back.' He handed the girl over to her mother. 'I'm not wasting another moment. Where's this entrance to the basement?' he asked Kane.

'There's a door off the largest room, in the centre of the building, marked with an electrical hazard sign. The hatch is on the other side.'

'Okay. I'll be back, one way or another.'

Thomas left. Connor watched him go, then went into the bathroom and ran a shower.

'Don't get the bandage wet,' Anne called. There was no reply. She swore, set her daughter down.

'I need to throw some clothes on.'

She went to the bedroom. It looked like the girl was about to cry again. Kane crouched, took a pencil from his pocket.

'Seen anyone bend a pencil before?'

She shook her head.

'First you try.'

She had a go, and then he took the pencil back and showed her the trick. She asked to check the pencil again.

'You're a Brit,' she said, sniffing, as if this explained his magic powers.

'That's right. Where are you from?'

'Here.'

'That's a special place to be from. I like your name.'

'It means stars.'

'Your name?'

'Look.'

She held out a hand and led him to the dining table.

'Put the chair by the shelves,' she said. He moved a chair to the bookshelf, and she stood on it and retrieved a pair of binoculars.

'Now put the chair by the window.'

'Are you allowed to use those?'

'They're mine.'

Kane set the chair up by the window. She climbed up and peered through the binoculars. Then she confessed: 'I don't know which one it is. Carina is up there. A million light-years away. It's a consolation.'

'A constellation?'

'Yes.'

'How many miles is a light-year?' Kane asked.

'A million million miles.'

'A long way.'

She offered him the binoculars. 'See if you can find it.' Her mother returned while he was searching the night sky. Anne Lindgren was in uniform now: a dark blue officer's uniform, but not like any he'd seen before. She saw Kane notice it and raised her eyebrows as if to say: *Well, this is me. This is the work outfit.*

'I was showing him my consolation,' the girl said.

'Very good. You go back to bed, or you'll be falling asleep all day tomorrow. And we might have some packing to do.' Anne checked the clock. It was half past four. Thomas had been gone fifteen minutes. Ten to drive to Georgetown, another ten to retrieve the equipment if he was lucky, then what?

'Is he contactable?' Kane asked.

'No.'

Kane listened for sirens. The night had quietened. Even the helicopter was down. If Thomas never returned? If those responsible ganged up to stop him in some way? Anne could establish US military support, perhaps. A few men at least. They might have to override the Administrator. That was going to get lively.

Anne took her daughter to the bedroom and re-emerged a moment later, closing the door quietly behind her.

'She's in bed, and she knows she's supposed to stay there. Thank you so much for this. I'll be right back. Connor?' Anne called through the bathroom door. 'I have to pop out. Edward's here. Try to get some rest. Connor?'

'I heard.'

'I'll see what I can do about the flight,' she said to Kane.

'Okay.'

Kane watched through the front window as Anne Lindgren walked deeper into the base. What was that uniform? The shower was still running. He started searching for a phone or computer he could use, but something caught his eye in Connor's room.

The room was closest to the front door, messy with what you'd expect: clothes, comics, some sketchpads and paints. Beside the bed was a framed photograph of a man holding a certificate, a boy beside him, both squinting into sunlight. This was what Kane had seen. He walked in, picked it up. The pair were outside, in front of a windowless building with manicured lawns. To their left, white letters on a curved brick wall spelled

FLIGHT RESEARCH TEST CENTRE. To the right was a sculpture of a rocket.

The boy was visibly Connor, aged five or six: grinning widely. Kane didn't recognise the man. He had his free hand on Connor's shoulder and was smiling, with neatly parted black hair, sideburns. He had Connor's deep-set eyes. Kane read the certificate: *The Association for Military Research Distinguished Scientific Award.* It was inscribed to Dr Jack Moretti.

'My dad,' Connor said.

Kane turned. Connor came into the room, a towel around his bare shoulders, a pair of jeans on. 'My real dad,' the boy clarified, with a grimace.

'It's a nice photo,' Kane said, processing this new information fast: recasting Thomas as a stepfather, reaching for its significance.

'Thanks.'

'Where is this?'

'California.'

Connor threw the towel onto the bed and found a T-shirt to pull on. Kane returned the picture to the bedside table.

'Where is he now?'

'He died when I was five.'

'I'm sorry.'

The boy shrugged, sat down on the bed. Kane thought back to Taylor's message. Rory had been interested in Jack Moretti just before he died. Taylor had said Moretti hanged himself a decade ago. One of the last messages the engineer had sent included his name. *What happened to Jack Moretti?* Had Rory seen the photo? Why did he think it was important?

'Where in California?' Kane asked.

'Where he worked.'

'Can I ask what happened?'

Connor stared at him.

288

'That's what Rory asked,' he said, finally.

'When?'

'When he was here.'

Kane watched the boy. He felt something slowly shifting in the fabric of the reality around him.

'What was he doing here?' he said.

'He'd come around sometimes. Him and Thomas were friends.'

'Really?' Kane tried to remember how Thomas had spoken about Rory. Not as a friend, that was for sure.

'He killed himself,' Connor said.

'Rory?'

'My dad.'

Kane glanced at the photo again. 'He looks like a nice person.'

'He was.'

A lot of images stirred in Kane's mind, prominent among them Anne's uniform, the windowless Flight Research Test Centre, and Thomas gazing across the Dew Pond on Green Mountain.

Kane returned to the living room, looked at other photos: in frames, on the shelves, in piles beside the books. He found Anne and Thomas's wedding, in a garden of some kind, a young Connor in attendance not looking much older than he did in the photograph by his bed. There were photos of Anne in her twenties, Anne pregnant among the surreal peaks of Ascension, then Carina as a baby surrounded by US Air Force personnel. There was a map of Finland with the Finnish flag in the top right corner.

'How did your mum meet Thomas?'

'Some green group.'

'Can you remember its name?'

'Antelope Valley Conservation, I think. They were involved in that a lot when I was little. When we were in California.'

'Weird question: Any idea which of them joined it first?'

Connor looked at Kane, puzzled. 'No.'

'Was it before your dad died?'

'Why?' he said.

'No reason. Just curious. Sorry.'

But something about this question had unsettled the boy. He wouldn't take his eyes off Kane now.

'Forget it,' Kane said. He looked out of the living room window, at the identical cabins, artificial-looking plants, the moon almost touching the horizon. He felt the boy watching him intently.

'Thomas said there are parties on this island,' Kane said. 'Secret ones. You saw one once and the Administrator's car was there. Does that sound right?'

'Not really.'

'No?'

'Everything was pretty normal until Petra went missing.'

'No invite-only parties? Guys messing around with young girls?'

'No. Why? Did Thomas say that?'

Kane went back to the photos and searched through them again, found one of a young and strikingly confident Anne Lindgren sitting in front of a round, triple-layered window, smiling at the camera. It looked like she was on an airplane, with the moon visible through the glass. There was something odd about the image, though. When Kane looked closer he saw it wasn't the moon – it was Planet Earth behind her. She was in space, and the earth hung in darkness over her shoulder. On the back, it said: *To Thomas. Maybe one day you'll come up here with me and we can watch the sunrise sixteen times a day.*

Kane replaced the photo, feeling a mixture of wonder and dread. He turned slowly back to Connor.

'What does your mum do on the base exactly?' Kane asked.

'Something important. I don't know exactly.'

'Important and secret, I guess.'

'That's why we have to be here.'

'Right.'

Kane went and checked on Carina. She lay very still in the dark with her eyes open.

'Where's Mom?' she said, without looking at him.

'She'll be back soon.'

Kane took the binoculars from the living room and returned to the boy's bedroom.

'I need to go and take a quick look at something. Are you able to keep an eye on Carina?'

There was no response. 'Are you okay?' Kane said.

Connor lifted the picture of his father and studied it. He looked up at Kane as if there was a question he wanted to ask but couldn't begin to formulate.

'I'll be back in one minute,' Kane said.

He walked away from the cabin, deeper into the base, in the direction Anne Lindgren had walked. It was the indigo hour before dawn, the sky beginning to pale at the edges. The base was all electronically monitored, Kane saw now. He would be stopped eventually, but he could say he was lost. Some of his association with Anne Lindgren would linger. And he wanted to see as much as possible while he could.

He passed a canteen, an officers' mess, and headquarters buildings. Then the domed observatory appeared in the distance, its shutters opening.

Kane walked toward it, watching as the dome rotated. What was it looking at? Who did it belong to? A few hundred metres before the observatory he got to a fence. Alongside the No Entry signs was a crest: UNITED STATES SPACE FORCE – WHERE SPACE SUPERIORITY BEGINS.

He lifted the binoculars. He could see signs of rapid recent construction, including cameras and sensors securing the telescope but also several new arrays around it. The guard posts here also bore the Space Force logo. People were streaming into the surrounding buildings.

A security vehicle in the distance began to move toward him.

Kane turned, walking swiftly back toward the Lindgrens' bungalow. As he got closer, he saw Thomas's Buick parked outside. A second later he heard shouting, then Connor stormed out, jumped on his bike, and pedalled.

The security vehicle was behind him now. Kane looked over his shoulder. The man in the passenger seat had a submachine gun trained on him.

'Stop there, sir. Keep your hands out in front of you.'

Two men disembarked, both in black T-shirts, both with guns at the ready. They were young, but had the swaggering authority of special forces. Kane kept his hands away from his body.

'What are you doing here?' one of the men asked.

'I'm a friend of Thomas and Anne Lindgren's. I was just going to that cabin there.'

The fact that he was a visitor alarmed them. He saw their expressions stiffen. One radioed in a check.

'Sir, please turn around.'

He did as instructed.

'We're going to need to see some ID, sir. Don't take it out, just tell us where it is.'

Then someone shouted, 'Hey!' and they all turned to see Thomas leaving the house with Carina in his arms. 'Hey,' he shouted at the guards. 'Wait.' He put the girl in the car and marched over.

'What's going on? This man just saved our son.'

'Step away, sir. This is not your business.'

'Not my business?'

'Mr Lindgren, sir ... '

'This is absolutely my business.'

Thomas reached into his jacket and pulled a Glock 19. That added a new element.

'Get into the car,' he said to Kane, gun on the security. The officers hesitated. Kane contemplated his fates. Arrest by US special forces was a cul-de-sac: game over. He climbed into Thomas's SUV.

'What's happening?' Carina said from the back seat.

'Good question, Carina. I don't know, but I'm sure everything's going to be okay.'

Thomas got in the driver's seat and started the engine, still holding the gun. He accelerated away and Kane turned to see the two guards standing there, both on their radios.

'What did they want with you?' Thomas asked.

'I think they were just being cautious. I appreciate the intervention.'

'They're not arresting you on my watch. Not after everything you've done.'

Thomas sped toward the front gates.

'Did you get to the tracking station?' Kane asked.

'Someone's set it on fire. I got there but it was too late.'

'Do the police know?'

'I think so.'

'Where are you going now?'

'Georgetown.'

'What's in Georgetown?'

'You'll see.'

THIRTY

The ship that had drawn Ian Latham's attention was the *Yantar*. It was what the Russians referred to as a research vessel and every other nation called an intelligence collection ship. It had been seen making erratic manoeuvres off the coast of Brazil the previous night. According to CNN, it wasn't using running lights or responding to communication from other vessels. The manoeuvres had taken it rapidly into the South Atlantic, in the direction of Ascension Island. It looked like it was armed.

Taylor left Latham a few streets from his home and drove away fast, searching for updates, but the story had suddenly been removed from the news, which made her very worried indeed.

She tried Kudus's line. She needed to find Gemstone. They were on Ascension, had been low-lying for years, maybe decades, with privileged access to state secrets. A situation like that was as high risk as can be and could explain the events that had happened – and suggested a lot more trouble to come.

Eventually Kudus answered.

'Did you find Ian Latham?'

'Yes. What's the situation your end?'

'We've got some developments.'

'The ship.'

'Yes.'

'Know anything about it?'

'No. Just that every department's been chased for relevant

insight. And there's some kind of communications blackout on Ascension. The technical team are in. It seems serious.'

'What kind of communications blackout?'

'I don't know. Maybe electronic jamming of some kind. Started around the time the boat began to approach.'

'That was around the time Lauren Carter went missing. What's she got to do with a Russian ship?'

'I've asked to be kept in the loop. Where are you? I heard there are police at your place.'

'Really?'

'Yeah.'

'I'm driving. Any update on Elliot?'

'He's not in custody anymore. The impression I get is that he escaped.'

'Oh, shit. Where is he?'

'According to what we've picked up from the island, he's on the US base with a family: people called Thomas and Anne Lindgren. It's not clear what role they have on the base, but the Ascension police don't have jurisdiction, so they're waiting for him to either leave or for some authority to grant them access.'

'See who Thomas and Anne Lindgren are, and if we can establish any kind of contact with them. I also want to know if there's a procedure in place for evacuating the island and how it's initiated – the Overseas Territories Department would be able to tell you. We need to think about involving Special Operations as well. There's an SAS unit on the Falklands. I think we'd have grounds to drop them in, but C would need to authorise. Get Special Ops informed of the state of play.' This was reserved for the most extreme of circumstances, but Taylor figured that was where they'd arrived.

'What did Ian Latham say?' Kudus asked.

'We've got the strong possibility of a Russian agent on the island, living deep cover, possibly within a space defence programme. So we need staff lists, previous security vetting files, everyone who's travelled on and off the island in the last few years. That includes as many working on the US base as possible. Try to access private contractor databases as well. Get security clearance lists for the bases, with dates and roles: air force, NASA, CIA. You wanted to risk your career, now's your chance.'

She checked the map, dialled the contact number for Markus Fischer.

'I have something for you, but I need help.'

'Know about the current situation in the Atlantic?'

'I have some ideas.'

'Can you get to West London?'

'I can get to the river. I want to stay where the roads are clear and I can see what's going on. Meet me at the south side of Wandsworth Bridge in an hour. Park by the Alma Hotel. If you think you've been tailed, drive by. I'll see you. We'll rethink.'

'Okay.'

'I need somewhere I can use a secure phone line and get internet access.'

'I can get you that.'

Taylor put the radio on news as she drove. Nothing on the BBC yet. The prime minister had had to pull out of an appearance at a new hospital. That meant an emergency meeting was under way. Things were moving quickly.

Fischer was already in place when she arrived, waiting in a BMW with tinted windows. He had an earpiece in. Taylor climbed into the passenger seat, saw another car pull out behind them as they began to drive. Fischer registered her concern.

'It's ours. We get an escort. You're a VIP now.'

'You think we might get jumped?'

'I think it's possible.' They swerved between traffic.

'What's the current situation in the South Atlantic?' Taylor said.

'Tense. Your people are going a bit crazy about this ship. Meanwhile something's very screwy on Ascension Island itself. You heard about that?'

'Some kind of signals disruption.'

'Right. Is it connected to the ship?'

'Possibly. If I can establish contact with my colleague in Vauxhall, I may be able to get you more.'

Fischer made a call in rapid German, then pulled a U-turn and tore toward the city. He didn't speak again until they got to Bishopsgate, where he stopped suddenly, double-parked, climbed out. She scrambled to follow.

'We're here,' he said, handing the car keys to a man on the pavement, who climbed in and had the BMW moving again before Taylor knew what was happening. 'Follow me.' Fischer led her into the marble foyer of what a glossy sign announced as MARWITZ-LEYEN PRIVATBANKIERS. They took an unmarked door off the foyer into a long corridor with oil paintings to a second door with a suited man in front of it. Taylor glimpsed a holster as he touched his thumb to the keypad at the side, then entered a pin. The door slid open. Fischer led her down a more austere corridor to a windowless boardroom, where a man and a woman sat before an array of communication devices: an older man in suspenders, a woman with a blond bob. As the door clicked closed behind her, Taylor saw it was a secure communications facility with radio frequency shielding on the walls. The intelligence officers looked at Taylor, but none seemed surprised by her presence. The man nodded.

On the screens were connections with the federal intelligence service HQ in central Berlin and the German embassy in Belgravia.

'The Foreign Office scheduled a six p.m. call with the White House,' the woman said. 'They will discuss whether to strike.'

Fischer glanced at Taylor, looking uncharacteristically tense.

He checked the monitors, then gestured for Taylor to sit down. Then he brought up aerial footage of the ship.

'The *Yantar*, usually found in the port of Severomorsk, attached to Russia's Northern Fleet. But we've seen it before in the Caribbean, usually near Cuba or Trinidad and Tobago, just outside of sovereign waters. Recently it's been sailing off the coast of Brazil. The size and the extensive array of sensors suggests it's purpose-built for signals intelligence gathering. But it's also armed with what look like two close-in weapon systems and what may be a surface-to-air missile launcher. Six hours ago it changed course, headed directly for Ascension Island.'

The Germans had data from NATO's Brussels HQ. The signals analysts there had picked up some mysterious communication between the island and this ship. It looked like a radio burst of some kind, coinciding with the ship's redirection.

'And there's some kind of interference on the island itself,' Taylor said.

'Yes, signals jamming. It looks like something's disrupted a lot of the electronic kit, possibly to allow the *Yantar* to do whatever it needs to do. Which no one can guess at.'

'Could someone on the island trigger all this themselves?'

'Possibly. The jammers are operating at the same frequency as other satellite communication systems to block their signals. It's basically thrown a bubble around the island, meaning external communications are down. We've seen devices as small as a briefcase that could have that effect, if there was someone in place to operate it.'

'What does the UK think?'

'That it's preparation for an attack. A Royal Navy patrol ship has been dispatched to shadow the *Yantar*, supported by air cover from the Falklands. US satellites are watching closely. But there's movement beyond this particular theatre.' He pointed to another map. 'We're seeing US carriers shifting deployment from the Middle East toward the Pacific. Activity around Maui, in particular, but also the Marshall Islands.'

'They all host space surveillance infrastructure,' Taylor said. 'Telescopes, observatories.'

Fischer nodded, studied the map again. 'That fits.'

'Fits what?'

'Your government is leaning toward the theory that there's going to be an all-out assault on their space capability – on the ground and in orbit. The relevant military and intelligence figures have been called into the Whitehall crisis centre. The attorney general's been asked to advise on the legality of any military actions. Our friends at the Free Space Foundation have turned up, advising the government directly now. Lawyers are working on the legal grounds for any first strike up there.'

He passed the printout of an email from the FSF to the Attorney General's Office, from Professor Adrienne York:

While it remains a cornerstone of the 1967 Space Act that use of space has to be peaceful, this does not override Article 51 of the UN Charter: 'Nothing shall impair the right of individual or collective self-defence.'

'They've used this before,' Fischer said. 'Does peace mean nonmilitary, or just nonaggressive. If they can frame a first strike as necessary for self-defence, then the belief is that it's justified. That all depends on a lot of clarity we're not getting right now. This is a nightmare approaching fast and we need you to think if there's anything you can do.'

'Show me the signal that came from Ascension.'

He passed over what they had. The data was raw, but Taylor could discern the spike representing the call-out to the ship. It looked like a beacon burst, an emergency signal. She'd been trained on devices that released a similar signal, to call in backup in the case of imminent death or discovery. They used it as a last resort for the really hairy jobs.

'It's a rescue signal. I think it's from an intelligence officer in trouble.'

'Someone already on the island?'

'Yes, that's what I believe. The ship is on a rescue mission. The officer's been under deep cover, but they're blown. The signals blackout is to allow for their escape. This is a manoeuvre to retrieve them before they fall into the wrong hands.'

'Does Vauxhall know any of this?'

'I doubt it.'

'All the noises from the MOD suggest they believe the sabotage is external, coming from off the island, possibly from the boat itself.'

He passed over copies of recent governmental cables – both UK and US – all pushing for intervention: Downing Street, British Forces South Atlantic Islands, the US Department of Defence's Combatant Command. Taylor looked through, checking the data they were drawing on, just to be sure of her own theory. Could she be missing something? The officer responsible for a lot of the instructions from the US side was a General Anne Lindgren. The name caught Taylor's eye. It was Kane's host.

'This woman,' she said. 'Do you know anything about her?'

'We believe she heads the Space Force over there,' Fischer said. 'Seems hawkish, ready to get their retaliation in first.'

'My officer on the island was with her,' Taylor said, puzzled. 'Anne Lindgren was sheltering him last night.'

It was starting to seem more than coincidence, and she wondered how and why Kane had ended up in their home.

'Get me a phone line,' Taylor said.

Fischer brought a phone over. She called Kudus and he answered on the first ring.

'Where are you?' he said.

'Somewhere safe for now. Thomas and Anne Lindgren, the couple that were with Elliot – did you get anything?'

'Yes. Anne Lindgren. Google her. Take a look.'

She turned to Fischer. He'd already typed it in. His monitor showed a woman in a space suit, her youthful face behind the curve of an astronaut's helmet. It was on the NASA website.

'Born Anne O'Shea,' Kudus said. 'Doctorate in laboratory astrophysics from the University of Pennsylvania, then joined the Air Training Corps. She transferred to NASA's Johnson Space Centre in 1995 as part of the Mission Operations Directorate, where she was selected for the astronaut programme.'

According to the website, Anne Lindgren had earned herself five NASA Space Flight Medals, two Distinguished Service Medals, and the Legion of Merit. She flew on four Shuttle missions between 1998 and 2005, served aboard the International Space Station as a member of the Expedition 18 crew. Next seen working at Lake Ravenna. The website didn't specify what she was doing there, just that she served as a consultant.

'Consultant for a defence company,' Taylor said.

'Presumably,' Kudus said. The site carried an interview with her in which she spoke about life in space, how she enjoyed the peace, how chocolate tasted like wax, how she used to sleep strapped beneath the windows so that when she woke she saw the whole world floating before her.

'But look at the next paragraph,' Kudus said.

It was at Lake Ravenna that Anne met and married the government scientist Jack Moretti.

Fischer saw Taylor staring at the screen.

'Does this mean something to you?' he asked. The other BND officers had gathered around, sensing a breakthrough. Taylor logged in to her own emails, found Perryman's cache, the interview with Moretti's colleague.

Someone said his wife was having an affair. She worked there too.

Jack found out a few days before he killed himself. I think she married the other guy a few months later. Lake Ravenna's full of black tech, but I'm not sure there's anything mysterious about Jack Moretti's suicide.

Taylor no longer felt sure that the final statement followed from the rest.

'She remarried. She's with someone on the island. Who is he?' Taylor asked. 'What have we got on her current husband?'

'Thomas Lindgren,' Kudus said. 'We have a full CV from when he applied to work in the Ascension Conservation Department, plus a scan of his passport. Finnish, came to the US a couple of decades back, studied environmental sciences at the University of California, then worked various jobs: lab assistant, landscape gardener, some teaching work. They married in 2010, around the same time she goes into the military. I can't get her exact role, but it coincides with the development of the US Space Force. It looks like she was helping put it together. Went to Ascension six years ago.'

'Send me what you've got on Thomas Lindgren.'

Kudus sent it through. According to the CV, Thomas Lindgren had completed his course at the University of California, San Diego, then got a job with a company called Green Desert Landscape and Gardening. He remained in LA for several years, doing a combination of gardening, tuition, some delivery driving, and general maintenance. He moved out to the suburbs in 1997: Apple Valley, then Santa Clarita.

Taylor was bringing up the map when Kudus said: 'They're both near Lake Ravenna.'

'Right.'

There was banging in the background at Kudus's end.

'What's going on?' Taylor said.

'They're trying to get in.'

'Where are you?'

'Your office. I got the feeling I might be taken off duties very soon. I've blocked the door.'

'Are you okay?'

'So long as the door holds.'

Taylor read Thomas Lindgren's CV as a narrative now, testing it for logic. Aged twenty-nine, he moves to the States, qualifies as an environmental scientist, then works a series of menial jobs that allow him to geographically circulate one of the most sensitive defence research sites in the country ... She heard more banging, then an alert flashed up on the BND monitor: Three Chinese-flagged fishing vessels had been stopped approaching the Marshall Islands. The US Coast Guard was holding sixty crew members. Fischer swore, spoke with his colleagues to one side, then returned to the monitor.

'Daniel, are you still there?' Taylor said.

'I'm here,' Kudus said.

'What do we know about Thomas Lindgren's childhood?' she asked.

'We're not going to able to get confirmation of much before his time in the States,' Kudus said. 'Thomas Lindgren attended a school called Turku Upper Secondary. I've had a look and there was a fire there in 1990 and they lost all their predigital records.'

Taylor exchanged glances with Fischer. She felt suspicion becoming certainty now. This was classic tradecraft.

'They've cut my internet connection,' Kudus said, then the line went altogether.

'Check this man's passport photo against the Soviet archive,' Fischer said to his male colleague. Taylor knew that the Germans had the world's most extensive archive of Soviet-era personnel: two million comrades dating from 1916 to 1991, leaked, hacked, purchased under the counter. They called them *Das Geister*: the ghosts. In the last couple of years, they'd hooked that resource up to some pretty sharp facial recognition software. It took less than five seconds to get a match.

Fischer angled the screen toward her.

'What do you reckon?' he said.

Nikolai Pravik. Directorate S, Foreign Intelligence Service, 1979.

The young Soviet intelligence officer stared out defiantly. According to their directory, Pravik had joined the air service in 1985, attended Chelyabinsk Higher Military Aviation School. Recruited out for special training in sabotage and stay behind networks, then moved to the SVR, Russia's Foreign Intelligence Service, specifically Directorate S, which trained intelligence officers to work under deep cover. Then, as you'd expect, he disappeared.

Some years in Finland spent crafting Thomas Lindgren would have been standard practice, as was claiming an education at schools with no trace potential. Of the five to ten years you needed to establish adequate cover to be a sleeper agent, it was common to spend time in third countries building up your identity; muddying your background, blurring the tracks behind you. Remaking yourself before circling in.

'And he's married to General Anne Lindgren? Jesus Christ.'

They studied the images side by side.

'The ship's coming for him,' Taylor said. 'They want to get their man back home.'

'A lot of people think it's part of an attack.'

'I have to go in and explain, before this escalates further.'

'Where?'

'Where they are. Whitehall. Give me a car.'

'You won't get out again.'

'I'll help you expose this, Markus, I promise. I'll blow every whistle there is. But I'm going to have to do this first. Give me some transport. Let me go in.'

THIRTY-ONE

Kane gripped the dashboard as they sped away from the base. Thomas drove with a focused ferocity, gun against the wheel. His eyes flicked to the mirror every few seconds, checking the road, checking his daughter. They veered around potholes, jolting over the rough surface, airfield to the right, the expanse of cawing birds to the left.

Kane thought fast. Rory had a predilection for children's secrets. He also had a spy's training, alert to stories about Russians turning up where they shouldn't be. He must have looked a bit closer, connected it to the man who had befriended him, the husband of a US general working on something beyond top secret. Everything Thomas had said to Kane about the island was misdirection. He hadn't passed on what Connor knew about that night to the police, because he was the man at the tracking station. He killed Petra. And when he learned that Lauren had seen what happened, he'd silenced her, too.

The Buick's wheels slipped on gravel.

'Slow down, Daddy.'

'Don't worry, sweetheart. You got your seatbelt on?'

'Yes. Where are we going?'

'I told you. We're going sailing.'

Thomas moved the gun into his left hand to wipe the sweat from his right on his thigh. Kane's mind reeled as he tried to decide his next move. How many years had Thomas Lindgren been living a double life? Fifteen, perhaps? Even to survive a month undercover, you have to convince your own heart. You bury a secret deep in your core and then forget it's there. You pray no one ever opens up a crack in that living facade. Connor had been running from his home just now. If that followed a confrontation over the past, over certain questions that Kane had placed in the boy's mind, then Thomas knew the threat Kane posed. He knew Kane was the only thing standing between him and escape. The question remaining was whether he'd shoot him in front of his daughter.

'Let's talk, Thomas,' Kane said.

'About what?'

'Maybe I can help. I owe you one now.' Thomas kept his foot down. The sun had broken from the horizon.

'What did you say to Connor?'

'I didn't say anything, I asked him some questions. I think both of us need to get out of here. You've been good to me. I think you're a good person. I don't think many other people are going to be on your side right now.'

'I don't know what you mean.'

A military truck tore past in the opposite direction carrying firefighting equipment. Thomas swung the car out of the way, bouncing them onto rocky ground before regaining the road.

'I've seen what you have, as a family,' Kane said. 'You can't fake that. It's real as anything. I don't think you can leave it behind.'

'Who are you?'

'You can probably guess who I am.'

'What are you offering?'

'I can get you on an RAF flight, all of you, and we can take it from there. But you wouldn't have to be separated.'

Thomas stared at the road ahead, sweat streaming. They were coming up to a crossroads: Georgetown ahead of them, a narrow track looping to the right into barren rocks. Thomas hesitated.

Kane could see him making a decision. Suddenly he wrenched the wheel and they swung north into the emptiness.

'Why are we going this way, Daddy?'

'Small diversion, sweetheart.'

'You said we were going sailing.'

'We are. Just got to drop Edward off.'

The lava plains stretched endlessly around them. It would be hours before Kane's body was found. Kane eyed the door lock, which was up, then the man's grip on the gun. The road they were on began to climb into the basalt hills. The gun didn't waver.

'We can get out of here our own way,' Kane said. 'There are options. I can speak to people, make an arrangement to ensure you stay with Carina.'

'What about me?' Carina said.

'We'd get you out of here together,' Kane continued. 'You'd have my word.'

'That's bullshit.'

'You got trapped. I understand that. You didn't have a choice.'

'You don't know anything.'

'I know this isn't what's best for the girl. What's she going to do in Russia? What's she going to do without her mum?'

They were still climbing, on the edge of a sheer drop now. Thomas pressed the accelerator down, throwing Kane back in his seat. He released the gun's safety catch. He was driving directly into the rising sun. Kane turned and saw the man was blinded by tears.

'*Poslushay menya*,' Kane said. *Listen to me.* He continued in Russian: 'There is a peaceful way out. For you, your children . . . '

'What's happening?' the girl said.

'Look at her,' Kane said. 'For Christ's sake.'

Thomas's eyes flicked to the mirror. Kane punched him in the throat.

The girl screamed. Kane grabbed Thomas's wrist and he fired

through the windscreen. The car swerved wildly. Kane couldn't get the gun out of his grip. They were on the edge of the drop now, with the windscreen cracked. Kane changed course; he opened the passenger door and jumped.

The ground never arrived. He tumbled down a slope of loose cinder, arms up to protect his head, heard a second shot that whistled past him, then the car continued away. When Kane eventually came to a stop, he looked up toward the road and it had gone. His left side was bruised agonisingly where he'd landed, clothes shredded at the knees and elbows. But he was able to stand, able to walk. That was a small miracle. Kane caught his breath and began up the slope.

It took him five minutes to get back to the road. A pall of smoke had begun to darken the sky. He heard sirens from the east and followed the sound, cresting the shoulder of another peak, then staggering down a rough foot path. After a few minutes he saw the golf course beneath him, which meant he was near One Boat. Another couple of minutes and the refuelling station came into view.

A cluster of British military vehicles had stopped under the canopy, with several RAF men and security contractors directing cars in some kind of evacuation, other officers in full combat gear fanned out across the lava, guns at the ready. Kane approached with his hands raised.

'Got him,' one of them called.

'Stay there.'

Kane stopped.

'Are you armed?'

'No,' Kane said.

'Who fired those shots?'

'A man called Thomas Lindgren. He's on his way to Georgetown with a girl who may be in danger. He needs to be stopped.'

A woman drove up to the fuel station shouting: 'What's happening? Can someone please tell me what's happening?'

They told her to drive directly to the airfield. Civilians were taking shelter in a bunker beneath the adjacent base.

'Why?' she said.

'Proceed to the airfield. Follow instructions.'

'Someone said they found them,' the woman said. 'At the fire.'

'Please proceed ...'

The woman sped off. Kane was searched. He heard their radios: It sounded like a lot of officers were up at Devil's Ashpit.

'What's at Devil's Ashpit?' he said.

'Two bodies at the NASA station. Someone started a fire there. Know about it?'

'No. But I suspect the man I told you about is involved. We need to get to Georgetown, fast,' Kane said.

'You need to come with us.'

Before Kane could reply there was the sound of a vehicle approaching quickly behind him. A Jeep appeared, speeding from the direction of the US base. It screeched to a halt and Anne Lindgren jumped out, still uniformed, gripping her radio transceiver. She ran over to Kane.

'Some security guys said you were with Thomas and Carina. Where are they?'

'Thomas has Carina. They've gone to Georgetown.'

'What about Connor?'

'I don't know about Connor.'

'What's Thomas doing at Georgetown?'

'Maybe trying to get away. His boat's there,' Kane said.

She looked baffled, turned to the British officer.

'Is anyone in Georgetown that you can contact?'

'Georgetown's been cleared,' one of the RAF officers said. 'There's no servicemen there. Everyone's busy getting people into shelter or up at the fire at Devil's Ashpit.'

'Someone said they found bodies there,' Anne said.

'Looks like Petra and Lauren.'

Anne turned to Kane. 'What's going on?'

'Let's go to Georgetown,' Kane said. 'I'll tell you what I know.'

'He's under arrest,' the airman said.

'Not right now he isn't,' Anne said. 'Come with me.'

Kane moved for Anne's Jeep. No one shot him, so he got in beside her.

'Who are you?' she said, turning the ignition.

'I work for the British government.'

'People are saying my husband might have started the fire.'

'He might have done. Let's get Carina safe first, then we can try to understand this.'

She pulled out fast, headed in the direction of Georgetown.

'You don't know where Connor is?'

'No.'

'You think Thomas is going to his boat? That's impossible. The sea's too rough.'

'We can explain that to him. He's armed, Anne. We're going to have to think how we do this.'

Then, very carefully, she said: 'Does this have something to do with the Russian ship?'

'Russian ship?'

'There's a ship coming – Russian signals intelligence, approximately twenty kilometres west of Ascension now.'

'I reckon it might.'

She looked straight ahead, taking the car to fifty, staring at the lava flows as if they might contain the explanation for her collapsing life.

THIRTY-TWO

The BND security team tailed Taylor as far as they could. For her protection, they said. After she crossed into Westminster, she didn't see them again. She had a sense of walking a tightrope between two burning buildings.

She drove past Charing Cross and Trafalgar Square, into government territory. It was a sunny day and Whitehall was crowded. Taylor ditched the car on Victoria Embankment with the doors open and the keys in the ignition, then circled back to the vast stone block of the Ministry of Defence headquarters: a pale, tomblike seven-acre sprawl of military bureaucracy. The main entrance was on Horse Guards Avenue, but she went to the one at the side. She'd hoped it might give her some privacy, but there was a group of tourists listening to a guide in Spanish. Taylor approached the MOD Police on the door, explained who she was, and why she needed urgent access. She watched as some communication went on inside their cabin. Then she was arrested at gunpoint.

There was a gasp from the tourists. The guide fell silent. The police checked Taylor for weapons and walked her inside with a grip on her arm.

The interior of the building was no less sepulchral, its oxblood marble suggesting cold butchery. Staff stopped as she was marched to the back of the ground floor, where she saw Skinner and Sir Roland Mackenzie advancing toward her.

'Kathryn.'

'I need to speak to you about what's happening on Ascension,' she said.

'You need to explain why both British and US special forces on the island are looking for a Dr Edward Pearce,' Mackenzie said. 'A man who escaped police custody last night and comes up on our records as your responsibility.'

'You've lost us the island,' Skinner said, before she could reply. 'In due course, we're going to ascertain what your game has been, but we have a potential war on our hands now and our priority is getting you as far away from this as possible. Put her somewhere secure,' he said to the police.

'There's a Russian intelligence officer on the island,' Taylor said as the police grabbed her arm again. 'That ship is coming to collect them.'

Skinner stared with a mixture of fury and disbelief. 'Spare us, Kathryn,' he said. One of the officers flicked a set of hand-cuffs open.

'Wait,' Mackenzie said.

'The *Yantar* is on its way to exfiltrate an intelligence officer who's been living undercover,' Taylor continued. 'We've known there was hostile penetration of the space defence programme on Ascension since last year. But we never got to the bottom of it, did we, Gabriel?'

The chief turned to Skinner. 'Is this something you know about?'

Skinner hesitated, but recovered quickly. 'This is a distraction. If you like, I can explain exactly—'

'Save it.' The chief turned back to the police. 'Bring her to the command room.'

Taylor was led to the lifts. The five of them squeezed in and plummeted down four floors beneath the pavement, where she was ushered through a security pod, past thick metal doors, into the tunnels. They must have passed back under Whitehall, under the Cenotaph, into the beginnings of War Command. There were several subterranean checkpoints, then a decontamination area. Two more armed police stood outside double doors signed DEFENCE CRISIS MANAGEMENT CENTRE. At a nod from Mackenzie they knocked, turned the handle and stepped back.

The room was bigger than Taylor expected, centred on a vast table with multiple sockets and fixed phones. Secondary workstations around the edges of the room included some form of communications hub with staff wearing headphones and mics. Thirty or so people in total, a handful in military uniform, most suited. She recognised the chief of defence staff, the head of MI6 military liaison, the secretary of state for defence himself. Screens in each corner showed live satellite maps, one tracing the *Yantar* as it crossed the South Atlantic, one, disconcertingly, showing the night sky. A monitor on the table linked with the military's Permanent Joint Headquarters in Northwood, another to a command centre with men and women in US military uniforms.

Taylor was ushered to the front.

'This is Kathryn Taylor from our South Atlantic team,' Mackenzie said. 'Tell us what you know.'

'I believe the *Yantar* is on its way to rendezvous with a Russian intelligence officer who's been operating under deep cover on Ascension Island. His cover's been blown. The signals blockage on the island is consistent with an exfiltration attempt and probably originates from a portable device operated by the officer himself.'

There was a second as they processed this.

'Who is he?' an American commander on the video link asked.

'He's been living undercover as Thomas Lindgren,' Taylor said, 'married to Anne Lindgren.'

'General Anne Lindgren?' the commander said.

313

'His face matches archived records for an SVR officer named Nikolai Pravik. I believe the discovery of his true identity connects to the death of a British intelligence officer on the island and possibly the disappearance of two children. It's been known for some time that Russia has a source there, code-named Gemstone, instrumental in the supply of space-related intelligence to China. Previous attempts to identify him have been complicated by the sensitivity of the joint US-UK arrangements.'

'Can you confirm this?' Mackenzie asked Skinner.

'I'll be briefing in due course,' Skinner said.

'Due course is now. I need to know exactly what happened, why a hostile agent has been allowed to continue operating in the heart of our defence programme. I want to know what you knew and when, and how extensive you believe the damage to be. A full report, today.'

Skinner looked sick. He gave a nod and left the command room silently. In his absence Taylor's credibility seemed to grow.

'What is the current situation on the ground there?' the commander asked. 'Where is Pravik?'

'It's not clear. I have one officer in place who may be able to do something, but it seems he's come under the suspicion of both US and UK security. I need them to be instructed to support him. He's in a position to bring about a peaceful outcome. But not on his own.'

Taylor felt the emptiness of the words in her mouth. What could Kane do? Where was he?

'Does your officer know about Pravik?' Mackenzie asked.

'Possibly. I can't say for sure. It's difficult establishing contact.'

'How would this rendezvous work?' the minister for defence wanted to know. 'If the ship is on its way to pick him up.'

'That's not clear either.'

There were rumblings of discontent. A few individuals turned back to their monitors.

'I think we can advise caution with regards to the ship,' the chief of defence staff said. 'Keep shadowing. Hold fire.'

'Hold fire only until we've ascertained more details,' the minister said. 'It's in our waters, well within striking distance, and we're authorised to neutralise it if we see fit.'

THIRTY-THREE

Anne drove as if possessed. For the second time that day Kane thought he might die in a car accident. They hurtled toward Georgetown. The only other vehicles they saw were racing toward Devil's Ashpit or carrying civilians to the airbase. Green Mountain sat wreathed in smoke, birds circling out in frantic clusters

Georgetown was in disarray. It had been evacuated fast, with the remains of last night's crisis littering the place. A couple of abandoned dogs remained beside the church. Terrified donkeys stumbled through gardens into the road. The rollers crashed in high, spray visible above the roofs.

'There's his car.'

Anne hit the brakes. The Buick with its bullet-cracked windscreen sat parked at the edge of the jetty.

'Jesus Christ. What happened?' she said, getting out and starting to run. 'His boat's still there,' she shouted, as they crossed the concrete. Then they saw Thomas and Carina.

The pair stood at the bottom of the jetty's steps, water lapping at them. Thomas was helping Carina on with her lifejacket. They looked absurdly fragile beside the vicious sea. The tide was in and their dinghy tossed fiercely.

'Thomas!' Anne called over the crash of the waves, starting down the steep steps toward him. 'This is insane. Stop it, whatever's going on.'

He straightened, pointed the gun at her.

'Get away, Anne. I'm sorry.'

Carina began screaming. 'Mommy!'

'Thomas, are you crazy? What the hell . . . '

Anne took another step.

'I'm serious. Don't come closer, Anne. Please.'

Thomas held the girl in one hand and the gun in the other. They ducked as a wave broke, drenching them. Kane began down the steps behind Anne, calculating options. The pair were unstable on the bottom step. Thomas needed to turn to climb into the dinghy, but the waves were getting more violent. He'd need both hands to help the girl in.

Anne was still moving, one step at a time.

'Talk to me. Thomas, please. Give me Carina.'

Thomas clung to the girl. If he fired, Kane would have two or three seconds to move. Could he reach him before he re-sighted? If Anne lunged first, it was anyone's guess. They'd all be an inch from the edge. But another factor had begun massing in the distance: a roller, slow and huge. Kane was watching it grow when another voice came from above them.

'Let her go.'

Connor stood on the quay. He let his bike drop to the ground, reached into his pocket, and pulled out the Beretta.

'Let her go,' he said again, aiming at Thomas.

'Connor,' Thomas said. 'You don't understand the situation and you don't know how to use that.'

Connor stood very still with the gun raised, both hands on the grip.

'Let Carina go,' he said.

'Connor, listen. You could hit your sister.'

'I don't give a fuck,' Connor said. 'Let her go or I'll shoot her too. I'll shoot her first. Would you let that happen?'

'Jesus Christ, Connor.'

Kane wondered if he'd reloaded. The original bullets were still in his pocket, but there would have been more at the cabin. If so, would he shoot? It depended on how much the boy had figured out. With both parents fixated on Connor, Kane moved past Anne until he was three steps away from the bottom.

'Put the fucking gun down, Connor,' Thomas yelled. 'You're out of your mind.'

'Connor,' Anne said. 'Do what he says. This isn't helping. Put the gun down.'

'You killed them,' Connor said.

'You don't know what you're talking about,' Thomas said.

'Don't I?'

Kane was inches away from them now. The wave was still building monumentally. No way he could disarm Thomas and secure the girl at the same time. It was going to be a question of risking a shot and praying it went wide. But unless Kane himself was secure, that would be for nothing. He saw an old mooring line wrapped around the rails at the side and began to unwind it.

'Connor,' Anne screamed. 'Please.'

The wave began to curl. Now Anne saw it too, and she swore. Thomas glanced over his shoulder, then turned back to them. He'd frozen. Kane twisted the rope around his arm, reached out to Carina.

'I've got her. Come on, Carina. Step toward me quickly.'

For a split second it looked like the girl might reach out, but then she turned and clung to her father.

It hit them like an explosion. Kane felt his feet swept from under him. The water drowned the steps, and when it drew back, Thomas and Carina were gone. Then two heads broke the surface of the sea, a few metres out: Carina flailing, borne up by the lifejacket; Thomas fighting against the water.

Kane kicked his shoes off and dived in. Thomas had grabbed his daughter and was trying to push her back toward the steps, but struggling to keep his own head above the surface. Kane took hold of the girl as her father sank back down. He clawed backwards through the water with Carina's limp body before the next wave hit. Anne had secured herself with the rope and reached for her, catching the girl's arm and dragging her up onto the steps. Connor appeared beside her and helped lift his sister out, then offered a hand to Kane. But another wave was growing, sucking the sea back and Thomas with it.

'Get her up to the top,' Kane said. 'Away from the edge.' Kane looked for Thomas. He saw a hand and launched himself toward it.

The undertow was unlike anything he'd felt before. It sucked him out with a sense of angry purpose, away from the island to within a few metres of the drowning man, before a wave threw him back. Kane twisted to use his feet to stop himself from smashing against the jetty, managed to fill his lungs and turn again. Thomas had disappeared from view. Kane dived down, kicking hard, trying to peer through the water as he moved. Small black fishes darted unperturbed around him. He couldn't see farther than a metre or so. Kane surfaced and there was still no sign of Thomas. Anne was calling.

'Edward! Come back!'

Kane sank a final time, saw nothing but the water churning clouds of fine white sand. And he knew that whatever he was trying to prove, it wasn't going to happen.

He thrashed his way back. The rope hit his arm. Kane pulled himself along it until he felt hands on him, dragging him onto the concrete.

'Quick,' Anne said. She helped him up the steps. Carina lay in the recovery position at the top, still in her lifejacket, vomit on the concrete beside her, watery blood over her face. Connor knelt beside her. Kane felt for the girl's pulse, then crouched and put his cheek beside her mouth until he could feel her breath.

'She's breathing.'

'Barely. She needs medical attention,' Anne said.

'I can try and call.'

'Are you okay?'

'I'm okay. You stay with her.'

Kane went to the harbour offices. They were locked but he smashed a window and climbed in, searching until he found a first-aid kit and foil blanket. He took them to Anne, then went back to the office and assessed the various communication devices. The digital comms were down, but the old analog telephone worked. No answer on the island's emergency number. He called the number for contacting Vauxhall Cross from overseas and asked to speak to Kathryn Taylor. Eventually his call was routed through to somewhere that wasn't Vauxhall but must have been on the governmental system.

'Elliot, is that you?' Her voice sounded miraculous in his ear.

'Yes.'

'You're alive?' He could hear Taylor's relief, and wondered where she was.

'I'm alive.'

'It looks like there's been some serious interference on the island. It centres on an individual going by the name of Thomas Lindgren. He may be working for Russia. Is that someone you've crossed paths with?'

'I crossed paths with Thomas Lindgren, yes.'

'Do you know his whereabouts? Is he still active?'

'He's no longer active.'

'Oh, Elliot. That's incredible. Well done.' He heard her breathe a sigh of relief. 'You arrested him?'

'He drowned.'

'I see.' Her voice grew a touch less confident. 'We've got a lot to catch up on. Who's with you now?'

'Lindgren's family,' he said. 'We need medical assistance, but

320

the emergency services are all attending other scenes. Are you able to contact the Administrator directly? It should be possible to arrange assistance from one of the bases. We're on the pierhead at Georgetown.'

'I can try. We're re-establishing a connection now. I can do that,' she said. 'The pierhead, okay. Are you able to stay on the line?'

'Not right now.'

The connection was breaking anyway. Kane hung up. He could see Anne through the window, looking toward the sea.

THIRTY-FOUR

Taylor passed on the good news to the Crisis Management Centre, who received it with a combination of relief and circumspection. In the aftermath of her briefing, the war room reached a crescendo of activity. Instructions were dispatched to the other command rooms and up the hierarchy of government itself. There was discussion regarding the channels via which the fate of Nikolai Pravik could be communicated to Moscow and onward to the *Yantar*. Then Taylor sensed a slight pause in proceedings as all the new information percolated through; a moment of sanity, perhaps. She felt she'd done her bit, and that she wasn't particularly welcome anymore.

'Let's get some air,' Mackenzie said.

They went back through the subterranean corridors, up to the equivalent maze on the ground floor. Finally, they reached a small door with one guard who nodded at the chief and released them into a courtyard. Taylor took a breath of air, looked gratefully up at the sky. There was a view of green landscape ahead that must have been St James's Park. It was behind locked gates, protected by two armed police with submachine guns. In her disorientation Taylor briefly wondered why the park needed such heavy security, then realised it was herself who was on the secure side. They were at the back of Downing Street.

Mackenzie walked her slowly toward the exit. Signal returned to her phone and she saw eight missed calls from Markus Fischer. She thrust it back into her coat pocket.

'Daniel Kudus,' she said. 'He's been assisting me. He's in headquarters now.'

'He's okay. Don't worry.'

'HQ know?'

'HQ have been fully informed. Daniel Kudus is safe and well.'

'Thank you.'

'Quite a few days you've had.'

'Yes.'

'How do you feel?'

'In all honesty? A little shaky.'

'I'm sure.'

The air was thick with peace: a day slowly softening toward its end without a war beginning. In the distance, tourists peered through the gate's ironwork. The chief slowed to a stop a few metres before it.

'Well, you know now. Ptolemy. It's not going to become any less critical. You've seen the future.'

'It's dramatic.'

'Potentially very dramatic.' Mackenzie nodded. 'Needs someone with a cool head.'

It took Taylor a second to realise what he was saying. 'I can see that.'

Her phone buzzed again. She reached into her pocket and switched it off, making a mental note to wipe Fischer's number when she got the chance.

'Find it interesting?'

'Space war?' she said.

'Space security.'

'I'm not sure I've got the technical know-how.'

'As you've seen, it's going to involve a huge amount of intelligence work on the ground. A new set of priorities.'

'Yes.'

'Would you work with a company like Quadrant? After these events?'

Taylor considered. Would she? Already she could feel the rationalisations arriving, smoothing a path for her conscience.

'I'd have to see. I wouldn't rule it out.'

'Why don't you come to my office on Monday and we can talk about it further. I can imagine you contributing significantly.'

Taylor nodded. She didn't even know where the space department was in Vauxhall Cross. Yet she could imagine herself contributing too. But then, success is easy to imagine. She'd been doing it long enough.

'I'll certainly have a think,' she said as the armed police nodded, angling their machine guns down and opening the gates back out to the real world.

THIRTY-FIVE

Connor had vanished by the time Kane got back to the jetty. Carina had begun shivering. Her eyelids fluttered and quiet groans escaped her pale lips. Anne rested a hand on her daughter's forehead and one on her trembling shoulder. Kane looked around for Connor and eventually saw the boy up on the fort beside the harbour, silhouetted against the sky.

Kane walked over, climbed up the old stones. The sun was high now and his clothes were already drying on his body. He realised how thirsty he was, and as the adrenaline seeped away he could feel his injuries, his left knee starting to seize up, hands throbbing where the skin had torn.

Connor sat on a rusted gun mount. He stared out to sea, and Kane thought he must be searching for signs of Thomas, but as he got closer he saw that the boy was looking at a ship. It was a few kilometres out from shore, long and narrow, with a small white radome and antennae that from a distance looked like masts. A spy ship.

'Ever seen one like that before around here?' Kane asked.

'No.'

'Looks like it's watching us,' Kane said. The boy nodded.

'It has to do with him, doesn't it,' he said.

'Maybe.'

The boy stared ahead.

'Are you going to ask for the gun?'

'No. Did you reload it?'

'No. It's empty. Is Carina okay?'

'She'll be okay. Want to come back?'

Connor shook his head.

'Mind if I stay up here with you?' Kane asked. The boy shook his head again. Kane sat on the gun mount beside him. He felt the heat off the old metal, and there was something comforting about it. The sea remained rough, but from their vantage point it was hypnotic. No traces of the life it had swallowed.

Eventually Connor said, 'Is it true? Did he kill Petra and Lauren?'

'I think so.'

'I should have done something. I should have seen.'

'There's not always something you can do.'

'Why did he do it?'

'Because he wasn't who he said he was, and when you're in that situation you can get desperate.'

'Who was he?'

'I don't know exactly. It's possible he didn't know either.'

'What do you mean?'

'I mean that people can be more than one person at a time. It doesn't make anything less real or less true. The time you spent with him, I mean.'

Connor considered this. Eventually he turned to Kane.

'You're not who you say you are either, are you?'

The assertion took Kane by surprise, even after everything that had transpired. In the chaos of the preceding few hours he'd overlooked the extent to which he'd abandoned all cover. Edward Pearce had departed the island for good.

'No, I guess not.'

Connor seemed on the point of asking more but must have thought better of it. Kane looked to see how Anne and Carina were doing, down on the jetty. They hadn't moved. Long plumes of smoke unfurled across the sky behind them. He thought of Anne watching the sunrise from outer space and couldn't match it to the woman bent over her daughter's body. No sign of any help arriving. The only thing now was to wait. Wait and try to stay sane.

'They would have gotten on the dinghy,' Connor said.

'I don't see how they would have managed that.'

'You don't think? They might have been okay.'

'I don't think so.'

'Will I be arrested?'

'No. I think people will say you did the right thing.'

They were silent for a while. Finally the boy said, 'So will we leave here now?'

'I imagine so.'

Connor took a breath and shut his eyes. Kane watched the sea. It could have been his imagination, but he thought he saw the ship begin to turn away. He thought of the men on board staring at the island, at the volcanic peaks gaining colour, at the miracle of the whitewashed church and the jumble of fever graves, and realising there was nothing there for them. That the ocean had its dangers, but you could move through it and you would find life elsewhere, and whatever that involved it would be less threatening than the lifeless rocks.

After another minute he saw he was right: The boat flattened, presenting a clear profile, then continued away from the island, growing smaller by the minute. Kane watched it go, feeling the heat of the metal beneath him and the slow breathing of the boy at his side. By the time Connor opened his eyes again he seemed calmer, as if he'd decided something, and the boat was a speck against the darkness of the ocean.

ACKNOWLEDEGMENTS

Many thanks to Michael Grist, Clare Smith, Sophia Schoepfer, Zoe Hood, Jaime Levine, Veronique Baxter, Sara Langham, Grainne Fox, Nicky Lund, Alice Howe, Heather Tamarkin, Alison Kerr Miller, Michelle Triant, Fariza Hawke.

Thanks also to New Writing North and my colleagues and students at Manchester Metropolitan University.

Most of all, thanks to Jihyon, for everything, and Taehee, to whom the novel is dedicated. Welcome.